Tell No Lies

A DETECTIVE
CAELAN SMALL NOVEL

TELL NO LIES

LISA HARTLEY

CANELO

First published in the United Kingdom in 2018 by Canelo

This edition published in 2019 by

Canelo Digital Publishing Limited
57 Shepherds Lane
Beaconsfield, Bucks HP9 2DU
United Kingdom

A CIP catalogue record for this book is available from the British Library.

Print ISBN 978 1 78863 387 1
Ebook ISBN 978 1 911420 67 5

Look for more great books at www.canelo.co

Printed and bound in Great Britain by Clays Ltd, Elcograf S.p.A.

iv

For Tracy, always.

Prologue

The first blow loosened a front tooth. The second jerked his head so savagely the impact ricocheted down his neck, jolting his spine and fizzing into his toes.

Still no one spoke. He forced open burning lips, sucked in some air. Shuddered. The men who had brought him here stood back, arms folded, faces impassive. Their boss was on his toes, grinning, holding up bruised fists. Blood already stained his knuckles.

His blood. Black under the flickering strip light. He watched a drop fall to the concrete floor.

He blinked, his right eye swelling, already closing. With his tongue, he worked at the loosened tooth. Maybe a dentist could save it. He didn't fancy having a gap. Then again, just now, it was the least of his worries.

'Ready to talk?' A smile, head cocked, eyes wide. When he didn't give a response, the man sighed, pursing his lips as though disappointed. 'Because I can do this all night.' He took a step back, nodded towards a black metal toolbox. 'Got some things in there you'd enjoy. Make you speak in seconds. Make you scream. No secrets then, am I right, boys?' Nods, snickering.

He took another breath. He was going to die in this place. He knew enough to make him dangerous. That was why he was here, after all. Why he'd been hanging around for the past few months. Tentative at first, head down, wallet open, buying their merchandise. Gradually forming acquaintances, risking a nod when he recognised a face at the bar. Treading carefully, never pushing. Slow and steady. Showing his face often enough to make his point, but not forcing the issue. He was there, available and interested, but not desperate.

It had worked. He had been trusted, beckoned a little closer to the inner circle with every passing week. Grunt work at first, anonymous and low-risk. Collect a bag, deliver a parcel. Never ask what's inside. Then the visits started. Polite and friendly, offering the option – pay up or your premises will be torched. As though it was as inoffensive as an offer of extra insurance, or more data on your mobile phone package.

As though he wasn't carrying a baseball bat.

A slap this time, open-handed, his nose leaking more blood, his good eye watering. His head lolled, his vision flashing white and then blurring. He forced his chin up, desperate to wipe the blood from his face but unable to raise his hands. His wrists and ankles were held tight, bound by plastic cable ties to the wooden chair he'd been forced into.

'Still not talking?' A tut. 'Stupid of you. Disappointing really.' The man hawked, spat on the floor. 'You might as well, you've nothing to lose.' The smile widened. He rocked back on his heels, hands in pockets. 'Our turn to ask the questions now, isn't it? My turn. And I can guarantee you'll give me answers before tomorrow.' He nodded, a quick, savage jerk of his head. 'Guarantee it, pal. Worming answers out of you like you did to us – cosying up to my boys, to my staff. But you won't be running back to base to tell tales. Not any more.' He leaned forward, smirking. 'Cover's blown, my friend. You're fucked, well and truly. And you know the best part?' He wriggled, clearly buoyed by the knowledge of what was to come. 'You know how we found out? Who grassed you up?'

He stared, right eye now swollen closed, blood still trickling down his face. Kept his mouth shut.

'Second thoughts, I'll let you guess. You know what, though?' The man chuckled, the sound echoing around the bare walls and stark floor. 'You can't trust anyone these days.'

'What?' It was a whisper, the sound grating against his throat. Then, 'You're lying.'

Leaning forward, a hand cupped around his ear. 'Sorry, mate? Didn't quite catch that.'

'Whatever's been said, whoever you've been talking to, they're winding you up.'

'You know you've given yourself away, you stupid bastard? You should have denied it, lied until you were in pieces on the floor.' He smiled. 'Then lied some more. You admit it then? You're a spy?'

'If you believe that, you're—'

His eyes bulged. 'Careful, pal. Not in a position to be a smart-arse, are you?'

'Who do you think I'm working for?' Stay calm, he told himself. Stick to the story.

That smile again as the man turned away, stepped across to the toolbox. He bent over it, opened the lid, took his time rummaging through the contents. Then he straightened, holding up a hammer with a grin. 'That's what we're going to find out.'

Caelan Small stood by the window, staring up at the sky. Still dark, dawn beginning to send a yellow and red glow across the horizon. The window was double-glazed, doing its best to mask the sound of the London traffic thundering by beyond, but not wholly succeeding. She turned away, closed the curtains. On the bed, the colours of the screen glaring bright against the plain white duvet cover, her phone began to ring again. She stepped closer, checked the caller's name. Shook her head and ignored the call. The fourth from the same number in as many hours.

'Take the hint, Nicky,' she muttered. Eventually they would have to talk, but not yet. The pain was too raw, too vivid. This was a new kind of heartbreak, one Caelan had no idea how to process. She lifted a hand to her bruised cheek, touched the dressing protecting the wound on her temple. The stitches itched, and she fought the urge to tear off the bandage. She needed clean clothes, but would have to buy them. Everything she owned was back at the flat in Rotherhithe, and she wouldn't be returning there any time soon. She also needed to eat, though she wasn't the least bit hungry. Her time was her own; her only instruction to rest and recover. Her injuries would take time to heal, and as for the resting, she had struggled to sleep for more than a few minutes. The ache in her chest had nothing to do with her cuts and bruises.

Her phone was ringing again. Irritated, Caelan snatched it up, glared at the screen. A different name, but someone else she didn't want to speak to. She sat on the bed, then lay back, the phone still squawking beside her. As a shrill beep informed her that the caller had left a voicemail, Caelan closed her eyes.

–

'No answer.' Assistant Commissioner Elizabeth Beckett shook her head as she set her phone down.

Across the table, Detective Nicky Sturgess bowed her head.

'I'm not surprised. When she left last night—'

'She was shocked and in pain. I understand. She'd had a difficult day. All the more reason for her to answer her phone this morning. I told her I'd be in touch.'

'She's hurt, ma'am. Emotionally as well as physically. In hindsight, me turning up unannounced wasn't the best move.'

Beckett held up a hand. 'Regardless, we need her here. Your personal relationship is irrelevant.'

Nicky looked up, folded her arms. 'Except if that were true, Caelan would be answering her phone.'

'You told me you wanted to get straight back out into the field.'

'And I do.'

'You know you can't go back to Edmonton, especially now.'

'Why not? Who's going to remember me?'

'We can't take the risk.'

'What aren't you telling me?'

Beckett's lips thinned. 'As I explained to you last night when you were released from the safe house, we have a major scandal to contain. If the press found out one of own officers was responsible for the murder of a ten-year-old child…'

'I see how it could be awkward.' Nicky's voice was ice. Beckett stared at her.

'It's not your concern. I had considered sending both you and Caelan to Edmonton to pick up where you left off.'

Nicky snorted. 'I'm sure she'd be delighted. Why both of us?'

'It's a complex operation.'

'No more than most.' Nicky inclined her head. 'Ma'am…'

Beckett tapped a fingernail on the table, considering. 'I think it would be best if we talked again later.'

Nicky got to her feet. She pushed her chair under the table, gripping the back of it tightly. 'You mean you want to ask Caelan whether she'll work with me?'

Beckett shot a warning glance. 'Not at all.'

'And there's me thinking you were in charge.'

'We'll speak later, Detective Sturgess.'

Contempt clear in her expression, Nicky strode from the room.

–

When she woke several hours later, Caelan listened to the voicemail. She slid off the bed and paced over to the window as she waited for Beckett to answer.

'Caelan. How are you? Good of you to find the time to call.'

She paused, rubbing her forehead. So this was how Beckett was going to play it. 'How's Ewan?'

'Two cracked ribs, bruising. He's at home, like you.'

'I'm on leave on your instruction. Take a couple of weeks, you said.'

A sharp exhalation. 'I remember.'

6

'And after I arrived home last night, I had an unexpected visitor.' Caelan swallowed, the words catching in her throat. 'I'm sure you can guess who it was.'

Beckett hesitated. 'It came as a surprise.'

'You think?'

'As I'm sure you can understand, Nicky's sudden disappearance was necessary, for her own protection.'

'It was cruel. Did you even think about her family? You didn't have to—'

'I had no other option. And when you've calmed down, had time to absorb it, you'll see it was the right decision.'

'With respect, ma'am, I doubt it.'

'Almost everyone else connected to the case is dead. Nicky going into hiding saved her. Remember that.' Beckett's voice was devoid of emotion.

'I'm not likely to forget.'

'We need to meet.'

'Why?' Caelan turned from the window. She had walked away from the Met once. Maybe it was time to do so again.

'We have a... situation developing,' said Beckett.

'You said you didn't want to see me for a couple of weeks. That was less than twenty-four hours ago.'

'I know, but there was an incident this morning. I'd like to discuss it with you.'

'What's happened? Is this about Nasenby?'

'I'm not going to talk about it over the phone. Are you at home?'

'Home?' Caelan laughed. 'I don't have a home.'

'What? But you—'

'Turns out I didn't inherit the apartment after all. I'm sure you can figure out why.' Caelan tried to keep the bitterness from her tone, but it was there all the same. There was a silence as Beckett thought about it. It didn't last long.

'Then where are you?' No sympathy, no warmth. Standard Beckett. Yesterday, when Caelan had identified and confronted a killer, been beaten and hospitalised by him, her boss had been concerned, courteous. Almost friendly. Today, she was back to cool and detached.

Caelan rubbed her eyes. 'A hotel.'

'I'll come to you.'

'I'm going to go out to get some food.' Caelan picked up her bag. Waited.

Another sigh. 'Fine. I'll meet you. Where?'

–

Ten minutes later, Caelan crossed a cobbled courtyard. In warmer weather, she would have had to weave around chairs and tables, but in the damp and drizzle, the area was deserted.

Inside, the Refectory was warm, welcoming. Part of the new wing of Southwark Cathedral, it was a place Caelan had visited several times. She never liked to frequent any one café or restaurant too regularly, because of the risk of becoming familiar and being recognised when on an operation. It was a slim chance, but a danger all the same, and Caelan had learnt to be cautious.

She approached the wooden counter, which was laden with cakes, scones, bagels and sandwiches. The smiling young woman behind it offered a greeting, and Caelan met her eyes, flashing a grin of her own. She saw sharp brown eyes taking in her bruises and bandage as the woman turned away to make Caelan's latte. The stitches were itching again, and she pushed her hand into her pocket to avoid the temptation of scratching them. She peered at the cakes, asked for a slice of coffee and walnut.

There were a few other customers already dotted around the room, chatting or reading. An elderly man met Caelan's eyes as she approached his table, then hurriedly looked away as he too noticed the injuries to her face. Caelan smiled.

'At least I won the fight,' she said.

He grinned. 'Wouldn't like to see the person who lost, then.'

Winking as she passed him, she carried her cup and plate to a table in the furthest corner. She eased herself onto the chair, her battered body protesting.

She had almost finished her cake when Assistant Commissioner Elizabeth Beckett pushed through the door. Her eyes scanned the room quickly. She acknowledged Caelan with a nod, mimed lifting a cup to her lips. Caelan shook her head, and Beckett turned back to the counter.

'Nice place,' she said when she arrived at the table. She set down a fruit scone and a mug of black coffee.

'Never eaten here before?'

'Didn't realise it was here.' Beckett cut the scone in two and buttered each half. 'How are you feeling?'

Caelan sipped her coffee. 'Stunned. Sore. Fucking furious.'

Beckett chewed, wiped her mouth on a paper napkin. 'As I said, I understand that seeing Nicky would have been a shock.'

'Some warning would have been nice. She was just there when I answered the door.'

'That was her decision. I phoned to tell her we'd arrested Nasenby, that she was free to leave. I sent a car to the safe house, told the driver to take her wherever she wanted to go. The rest was down to her.'

And she had chosen to come straight to the flat, knowing Caelan would be there, totally unaware that Nicky was still alive. A flicker of unidentified emotion sparked in Caelan's chest, but she ignored it. Now was not the time to sift through her feelings for Nicky. She set her cup on the table with more force than she had intended. 'You should have trusted me. Nicky should have, at least.'

Beckett shook her head. 'We couldn't tell you. Nicky's life was at risk, and if you'd known of her whereabouts, yours would have been too. She had to disappear.'

'Which I understand, but—'

'I made the decision with the intention of protecting my officers, and the investigation. I believe I made the right call, and I'm not prepared to discuss it further.'

Caelan glared at her. 'And I have to accept that? What if I don't want to listen to you either?'

'Your decision. You've resigned once, why not again?' Beckett drank some coffee. 'This time, though, there'd be no pay, no pension. No comeback. We're being forced to rebuild the team, Caelan. Either you're a part of it, or you're out.'

'That's all you can say? You've dragged me back from leave once; now you're doing it again, to tell me that if I don't fall in line, I won't have a job? And I'm supposed to accept that without complaint?'

'Like I said, it's your decision.' Beckett spoke calmly. Her expression hadn't changed.

'What do you want?' Caelan folded her arms. 'Bearing in mind the last opportunity you offered almost got me killed.'

Beckett smirked. 'Hardly. Anyway, it's your job, what you thrive on.' She ate the last of her scone and took her time wiping her hands. 'A body was found this morning.'

'Whose?'

'It's… difficult. He's a mess.'

'How do you mean?'

Leaning closer, Beckett lowered her voice. 'We suspect he was tortured.'

Caelan winced. 'Who was he?'

'We've not confirmed his identity.'

'But you've an idea.' Caelan watched Beckett's face, but the other woman was giving nothing away.

'The post-mortem is later today. We'll know more then.'

'Where was the body found?'

'In an empty house.'

Caelan waited for Beckett to elaborate, but she raised her mug and concentrated on her coffee.

'Where?' Caelan asked eventually.

'It doesn't matter.'

'You mean you don't want to tell me. Why not?'

Beckett sighed. 'Not here.'

'Why ask to meet me then?'

'I wanted to see you, Caelan. You were beaten pretty badly yesterday.'

Caelan laughed. 'And you were concerned?'

'Of course. You're under my command.' Beckett put her empty cup down on the table. 'Are you willing to get straight back to work?'

Caelan sat back. Was she? She was in pain, yes, but not enough to keep her away from her job. Staying in the hotel was impractical and expensive. She couldn't go back to the apartment – she would need to look for a place of her own, and without a regular income, she would struggle. Perhaps she should hear Beckett out.

'What would you need me to do?'

'The operation Nicky was assigned to before she disappeared? We need someone back there.'

'And you want to send me?'

Beckett blinked. 'Not exactly.'

'What then?'

'We want both you and Nicky on it.'

Caelan was already shaking her head. 'No way. I can't work with her now. You think it wouldn't be obvious we have a history?'

'You're both too professional for that.'

'I wouldn't bet on it.'

'Then I'll have one or both of you transferred out of the department.' Beckett narrowed her eyes. 'Time to grow up, Caelan. Toe the line, or leave. Your decision.'

'Mine?' Caelan snorted. 'You've ordered me to do as I'm told or I'll be out of a job.'

'No, I said if you walk away now, it would be your final decision. No second chances, no comeback, no financial compensation. You'd be free to pursue other career paths, of course.' Beckett's expression made it clear what she thought of Caelan's chances of succeeding elsewhere.

'You think I haven't thought about it? Working regular hours, living life as the person named on your own birth certificate? Not having to constantly look over your shoulder, worry about every word you say?' Caelan made Beckett meet her eyes. 'Lying to everyone you meet? You think I wouldn't welcome a change?'

Beckett gave a tiny shake of her head. 'I think you'd be bored before your resignation was processed. You think you could stroll into an office job and be content? Think about it. Think about the criminals you've been close to, the lies you've told them. The money they've lost, the sentences they're serving. There are a few who'd love to know who you really are, I'm sure.'

Caelan laughed. 'You're threatening me. Perfect.'

'Don't be ridiculous. You know we would never compromise your safety. All I'm saying is, we can't protect someone who's no longer part of our operation.'

'Which is still a threat, you've just worded it differently.'

'Caelan, let me spell this out. You accept this opportunity, working with whoever I deem appropriate, or you'll find yourself transferred. Frankly, I don't have the time to argue.'

There was no choice. Caelan sighed. 'Fine. Give me the details.'

'Go to Enfield police station. This is a joint operation; there's a meeting at noon to discuss the details. You'll need to be ready to go immediately.'

'Come on, ma'am, you know I need more than that. Street clothes, business suit, what?'

'Casual. Scruffy, if you like.' Beckett's eyebrows danced. 'The clothes you're wearing now are perfect.'

Caelan glanced down at her comfortable old jeans, her creased hoody. 'This is all I have. I need to go shopping.'

'All you have? How do you mean?'

'Everything's back at the flat – Nicky's flat.'

'Then go and get what you need.' Beckett pushed back her chair. The conversation was over.

–

Caelan didn't make the call until she had left the train at Canada Water and was approaching the apartment building she had, until the previous evening, called home. Nicky answered immediately and Caelan began to talk, not giving her any opportunity to interrupt.

'Listen, I'm five minutes away, can you let me in so I can grab some of my gear? I'll be in and out, don't want to disturb you. See you soon.'

She ended the call and shoved the handset into her jeans pocket, cutting off Nicky's voice and ignoring the sting of guilt. Beckett had demanded professionalism, and that was what she would get.

She marched towards the building, six storeys of pale-yellow bricks and immaculate royal-blue paintwork. She smiled up at the CCTV camera on the corner of the building as she walked beneath it, knowing Peter would be manning the reception desk at this hour. The glass door already stood open and she stepped inside. When she had left the previous evening, she had had no intention of ever returning. Now, less than twenty-four hours later, she was back.

'Caelan.' Peter was on his feet, clearly confused. 'Ms Sturgess is here, she's upstairs.'

Caelan forced a smile. 'It's okay.'

'I wasn't sure if you knew...' His voice trailed away and he ran a hand over his mouth, embarrassed.

'I saw her last night. She's moved back in.'

'But...'

Caelan kept walking. 'I'll keep in touch, Peter. Say hi to your wife for me.'

He nodded, sensing she didn't want to talk.

Nicky's apartment was on the sixth floor. Despite her aching, bruised body, Caelan made herself walk up the stairs. She usually took the lift, but the stairs would take longer, and today, giving herself extra time mattered.

On each landing was a huge window offering a view of the Thames. Caelan paused, looked down at the green-grey water. Peter would have rung to tell Nicky she had arrived. The temptation to turn and run was almost overwhelming. She took a breath, steadied herself. She had done nothing wrong. She had mourned someone she believed to be lost to her, someone she had begun to love. There was no shame in that. She looked up to the floors above, began to move again.

As she approached, the door to number 135 opened. Nicky stood there, dressed in jeans and an old T-shirt Caelan recognised, because it was one of her own. Nicky said nothing, but stepped back, allowing her to enter. Caelan nodded.

'Thanks. I won't be long.' Her chest was tight, her throat feeling choked. She didn't trust herself to say any more. She still couldn't quite believe Nicky was here, alive and well though clearly exhausted, her eyes shadowed and watchful. She hesitated, wanting to speak but with no clear idea of what to say.

'I'll be in the kitchen.' Nicky's face was closed, her arms folded. She turned and walked away. Caelan watched her go, her jaw clenched. She wouldn't break down again. She was a professional, and she was working. There was no room for emotion.

In the bedroom, she pulled her rucksack out of the wardrobe, filling it with tops and jeans, a couple of hoodies. Underwear, socks. Enough for a few days. She pushed her feet into a pair of gaudy pink and purple Air Max trainers, pulled on a padded jacket. In the bathroom, she grabbed shower gel, toothpaste and her toothbrush. She'd go back to the hotel to shower. The apartment seemed smaller somehow, the atmosphere suffocating. She had enjoyed living here, though it had never felt like her own. Now she knew why. It wasn't, and never would be. Whatever legal processes had resulted in the property being signed over to her would have to be reversed now that Nicky had reappeared. It didn't matter.

She heaved the rucksack onto her shoulder and forced herself to approach the kitchen. Nicky sat at the table, shoulders hunched, drinking a glass of orange juice. Orange juice Caelan had bought. She frowned, realising she was being petty, and pushed the thought away.

'I'm going now,' she said.

Nicky set down her glass. 'Caelan, listen. I want you to stay here. This is your home, not mine. I'm going to rent somewhere else.'

Caelan stared. 'No. I can't.'

'I've never felt comfortable here anyway.' Nicky glanced around, her eyebrows drawn together. 'I don't want to live here. I've spoken to my solicitor. It's yours.'

'I don't want it.' Caelan hitched the rucksack higher on her shoulder as she turned away. Nicky stood abruptly, the chair legs screeching on the floor, but Caelan didn't look back as she pulled the door closed behind her.

2

The sleeping bag was thin and threadbare, offering little warmth and less comfort. Ryan drew his knees towards his chest, wondering how long he'd been asleep. He raised his head, slid his arm out from beneath it. Tried to remember when he'd last slept in a proper bed with pillows and a duvet. Reaching down to his jeans pocket, he pulled out his phone, the smell of his unwashed body drifting up from inside the sleeping bag and making his nose wrinkle. Ten thirty. He'd had about three hours' sleep. Not bad.

He sat up, rubbing his hands over his face, and leant back against the wall. He'd fallen asleep in a corner, out of the way at least. Who knew how many people had tramped through the room while he lay there, completely out of it. He had few belongings, but he always made sure they were pushed down inside the sleeping bag when he slept, with his body on top of them, not left out where anyone could see them. They wouldn't be there when he woke otherwise.

There was a battered sofa on the other side of the room. A young man and woman, probably still in their teens, lay on it, their limbs entwined. Ryan recognised the dazed, unfocused eyes; saw the pipe, made from a whisky miniature bottle, in the girl's hand. He felt the familiar tug of need and pushed himself to his feet.

In the kitchen, standing over the cooker and preparing the next batch, was Mulligan. The room was stuffy, hot, and

Ryan licked his lips, sweat beginning to dampen his palms. Mulligan turned, threw him a smile. Ryan stuffed his hands in his pockets. What was he grinning about? The rumour was he'd killed his own cousin over a drug debt, and Ryan could believe it.

'Morning, sunshine,' said Mulligan. 'Full English, or Continental?'

Ryan coughed, his chest rattling, pain thudding through it. 'Not hungry.'

Mulligan smirked. 'You want to lay off the smoking.'

'Funny.'

'Would if you could, I know.'

'How would you pay your rent if I did?' Was he slurring his words? Ryan couldn't tell.

His stomach churned as he gazed at the frying pans on the cooker top. Crack. He hated it.

He loved it.

'Looks like we're boiling.' Mulligan pointed to the nearest pan. 'Looking good, boyo.'

'Haven't you got some that's ready?' Ryan heard the desperation in his own voice, and flinched.

Mulligan tilted his head. 'Ah, pal. Is it bad? Need a helping hand this morning, is that it? You know, for a change?'

'Come on, man…'

Laughing, Mulligan turned back to his pans. 'I've only got a few rocks left, reserved for a special customer. Can't let you have them, I'm afraid.'

'Who? Whatever they're giving you, I'll pay double.' The words fell out of Ryan's mouth before he knew what he was going to say. Did he even have the money? He was pathetic, he knew it, and he didn't care. Mulligan held him and many others in the palm of his hand. They all danced to his tune, would get on their knees and beg if he asked them to. And while they were down there... Anything.

And Mulligan knew it. Played on it, as often as possible, for as long as he could.

'Mulligan? I'll give you double.'

'What?' Mulligan's lip curled. 'Twice fuck-all is still fuck-all. No can do. It's business. You'll have to wait until this lot's ready.' He nodded at his pans. 'I'm starting to cool it now, it'll only be a wee while.'

Ryan clenched his fists, knowing as he did so he was making a mistake. Sure enough, Mulligan turned, saw the movement. Cleared his throat. In a second, two heavyset men stood either side of Ryan. They didn't speak, didn't even look at him, but there was no mistaking their message. Shut the fuck up.

'Not going to have any unpleasantness, now are we?' Mulligan was totally unconcerned, humming as he worked. 'You're one of my best customers, Ryan. In fact, I'm thinking of giving you a loyalty card. You wouldn't want to spoil this perfect working relationship, would you?'

His chest heaving, Ryan forced himself to remain calm, knowing he had to bide his time. Mulligan was a sadistic fucker, and he liked to make people wait, purely for his own amusement. He was a businessman, and knew his customers well enough to take liberties, especially with those he allowed to doss down in his flat. Those were fair game, usually homeless and hopeless, their thoughts never wandering further than their next fix. Mulligan knew their desperation, and revelled in it. He needed them as much as they needed him, but he would never admit it.

Ryan held up his hands, and the two minders moved away. Mulligan grinned.

'That's better. I prefer to keep things friendly, you know that. We're pals, you and me.'

They weren't, but Ryan managed a nod. 'Could I have a glass of water?'

'Help yourself.' Mulligan jerked his head towards the cupboards. Ryan nodded his thanks, filled a mug, gulped down a couple of mouthfuls. He should think about going out to get some food, but… not yet. Not until… Not yet.

'So, who's this special customer?' he asked.

Mulligan lifted his shoulders. 'Someone who could put some extra business my way. Buy an extra cooker, splash out on some new pans.' He laughed, clearly at himself. 'Billy Big Time, that'll be me.'

'They coming for a sample, then? Testing the product?'

Mulligan rounded on him, all traces of laughter gone. 'Mind your mouth, you scrawny little shit. What's it to do with you?'

'Nothing, I… Nothing. Sorry.'

'Fucking think so. You're a junkie waster, Ryan. You don't ask me questions about my business.'

'All right. I said I'm sorry.'

Ryan turned away, wandered back to the living room. The young couple had gone.

So had his belongings and his sleeping bag.

3

Enfield police station reminded Caelan of a model a child had made by sticking cardboard boxes together. One shoebox on the bottom with two more piled on top. The small car park in front of the building was almost full, and she had to make several attempts at manoeuvring into a space. As she slammed her door, another vehicle entered the car park, reversing neatly into the last available parking spot. Caelan paused as she recognised the vehicle.

'Hello, stranger,' she called as the driver emerged. Tim Achebe was a few years older than Caelan – she guessed mid-thirties. There weren't many black police officers in the country who held a rank above that of inspector, but Achebe had risen to DCI in record time, and was widely tipped as a future Commissioner. She had first met him a few days ago, though with all that had happened, it felt longer.

Achebe grinned at her. 'Morning. We meet again.' He pointed to her battered face, wincing. 'Looks nasty. How are you feeling?'

'I've been better.'

'But you're here.'

'No point sitting around feeling sorry for myself.' She didn't add that she had nowhere to go except a hotel, even if she had wanted to take some time off to recuperate.

'No one could blame you, not after Nasenby, and...' He paused. 'You know.'

After she had discovered that Nicky, her colleague and former lover, whom she'd believed she'd seen killed, was still alive and had been hiding in a safe house. Caelan didn't trust herself to reply, and was thankful when Achebe didn't push for a response.

As they crossed the car park together, Caelan said, 'I wasn't sure who would be here.'

'One of my DIs has been involved, but she's off sick – had a car accident on her way home last night.'

'Shit. Is she okay?'

He held the door of the station open for her. 'Yes, thankfully. I spoke to her husband. Cuts and bruises.'

Caelan nodded, hesitating just inside the door. 'Who are we here to see?'

Achebe glanced around, lowered his voice. 'This is an Organised Crime Partnership operation.'

'We're working with the NCA?'

'Yeah. They've been sniffing around in Edmonton for a while, but haven't got very far.'

'Edmonton?' Caelan ran through the possibilities, didn't like any of them. Though she wasn't an expert, she knew of several gangs in the area, and anything linked to their activities could be dangerous. What was she walking into here?

'We're meeting with a couple of NCA officers, and... I understand you've been told about Nicky Sturgess?' Achebe glanced at her, then averted his gaze.

Caelan stepped closer to him. 'Did you know?'

Achebe raised his head. 'That she was alive, in hiding? No. I had no idea.'

She nodded, believing him. 'Who's questioning Michael?'

'Nasenby? I don't know. Still can't believe he was behind it all, to be honest.'

Caelan managed a short laugh, but it was an effort. 'You can't have been as surprised as I was. I thought I knew him.'

'Did he do that to your face?' Achebe touched his own cheek with a fingertip.

'Yeah. He didn't take kindly to being accused of murder. Several murders.'

'Including that of a ten-year-old child.' Achebe's face was blank, his voice little more than a whisper. Caelan touched his arm.

'We couldn't have known, Tim.'

Achebe rubbed his eyes. 'Just makes me sick to think of him sitting there, watching us run around trying to figure out what had happened, all the time knowing he'd done it. Enjoying watching us struggle.'

'You think that's what he was doing?'

'Fuck, I don't know. He was so... smooth, you know? Self-assured. But he had to know the truth would come out eventually.'

'I don't think he did. I think he believed he'd get away with it, even while I was listing all the evidence we had.'

'Arrogant prick.'

Caelan laughed. 'I think that's what he thought of you.'

Achebe's eyes opened wide. 'Bloody cheek.'

'Detective Small, DCI Achebe?'

The voice came from behind them. Caelan turned, looked at the man who had spoken. Stepping forward, he held out his hand, smiling at her. 'I'm Spencer Reid, NCA. It's good to meet you. I've heard... Well, I've heard about you.'

Caelan shook his hand, stepped away as he turned to greet Achebe. She hadn't worked with the National Crime Agency before, though she had been involved in a couple of joint operations with the organisation it had replaced. The NCA existed to bring to justice serious and organised criminals, including those involved in drug trafficking, the sexual abuse and exploitation of children, and money laundering. Its representatives worked in partnership with other organisations in the UK and internationally. Caelan wondered what they wanted with her.

Reid gestured towards the door he had emerged from. 'We're through there.'

Caelan and Achebe followed him into a dingy corridor. The walls were painted grey, scuff marks visible above the skirting board. The floor was carpeted in navy blue, with a path trodden down the centre. Battered wooden doors were set along the corridor at regular intervals. Caelan kept her eyes on the back of Reid's head as he marched along in front of her. She had promised herself once before that she would not be dragged back into this world, but she had allowed it to happen. Had that been a mistake? As they walked, she decided that if she had the slightest reservation about whatever they were here to discuss, she would leave. She would go back to Beckett, ask for the transfer she'd threatened. Major Crimes, Protection or Security... There were possibilities. As Reid stopped outside one of the doors and pushed it open, Caelan set her jaw. Elizabeth Beckett had lied to her before, or at least hadn't been entirely honest about what she knew. Caelan felt little loyalty to a woman she did not trust.

Reid stood back, allowing Caelan and Achebe to enter the room before him. It wasn't large, around four metres square, with one window on the back wall. An oval table stood in the centre, three people already seated around it. Caelan's stomach dropped as she saw Nicky beside Richard Adamson. The other man, she had never seen before. Though she had half expected Nicky to be here, seeing her again so soon was like a punch to the stomach.

Richard smiled as Caelan pulled out the chair beside his, clearly uncomfortable to be sitting between her and Nicky. 'Come to join the party?' he said.

She nodded at him. 'Apparently.'

Nicky kept her eyes fixed on the far wall, not acknowledging Caelan. Richard cleared his throat.

'I didn't think you'd be at work, not after...' He flushed. 'After yesterday.'

'Forget it.' Caelan raised a hand to the dressing on her temple, desperate to remove it. 'I have.'

She heard Nicky sigh, but didn't look at her. The comment had been about Michael Nasenby, but if Nicky wanted to take offence, let her. Guilt could skew your vision, as Caelan knew only too well. Nicky wasn't stupid; she would know how badly Caelan was hurting. No doubt Nicky was too, but Caelan put the thought out of her mind. They were here as professionals, the best in their field. This wasn't the time for bickering.

Spencer Reid took a seat, setting an iPad on the table. He nodded towards the man sitting beside him. 'This is my colleague, Phil Webster.'

Webster nodded. 'Good to meet you all.'

Reid leant forward. 'Nicky, do you want to brief your colleagues on the basics?'

Nicky ran a hand through her hair, glancing at Richard but not Caelan. 'Okay. A few months ago, we had word from an informant who knew the drug scene around here. He couldn't tell us much, just that a couple of the local street dealers had been offering different drugs – coke and crack when they'd only had cannabis before. Nothing concrete, but worth keeping an eye on. I was asked to spend some time on the streets, see what I could dig up. A major dealer had been jailed, potentially leaving a gap for someone else to move into.'

'And?' Caelan said. Nicky lifted her shoulders, let them fall. 'Nothing. The street dealers? I hardly saw them.'

Achebe frowned. 'What about the informant?'

Nicky shot a look at Reid and Webster. 'He's dead,' she said.

Realisation hit Caelan. 'The man they found this morning.'

Nicky turned to look at her, and Caelan forced herself to maintain eye contact. 'Yes. Did Assistant Commissioner Beckett tell you—'

'That it appeared he'd been tortured?' Caelan nodded. 'She mentioned it.'

'It's been confirmed.' Reid's face was expressionless. 'He hadn't been dead long when his body was discovered. A matter of hours, according to the pathologist. His fingers had all been broken by hammer blows. Most of his toes too. Boiling water had been poured into his mouth, and on his back...' Reid paused. 'On his back, he was severely burnt. They'd used an iron.'

There was a silence as everyone in the room visualised the agony.

'What was his name?' Caelan asked softly. Reid didn't need to check.

'Anthony Bryce.'

Caelan said nothing. The name prodded at a memory, but she couldn't recall where she'd heard it before. Someone from school? Someone she'd arrested? She knew it would irritate her, catching like a broken fingernail until she remembered where she had heard it.

'Does he have a record?' she asked.

Reid shrugged. 'Minor drug stuff. He's never been inside.'

'How did he end up as an informant?'

'He'd only contacted us once, with the information about the possibility of a new supplier or major dealer arriving in Edmonton.'

Caelan considered it, pinching her lower lip between her finger and thumb. 'Then why was he tortured? He must have known more than he told us.'

'Or someone thought he did,' said Nicky. 'His death was unexpected, and—'

'And we need to find out what happened,' said Reid. He spoke quietly, but Caelan could see he was rattled. She wasn't surprised. Murder, torture. Most people wouldn't have the stomach for it. This wasn't about minor drug dealing.

'Do we know anything else about Bryce?' she asked. 'Was he a dealer himself?'

Webster folded his arms, the material of his shirt tightening over his bulky shoulders. 'We don't think so.'

Caelan gave him a hard stare. 'Why did you think it was necessary to send an undercover officer in? I was told Nicky had been attempting to infiltrate a major drug gang. It sounds more like you were looking at low-level street dealing at first.'

Reid shot Webster a glance. 'Maybe, but the drugs are coming from somewhere. We wanted to poke around, see what fell out of the woodwork.'

Caelan snorted, pushed back her chair. 'I've heard enough. Good afternoon.'

Beside her, Richard Adamson was also on his feet. 'We're wasting our time here,' he said. Nicky didn't move, staring at Reid and Webster with something like contempt.

Reid held up his hands. 'Wait, the plan was we work together, wasn't it?'

'Then tell us what you know.' Caelan pushed her chair beneath the table and picked up her bag. She'd give them another thirty seconds, and no more. 'You've a dead body now, a man who was tortured before he died. You don't think it's time to take this more seriously? This isn't kids playing at being gangsters.'

Reid sighed. 'We know. Why do you think we asked for more officers?'

'I've no idea, but if we're going to work together, you need to be open with us. It's our lives on the line, not yours.'

Webster was watching her. 'What my colleague means is, we're aware of the seriousness of the situation. We're told you lot are the best in the business. I'll be honest, this thing has blown up in our faces.'

Achebe said, 'Another man died, a few weeks ago now.' He looked at Reid, at Webster. 'Tell them.'

'He was tortured too,' Webster said softly. 'The same injuries as Anthony Bryce suffered. The difference is...' He allowed a silence to develop, as though unwilling to complete the sentence.

'The difference is the first victim was a police officer,' Reid finished for him.

Caelan's stomach dropped. 'What?'

'A young constable. He'd only been in the job nine months. We've no idea why he was targeted. His patch was miles away. He didn't turn up for his shift at Limehouse station, and no one knew where he'd gone. A few days later, his body was found in an empty house.'

'The same one where Bryce's was discovered?'

'No, a few streets away.'

'Other than the manner of their deaths, what's the connection between the two victims?' asked Adamson.

'We don't know.' Reid's frustration was evident in his voice, in his frown. 'The PC – Ben Rainey was his name – wasn't a drug user. His mobile phone gave us no clues, neither did his laptop. His family and friends know nothing, his colleagues and sergeant are as bemused as we are. No one can understand what he was doing in Edmonton.'

'That's where he was found?' said Caelan.

'Same as Bryce.'

'If they were both tortured, we could assume the two of them knew something,' said Richard Adamson.

'But what? We spoke to Bryce when Rainey's body was found — discreetly, of course. Bryce didn't know Rainey. He'd never heard of him, didn't recognise his face.' Webster grimaced. 'Not that his own mother would have done when his body was found. Bryce hadn't heard any whispers about a copper poking his nose in where it wasn't wanted, or rumours about what had happened. It's a mystery.'

'And now Bryce is dead too.' Caelan sat back down, though her instinct was to head for the door. This situation was more complex than she had imagined, and more serious. People who were willing to torture and kill were not ones she wanted to meet, much less infiltrate.

'When Nicky was taken off the case, we lost our eyes on the ground.' Reid kept his voice level, but the implied criticism was clear. 'Maybe someone was spooked.'

'I didn't—' Nicky began.

Reid spread his hands. 'I don't mean by you, Detective Sturgess. Possibly by Bryce himself, or maybe it was just paranoia. You know how careful the people at the top of these gangs are.'

'But they knew to target Bryce. That wasn't accidental,' said Caelan.

'It doesn't mean they knew he'd spoken to us,' Nicky pointed out. 'He could have pissed them off in any number of ways. We're assuming the torture was because he grassed, but it doesn't have to have been.'

'A punishment for something else?' Reid frowned.

'Or just someone's idea of making a point. Torture makes people sit up and take notice. Maybe Bryce's death was a warning,' said Nicky.

Caelan glanced at her. 'A warning to whom? About what? Bryce got more than a slap on the wrist.'

'I don't know.' Nicky folded her arms. 'I'm making suggestions.'

'You've spent time in the area, you know people. Who could have done this?' Caelan knew she was being unfair, forcing Nicky under the spotlight, but she didn't care. There had been enough focus on her own job performance recently. Time for someone else to feel the glare of attention.

Nicky scowled at her. 'That wasn't what I was here for, Caelan, as you've been told.'

'Still...'

Reid was studying them, face impassive. Caelan shut up, not wanting him to pick up on the issues between them. Richard Adamson sat forward. 'Maybe you could explain why the three of us are here?'

Webster nodded. 'Obviously something's brewing in Edmonton. My guess is that the new dealer who seems to have moved in has ruffled some feathers. We think someone's making a statement, trying to warn everyone in the area not to mess with them. We need to know who it is, so we can shut them down.'

'And that's where we come in?' asked Adamson.

'That's the idea. It could be risky, though. Two deaths already, the victims tortured for a prolonged period before-hand...'

'You're really selling it to us,' said Caelan. Webster laughed.

'Telling it how it is. I wouldn't want to go in there, but undercover work isn't our bag. You know as well as I do what sort of reputation the area has. Gangs, violent crime, antisocial behaviour...'

'Crimes that happen everywhere.'

Webster widened his eyes, an exaggerated gesture of incredulity. 'You're saying gangs are everywhere?'

'We'll leave them alone.' Irritated, Caelan spoke with more confidence than she felt. Webster responded with a smirk.

'And hope they do the same to you when you're in their territory, asking questions? Big ask, wouldn't you say? We're talking about hardcore criminals, people who've already tortured and killed.'

'I thought you wanted to find them? Shut them down?'

'Yeah, but...' He shook his head. 'It's a risk, is all I'm saying. These people could be bankrolling the Edmonton gangs. We're talking serious money here.'

He wasn't telling Caelan anything she didn't already know. She ignored him.

Reid frowned at his colleague. 'They won't barge in and start asking questions,' he said. 'I think they're subtler than that, Phil.'

'Just saying. They need to be prepared.'

'I'm sure they will be.'

'How would the operation work?' Nicky demanded.

'The flat you stayed in before is still vacant. We thought you could go back there, make out you'd been away for a while. A short prison sentence, maybe?'

'Not a good idea. It's not wise to pretend you've done something when you never have,' Nicky told him. 'Too many chances to be found out.'

'How do you mean?'

'Say I met someone whose sister, unbeknown to me, really had been in the same prison I'd pretended to have served time in. They could ask about me, she'd never have heard my name, wouldn't know my face. I wouldn't be able to explain it, and at best, it'd be awkward. At worst, it could show I'm pretending to be someone I'm not.'

Webster thought about it. 'You could have been on different wings.'

'But there'd still be things that would be common knowledge, and I wouldn't have a clue about them. The governor, the food, what the visitor centre was like...'

'In our game, staying as close to the truth as possible is generally the best idea.' Caelan spoke to Webster, but watched Nicky's face. Nicky didn't react, but Caelan was aware of Adamson shifting position beside her. Reid was grinning, obviously enjoying his colleague being taught a lesson in undercover policing. Webster held up his hands.

'All right, point taken. You say whatever you want.'

'What are we looking for?' Adamson asked.

'Honestly? We don't know. It might be nothing, but we've got two dead bodies. We don't want a third.'

'What finally killed Rainey and Bryce?' Caelan wasn't sure she wanted to know.

Tim Achebe sat up straight. 'Bryce was strangled. We don't know what with. Whatever it was left no trace evidence. Rainey bled out after someone rammed a screwdriver into his chest.' He stopped, rubbed his face with both hands. Blinked. 'They'd both been beaten, punches and slaps to their faces. Abrasions and cuts on their wrists and ankles showed they'd been tied to chairs.'

Caelan stared at him. 'You're SIO?'

'Yeah. Like I said, one of my DIs was involved.'

'Why?'

'Because we work together as necessary,' Reid said quickly. Caelan raised an eyebrow.

'And the truth?'

Reid flushed. 'Come on, Detective Small...'

'If we're working together, we need to be honest with each other.'

'Okay.' Achebe sat back in his chair, his eyes on Caelan's. 'The DI is called Liv Hobbs. She transferred into my team about six months ago. Heard of her?'

Caelan thought about it. 'No.'

'Sister of Jackson Hobbs,' Nicky said, 'who's currently serving sixteen years for drug offences. He's the jailed dealer I mentioned a few minutes ago.'

'Meaning?'

'Meaning, Liv grew up around here,' Achebe told her. 'Drugs has been the family business for a couple of generations. In fact, Liv reckons she was only conceived because her dad broke out of prison and spent a few hours at home with her mum before being captured and locked up again. She knows this place, and she knows the people. She can help us.'

'What do her family say about that?'

'Strangely enough, she's estranged from them. They didn't take kindly to her joining the force.'

'Imagine.'

'And she came from Limehouse nick.' Achebe paused, eyebrows raised.

Caelan saw the connection. 'She knows Ben Rainey?'

'Not well, but she'd seen him around the station.'

'Interesting. Who's investigating the deaths of Rainey and Anthony Bryce?'

'As we've established, I'm SIO, but a local team will be doing the legwork. They won't know about you three.'

'Why do you want us all?' asked Adamson. 'Who are we supposed to be? What are our stories?'

'Nicky already has one. You two – I don't know. A couple who've just been given a flat on the estate?' Reid snapped his fingers. 'You could move into the one Nicky had.'

'Handy. You ready to be my boyfriend again, Richard?' Caelan nudged him. It was the kind of comment she usually rolled her eyes at, but it was a chance to needle Nicky again. It was pathetic, she knew, but she wasn't going to let the opportunity pass by. Adamson grinned.

'I'm sure I'll cope. Will you?'

Caelan watched Nicky's cheeks flush as the others laughed, feeling a tiny jolt of shame.

'What's my link to Caelan and Richard?' Nicky demanded when they had quietened down.

Reid clicked his tongue as he considered it. 'Caelan could be your sister?'

'It's an idea.' Again, as Nicky spoke, Caelan's eyes were drawn to her face. Her expression gave nothing away, but Caelan knew she was irritated. Webster was smug, Reid was slick, and neither of them appeared to know what they were hoping to achieve. As collaborations went, it wasn't ideal. She had been determined to remain professional, and here she was acting like a schoolkid. What had Beckett said? *Time to grow up.* Caelan folded her arms, forced Reid to meet her eyes. He smiled at her, clearly believing himself to be in charge.

'Richard asked why there needs to be three of us. You didn't answer him,' she said. Reid forced a laugh.

'We need answers. Three people should get the job done quicker than one or two, wouldn't you say?'

She tipped her head to the side, watching him steadily. 'No, I wouldn't.'

Achebe shot her a look, his eyebrows lifting, mouth struggling to fight off a grin.

'Even if Caelan and I are supposed to be sisters, we'll have to be careful,' said Nicky. Reid frowned, beginning to interrupt; Caelan talked over him.

'Exactly. In fact, I think it'd be best if we pretended we don't know each other at all.'

Nicky was nodding. 'Richard? What do you think?'

He cleared his throat. 'I agree. We should avoid each other. We can meet up if necessary, out of the area.'

For a second, Webster looked as though he might argue. Then he said, 'You know what, you're the experts. We'll leave the details up to you.'

'Good of you.' Caelan smiled to take the bite off the comment. It wasn't entirely successful. Webster set his jaw, but said nothing.

Reid was fiddling with the iPad. He held it up, turning it so they could all see the mugshot on the screen. 'This is Frankie Hamilton. He's due to be released from prison in a few days' time. He was a well-known drug user, though he's supposed to have cleaned up his act inside.'

'Really. Found Jesus, did he?' Webster sniffed. Reid ignored him.

'His girlfriend's moved on since Frankie went to jail. Had two kids with someone else – Frankie's brother, as it happens. She hasn't bothered to tell Frankie about her change of living arrangements, and we're guessing he'll be miffed when he finds out.'

'Miffed?' Caelan couldn't help repeating.

Reid grinned. 'We're hoping it might prompt a relapse.'

'You're all heart. The idea is Frankie leads us to a dealer?'

'Well, he might. Who knows?'

Nicky heaved a sigh. 'But you *know* who the dealers are. You showed me photographs of them.'

Reid nodded. 'And you said yourself you haven't seen them. Where are they?'

'A shallow grave. Prison.' Caelan counted them off on her fingers. 'Selling in a different borough, even a different town. Found a job with less chance of doing jail time or being killed.'

'Point taken. We heard Frankie was coming out, and thought… Well, it seemed like something we could use.'

'We'll keep it in mind.' Caelan smiled. Reid exchanged a glance with Webster.

'Thanks, everyone, but we need to leave – we have another meeting,' he said. 'We'll be in touch again over the next few days.'

After handshakes and exchanges of contact details, Reid and Webster left. Caelan pushed back her chair, crossing her legs.

'A conference call would have done. I thought we were heading out today?'

'That's what I was told,' said Adamson. 'Nicky?'

She puffed out her cheeks. 'No idea.'

Achebe was checking his phone. 'I've got to shoot off too.'

'Tim – Ben Rainey,' Caelan said.

'What about him?'

'There's been nothing in the news about his death, has there?'

'Not that we've seen. No details, anyway. Not that we'd want there to be. The press decided he'd overdosed, or it was some gang-related dispute that wasn't worth reporting.' Achebe gave a grim smile. 'A young black man found dead – what else could it be?'

'The reporters didn't know he was a police officer?'

'I guess not. If they did, they didn't care.' Achebe pushed back his chair, began to stand.

'A police officer murdered, and no press baying for blood? No public outcry?'

'Like I said, it's how we wanted it. His family agreed – they preferred to be left to grieve in peace.'

'It's understandable, but...'

Achebe was buttoning his jacket. 'I'll be honest – the investigation into Rainey's death has been ongoing for three weeks. In that time, we've discovered nothing.'

'You mean the investigation's stalled?' Caelan had only known Achebe for a few days, but she'd already formed an opinion of him and the way he worked. Allowing the death of a police officer to go unpunished would be unacceptable to him.

To them all.

He met her eyes, his irritation clear, though when he spoke, his tone hadn't changed. 'Believe me, we've been trying. I've been busy with other matters, as you know, but Liv, my DI, has been keeping me updated. Now that she's out of action, I've been asked to lead the team looking for the people who killed Ben Rainey.'

'And Anthony Bryce.'

'Of course. That goes without saying.'

Does it? Caelan wanted to say. 'You're certain the two deaths are linked?'

'Hard to believe they're not.'

'But you've found nothing the two of them have in common?'

He checked his watch. 'Not yet. Caelan, I—'

'Assistant Commissioner Beckett didn't mention Ben Rainey's murder.'

'No doubt she was expecting me to tell you. Like I said, it's been hushed up.'

Caelan snorted. 'I suppose I shouldn't be surprised. Beckett's good at withholding information.'

'She does what she has to.'

'You think? Since it appears we're not needed by our friends at the NCA today, I'd like to join the investigation into Rainey's death. Is that okay?'

Pushing his hands into his trouser pockets, Achebe rocked back on his heels. 'People who knew Rainey have already given statements, and no one could help us. We've no sightings of Ben Rainey the night we believe he was killed. CCTV cameras around the area he was found are scarce, and the footage we do have is useless.'

'Where did he live?'

'Northolt.' He raised his eyebrows.

'My favourite place.' It wasn't. A few days before, a young man Caelan was supposed to have been tailing had been shot and killed there. It hadn't been her finest hour.

'We've managed to find footage of him going into Northolt Underground station, and we've seen him on the train. He's alone, talks to no one. He gets off at Oxford Circus, then we lose him.'

'What about at Edmonton?'

'The station there? No, we've not spotted him.'

'But you think he travelled there on the Tube?'

'From Oxford Circus, he could have taken the Victoria Line, gone to Seven Sisters. From there, you get on the Overground to Edmonton Green.'

'But?'

'Well, we haven't picked him up anywhere, so perhaps he didn't. Maybe he got a taxi, or a lift. I don't know.'

'Or maybe he was only taken to Edmonton after he was killed. What about his Oyster card? Have we checked if he used it that night?'

The look Achebe gave her was hard to read. 'Yes, Caelan, but he didn't. When his body was found and we searched his bedroom, we found the Oyster card.'

'Meaning he used a Travelcard on the day he was killed?'

'No one remembered selling him one – yes, we checked. He didn't use his debit or credit card to buy one either.'

'Then it's possible he used cash, that he was being careful, covering his tracks. Interesting.'

'Or it means nothing.' He took a step backwards. 'I need to leave, Caelan.'

'Two seconds, Tim. Please?'

A sigh. 'All right.'

'What do we know about Bryce?'

'As you know, it's early days. He didn't have a fixed address – the one he gave when he contacted us is empty. We've tried to track down his mother, who we assume is next of kin, but no luck so far. Listen, go to South Harrow. That's where the incident room is. We didn't want to base it here – too close for comfort. I'll let them know you're coming.' He looked at Nicky and Richard. 'What about you two?'

Nicky was frowning. 'We should all report back to Commander Penrith.'

'Is he in charge now?' Achebe asked.

'Since our old guv'nor's been arrested for murder, yes,' Richard told him. Achebe screwed up his face.

'Fair point.' He was halfway through the door. 'Seems I'll be speaking to you all soon.'

4

Ninety minutes later, Caelan stepped off the train at Northolt and hitched her rucksack onto her shoulder. As she left the station and crossed the road, she didn't allow her eyes to stray towards the entrance to the underpass where the man she had been following, the man she should have kept safe, had been killed only a few days before. Standing at the bus stop, she kept her head turned away as though looking out for a bus approaching. She had done her best to keep him alive, her hands and clothes stained with his blood when the paramedics arrived, but it had been futile. He had died on the operating table as the surgeons fought to save him. She blinked away the memory of the blood, and his mother's devastated face. She was here to speak to another grieving family, and they deserved her full attention.

A bus took her close to Radcliffe Way, where PC Ben Rainey had lived with his parents and younger brother and sister. Large blocks of flats and maisonettes dominated the area. The Rainey family's home stood at the edge of an expanse of concrete, facing a row of garages. There were ten properties, and Caelan found the number she was looking for on the door of the house on the bottom left of the block. Drifting from the property above through an open window came beautiful, haunting music and a voice singing in a language Caelan couldn't understand. She stood and listened, the sounds of the street, of busy modern London, fading into the background.

'Any reason you're waiting outside our house?'

The question came from behind her. Caelan turned to see two teenagers. They wore black blazers and trousers, white shirts, blue-and-black-striped ties and quizzical expressions. Joseph and Miriam, Ben Rainey's siblings. She smiled.

'Yeah, sorry. I'm a police officer.' She remembered her outfit – the jeans, the gaudy trainers. 'Though I might not look like one today.'

Joseph inclined his head. 'You got ID?'

Caelan unzipped her jacket and reached into the inside pocket. Usually, being undercover meant leaving your warrant card at home. Since she'd had to pack as much as she could carry at Nicky's flat with no idea when she might be able to collect the rest of her belongings, her warrant card had been the first item she grabbed. She'd just have to be careful, or give it to Achebe or Beckett to lock away safely.

The boy took it, and he and his sister peered at it. Miriam looked Caelan up and down.

'Why are you here?' she asked.

'I need to speak to your parents, and the two of you.'

'About…' She stumbled over the name, was unable to say it. 'About my brother?'

'I'm afraid so.'

Miriam screwed up her face. 'More questions?'

'Why haven't you caught this…' Joseph frowned, his mouth working. 'Why haven't you found him?'

Caelan took back the warrant card, pushed it into her pocket. 'Honestly? I don't know. I've only just been drafted onto the case.'

'And what, you couldn't read up on what we've told you people already? You had to come here to upset everyone all over again?' Miriam's voice was harsh, but Caelan could see

41

tears in her eyes. Her brother stepped closer to her, the two of them moving towards their front door, blocking it from Caelan's view. 'We don't want you to come in. Our mum and dad...'

'They're devastated.' Caelan made it a statement, not a question.

Joseph scrubbed his eyes with his knuckles. 'Can you blame them?' He folded his arms across his chest. 'They won't want to see you, or talk to you. Can't you leave us alone?'

Caelan paused. 'I want to find the person who killed your brother, who did this to your family. I wouldn't be here disturbing you if it wasn't important, if I didn't believe you can help me.'

Miriam pulled her bag higher on her shoulder. 'We've answered questions, given statements. There's nothing more we can tell you.'

'Read the reports.' Joseph twisted his features into a sneer. 'You're not coming in.'

'Miriam? Joseph? What's going on?'

Behind them, the door had opened, a man's face appearing. Seeing Caelan, he stepped outside, slid an arm around each of his children's shoulders. The gesture could have seemed like a warning, either to her or to his son and daughter, but there was no anger in his face. Weariness and defeat, but nothing else. Caelan turned as she heard footsteps behind her. A young constable was approaching – the uniformed presence she had requested. She didn't know him, but it didn't matter. He was here to observe, nothing more.

'She's from the police,' Joseph was saying. 'She wants to talk to us again. We told her—'

'That you would fetch one of your parents, I hope?' Charles Rainey spoke quietly, but with authority. Joseph bowed his head.

'Sorry, Dad.'

His father smiled, took a step back. 'Your mother and I don't need looking after, you know.'

Miriam looked at Caelan. 'Sorry. We just…'

Caelan smiled. 'I understand. No problem.'

As Miriam and Joseph disappeared inside, Mr Rainey held out his hand for Caelan to shake. 'I apologise. It's been… a huge blow to our family. My children were trying to protect us, that's all. A role reversal. Though we couldn't protect Benjamin.' He swallowed, blinking rapidly. Caelan waited, giving him time. 'I'm sorry,' he repeated.

'Please don't apologise. I wish it wasn't necessary to disturb you again, but…'

'There's been another murder.' Charles Rainey choked on the word. 'They told me on the phone.'

'I'm afraid so.'

'Come inside, please, both of you.'

He stepped back to allow her into the house first. Inside, Caelan slipped off her shoes, nudged the uniform to do the same. Charles Rainey went into the kitchen, saying he'd make some tea.

'What's your name?' Caelan whispered.

'PC Daynes, ma'am.'

'No need for the ma'am. First name?'

'Jordan.'

Caelan blinked at him. 'We really are getting younger.'

She led the way down a carpeted hallway to the living room.

'Some police officers are here, Abigail,' Charles Rainey called. As Caelan entered the room, Mrs Rainey was getting

43

out of her chair, her hand outstretched. Caelan took it between both of her own.

'I'm so sorry about your son,' she said, as Mr Rainey came to stand beside his wife. Mrs Rainey managed a smile as they sat, waving Caelan into an armchair.

'Thank you. Have you... Is there any news? Charles mentioned another murder.' Her expression was fearful, her eyes tired, the lids appearing swollen. Caelan now wished she had stayed away. Ben Rainey's parents had answered too many questions already.

'That's correct, I'm afraid,' she said. 'I understand this is painful and difficult, but it's possible that the victim discovered today was murdered by the same people who killed your son.' Her stomach clenched as she said the words. They sounded stark, unsympathetic, but she could think of no other way of approaching the possibility of a link.

Charles Rainey was frowning. 'Was this poor man a police officer?'

'No, sir, but he was known to the police.'

'You mean he was a criminal?' Rainey's lips thinned. 'Our son didn't know any criminals, Officer, except those he had contact with through his work. I'm not naïve, or stupid. I know there are gangs, drugs. Crime. But my children... My children would never get involved. They know right from wrong, they respect people, they attend church. They're good kids.'

Caelan looked at him, seeing how much he needed to believe what he had said. All he had left to cling to was his belief in his family's future.

'I understand, sir. The man whose body was discovered today was called Anthony Bryce. Does the name mean anything to either of you?'

They looked at each other, thought about it. Then Abigail Rainey said, 'No.'

Caelan pulled her phone from her pocket. 'I have a photograph...' She stood, handed Charles Rainey the phone.

He stared at the image on the screen, tilting the handset so his wife could see it too. 'A mugshot?' He looked up at Caelan, his disapproval clear.

She tried a smile. 'It's all we had.'

'I don't recognise him. You're asking if our son knew this man?' Rainey returned the phone. 'We raise our children to have respect for the law, Officer. None of them have criminals for friends.'

'I understand, but you'll appreciate I need to ask.' Caelan cleared her throat to give herself a second to phrase the next question. 'You see, Anthony Bryce was the same age as your son.' She looked at them, chose her words carefully. 'I'm wondering if it's possible they could have known each other at school, or maybe through a youth club or sports team? Bryce grew up in Hounslow, and still lived there.'

Ben Rainey's parents exchanged a glance. 'Benjamin went to the same school Miriam and Joseph attend,' Charles Rainey said. 'He used to run, but not competitively. He played for a local boys' football team for a few years, but... I don't remember anyone called Anthony.'

Caelan looked at Benjamin's mother, who was frowning. 'Mrs Rainey?'

'No, there's no one.' She spoke quickly, her eyes on the carpet, her hands tightly folded in her lap.

Was she holding something back? Caelan waited, allowed the silence to stretch. No one spoke. Mr Rainey looked at her, his eyebrows raised, his eyes pleading with her. Leave us alone. He stood up slowly.

'I'll make that tea.'

Caelan smiled. 'I'd like to talk to Miriam and Joseph too.'

'Is it really necessary?' Abigail Rainey picked up a cushion from the sofa, held it close.

'This property has three bedrooms, does it, Mrs Rainey?'

'Yes. Benjamin and Joseph shared a room.' Her chin trembled. 'Benjamin was saving to get a place of his own, but…'

'London prices,' Caelan said quickly.

'That's right. He looked for a house share, but with his job… He wouldn't have wanted to disturb people, coming and going at all hours. Ben was so…' The tears were falling now. Caelan shot Daynes a glance, and he jumped up, hurried out of the room. 'He was considerate. He always wanted to be a police officer, you know. Since he was a boy.' Emotion overcame her; she covered her face with her hands.

Mr Rainey hurried back in, handed out mugs of milky tea. He sat beside his wife and wrapped his arms around her. PC Daynes followed him with a box of tissues. He passed them to Mr Rainey, who nodded his thanks, his own mouth trembling. Caelan took a polite sip of her tea, tried not to grimace. Too weak. Daynes picked up a cup and sat down, his face showing his discomfort. Caelan wondered how long he'd been a police officer, whether he'd had to visit the family of a victim of violent crime before. She was guessing not.

Mrs Rainey gently pushed her husband away, a wad of tissues clutched in her hand.

'I'm okay, Charles,' she said. 'Let's try to answer their questions.'

'Thank you,' Caelan said. Charles Rainey nodded.

'You're CID, aren't you?' he asked, taking in Caelan's outfit.

'I am. I apologise for my clothes – I'm not usually so scruffy.'

Mr Rainey tried to smile. 'Called in on your day off?'

46

'Something like that.'

'Ben wanted to be a detective,' Abigail Rainey told them. Caelan sat forward. 'Out of uniform within a couple of years, he'd say.' She reached for her husband's hand. 'We were happy to hear it. We thought...' She swallowed a sob. 'We thought he'd be safer, off the streets.' Pressing a tissue to her eyes, she bowed her head, her shoulders shaking. Her husband pulled her close again. Caelan got to her feet.

'I'll give you a moment. May I see Ben's room?'

Mr Rainey's head jerked up. 'Are you going to talk to Joseph and Miriam? Shouldn't we be present if so?'

Caelan held up a hand. 'I'm not going to ask them any questions, sir, I promise.'

Rainey frowned, clearly torn between his need to comfort his wife and the desire to protect his children. Caelan kept walking. She nodded at Daynes. He remained in his chair.

She passed framed family photographs, including one of PC Benjamin Rainey standing proudly in his uniform, halfway up the stairs. She paused, studied his face. Touched a fingertip to his cheek.

On the landing, there were four closed doors. The only sound was Mrs Rainey's muted sobbing downstairs. Caelan stepped up to the nearest door and tapped on it. Miriam opened it instantly, as though she had been waiting for Caelan's knock.

'Sorry. I was looking for your brothers' room.'

Miriam gave a tiny laugh. 'Next door. You usually just need to follow the music.'

'But not today.'

'Not since Ben died.' Miriam stared into Caelan's eyes as though challenging her. 'We're all creeping around the house trying not to upset each other.'

'It's understandable.'

The girl's eyes flared. 'It's suffocating.'

Caelan took a step back. 'I can't imagine—'

A breath, drawn in quickly, sounding like the hiss of a snake. 'No. You can't.' Miriam's gaze was hard as she closed her door.

Caelan paused, pushing her hands into her jeans pockets as Joseph appeared beside her.

'Still here?' His voice was taut. Clearly, he wished she wasn't.

'Could I have a look at your room, please?'

He frowned at her. 'Our room? Why? It's already been searched.' He hunched his shoulders as though expecting an attack. 'My stuff as well as Ben's. They went through everything.'

'I'm sorry.'

'Are you? What were they looking for? What did they think Ben had done?' His eyes shone with tears. 'All he wanted was to be a police officer. Even when he was a kid, it was all he could talk about. He loved his job. Loved it. And now he's dead.'

'Your mum said Ben wanted to be a detective?'

A flicker of his lips. Not quite a smile, but the ghost of one. 'Yeah, he did. He'd have done it, too. He was like that – determined.'

'Ambitious?'

Joseph shuffled his feet. 'He knew what he wanted. Nothing wrong with that.'

'I'm not saying there is.' Caelan tried to meet his eyes, but he was staring at his socks. 'Did he talk to you about his work?'

His head shot up. 'No. No, it was confidential, wasn't it?'

'I mean generally. Listen, Joseph, I'm hoping you can help me. Help us find the person who did this to your brother.'

Movement at the bottom of the stairs. Charles Rainey's voice: 'Excuse me? I'd like to be present if you're questioning my children, as I've already explained.'

48

Joseph leaned over the banister. 'It's fine, Dad. We're just talking.'

Mr Rainey started up the stairs. 'Even so, I should be with you.'

'It's okay, I'm leaving.' Caelan lowered her voice. 'Joseph, if you think of anything, please call me.'

He shook his head, screwed up his mouth. 'There's nothing.'

'Let me give you my number...'

'Detective Small, I'd be grateful if you'd leave now.' Charles Rainey strode across the landing. 'You've upset my wife, and my children. I...' He swallowed hard. 'Please. Please, just leave.'

'It's okay. We're going.'

PC Daynes was already by the front door. Mrs Rainey stood in the kitchen doorway, blowing her nose. Caelan met her eyes, saw the agony in them. She turned away, knowing she never should have come here to trample over their grief.

–

Back on the train, she found a seat, allowed her head to fall back as she attempted to relax. The visit had been difficult, draining. Had it been worthwhile? What had she discovered? Ben Rainey had harboured ambitions to be a detective. Joseph had said his brother had loved his job, seeming to blame Ben's career for his death. Was he correct? Had Ben been killed because he was a police officer? And if so, why? There had to be more. The brutality, the torture... It had been no accident, no random attack. Ben's killers had taken their time. People who knew what they were doing, who had no qualms about inflicting suffering.

Caelan stretched out her legs. Did Joseph Rainey know more than he had been willing to say? Did Mrs Rainey,

Miriam? And if so, how could she encourage them to admit it?

5

It was always worse to go down the stairs than to climb back up. Downstairs, outside, was reality. Up here, you could escape as many times as you were able to afford.

Ryan stood on the concrete landing, oblivious to the stench of piss and decay, one hand on the cold metal banister. The stairs unfolded below him, and he stepped down, breaking into a jog as he neared the bottom of the first flight. Bounced across to the glass door that led outside, stood on the scrubby brown grass looking left and right.

Where to? He had to find some cash, and quickly, but also food. He had a couple of quid left in his pocket, but he wanted to save that. Now that his wallet and phone had been nicked, he needed every penny. Mulligan had laughed when he'd told him. Ryan had lost his temper, demanded to know who the kids who had legged it with his property were. Mulligan's two heavies had reappeared, only leaving the room again when Mulligan chucked Ryan a wrap, told him to have it on the house and shut his mouth.

Moving quickly, he hurried along, the shadows of the highrise blocks falling across the scruffy tarmac. There were plenty of people around, and Ryan kept his head up, looking for someone he recognised. He wanted to talk, have a laugh, something that was in short supply at Mulligan's place. But most of those he passed kept their eyes averted. Ryan knew what they were seeing: a crackhead, venturing out between fixes.

He didn't care. A grin split his face, the winter sun just managing to warm his cheeks. He approached a discount shop, everything from batteries to fruit for sale on the wooden tables that stood at either side of its door. A man in a red polo shirt was serving, laughing as he counted oranges into a paper bag for an elderly woman. She took them with a smile, speaking quickly in a language Ryan couldn't understand. From the restaurant next door, the smell of spices, frying onions. A memory chased through his head – his mother making a curry: mysterious-looking pods and exotically coloured powders sizzling in the pan before she added the chicken. How long had it been? Years. Before his dad died, before Ryan had given up on school. Given up on life. He smiled again, knowing he was wrong. This *was* life, his life. Marching down the street, answerable to no one, ready to grab what you could. Living on your wits.

He kept moving, his hand whipping out as he passed the shopfront, grabbing two bananas. He pushed them under his sweatshirt, curving his arm around them as though he had a stomach ache. Waited for a shout of outrage from the shop-keeper or one of the people gathered around him, knowing at the same time that it wouldn't come. No one had seen, no one could touch him.

He waited to cross the road, watching the cars and buses thunder past him. Noticed the woman in front of him.

Saw the leather handbag.

She wasn't wearing the strap across her body; the bag was hanging from her right shoulder. As she turned her head, looking at the traffic, trying to judge if it was slowing, he reached out and—

'Oi!'

A hand around his wrist, tight, hurting. Ryan jumped, looked down. A man behind him: bald head, squat but well-muscled. He was twisting Ryan's arm, forcing him to turn around.

'The fuck you playing at, sunshine?'

Ryan squirmed, tried to prise the man's fingers open with his free hand. The bananas fell onto the pavement. 'Nothing, I—'

He sneered. 'Don't give me that bollocks. You were going to nick her purse.'

The woman had also turned now, hand clamped around the strap of her handbag. A few other people had stopped to see what the commotion was. Ryan licked his lips, despair already beginning to creep into his gut. He kicked one foot backwards, knocking the bananas onto the road.

'I wasn't, I swear. I don't...'

The man looked him up and down, disgust evident on his face. 'Yeah, mate, I know what you were up to. Time for your next fix, is it? Fucking smackhead.'

He let go of Ryan's arm, wiping his hand on his jeans as though it was dirty. Which, Ryan had to admit, it might have been. He couldn't remember the last time he'd showered. The crowd of people were surrounding him now, jostling and jeering. Someone said, 'I've called the police.'

'You hear that? Going to be a long night in the cells, isn't it?' The man stepped forward, prodded Ryan's chest. 'Nothing to shoot up with in there.'

Ryan twisted away, trying to push down the panic. He had to run. Trouble was, there was nowhere to go. Typical. Couldn't even snatch a bag without making a mess of it. He had to go, get some money, head back to Mulligan's place. He was wasting time standing here, and if the police came, he might be looking at a jail sentence. He'd been warned before. In the distance, he could hear a siren. Already? It couldn't be for him.

A few people turned, looking for the source of the noise. It gave Ryan the second he needed to push through the crowd and sprint away. He heard shouts, but no one seemed to be chasing him. After a couple of hundred yards, his lungs were aching and his throat burned. He jogged across the road, horns blaring as he zigzagged through the traffic. Down a side street, and Mulligan's building loomed in front of him. Should he go in? If the police had his description, if they'd seen him, followed him inside... Mulligan would kill him.

He leaned against a wall, took some deep breaths. No cash. What was he supposed to do now? He could find a paper cup in a bin, go and do some begging, but it could take forever to collect enough money. Sympathy was often in short supply, and plenty of those living in the area barely had enough to feed themselves. Plus, he needed to stay away from the street for a while.

He stared up at the sky, watched the sun sidle behind a grey cloud. Felt the vibration begin beneath his skin, hardly noticeable yet, but there all the same.

Across the road were some concrete steps leading up to a delivery door. Ryan wandered across and sat down, running grubby hands over his face. He stretched out his legs, eyes on the busted toes of his trainers. Rain came in, filthy socks hung out. He thought of his mum again, what she would think if she could see him now. He should phone her, see how she was.

See if she could lend him a few quid.

Wrapping his arms around his body, he closed his eyes. She'd be ashamed, probably wouldn't even let him in the house. Who could blame her?

A sound roused him, and he blinked as a kid sped by on a moped, a messenger bag slung across his back. Ryan watched him disappear, wondering. Pushing himself to his feet, he hurried towards Mulligan's building, his worries about the police forgotten.

6

The house was semi-detached, rendered and painted white. In place of a front garden there was a short brickwork driveway with an estate car parked diagonally across it. The parking bays marked on the road were for permit holders only, but Caelan reversed into the nearest space. She didn't intend to be long. She'd travelled back to Enfield to collect her car, against her better judgement. This was why she hated driving in London.

She knocked on the front door, watched a shadow move behind the frosted glass pane. The man who appeared, dressed in running shorts and vest, frowned at her.

'Can I help you?'

'I'm here to speak to DI Hobbs?' Caelan tried a smile.

'Sorry, Liv's on sick leave. She's not well enough to see anyone.'

'I only need a few minutes of her time.'

He shook his head. 'Like I said, she's shocked and hurt. Sorry you've had a wasted journey.'

'Sir...' Caelan took a step forward, but he'd already retreated, his face set in a scowl.

The door was almost closed when she heard a woman's voice call, 'Who is it, Adam?'

He didn't have time to reply before she was standing beside him. Slim and athletic-looking, DI Liv Hobbs was almost as tall as her husband, whose head wasn't far from the top of the door frame. She pushed in front of him, squinting at Caelan. Dressed in jogging bottoms and a T-shirt, she moved gingerly, clearly in pain. She wrapped her arms around her body, wincing.

'You're here to see me?'

Caelan raised her warrant card. 'Do you have a few minutes?'

Her husband muttered something, and Hobbs turned. 'I'm fine. I told you someone was coming to talk to me. Why don't you go for your run?'

She stepped back and he emerged, his expression making his disapproval clear. Caelan smiled at him as he passed and began to jog.

'He thinks I should be in bed.' Hobbs rolled her eyes. 'Overprotective. He's a paramedic, attended way more RTAs than I have. You'd think he could see I'm okay. Anyway, come in. Can I get you a drink?'

'Don't worry, thank you. I won't take up much of your time.'

'It's fine. To be honest, I'd rather be at work. Doing nothing drives me crazy.'

Caelan followed her into the living room. It wasn't large, but the white walls and wooden flooring made it seem spacious. Hobbs waved Caelan onto the two-seater sofa and took her time lowering herself onto a dining chair.

'Less painful this way,' she explained. 'I tried the armchair, but getting back up was agony. Too low.'

'Your ribs? A friend of mine hurt his yesterday.'

'Yeah? What, did he have a car crash too?'

Caelan shook her head, wishing she hadn't mentioned Ewan's injury. 'No. He was shot.'

Hobbs looked horrified. 'Shit.'

'He's okay, he was wearing a bulletproof vest. Cracked ribs.'

Hobbs nodded. 'Mine aren't broken, but they're bruised. Adam – Adam Waits, my husband – wants me to take my time, get better, but I've only been home four hours and I'm going stir crazy already. I want to get back to work.'

'DCI Achebe phoned?'

'Yeah. Said he'd given you my address, that you wanted to speak to me.'

'You know about Anthony Bryce?'

She dipped her head. 'I do. I never thought...'

'What?' Caelan sat forward, watching the other woman's face.

'He came to us with information, he trusted us. We should have protected him.'

'But the details he provided were vague, from what I've heard. No one could have predicted he would be killed.'

Hobbs looked up, met Caelan's eyes. 'You know who my brother is, where I grew up?' Caelan nodded. 'Well then. I know how these bastards work. Someone knew that Anthony had spoken to us, and went running to grass on him.'

'They informed on the informant?'

Hobbs snorted. 'If you like. At least, that's the way I see it.'

'Who?'

'I don't know. Wish I did. Someone who wanted a foot in the door. Low-level dealer, a young kid... Both, maybe. When I lived there, I'd have been able to guess, possibly find out for sure. Now, though...' She shook her head, dark curls flying. Wincing, she raised a hand to the back of her neck. 'Now, I'm out of touch. No one will speak to me. The way they see it, I betrayed them, turned my back on my roots. I'm a traitor, I joined the enemy. That makes me the lowest of the low.'

'Would your brother—'

'No.' Hobbs spoke abruptly, then held up a hand. 'Sorry. Jackson's inside, and he wouldn't speak to me anyway. The last thing I want is for him to be dragged into this. I'd not be allowed back near the case.'

'I'm guessing your brother's the kind of person who doesn't stop working because of a prison sentence, though?'

Hobbs's eyes narrowed. 'What does that mean?'

'Doesn't he have someone running his business until he gets out?'

'I wouldn't know.'

'Right-hand man?'

'Anyone who worked with him was arrested when he went down.'

Caelan nodded. 'Leaving his turf free for someone new to move in.'

'Jackson wouldn't have been the only dealer in the area. You know how it is, they're like flies. You swat one, turn around, and three more have flown in to spread shit around.'

'Good analogy.'

'Thanks.'

'What about Frankie Hamilton?'

'Frankie?' Hobbs laughed. 'Haven't heard his name for a while. I went to school with him. At least, I went to school. Frankie didn't usually bother.'

'He's being released in a few days.'

A pause, then, 'Right.'

'His girlfriend...'

Hobbs was already nodding. 'Frankie's not going to be happy.'

'You know?'

'Look, my family don't speak to me. Doesn't mean I have no friends left over there.'

'Can't be easy.'

'It's not.' Hobbs gazed at the floor, then raised her chin. 'But I made the right choice. If I hadn't joined the police, what would I be doing? Time, most likely.'

'Really?'

Hobbs lifted her shoulders, grimaced, and let them fall. 'I'd like to think not. But two of my cousins are, my brother is. Drugs, theft, fifteen kids? Who knows?'

'What did you think of the officers from the NCA?'

'Reid and Webster?' Another snort. 'More like Dumb and Dumber.' She looked at Caelan from beneath thick eyelashes.

'You weren't impressed.'

Hobbs waved a hand, dismissing the subject. 'All right, listen. Honestly, I think we're wasting our time with Frankie Hamilton. He's a user, not a dealer. If we're thinking about people who could have killed Ben Rainey and Anthony Bryce, Hamilton wouldn't even be in the top one hundred. He's in jail, plus he's a lowlife, a follower. No one respects him, no one would do anything on his say-so. He has no authority.'

'And whoever murdered our victims has?'

'Must have. Even if they killed Ben Rainey and Bryce them-selves, they'd have needed help. If they ordered others to do it, well, then they have people working for them. People who'll do whatever they're told to. Rainey was a police officer, for Christ's sake. Whoever murdered him means business.'

'We're looking for someone surrounded by people who are loyal.'

'Or they're being paid part of their wages in weed, or coke. That can be persuasive. Or maybe they're scared – either they or their family could be being threatened. We're not talking about stealing a few items from a pound shop here. This is serious. People get hurt.'

'I realise that.'

'People get killed.'

The words hung between them for a second. Caelan allowed the silence to develop, then said, 'Can you give me some names?'

'Not any more. Twenty years ago, maybe. But I would have kept my mouth closed, nevertheless.'

'DCI Achebe said you knew Ben Rainey?'

Hobbs blew out her cheeks. 'I spoke to him in passing. Doesn't matter if we weren't best friends; he was one of us, and no one should die like he did.' She met Caelan's eyes. 'I see you agree.'

'All right. Tell me about your accident.'

Hobbs looked thrown. 'My accident? How's that relevant?'

'I'm curious.'

'Well, okay... I was driving home, it was late, I was tired. I stopped at a junction, the car behind shunted me.'

'Did it stop?'

'No. I smacked my chest on the wheel, hurt my neck, banged my head somehow. Must have lost consciousness for a second. Whoever hit me had driven off.'

Caelan was quiet, considering what Hobbs had said. 'You didn't see the car?'

'No. It was dark, I could only see headlights. Then... they'd vanished.'

'Is your car damaged?'

'Oh yeah. I managed to drive it home, and the garage collected it this morning. It needs some work.'

'Then it's safe to assume that the car that hit you is damaged too?'

Hobbs stared at her. 'Possibly. Why?'

'Are we trying to trace the vehicle?'

'I don't know. I gave a statement. It happened by the shops on Northolt Road – there must be cameras.'

'I'll check with DCI Achebe.'

'What are you saying?'

Caelan hesitated, wondering if she should voice her suspicions. 'This crash of yours – what if it wasn't an accident?'

Hobbs opened her mouth, her eyebrows drawn together. 'What do you mean?'

'Think about it. Why wouldn't the driver stop? If you were in your own car, he or she wouldn't have known you were police.'

Shifting in her seat, Hobbs spread her hands.

'You know there could be any number of reasons. Maybe they had no insurance, no tax. Maybe they were pissed, or high. Or both.'

'Possibly. Probably, even. But I think it's worth following up.'

'Seriously?' Hobbs looked sceptical. 'Why would you even consider it could have been deliberate?'

'You're working on a drugs operation on your old patch; two men are found dead, one of whom was a police officer. Both have been tortured. Both men you knew, or at least had met.'

'No one knows about my involvement. How could they? I've stayed away from Edmonton.'

'You know as well as I do that information gets leaked. People sometimes hear about things they shouldn't.'

'Listen, I don't know what happens where you're from, but I trust my guys, and they trust me.'

'Yeah, well I thought I could rely on my colleagues too. Turns out I was wrong. Sometimes, they turn on you.'

Hobbs tipped her head to the side, gazing steadily at Caelan. 'You know, you're beginning to sound a little paranoid. I can see you've had a bang on the head, but...'

Caelan took a breath, forced herself to calm down. 'Okay, I'll shut up, but I'd like to mention it to DCI Achebe. At least give him the chance to hear me out.'

Hobbs exhaled sharply. 'Fine. Adam won't like it, though. He already wants me walking around wrapped in cotton wool.'

Caelan wondered why, but didn't want to ask. 'Don't tell him. It's probably nothing.'

The glance Hobbs shot her was shrewd. 'You don't believe that.'

'But I'm willing to be convinced.'

'Strangely, I don't find that reassuring.'

Caelan stood. 'Thanks for seeing me. I'll leave you to rest.'

Hobbs nodded towards the sofa. 'Could you pass my mobile, please? Can I take your number?'

Handing over the phone, Caelan dictated it. 'I'll stay in touch.'

'Thanks for coming, even if you've given me something else to worry about. Do you mind if I don't come to the door with you?'

'It's fine.'

As Caelan stepped onto the driveway, she saw Adam Waits, Hobbs's husband, jogging slowly past on the other side of the road. Seeing Caelan, he raised a hand then sprinted away. He'd waited, looking out for his wife. Who could blame him?

Caelan unlocked her car, thumbing out a text to tell Achebe she was on her way back to the station before starting the engine. Hobbs was clearly fit, and could no doubt look after herself. If needed, her husband could also be an intimidating presence.

All the same, Caelan felt a dig of unease as she drove away. She hoped she was wrong about the car crash.

7

When Caelan arrived in the incident room at South Harrow police station, Achebe was standing beside a uniformed constable who was pointing at something on his computer screen. Caelan stepped closer, but didn't interrupt. Achebe acknowledged her with a nod, held up a hand. Five minutes.

Caelan asked the nearest person where she could get some coffee, followed their instructions to a dingy kitchen with an ancient kettle and an assortment of dirty crockery. A woman wearing charcoal trousers and a white shirt stood by the window, arms folded. She turned as she heard Caelan flick on the kettle.

'I wouldn't bother,' she said, with a smile.

'Sorry?'

'It's broken.'

'Oh.' Caelan looked down. Sure enough, the kettle was silent, the red light near the handle refusing to light up. 'They didn't tell me that.'

'Mug of water's as good as it gets, I'm afraid.' She indicated a cupboard with a jerk of her chin. 'In there. I wouldn't like to say how clean the cups are. Hope you've had your injections.'

Caelan laughed. 'Maybe I'll pass.'

'A wise decision.' She grinned. 'DS Somerville. Call me Jen. You've been in the wars.'

'It looks worse than it is.' Nevertheless, Caelan's hand strayed again to the bandage on her temple. Maybe she should take it off. It was too noticeable, as were her casual clothes and gaudy trainers. Liv Hobbs hadn't commented, but Caelan had seen her eyes widen as she'd taken in her outfit. Maybe it hadn't been wise to go rushing over there dressed as she was. Even after their brief meeting, Caelan knew Hobbs was sharp enough to join the dots. Caelan wasn't in uniform, but she wasn't dressed in the smart office clothes of the average detective either. So who was she? It wouldn't take much thought to make the connection to covert policing. Caelan's official rank was detective sergeant, but it had been a while since she'd introduced herself as such. She decided to now.

Achebe pushed open the door as she and Somerville were shaking hands. 'Caelan. I've only just seen your text.' He nodded towards Somerville. 'Jen's part of Liv's team; she'll be covering for her until she gets back.'

'Which knowing Liv will be within the next five minutes,' Somerville added.

Caelan outlined her conversation with Hobbs. Achebe listened, hands on hips. He raised a finger.

'Wait a second. You think Liv's car was hit deliberately?'

Did she? Or was she jumping to conclusions, seeing things that weren't there? She made the decision.

'I think it's a possibility we should be considering,' she said.

Somerville's cheeks were red. 'What the hell? Why would someone do that?'

Achebe gave Caelan a long look, frowning.

'We need to locate the vehicle involved,' he said. 'Jen, can we get someone onto it, please?'

She nodded. 'With pleasure. I'll do it myself.'

She strode from the room, lips pressed into a line. Achebe waited for the door to close.

'They're a tight-knit bunch.'

'Understood.' Caelan pushed her hands into her jeans pockets. 'I could be overreacting, of course.' It wouldn't be the first time. The job could make you paranoid.

'We need to be sure. Why would anyone do that to Liv, though?'

'To warn her, or scare her? To send a message to her brother?'

'Jackson? She hasn't spoken to him for years.'

'I could be wrong.'

He met her eyes again. 'You weren't yesterday.'

She scowled at him. 'Nasenby? Like I said earlier, forget about it. I'm going to.'

'All right.' Achebe didn't look convinced, but he'd clearly decided it wasn't worth arguing the point. 'How did it go with Ben Rainey's family?'

'It was... difficult.' She told him what Mrs Rainey and Joseph had said about Ben wanting to be a detective.

'You think it's important?' Achebe asked.

Caelan shrugged. 'I don't know. Did any of his colleagues mention it?'

'Don't think so, but I'll check. He might have seen himself as too much of a new boy to start talking about his future in the force.'

'Maybe.' Caelan pinched her lower lip, thinking about it.

'We can speak to his sergeant again, his colleagues. It shouldn't take long.'

'What do you want me to do?'

'Do?'

She grinned. 'You said I could join the investigation team. You're the boss, aren't you?'

Achebe laughed. 'Dressed like that? How about going to Edmonton after all? Have a look at the information we've got so far. There's not much yet on Bryce. We only knew who he was because he had a bank card in his wallet. We were able to confirm his identity using his fingerprints, because he's in the system.'

'The wallet was left on his body?'

'Yeah. No cash inside, but then he probably didn't have much. No point trying to make it look like a mugging gone wrong when you've moved him into a house.'

Caelan nodded. 'And smashed his fingers and burnt him beforehand.'

'That too.'

'He definitely wasn't killed in the house?'

'We don't believe so.' Achebe didn't elaborate. It was early days, and the results of the forensic investigations would take time. Making assumptions or guesses would only complicate, or even jeopardise, their progress.

'Who owns the property?'

'A local businessman. He has a couple of restaurants, plus some residential properties. We've contacted him by phone – he and his wife are visiting family in Turkey.'

'Convenient.'

'They're flying back in a couple of days. He says he's never heard of Anthony Bryce. Said he was happy to cooperate with us, and was furious that his house had been used to dump a body. His words, not mine.'

'Worried about his reputation? The effect on his businesses?'

'I'm guessing so. The house has been empty for a few weeks. A new tenant was due to move in next month. This might change their mind.'

'What about his family?'

'He has two sons, one in his early twenties, the other younger. One daughter, late teens. None of them has had so much as a speeding fine. Neither have the parents.' Achebe lifted his eyebrows.

'The younger son's age?'

'Fifteen.'

'Old enough, then.'

Achebe rolled his neck, then his shoulders. 'Easily. Don't worry, we're not going to forget about him.'

'What about the elder son? What does he do?'

'He's a plumber.'

'So, he could have access to a van?'

'Maybe plastic sheeting too, plus some strong mates. We're checking.'

'Any intel?'

'Nothing. Either they're all as squeaky clean as they appear to be, or...' Achebe left the sentence unfinished.

'Seems unlikely any member of the family would leave the body in a property they own, though.'

'Agreed, but you never know.'

Caelan nodded. It was true. Under stress, rational thinking could disappear, and few situations were as stressful as having a dead body to dispose of. 'Who found Bryce?'

'A window cleaner knocking on doors, looking for business. There are still curtains up at the windows; he hadn't realised no one was living there. He approached the front door, saw a few drops of blood on the step. He looked through the nearest window, saw Bryce sprawled on the carpet.'

'He was in the living room?'

'Looks like they'd literally thrown him in there. On his back, arms and legs spread wide. Like a rag doll.' Achebe blinked as though trying to rid himself of the image.

Caelan considered his words. 'They were in a hurry, then? Panicking? Or they just didn't give a shit?'

'Probably both. Anyone who can torture someone isn't going to be too worried about treating their body with respect afterwards.'

'Fair point. If there was blood on the step, whoever left him there would have had some on their clothing, in their vehicle.'

'You'd think. It's an end terrace, one set of neighbours who predictably saw and heard nothing. We're still knocking on doors, but I'm guessing it'll be the same story all down the street. There's a patch of waste ground next to the house, and a side gate into the property. They could have backed a vehicle right up to the gate, opened the doors and carried him in.'

'No witnesses.'

'Or none that will talk.' Achebe ran a hand around his jaw. 'Hopefully Scenes of Crime will pick up some tyre tracks.'

'Fingers crossed. There had to be more than one person to lift him, though.'

'At least. Bryce was scrawny, but also tall. There may be trace evidence on his body, we don't know yet. There were plenty of wounds for fibres or other stuff to stick to.'

A silence. Caelan hadn't seen Bryce's body yet, or the photographs and video footage that would have been taken at the scene, but she could imagine the devastation the torture would have wreaked on his body. Achebe cleared his throat.

'Scenes of Crime should be finished at the address soon, but we'll leave someone there. Might have people trying to get in to take photographs or whatever. There'll be lots of gossip, theories flying around. You know how it is.'

She flashed him a grin. 'All right.'

'I'll make a few calls, clear it with Beckett and our NCA colleagues.' Achebe took out his phone.

Caelan wandered back into the incident room, looking for Jen Somerville. She couldn't explain why the idea that Liv

Hobbs had been deliberately targeted had come into her head, but the more she thought about it, the more convinced she was that she was correct.

'Caelan?' Somerville was waving to her from a desk in the corner. Caelan went over, exchanging nods and smiles with a few of the people who were busy at keyboards or on calls. Ben Rainey had been one of their own. They would keep searching for his murderers until they found them. The news of Anthony Bryce's death would have made them all the more determined, Caelan knew. The torture disturbed and worried her. It was abhorrent and frightening. Were they attempting to extract information from their victims, or were the grisly deaths a warning? Why had Rainey been in Edmonton? What was his involvement?

As she reached Somerville's side, she blinked the questions away. She would have time to consider them again later. Now, she needed information.

'We're going to have to go to the shops nearby, ask if they have CCTV footage,' said Somerville. 'Are you—'

'I can't,' Caelan said quickly.

Somerville raised her eyebrows, surprised. 'I wasn't going to ask you to go. I'm sending a couple of my DCs. I was going to say, are you sure about the location of the crash?'

Caelan felt a blush start in her cheeks. 'Sorry. Yes, I am. DI Hobbs made a statement too.'

'I'll check it.' Somerville turned away, leaving Caelan feeling ridiculous.

Achebe was in the doorway, holding up a thumb. She moved towards him, hands in her pockets.

Time to go.

She turned left out of Edmonton Green station, following the pavement around the corner and under a bridge. Shops on both sides of the road, their windows advertising kebabs, property, haircuts. Further along, houses, then a post office; several Royal Mail vans were parked at the side of the road. Caelan kept her head up, her hands in her jacket pockets as people passed her without a second glance.

She kept walking, noting road names she remembered from statements and briefings or from the news. There had been stabbings, mass brawls, shootings. As she'd told Reid and Webster, those crimes happened everywhere. But here... here, she felt fear clutch at her belly. Two men were dead. Could she be sure she was safe? She knew she had to deal with her anxiety immediately, before it had a chance to take a hold. She spotted a bus stop and headed towards it, stood with her back to the road, pretending to look at her phone as though waiting. Breathing slowly, she waited for her hurtling thoughts to become calmer. She remembered her days in uniform, being summoned to streets like these, not knowing whether a domestic disturbance might turn deadly, a fight in a pub end up a murder scene. She had survived, never been injured. At least in her undercover role she was in control, could decide whether to keep going or back away. It was nerve-racking, exhilarating, and occasionally terrifying. She thought again about the ultimatum Elizabeth Beckett had given her, and knew she had made the right decision. Her job was all she had. She lived for it, whatever the cost.

A kid zipped by on a BMX, hood up, head down low. He'd been close enough to touch. Caelan watched him jam on the brakes, bringing the bike to a halt at the side of the pavement, outside a church. He pulled his phone from his pocket and held it up to his ear. She slowed her pace, wanting to hear what he was saying, but soon he was off again, waiting for a gap in the traffic before disappearing across the road.

She kept walking, not going directly to where she knew Bryce's body had been discovered but taking the longer route she had planned before leaving the incident room. She needed to look like she belonged, not to have to keep checking where she was on her phone.

Another residential street, semi-detached houses and cars lining both sides of the road. Speed bumps.

Then, footsteps behind her. Not hurrying, not running, but close enough to cause concern. A muffled comment, a burst of laughter. More than one person. Local accents. Male. Young.

Her stomach tightening, Caelan maintained her pace. She wouldn't allow them to intimidate her. As she walked, she listened carefully, trying to determine how many there were. They weren't speaking now, and she guessed they were concentrating on getting as close to her as possible.

If there had been a shop or pub on the street, she would have turned into it, regardless of her plan. There wasn't. The road stretched in front of her, battered fences and overgrown hedges separating the houses from the street. Caelan licked her lips, suddenly dry, and slid her hands out of her jacket pockets. She doubted they would try anything on the street, but who knew? She had been trained in unarmed combat, was confident in her ability to keep herself safe, but if there were four or five of them, what chance would she have? She had zipped her phone into the inside pocket of her jacket too. She could get it out, but perhaps that was what they were waiting for. Maybe the idea was to intimidate her so she felt she needed to call for help, then grab the phone from her hand. There was a police station nearby, but from what she remembered of the street view, she would have to turn and walk the other way. There was no through route from here.

Another burst of laughter. They were even closer. Caelan felt fury build in her chest. They were halfway along the street now. Abruptly she turned to her right and marched out into the road. She heard scuffling feet as they changed course behind her. As she approached the end of the road, cars speeding by on the street it joined, she made up her mind.

She stopped, spun around.

There were three of them, boys aged around sixteen, all wearing tracksuit bottoms, trainers, sweatshirts with the hoods up. Two of them had bandannas tied around their necks, ready to pull up to conceal their faces if necessary. Caelan kept her expression blank, knowing that to show any fear would be a mistake. The boy in the middle grinned at her.

'What?' he sneered. 'Where you going? You're not from around here.'

Caelan paused, knew her accent had to be convincing. 'Visiting my mate.'

'Your mate?' He took a step towards her, baring his teeth in an approximation of a smile. 'Where's this mate of yours live then?'

Thinking quickly, Caelan recalled a name from the streets she'd looked at earlier. 'Leonard Road.'

He laughed, spat on the pavement at her feet. 'Yeah? Going the long way round, are you?'

'I got lost, all right? I've never been here before.'

Looking her up and down, he smiled. 'Yeah, I can see that. 'Cos if you had, you'd know there are streets in this area you stay away from. And this is one of them.'

'I didn't—'

'Why don't you go back where you came from?' He nodded down at her trainers. 'Nice shoes. Ever use them for running?'

Caelan stared at him. 'What?'

He shoved his hands into his trouser pockets, rocked back on his heels, his eyes half closed. Enjoying her discomfort. 'I want to see you run. Go on, fuck off. Don't let us see you round here again.'

She narrowed her eyes, wanting to drive her fist into his face as he stepped even closer. He lifted his hand. Caelan tensed, knowing she could have him on the ground in seconds, also aware that his friends would be on her soon after. It would be suicide.

He touched her bruised cheek with a fingertip almost tenderly, then shoved her shoulder so she staggered backwards. Caelan was silent, not reacting as she straightened up. 'Go. Now.' He laughed. 'And fucking run!'

Rage building in her belly, Caelan did so, sprinting for the end of the street. Their laughter chased her along. She ran around the corner and stopped dead. People were staring, and one car tooted its horn, the man in the driver's seat sticking his thumb out of the window at her. Caelan risked a glance down the street, wondering if they were coming after her. They weren't. They'd turned around, sauntering back the way they had come, no doubt believing they'd scared her off. She saw a café across the road and headed towards it. She wasn't far from the road where Anthony Bryce's body had been found, but a break wouldn't hurt. The encounter with the three youths had shaken her more than she wanted to admit. She didn't believe she had ever been in real danger, but their casual certainty that they had the right to say who walked around here made her furious.

The café was run-down, empty. Specials were scrawled on fluorescent cardboard stars, Blu-Tacked to the wall. Behind a chipped wooden counter, a sulky-looking girl stood staring at her phone. Caelan took a bottle of water from the fridge in the corner and scanned the meagre display of chocolate bars and cellophane-wrapped biscuits and flapjacks. She selected a chocolate chip cookie and set it and the water on the counter. The girl took her time ringing the items into the till. She stared at Caelan without speaking as she handed over a five-pound note, leaving her change on the counter and going back to her phone.

Caelan flashed her a smile. 'Thanks so much.'

The girl scowled, managed a nod.

At a table in a corner, Caelan sipped her water and took out her phone. Two missed calls from the new head of their unit, Commander Ian Penrith. Shit. No doubt he wanted to see her, to ask why she'd gone haring off to Edmonton despite the operation she had been dragged back to work for being delayed. She put the phone back in her pocket. She would have to speak to him, but not here, and not yet.

Out on the street, a fine drizzle had begun to fall. Hunching her shoulders, she began to walk. Cars sped by, but there were fewer pedestrians now, no doubt driven inside by the rain. As she turned the corner into the street where Bryce's body had been found, Caelan saw the crowd. Undeterred by the weather, a group of twenty or so stood in the middle of the road, where a marked police car was parked. Some were drinking from beer cans; most were smoking or vaping. Caelan strode up as though she belonged. If the three lads who had followed her were around, she'd have to keep her head down, but they weren't going to stop her following Achebe's instructions. Two men were dead, and the people who had tortured and killed them were probably still walking these streets. Maybe they were even part of this crowd.

She pushed closer, standing on tiptoe to try to see over the heads of the people in front of her. She spotted the familiar blue and white POLICE LINE DO NOT CROSS tape preventing bystanders from pushing too close to the crime scene. A male uniformed officer stood just beyond the tape, his hands behind his back. Caelan didn't envy him as the rain fell harder.

'What's happened?' She turned to the woman standing beside her, who had two sleeping babies in a huge pushchair and was eating a sausage roll from a paper bag.

'There's a dead body. Murdered, they're saying.' She spoke with relish, through a mouthful of pastry.

Caelan altered her expression so she looked suitably shocked. 'Who is it?'

The woman took another bite, chewed vigorously. 'Don't know. Some bloke.' She swallowed. 'I've been here half an hour, and no one's come out. Reckon it's a wind-up?'

'Could be. But why would they have taped the road off if it was?'

An elderly bearded man in front of them turned. 'I heard it's a stabbing.'

The woman rolled her eyes. 'Another one? I'm not hanging around then.' She screwed up the now empty paper bag and dropped it onto the pavement. 'No TV cameras, no armed police, nothing. Fuck this, I'm getting soaked. I'm going home.' She gave the pushchair a shove, turned it around and disappeared.

Caelan glanced about her, scanning the nearby faces. No one familiar, no one talking furtively on their phone or to their companion. No one looking frightened or traumatised. Not even anyone with blood stains on their clothing or an iron in their hand. She stepped to her right, trying to inch her way closer to the police cordon. Murmured conversations were going on all around her, but she heard nothing suspicious. Maybe she was wasting her time here. Her phone was ringing, and she checked the display. Ian Penrith again. She switched it to silent without answering.

Caelan waited ten minutes longer, but there was no movement behind the cordon. People were beginning to drift away, talking about collecting children from school and what they were going to have for dinner. She checked her phone and made the decision.

–

'Where the hell have you been all day?' Ian Penrith folded his hands over his belly as he leaned back in his chair. He wore a crumpled white shirt, his navy tie loosened. Looking her up and down, he said, 'Nice outfit. Is that what all the bright young things in Edmonton are wearing this season?'

Caelan sat opposite him, crossed her legs.

'If you know, why are you asking?'

'What?'

'You wanted to know where I'd been.'

'I was informed you were needed. Then, suddenly, you weren't. Was it unreasonable of me to expect you back here? You know, where you're supposed to be based?'

'I'm *supposed* to be on sick leave.'

He waved a hand, dismissing the idea. 'We all know you've no life outside your job, Caelan.'

'Too kind. And you have?'

A smirk. 'Never claimed otherwise. You, on the other hand, had a stab at happiness.'

'You knew, Ian. You knew Nicky wasn't dead.'

He didn't deny it, just sat looking at her, his head tipped to one side. 'No comment. Anyway, she's back now. You can play happy families.'

Caelan stared at him. 'What? Are you joking?'

'Not welcoming her with open arms then?' He sniffed, pulled a grubby handkerchief from his trouser pocket and blew his nose. 'She had no choice, Caelan.'

'Of course she did. I'm not going to discuss this with you.'

'Fine.' His voice changed. 'Why are you getting involved in the death of Ben Rainey?'

'Getting involved? Elizabeth Beckett asked me—'

He held up a finger. 'No, Caelan. Assistant Commissioner Beckett asked you to assist with gathering information about the drugs scene in Edmonton.'

'You've heard about Anthony Bryce, whose body was found today? His death and Rainey's are linked.'

'Because you say so?'

'What? No, because they were killed in the same way.'

'But they weren't. Bryce was strangled, Rainey was stabbed.' He grinned at her. 'Come on, Caelan, this is basic stuff. Making assumptions, surmising. Is there proof the same person or people killed them both?'

She wasn't going to allow him to provoke her. 'Achebe said—'

'That they were both tortured. I know. Listen, Caelan, you're needed this evening.'

'Needed? What do you mean?'

He sat up straighter, ran a hand over his sparse hair. 'We've had a request for an undercover officer. One night only.'

'Doing what?' Caelan rubbed her brow, a headache beginning to make its presence felt.

'Oh, lying around.' Penrith didn't bother to hide his smirk.

'What?'

'There's a hotel in Hackney that some of the Stoke Newington lot have been sniffing around. It's a dump. I wouldn't let my dog sleep there.'

'You don't have a dog.'

'All right, I wouldn't let my ex-wife sleep there.' He bared his teeth. 'No, of course I would. I'd book her in for a fortnight.'

'I get the idea. What's our interest?'

'It's a cover for a brothel. The whisper is, some of the girls aren't there by choice.'

'Trafficking?'

'They think so. Stoke Newington have an informer inside. Bouncer type, throws out clients if they get too rough. Seems he has a conscience. He'd not been working there long when he guessed what was really going on.'

'And he came to us?'

'He'll be protected, after we arrest him for show, of course. As well as renting out rooms complete with prostitutes, they also let them by the hour to working girls.'

'Let me guess. I'm going to be one of those girls?'

'Bingo.' He pointed a meaty finger at her. 'Maybe you could lose the bandage? Not very glamorous.'

She lifted a hand to her cheek. 'And the bruises are?'

'Blame a client.' His face hardened. 'The girls will understand, that's for sure.'

'Can't Nicky—'

'No.'

'Why not?'

Penrith rubbed his mouth. 'She's in Edmonton.'

Surprised, Caelan leaned forward. 'Nicky is? Why?'

'Don't ask me. I'm only her commanding officer.'

What the hell? 'We were told the Edmonton operation wasn't happening yet.'

'I know. And yet you were there earlier today.'

'Come on, Ian, what was I supposed to do? Come back here, wait around? I'm a police officer. If I'm not required on an undercover operation, I'm supposed to be working on other cases, aren't I?'

'I'm not disputing that.'

'Then what's the problem?'

'Why did you go to see Ben Rainey's family? DI Hobbs?' He was watching her face. Caelan shook her head.

'You know about that?'

'Telling DI Hobbs that a car deliberately crashed into her?' He snorted. 'You're complicating matters, Caelan. Sticking your oar in. Looking for conspiracies. Just because Nasenby was dirty doesn't mean every officer in the Met is.'

'I'm aware of that. But why was Ben Rainey tortured? He must have known something.'

'You're doing it again. There's no "must". How do you know he wasn't grabbed by someone who just enjoys hurting people? Who knew he was a copper? A gang initiation, or even a case of mistaken identity? We don't know why he was killed, and you upsetting his family and rattling cages all over London isn't going to help.'

'DCI Achebe said they have nothing. No clue who killed him, or why. Then another body's found and I'm supposed to ignore the link?'

Penrith's cheeks reddened. 'Yes, that's exactly what you're supposed to do. It's not your case, not your problem. Let Tim Achebe worry about it. You're going to be busy in Hackney.'

Caelan stood, knowing this was an argument she wasn't going to win. Bickering with Penrith was a waste of her time.

'Where's this hotel?'

He didn't need to check. 'Be at Finsbury Park tube station at nine this evening. You'll be picked up nearby.'

'By?'

'A DC Bailey. He's your client for the evening.' Penrith waggled his eyebrows.

'And what, we rent a room then go wandering through the premises?'

'You've done this type of thing before. Let Bailey take the lead.'

She snorted. 'Depends on what I think of him.'

Penrith pushed back his chair. 'I have a meeting, Caelan. About Michael Nasenby. Don't let me keep you.'

Her stomach jolted. 'Michael? What has he... Has he admitted to anything?'

'I've no idea.' Penrith checked his watch. 'Hard for him to deny his involvement after the conversation you had with him.'

'He'll try.'

'I've no doubt. How's your assistant, by the way?'

'Ewan? I'm told he's recovering at home.'

Penrith yanked his suit jacket from the back of his chair. 'You mean you haven't been to see him? Poor show, Caelan.'

'Now you sound like Nasenby.'

He grinned. 'Entirely intentional, I assure you.'

'Don't tell me you're missing him?'

'No, I'm seeing plenty of him.' Penrith pulled on the jacket, straightened his tie. 'Lucky me. Remember what I've said, Caelan. Leave the Rainey case to Achebe.'

She ignored him, took out her phone as Penrith lumbered past her and left the room, thumping the door closed behind him. She found Ewan's number, and he answered on the second ring.

'Caelan? How are you?'

She smiled. 'I was going to ask you the same thing.'

8

Ryan knew that Mulligan carried a knife, because the first time he had come here, Mulligan had held it against his throat. He'd stumbled up the stairs, desperate, his mate Jonny telling him about this new dealer he'd found. Jonny had knocked on Mulligan's door, and eventually the letter box had opened. Jonny had dropped to his knees, peering through, begging to do business.

Mulligan's man had laughed, told him they'd have to come in and wait like everyone else. Then the door had opened. Ryan had never been in a crack house until then, and he remembered his first visit to this flat vividly. The smell – like… burning plastic? Not quite. The bare floorboards, the rubbish piled high in black bags in the corners. Empty plastic bottles, food wrappers.

Then the people, all demanding to know when Mulligan would be there. When their orders would arrive. Bad skin, bad teeth, and the stench of desperation. This was a while ago, when Mulligan was much further down the hierarchy than he was now. When he had one scrawny, strung-out assistant, not two full-time minders. When he lived in this shithole, as well as trading from it.

Mulligan had sauntered in forty minutes later, carrying a black sports bag. He made certain the door was locked and bolted behind him before he unzipped the bag. Ryan had hung back, still fooling himself he was in control of his drug habit, and not the other way around. Jonny made his purchases and scurried off to a corner like a kid leaving a sweetshop. All around, people were smoking, rolling, beginning to pace and circle. It was pitiful, but at the same time, exhilarating. Ryan became aware of Mulligan staring at him expectantly.

'Do you want something, pal, or are you just here to see the sights? Fucking paradise, isn't it?'

'No, I want… I want…'

'Spit it out then.'

'A couple of rocks.'

Mulligan had raised his eyebrows. 'And I'm supposed to hand them over? Who are you here with? How do you know who I am?'

Ryan turned to point to Jonny, but he had vanished. 'I'm with Jonny. He says your stuff's the best.'

Mulligan had stepped closer. Ryan smelt dope and sweat, unsure whether the odour was coming from Mulligan or from himself. 'I don't know anyone called Jonny.' Mulligan's voice was soft. 'Let me look at you.'

Ryan waited, fear beginning to inch and crawl its way around him. Where the fuck was Jonny? Mulligan took another step nearer.

'Who are you?'

Ryan's mouth was dry. He whispered his name, and Mulligan lifted a hand to his ear as though he couldn't hear.

'Who? Tell me why I should sell to you. How do I know you're not a cop?'

'A… what?' Ryan had almost laughed at the idea, but guessed Mulligan would take offence. 'I'm not, I swear.'

'Yeah, that's what they all say.' Mulligan's mouth was right by his ear, and then Ryan felt a coldness against his skin. A pinprick, like an injection, then pressure. 'Tell me the truth or I'll rip your fucking throat out,' Mulligan had hissed.

'I'm not police, I swear. Swear on my mum's life, on mine. I just want to buy, I promise.' Ryan felt his bladder clench, heard the pleading in his voice.

Then, instantly, the blade was removed and Mulligan was smiling, holding out his hands. 'Here you go, mate. Two rocks.'

Ryan had fumbled in his pocket, brought out two dirty and creased banknotes. Mulligan had taken them, his lips twitching at the state of them.

'Had to work hard for these, I bet,' he'd smirked. 'Now get out. Next time, bring more money.'

Ryan had fled, running as fast he was able, not stopping until Mulligan's building was out of sight. Then he'd found a doorway, and had his smoke. And Jonny had been right. Mulligan's stuff knocked the shit out of anything he'd had before.

Two hours later, he went back.

9

The car was a new Mercedes, silver, smart enough to impress, bland enough to be inconspicuous. Caelan watched it stop on double red lines, and hurried over. The driver wound down his window as she approached. He was in his thirties, blonde-haired and handsome.

'Kay?' he said.

'That's me.'

'Thought you might want to check my warrant card before you got in.' He smiled, and Caelan realised he was nervous. She opened the passenger door, picked up the warrant card. DC Liam Bailey.

'Looks good to me.'

Caelan slid into the passenger seat, put his warrant card in the glove box. The interior was immaculate, smelling of leather and lemon air freshener. She kicked off her heels, pulled down her skirt so it covered more of her thighs.

'Sorry,' she said. 'I hate these clothes.' A blush rose in Bailey's cheeks, and Caelan smiled, looking at his profile. 'Never picked up a prostitute before?'

His Adam's apple jumped. 'No. Not even a pretend one.'

'Do you want to tell me what to expect tonight?'

He nodded, his eyes on the road. 'The hotel is called the Palace. I think the name's ironic – the Shithole would be more appropriate.'

'My boss did mention it was a dump.'

'I've been in the bar next door a few times, seen geezers coming and going with young girls.'

'What's the bar like?'

'Pretty much what you'd expect for a place next door to a brothel. Always feel I need five showers when I've been in there.'

'What's the plan?'

Bailey braked, stopped at a red light. 'We'll need to rent a room. I assume they charge by the hour.'

Caelan grinned. 'I know I do.'

He laughed, his cheeks reddening again. 'I'm guessing the girls negotiate the price, and the men pay. I don't know.'

'All right, so we get a room, go upstairs. Then what?'

'Well, I have a look around.'

Caelan looked at him. 'Really? You're going to wander off? You don't think you'll be noticed?'

'I'll have help. There's a man who works there...'

'Okay, and what will I be doing?'

He glanced at her as the lights changed, and slid the car into gear. 'You'll... just be waiting.'

'I'm your excuse to get into the building, and nothing more?'

'That's right.'

She puffed out her cheeks. 'How about if I try to talk to some of the girls?'

He shot her another glance. 'I'm not sure...'

'They'd probably rather talk to me than you.'

'Well, I—'

'Shall we see how it goes?'

His jaw tightened. 'That's not what we agreed.'

'I wasn't aware I'd agreed to anything.' Caelan turned her head to look out of the window. She knew she was being unfair, but Bailey's vagueness was infuriating. She had been on operations before with no clear goal, no expected outcome, and they were always more nerve-racking than those planned to precision. Bailey was here to do some fishing, nothing more, and he could have asked any female colleague to accompany him. She wasn't needed for this assignment. They could have sent someone in posing as a plumber or electrician to poke around, although a tradesman turning up at night might have raised some eyebrows. She turned back, folded her arms.

'Okay, we'll do it your way.'

Bailey let out a breath, clearly relieved. 'Great.'

'Will we have backup?'

'A couple of guys in the bar.'

'Have to hope nothing kicks off then.'

'It won't.' Bailey sounded as though he was trying hard to convince himself. 'We're about five minutes away. I'm going to find somewhere to park.'

–

As they walked away from the car, Caelan slid her arm through Bailey's. She felt him tense.

'Why are you...?'

'We have to look like we're together. If we're going to pull this off, you need to relax,' Caelan told him in an undertone. 'I'm not going in there until you do.'

'I'm sure loads of men who pay for sex are nervous.'

'But you can't be. The whole operation's at risk if you don't calm down. The women will be moved out of here, and any chance we have of rescuing them will be gone.'

'All right, I get it.' He exhaled. 'Let's go.'

Caelan's gut was telling her to run for the nearest Tube station. She could – but the idea of turning her back on the women being forced to work in the brothel was unthinkable. She kept walking.

'There it is,' said Bailey.

The ground floor of the hotel had obviously once been a shop, with three large windows. Lurid pink metal shutters covered two of them, while the third had a grubby white metal blind hanging in it. The sign above was purple, with the hotel's name in thick black lettering. On the two floors above, the same violent shade of purple had been used to paint the window frames. Next door, people were smoking on the pavement outside the bar Bailey had mentioned.

'Okay?' Caelan spoke as quietly as she could.

'Fine,' Bailey replied. His voice was steady, and Caelan felt reassured. Perhaps he wasn't the amateur he had appeared to be.

She pushed open the hotel door and stepped inside. Dirty laminate on the floor, a stale smell in the air. Bailey followed so closely he bumped into her as she stopped at the reception desk. Behind it sat a man whose grey polo shirt strained over his belly. He was eating a takeaway pizza from the box, staring at his phone. On the desk, a battered TV displayed CCTV images of the outside of the hotel, and a short corridor. Behind him, a wooden board held keys hanging on hooks, room numbers scrawled in black marker pen above each one. Classy. Caelan cleared her throat, and the man looked up with a knowing smile.

'Want a room?' His accent was hard to place. Caelan dropped into her best London.

'Yeah, mate. How much?'

He waited, his eyes travelling over her body. Caelan stared back, unfazed. Let him look. He'd have plenty of time to fantasise when he was in prison.

'For the night?' he said. Caelan began to protest, but he held up a hand, made them wait while he chewed through another mouthful of pizza. 'I don't know you. You pay for the night, no matter,' he winked, 'how many hours you stay.'

Bailey stepped forward. 'Fine.'

'One hundred pounds.'

Caelan was going to argue, but Bailey laid a hand on her arm as he handed over some banknotes. The man took them without a word, tucked them into his trouser pocket. He turned, unhooked a key from the board behind him.

'Room Three. One of our best. The bed is... very comfortable.' He held out the key to Caelan, who forced a smile.

'Thank you. I'm sure it'll be just what we need.'

The man laughed unpleasantly and waved towards the staircase at the back of the room. 'Go up. Enjoy.'

Caelan took Bailey's hand, put it on the small of her back. 'Oh, we will.'

The stairs were grimy, and each step creaked. There was silence as they reached the first landing. They passed two doors, found the one with a white plastic '3'. Bailey unlocked it, poked his head inside.

'Brace yourself,' he said.

Caelan stepped inside and turned on the light. The room was small, just big enough for the double bed with a faded blue floral cover. The carpet was pink, dirty. In one corner was a shower cubicle, but there was no sink or toilet. Two pillows on the bed still had the indents caused by the previous occupants' heads. The room smelt musty and damp. Caelan moved round the bed.

'I don't even want to sit on it,' she said. Bailey came into the room, closed the door behind him.

'Do you think they bother to change the sheets between guests?'

'I think they should burn them.' Caelan looked up at him. 'What now?'

Bailey shrugged. 'We'll give it five minutes, and then I'll go and have a nosy.'

'You don't think it's weird there's no one around?'

'Maybe we're too early.'

Caelan heard feet on the stairs, voices. She held up a hand. 'Perhaps we should be making some noise?'

Bailey looked horrified. 'You mean…?'

The door to the room next door slammed, and a woman began to giggle. Then a man's voice, low and urgent. A pause, then a bed creaking.

'I can't stay and listen to them… I'll see you soon.' Bailey slipped out of the door, leaving Caelan staring after him. In the next room, the man began to moan. She made up her mind. Caelan made up her miEasing the door open a fraction, she listened, wondering where Bailey had gone. She'd give him a count of a hundred, then do some sniffing around of her own.

Downstairs, the man on the reception desk had finished his pizza. He looked up as Caelan clattered down the stairs in her heels, then leant back in his chair and laughed at her.

'Did you frighten him?'

'Has he gone?' She put her hands on her hips. 'He owes me.'

He pointed upstairs. 'Second floor.'

'What's up there?'

A chuckle. 'More rooms.'

Caelan flicked her hair.

'If he doesn't want me, there's plenty of men out there who will. I've a living to make.'

He yawned. 'Maybe he found someone he liked better.'

'Do you have girls up there, is that it?'

'Why don't you leave? I think you've lost your client.' He was laughing at her again. 'Go on, get out.'

Caelan was torn. She shouldn't leave Bailey alone here, but coming downstairs had been a mistake.

'I'll go back and wait for him.'

He pushed back his chair, heaved himself out of it. 'Leave, now. Otherwise...'

'Yeah?'

At the bottom of the stairs, he bellowed, 'Piotr!'

Caelan waited. Was Piotr the man who had raised concerns about the place?

There was no reply. Should she intervene? If Bailey was talking to Piotr, the receptionist's suspicions might be aroused if he didn't appear. She sidled over to him.

'Listen, the room's paid for, isn't it?'

He glared at her. 'So?'

'So why don't you and I go up there?' Caelan had no time to think about what she was saying.

'I'm working.' He was tempted, though, she could see it in his eyes.

'Your loss.' She smiled and turned away.

'What's the problem?' A shout from the floor above.

'Got a girl here who needs to leave.'

Another man appeared, six feet tall, broad and toned. Caelan grinned at him.

'Hello. If you're the muscle, is this joker the brains?'

They both stared at her. 'Bitch,' spat the receptionist. 'Get her out of here.'

Piotr strode across the room, seized Caelan's arm. 'Come on.'

She allowed him to march her towards the door. As he opened it and propelled her onto the street, she said, 'What about my client?'

Piotr frowned at her. 'Forget him. He's having some fun.'

'But he owes me…'

He lowered his voice, gave her a gentle push. 'Back door.'

Caelan nodded her thanks, but he was already closing the door behind her. Wishing she could step out of her heels, she made her way around the side of the building, hoping she wasn't walking into a trap.

There was a black-painted door set into the wall. It stood ajar, and Caelan stepped closer, attempting to see through the gap.

'Here.' It was a female voice, no more than a whisper.

'Who are you?'

'Please.'

Caelan eased the door open, revealing a paved yard about fifteen feet square, three overflowing dustbins polluting a corner. A girl stood there, thin and pale, wrapping her arms around her body as she shivered. She wore a tight lacy top and a short skirt, her feet bare despite the chill of the evening. Caelan fought the urge to grab her and run. She stepped closer.

'Can you tell me your name?' She spoke softly. The girl lifted her eyes and Caelan flinched at the bleakness in them, the desolation. 'I can help you. Do you understand?'

No reaction. The girl began to shiver, and Caelan tried to slide an arm around her shoulders. She froze, let out a cry of distress, and Caelan held up her hands, attempting to show she wasn't a threat.

'Okay, it's okay. I'm not going to hurt you.'

'You've seen her then?' It was Piotr, his arms folded, his expression grim. 'There are five more girls up there. Can you get someone to come for them? They've been here two weeks. They'll be swapped any time.'

'Swapped?' Again Caelan glanced at the girl. She stood silent, as though waiting to see what was going to happen to her next.

'They bring different girls, swap them around. Stops the customers becoming bored.' Piotr's mouth twisted. 'It will be tomorrow, in the morning. Always the same.'

'Who brings them?' Caelan's mind raced ahead. Officers would be waiting. No way was she going to let these bastards get away with what they were doing.

'No one. They arrive alone, a group of four or five girls.'

'But someone must come with them, watch them. They could go to the police.'

He shook his head. 'With no papers, no passports? No. The girls know what will happen to them, to their families back home, if they dare to try and escape.'

Caelan clenched her fists. She had expected as much. 'Where's... the man I came in with?' she asked. Piotr nodded.

'With one of these girls – asking her questions, I hope. The man at the desk, Felipe, he offered him something special. I think he means underage. They're prisoners up there. I only got this one out because I watched him enter the door code.'

Caelan's throat tightened. 'Do you know where they're from?'

'Does it matter? They shouldn't be here, not like this.' Piotr glanced over his shoulder. 'I don't trust the police, they won't listen to me, but can you do something? Speak to someone?'

Caelan nodded. 'I'll go now.'

He stepped back. 'Good. I should take her inside. If they see we're gone...'

'Okay.' On impulse, Caelan reached out and grabbed the girl's hand. She flinched, but allowed Caelan to take it. Gently Caelan eased it away from the girl's body, turning it to the side to examine the inside of her forearm, the crook of her elbow. 'Listen, I'm going to help you. Do you understand?'

The girl blinked. 'Ardiola.' She removed her hand from Caelan's and tapped her own chest. 'Ardiola,' she repeated.

'That's your name?'

Piotr shifted his feet, glanced over his shoulder. 'We need to go inside. Remember – tomorrow morning.'

Caelan didn't want to leave the girl in this place, but she knew she had to. If she took her now, their captors would spirit the others away. 'I'll help you. Okay? Trust me.'

The girl allowed Piotr to lead her back inside, giving no sign that she had heard Caelan, much less understood. Caelan walked away, raging at the situation and the abuse the girl had endured that had left her so passive, so compliant.

Or maybe it was the drugs.

She made her way back to the car, hoping Bailey wouldn't be long. Hanging around on the street at night wearing these clothes wasn't her idea of a good time. She pulled her phone out of the tiny handbag she'd brought along and stepped into a doorway. Ian Penrith answered on the first ring.

'Caelan?'

'The hotel you sent me to? We need to raid it, immediately. It's got to be shut down tonight. I've been told more girls will arrive tomorrow. We could grab whoever brings them.'

'It's not our operation, as you know.'

'Then talk to someone. Please, Ian. The girl I saw looked about fifteen. She was probably even younger.'

He clicked his tongue. 'All right. I'll see you tomorrow.'

'Will you call me back? I want to know what—'

Caelan broke off as she saw Bailey staggering towards her. He held out the car keys, and she saw that his left eye was swollen and bruised.

'Would you mind driving?' He leaned against the side of the car, holding his stomach. 'I'm not sure I can.'

'What the hell happened to you?' She held the phone back up to her ear. 'I'll talk to you soon, Ian.' She put the handset away and grabbed the keys from Bailey's hand. He turned away, and Caelan knew he was embarrassed.

'Can we just get out of here?' he said. 'Please?'

Caelan unlocked the doors, started the engine. 'Fine.'

Bailey winced as he slid into the passenger seat. 'Shit, that hurts.'

'Are you going to tell me who did this to you? Where are we going?'

'Can you take me to the station at Stoke Newington, please? I'll direct you. I need to speak to my boss.'

'And get those girls out of there?'

'Left here. Yeah, we're soon going to be battering the door down.' Bailey spoke with bravado, but Caelan wasn't convinced. What he had witnessed in the hotel had affected him.

'Who hit you?'

He attempted a laugh. 'The bouncer, Piotr. I was talking to him, and the receptionist bloke came storming in. Piotr had to pretend he was throwing me out and,' he pointed to his eye, 'this is the result.'

'And he was only pretending?'

'Had to make it look convincing. You need to take the next right.'

'Well he definitely succeeded. What did you find out?'

'The girl couldn't tell me much – her English was limited, and I can get by in German but nothing else. The girls were locked away, though, that's all I needed to see. We'll be going in as soon as we've got permission.'

Caelan told him how Piotr had brought one of the girls out to her, and what he had said about the new girls arriving. 'How did he know who I was?'

She glanced at Bailey, who had turned his head away. 'DC Bailey?'

'I told him. I said a colleague of mine was in the building.'

Her hands tightened on the steering wheel. 'And you thought that was acceptable?'

'I trusted him… I mean, he came to us. He's an informer.'

'And?'

'Well, it's in his interests to work with us.'

'And if one of his bosses had found out he'd blabbed and had a gang of five men with baseball bats waiting for me?'

Bailey's hands clenched in his lap. 'I… I hadn't thought of that.'

'No, you hadn't. Which means we're lucky to be going home at all.'

'All right, I fucked up. Didn't matter, though, did it? We got what we came for. Evidence.'

Caelan fought to keep the fury out of her voice. 'And if you and your boss don't move quickly, you might lose it again.'

'We will. Those girls will be free by breakfast time.'

'Physically, maybe.'

He held up his hands, shaking his head. 'We'll get them the help they need. I have a thirteen-year-old niece. Believe me, I'm as angry as you are.'

'Just… get them out of there, and catch the fuckers responsible.'

'We will. You can park here.'

They drew up outside Stoke Newington police station. 'Come inside,' Bailey said. 'I'll get someone to drive you home.'

Caelan dropped the keys into his palm. 'Thanks. I don't fancy getting on the Tube in this outfit.'

10

Back in her own hotel room, Caelan stepped into the shower, lathering and rinsing her body and hair three times before she felt remotely clean. She was furious with Bailey, angry with Ian Penrith. He hadn't called back. She knew she had to trust them, allow Bailey and his colleagues to complete the job they had started. It didn't make her feel any better, not when she remembered the girl she had seen, and the others who had been inside the hotel.

She knew there must be hundreds, probably thousands of women, and men too, in the same situation up and down the country. Lured to the UK by promises of a better life, employment opportunities. Only when their passports were taken away did the ugly truth begin to emerge. Forced into prostitution, introduced to drugs to keep them dependent and compliant. Beaten, raped, abused in ways Caelan, even with her years of experience, probably couldn't begin to imagine. A nightmare, a life sentence that some didn't survive.

She pulled on clean jeans and a T-shirt, forced herself to stop thinking about it. She was doing what she could. What had Liv Hobbs said? *You swat one, turn around, and three more have flown in to spread shit around.* It was true, though not easy to accept. Sometimes the tide of filth felt overwhelming.

She paced around the room, glanced at the TV, knew there would be nothing she wanted to watch. Picked up her phone, checked the time. After midnight. Late, but then he could ignore the call.

'Caelan. Can't you sleep either?'

She smiled. 'I haven't tried yet.'

A pause. 'We could meet up. There's a twenty-four-hour café near here…'

Caelan was already pulling her coat on. 'Text me the address.'

–

Ewan sat in a corner booth, well away from the counter. As Caelan approached, he made to stand up, but she waved him down and went over to buy their coffee.

Sliding the tray onto the table between them, she pulled out a chair. 'I was worried I'd wake you.'

'No chance. It's difficult to lie comfortably.'

'You look pretty good for someone who almost died yesterday,' she said as she handed him his cup. He grinned.

'Could say the same for you.'

Caelan raised her mug in a mock toast, drank some coffee. 'Why have you brought a pillow with you? Or shouldn't I ask?'

'In case I need to cough. Sounds weird, but if you hold the pillow to your chest, it makes it less painful.'

'What if you sneeze?'

Ewan grimaced. 'Haven't needed to yet. I'd probably burst into tears.'

She watched him wince as he lifted the cup to his lips, saw the white gauze dressing on his temple where he'd fallen and hit his head following the shooting.

'How long do you have off work?' she asked.

He set his cup on the table. 'As long as I need.'

'Aren't you bored yet?'

Ewan laughed. 'Aren't you?'

'Not exactly.' She told him about her meeting with Elizabeth Beckett, then Tim Achebe and the others, not disclosing details, but giving him an idea of what had happened. She wanted to tell him about Nicky, but found the words wouldn't come. Ewan had quickly become a friend when she had asked him to partner her in her last assignment. He had joined the Metropolitan Police after his career in the army ended, and currently worked in protection. Caelan had met him when he was sent to collect her from the airport and escort her to a meeting. He had already proven himself to be capable and trustworthy – something she couldn't say for some of her other colleagues. Ewan listened, his head on one side.

'What are you thinking?' he asked when Caelan fell silent.

'I don't know. Ben Rainey's family say he didn't know Anthony Bryce. They're the same age, and Bryce grew up about seven miles from where Rainey lived. There has to be a link between them, but we haven't found it yet.'

Ewan picked up his coffee, took another sip. 'They could have met in any number of ways, even just hanging around on the streets. Their parents might never have known.'

'Could be. Or I'm wrong, and the attacks are random.'

Meeting her eyes, Ewan frowned. 'That would be worse?'

'Yes, because it makes our job harder. If there's a link, there will be lines of investigation to follow. Random attacks are rare, and it can be more difficult to find leads.'

'There are loads of places where they could have met in a city this size. Sports teams, religious groups, school, college, Saturday jobs…'

Caelan held up her hand. 'Wait a minute.'

'What?'

'Religion. Ben Rainey's father mentioned his children going to church.' She sat back, considering it. 'And their names...'

'What about them?'

'Benjamin, Miriam, Joseph – aren't they all Biblical?'

'Yeah, I think so. Does that matter?'

'I don't know. It might suggest the Bible and their religion is important to Abigail and Charles Rainey.'

'I think the name Abigail is in the Bible too.' Ewan finished his coffee. 'You see, I knew going to Sunday school would come in handy one day.'

Caelan had her phone in her hand. 'I'll email DCI Achebe. It's probably irrelevant, but...'

'Worth checking. What about the other victim, the one found today?'

'Anthony Bryce? I don't know anything about his background.'

Ewan glanced at his watch. 'Caelan, listen. There's something I need to say, about yesterday.' Caelan tried to interrupt, but he held up a hand. 'Please. I wanted to apologise. I was there to back you up, and I ended up flat out on the floor. Not my proudest moment.'

'It was my fault. I underestimated Nasenby. I should have known better.'

Ewan cleared his throat, holding his ribs. 'Well, we survived and Nasenby's looking at spending the rest of his life in prison. I'd say job done.'

Caelan grinned at him. 'Me too.'

'There's something else.'

'That sounds ominous.'

He blushed, lowered his voice. 'No, it's a good thing... At least, I hope it is. I've applied for a transfer.'

She stared at him. 'A transfer to…?'

'Specialist Crime and Operations – your department. I know it won't be full time, but working with you really opened my eyes.'

Caelan stood, leaning over to give him a gentle hug. 'That's brilliant news. What did they say?'

He winked. 'Hard to say no to a man who was shot yesterday in the line of duty.'

'Who did you speak to?'

'Elizabeth Beckett. She said something about rebuilding the department.'

Caelan nodded. 'They'll have to. Wait until Penrith hears.'

'I'm seeing him tomorrow.'

'You're coming back to work then?'

'Like you said, I'm bored at home.'

They smiled at each other. 'Lots of training to do,' Caelan warned him.

'I know. I'm looking forward to it.'

–

DCI Tim Achebe stood at the back of the briefing room in South Harrow, watching his officers file in rubbing their eyes and sipping coffee from cardboard cups.

'They're knackered,' said DS Jen Somerville, who was standing beside him. Achebe looked shattered too, she realised. It was early – she could sympathise. 'We've made no progress on the Ben Rainey investigation, and they know it.'

'We all do.' Achebe straightened his tie. 'It just means we work harder.'

'Agreed.' Jen glanced at her boss. 'What about the church?'

Achebe had forwarded her the email from Caelan Small. They had asked Mr and Mrs Rainey about their church before, but the couple had said Ben didn't go with them now. They were disappointed, they'd said, but Benjamin was an adult, and his job meant it wouldn't always be possible to attend the services in any case. They had thought it a dead end. Now, it was possible they had been wrong, and Jen wanted to know for sure.

'Did you speak to the pastor again?' Achebe asked.

'Yeah, he doesn't remember Anthony Bryce ever being part of the congregation. Then again, he's only been there four years, so I asked for the details of his predecessor.'

'What did he say?'

'I got a mobile number. Haven't had a chance to call yet.'

Achebe looked up at the clock on the wall. 'Could you do it now?'

She looked up at him. 'Well, yes. I thought—'

'It won't take long. Please, Jen. This case...' He shook his head. 'I want to find these fuckers.'

'We all do. And we will.' Somerville took out her phone, left the room, ducked into an empty office. She found the number, waited for it to connect. Four rings.

'Hello?' The voice was female. Somerville frowned.

'Good morning. I was hoping to speak to Pastor Miles. This is DS Somerville from the Metropolitan Police.'

A pause. 'I'm Pastor Miles.' The woman laughed. 'You were expecting a man, weren't you? Typical.'

Somerville ignored the comment, though she was blushing, knowing she was guilty of making the kind of assumption she'd berated colleagues for in the past. 'I need to speak to you, ma'am. Would later this morning be convenient?'

'Well, yes, but can I ask what it's about?'

'An ongoing investigation, ma'am. Shall we say ten thirty?'

'Fine. I'll be at home. I assume you know the address.'

'I'll find it. Thank you.'

Somerville ended the call, went back to the briefing room, not looking forward to the interview. Miles would already feel she had the upper hand, having caught her out.

Achebe was at the front, encouraging the officers in front of him. Somerville had to admit, he was a good motivator. As he told them he knew how hard they were working, that they were the only people who could bring the murderer of one of their own to justice, she saw backs straighten and shoulders lift. Achebe was the right blend of mate and boss. His team wanted to impress him, please him. As he turned away, though, the assembled officers going back to their desks, Jen saw the mask slip. Achebe stood still, hands by his sides, face blank. She went over, touched his sleeve.

'Tim?'

He blinked. 'Sorry, Jen. Just wondering what I'm going to say to the Chief Super. How'd it go?'

She filled him in. 'Pastor Miles?' He raised his eyebrows. 'What sort of church is this?'

'Well, according to their website—'

'Churches have websites now?'

'Of course. It's a Christian movement—'

He held up a hand. 'I know the sort of place – tambourines, lots of singing… My parents are members of a place like that.'

She stared at him, unsure how to respond. He grinned at her.

'I'm sorry, Jen, I'm not being dismissive – at least, not of you. Rather you than me, that's all I'm saying.'

–

Having managed to finally grab a few hours' sleep, Caelan was up early. She had just left the Tube station when she received the call. She stepped into a doorway to listen to what Liam Bailey had to report. As promised, he and his boss had organised a raid on the hotel in Hackney at first light.

'We arrested the receptionist, the bouncer, Piotr, seven women, including the girls who were behind the locked door, and two punters.' Bailey sounded exhausted, and Caelan could imagine how he would be feeling. The adrenalin of the raid leaking away, replaced by the familiar crawling reminder that however many you saved or arrested, there would be thousands more you could never reach. Or perhaps she was wrong. Perhaps Bailey never thought about the endless, bottomless struggle of the job. When your best was never quite good enough. She thought of the girl she had met, Ardiola; her bird-like limbs and the wide gaze that saw nothing. But all she said was, 'Thanks for letting me know.'

Bailey huffed. 'We thought it was a good result.'

'It is, of course it is. Congratulations. What about the girls who were supposed to arrive today?'

'We... that is, it was decided we should close the place down immediately. I'm not sure what will have happened to them.'

'Then they're still out there.'

'It wasn't my call. The girls we arrested are illegal immigrants, no surprise there. They were taken to hospital. I'm sure you can imagine the injuries and trauma we're expecting them to have suffered.'

Caelan swallowed. 'Yes.'

'When we've spoken to them, they'll be taken to a centre, where either they'll be helped to get home, wherever that may be, or they'll be found housing.' He paused, and when he spoke again, his voice had changed. 'I'll make sure of that.'

'What about whoever trafficked them into the country?'

'Piotr, the geezer who contacted us in the first place, is going to tell us what he can. We're also leaning on the receptionist, because he's terrified of going to prison, and we want to use that. We seized the CCTV recordings, and there were some records in his desk. It looks like he made notes about the punters – maybe he was planning a spot of blackmail. We don't know yet. It's all hand-written, and not in English, so it'll take time to go through and see if there's anything useful.'

It wasn't what she had hoped for, but it was a start. 'All right. I'll keep in touch. Let me know if there's anything I can do.'

'Will do.' Bailey coughed. 'Thanks for last night. I know I fucked up, but at least we got those girls out of there.'

Caelan pulled her coat around her body as rain began to fall. 'But if you don't find the bastards who are in charge, there'll be six more to replace them in another hotel before the end of the week.'

'I know, I get that.' Bailey sound more annoyed than contrite, and Caelan knew she had to back off.

'Which hospital were the women taken to?'

'Homerton.'

'Okay, thanks.'

'Wait a minute, you're not planning on—'

Caelan ended the call on his spluttering. She wanted to reach South Harrow police station quickly. Achebe hadn't replied to her email and she wanted to speak to him, as well as ask Jen Somerville if she had traced the car that had collided with Liv Hobbs's vehicle. Ian Penrith had told her to leave Achebe's investigation alone. How could she? She hadn't been asked to go to Edmonton yet, even if Nicky had. As she marched along, another thought struck her, and she pulled out her phone.

'Dare I ask where you are?' Penrith yawned.

'Is Richard in Edmonton as well as Nicky?'

Penrith was eating, the sounds of biting and chewing all too audible. Caelan grimaced as she heard him swallow.

'Why do you want to know?'

'Come on, Ian. Either I'm wanted on the operation, or I'm not. Why send them, and not me?'

'You were needed last night. The job in Hackney—'

'Anyone could have done it. They didn't need me.'

'You know how it is. If someone asks for a woman, you're top of my list.'

She snorted. 'I'm sure.'

'Yes, Richard and Nicky are in Edmonton. They spent the night there after showing their faces in a couple of the pubs.'

'They're working together?' Caelan stepped around an elderly woman who was walking a barrel-shaped Jack Russell. 'I thought it had been agreed we'd go in separately.'

'Overruled. Safety in numbers and all that.'

'Nicky was working on her own before, though, wasn't she?'

'That was before two dead bodies turned up.' Penrith was clearly now slurping liquid. Caelan pictured him behind his desk, his coffee cup resting on his belly. 'We thought it best to be cautious this time.'

'When do you want me there?'

Penrith was silent for a few seconds. 'Let me speak to the fellow from the NCA – Reid, isn't it?'

'Reid and Webster.'

'I prefer Reid. Webster looks like a long-lost Mitchell brother. I can't take him seriously.'

Caelan laughed. 'Now you mention it…'

'If it was my decision, Caelan, you'd have gone with Nicky and Richard last night.'

'Then it's not?'

Penrith clicked his tongue. 'Have I officially been promoted? Do I have a shiny new office, a new job title, a pay rise? A parking space that's less than forty minutes' walk from the building? No. And until I have those things, Assistant Commissioner Beckett makes the decisions.'

'And takes the shit.'

His tone sharpened. 'Only from you. You didn't answer when I asked where you are.'

Caelan glanced around as she walked. 'Because I don't want to tell you.'

'No doubt on your way to South Harrow, disregarding my express instructions to stay away?'

'Lucky you're not my boss really.'

'I've already spoken to Tim Achebe.'

'And there was I thinking I'd woken you.'

'I've been in the office since seven. I'm on my second break-fast.'

'A copper's dead, Ian. Reid and Webster started this, now they're backing away. I know you're going to say we've no proof Ben Rainey's death is linked to the operation in Edmonton, but why was he there if it isn't?'

'We've discussed this. His body was found there. That doesn't mean he was ever in the area when he was alive.'

'I was thinking—' Penrith interrupted her with a loud groan. 'Hear me out, Ian. Ben's family said he wanted to be a detective. What if he'd heard about the new dealer in Edmonton? What if he decided to nose around himself?'

Penrith sucked his teeth. 'And why would he do that?'

'Maybe he thought if he found some answers, it would look good on his record. His brother told me Ben was ambitious.'

'We all were, once. How would he have known where to look? He lived in Northolt, was based in Limehouse. Why would he know anything about Edmonton? You're reaching, Caelan. How would he even know we'd been asking questions?'

'Anthony Bryce knew.'

'You think he told Rainey, even though we've no evidence they knew each other? How? When?'

'I don't know.' Caelan shook her head, frustrated. Penrith gave a heavy sigh.

'Have you told Tim Achebe this bright new idea of yours?'

'Not yet, though I mentioned that Ben Rainey had ambitions of being a detective. I *was* on my way to South Harrow to talk to him.'

'Phone him. Let him and his team investigate the possibility. Listen, Caelan, I'll say it again in the hope you listen – this is not your case.'

'What else am I supposed to do?'

'Go back to your flat. You know Nicky's not there. Prepare for Edmonton, and wait for my call.'

She said nothing, kept walking.

'Hello?'

'I'm here.'

'You said you *were* going to South Harrow. You're not heading for the hospital?'

Caelan remembered the girls from the brothel, imagined their fear, their confusion. She thought of the expertise and understanding of the medical staff who would be caring for them. She had done her part; she had helped as she had promised Ardiola she would. She had to walk away from them now, though it went against every instinct. Going to the hospital, meeting them all, giving assurances that they were safe – it was out of the question. And yet, knowing where her responsibilities ended was something she had struggled with since her days in uniform. Having to walk away after being called to a domestic disturbance, aware that the abuse would begin again as soon as the squad car disappeared. Promising an elderly man whose wife had been mugged and left for dead on a freezing pavement that those responsible would be caught, while knowing that finding the perpetrator was next to impossible. Becoming friends with the girlfriend of an East End gangster; tricking her, lying to her every day until he could be arrested, and then disappearing from her life without a word. Fooling people, using them, spending days, weeks and months living as someone she usually despised. It was a strange way of meting out justice, and she had to wonder, was she making any sort of difference?

'No. I'll be at South Harrow in five minutes,' she told Penrith.

11

Mulligan was standing at the filthy kitchen window, his hands on his hips, gazing down at the street far below. In the next room, the men he paid to watch his back were playing cards. He had spent all night cooking, and hadn't slept. It was early, too early to be thinking about business. He should be at home, in bed, getting a few hours' rest before calling for some company, having one of the new girls brought over. The voice in his brain he no longer obeyed was telling him exactly what he needed to do, and as always, it was tempting. He knew there would be no way back if he did, though. He was clean, hardly even had a drink these days. Too risky. One thing could easily lead to another, he knew.

'Is it clear out there?' he called. Silence. He turned, jamming his hands into his jeans pockets. What the fuck? He marched through the door, stood glowering at them.

The nearest man turned. 'What's the problem, boss?'

Mulligan stared around. 'Where are they?'

'Who?'

'My regulars, my resident crackheads. Where did Ryan go?'

Two matching frowns. He was confusing them.

'I thought you wanted them gone? Got a meeting, you said.'

'Yeah, I did, but Ryan's got some of my merchandise. He's making a delivery, his first one, and I don't know if I can trust him.'

'Maybe you should have thought of that before you let him leave.'

Mulligan narrowed his eyes. 'You getting smart with me, pal?'

The man shook his head, his face solemn. 'Only saying.'

Mulligan paced the room. 'Ryan's a crackhead, delivering crack. What could go wrong?' He laughed. 'You know what to do.'

'You leaving then, boss?'

Mulligan stopped in the centre of the room. 'Yeah, business meeting, like I said.'

'You need us with you?'

'Only one of you.' He pointed. 'You. Go and find Ryan.'

Obediently the man set down his hand of cards, heaved himself to his feet. 'What do you want me to do with him?'

Mulligan smiled. 'I'm sure you'll think of something.'

–

Ryan hadn't been on a bus in months. Nowhere to go, no one who wanted to see him. No money, at least not to waste on bus fares.

He held the rucksack on his lap, his hands clenched around the straps. Was he being too obvious? He licked his lips, leant back in the seat. Crossed his hands over the bag instead. He sat near the front, eyes scanning the other passengers. There were a few who looked as though they were familiar with what he was carrying. More than a nodding acquaintance, he reckoned.

Mulligan had told him where he needed to get off, and Ryan tensed, knowing they were almost there. He'd memorised the address, the route he had to take. Mulligan hadn't allowed him to make a note of it. 'You're telling me you can write now, wee man? Not sure I believe you.'

Laughing at him, same as always. Ryan was fed up with it, but at least Mulligan had listened when he'd said he needed to earn a few quid. This was a chance, Ryan knew, an opportunity. If he made the delivery, Mulligan had promised him more work. He'd have to stay off the crack, of course, but it was killing him anyway. Time to move into supply, provide the means to allow some other poor fucker a few minutes' escape from the world.

One more stop. He shifted in his seat, thinking of the contents of the bag. How much was it worth? Mulligan had told him the goods were paid for, he already had the money. All Ryan had to do was make the drop. His hands were shaking now. Would anyone notice if he helped himself, just enough to take the edge off? Would they know? He shut down the thought immediately. No. Mulligan was trusting him, and if he fucked up, he'd be dead, no questions asked. Stealing was not an option.

He got to his feet, stepped off the bus. Stood for a second on the pavement, getting his bearings, remembering what Mulligan had told him. Go to the end of the road, turn left. Left again, cut down an alley behind a row of shops. Turn right at the bottom, find the house. Three knocks, then four. Hand over the goods. Couldn't be simpler. So why was his mouth dry, his heart thumping?

He began to walk, focusing on putting one foot in front of the other and nothing else. He hadn't travelled far, but here, the air seemed charged. He laughed at himself, knew paranoia was creeping in. He was okay, he was fine. Just out for a stroll. He adjusted the bag on his shoulders, kept striding along. Bottom of the road, and he turned left. Saw the shops, found the alley.

Heard the footsteps.

He hesitated, stopped. Nothing but traffic noise. Took a deep breath and moved off again. The alley was narrow, lined with piles of rubbish and industrial bins. Ryan glanced around. Why had Mulligan sent him down here? No one would see him, sure, but it was horrible. No doubt there were mice, maybe even rats waiting to jump on him. They went for your throat, he had heard. He swallowed, shitting it now. Rats, fucking rats. With each step he might disturb one. He tried to move faster, pulling the rucksack from his shoulder and clutching it to his chest. He couldn't do this again. He'd get rid of the bag, go back to Mulligan and tell him he wasn't up to the job.

His pipe was in his pocket. He could stop now, here, make all the fear go away. The rats wouldn't touch him then. He moaned, long past realising he had made a sound. He grabbed the bag's zip, wrenched it open, shoved his hand inside.

The blow came from behind, a hard slap to the back of his head. Ryan cried out, fell to his knees, the bag disappearing. As he hit the ground, a kick thudded into his ribs. A hooded figure loomed above him. Ryan squirmed on the floor, his hands in the filth, searching for the rucksack.

Too late. It was snatched away, held up in front of his eyes. Fucker. Ryan flailed, trying to grab it. No chance. The figure turned, disappeared, leaving him on his knees. Ryan closed his eyes, a sob starting in his throat.

He'd lost it.

He was dead.

12

As Caelan entered the incident room, Jen Somerville waved her over. She was sitting at a desk in a corner, a mug of black coffee in her hand.

'Morning. Got something to show you.' She pointed at the computer screen. 'Watch.'

Caelan bent closer. It was CCTV footage. A car stood waiting at a set of traffic lights, its colour and model impossible to make out in the gloom.

'Is that DI Hobbs?' Caelan squinted, but couldn't tell.

'Yep, it's her. I've checked it all out. And… here comes the other vehicle.'

They watched as a dark-coloured van sped into the shot. It slowed for a second, then accelerated directly into the back of Hobbs's car, reversed at speed and disappeared. Caelan frowned.

'Can we watch it again, please?'

'You want me to slow it down?' Somerville clicked the mouse a few times, and the footage played once more.

'For me, this adds weight to the idea that the collision was deliberate,' Caelan said. 'The van driver braces himself, rams into DI Hobbs, then gets out of there as quickly as he can. What do you think?'

'I agree.' Somerville's tone was measured, as though the admission gave her no satisfaction. Caelan understood: watching someone deliberately smash into the car being driven by one of your colleagues was hardly a pleasant way to start your morning. 'I checked the ANPR,' Somerville continued. 'It's definitely Liv's car, and the crash happens just as she described it.'

'Was the van following her before the collision?'

'It's hard to be sure, but I didn't see it, and I've checked the cameras we know about along her route.'

'Which suggests it was random after all.' Suddenly exhausted, Caelan pressed her palms against her cheeks. 'Maybe it was accidental and the other driver panicked. Maybe I've wasted your time.'

'I'd have had to check it out anyway.' Somerville looked up, pushing her hair out of her eyes. 'I'm not sure it was random, though. I think you're right, and it was deliberate. Maybe they were waiting in a side street, knowing the route Liv would take home.'

'It's a possibility.' One Caelan had already considered; one she didn't like. She hadn't wanted to believe that Hobbs's 'accident' had in fact been deliberate, but after watching the footage, there was little doubt. The driver had hesitated as if picking his spot, lining up his own vehicle to maximise the impact. 'I don't suppose it's worth asking if the number plate of the van was picked up anywhere?'

In theory, each time a vehicle passed an automatic number-plate recognition camera, its licence plate was read and checked against databases to see if it was a vehicle of interest. Caelan wasn't holding out much hope of recognising the van, much less its owner, and wasn't surprised when Jen Somerville shook her head.

'No chance. As I said, I didn't see the van on any of the routes approaching the traffic lights. I can't make out who's driving, and the plates were impossible to read during the collision. Covered in mud or something.'

'How convenient.'

'They were probably cloned anyway.'

'No doubt.'

'There's more.' Somerville clicked away again, and brought up an email. Caelan read it quickly – a report about a vehicle fire the previous evening.

'This is the van that hit DI Hobbs?'

'I'm waiting for confirmation, but it's a black Transit, reported stolen the day before the accident.' Somerville lifted her shoulders, spread her hands. 'It was torched, plenty of petrol thrown around. I'd say it's a safe bet.'

'Who owned it?'

'A plumber in Milton Keynes. We're checking him out, but I'm confident he knew nothing about this.' She gestured towards the screen. 'He only bought the van last week, hadn't even transferred his tools into it.'

Caelan straightened again, hands on hips. 'I didn't want to be right about this.'

Somerville swivelled her chair so they faced each other. 'Well, it seems you are.'

'Has DCI Achebe seen the footage?'

'The whole team has. Forensics have the vehicle, but as you can imagine, there's not a lot left for them to work with. I'm expecting a preliminary report later today.'

Caelan nodded. 'There's something else.' She told Somerville about Ben Rainey's ambitions to be a detective. Somerville nodded, wrinkling her brow.

'The boss mentioned it, but we hadn't considered the possibility of him going out on his own and asking questions.'

'Where is the DCI?'

'Tim? In a meeting with the Chief Super.'

'Adele Brady?'

'You know her?'

Caelan snorted. 'We've met.'

Somerville grinned. 'I won't ask.'

'That… might be wise.' Caelan didn't elaborate, though her feelings about Detective Chief Superintendent Adele Brady were far from clear-cut. 'Did the DCI say anything about the Rainey family's church?'

A pause. 'Why do you ask?' Somerville sounded wary, and Caelan wondered what she had been told.

'I emailed DCI Achebe last night, mentioning the church. I wondered what he thought, that's all.'

'I spoke to the pastor. I'm heading off to see her shortly.'

'She couldn't discuss it on the phone?'

'Apparently not.' Somerville screwed up her face. 'Meeting her should be interesting.'

'Could I come with you?' Caelan regretted the words as soon as she heard herself say them. Why was she begging?

Somerville took a step backwards. 'I'll speak to the DCI.'

Caelan held up her hands. 'Look, it doesn't matter. I probably shouldn't be here anyway.' Somerville waited. Caelan blew out her cheeks, stared at the carpet tiles. 'I'm going to head back to my own station. See you around.'

She turned, walked away. No doubt Somerville would talk to Achebe; they'd shake their heads and get on with their jobs. They didn't need her.

-

Out on the street, Caelan tipped her head back, gazing up at the grey sky. She didn't want to go back to the flat. Penrith had promised to call her, but she didn't believe him. She was being sidelined, not for the first time recently. Nicky and Richard were already in Edmonton, while she was here, kicking her heels. Why? Penrith had said it was Beckett's decision. Bailey hadn't needed an expert the previous evening, though Beckett might use the request as justification for keeping Caelan out of Edmonton until she gave the word. She was probably just reminding Caelan and Penrith who was in charge.

Caelan took the tube to Westminster, knowing there would crowds of people to disappear into there. In a coffee shop, she ordered tea and took it to a corner table. She checked her phone, knowing what she would find. No texts, no missed calls. Her social media presence was non-existent, except for the fake accounts set up in the names of some of the identities she used. Even those had probably been deleted. Since she had agreed to return to work, the feeling that she was half a person had dogged each step. Her family and friends knew nothing of her real job. She lived her life in the shadows, and it had taken its toll. She drank the last mouthful of tea, told herself to snap out of it. This was normal when she wasn't on an active operation. Doubt set in, creeping around her head, eroding confidence and self-belief.

Nicky had understood. No doubt Richard would too, if she spoke to him about it. She had been told during training about officers who had burnt out, had breakdowns, walked away from marriages and children. She had told herself she was different. Now, she wondered.

On the next table, a group of tourists chatted and laughed. Caelan envied them, carefree and happy. Her last holiday had been taken alone, interrupted by a visit from Richard Adamson and an offer she now wished she had never accepted. She took out her phone.

'What now, Caelan?' Penrith was gruff. 'I told you to wait for my call. I haven't spoken to the boss yet.'

'I'll come in then. I can't just wait around, Ian. Isn't there something else I could be doing?'

'No. You'll be on your way later today.'

He hung up. Caelan set the phone on the table, wondering whether she should have told him where to stick his job.

–

In her kitchen, Liv Hobbs picked up her bag, ignoring the ache in her ribs as she pushed her feet into her shoes. Adam had gone to work, and there was no way she was spending another day sitting around at home. The garage hadn't dropped off her courtesy car yet, but the gym was only a fifteen-minute walk away. It would do her good to stretch her muscles with a swim after so many hours spent sitting down. Maybe some time in the sauna would help her aching body too.

She went out of the front door, locked it behind her. She would have to be sure she was home before Adam. He wouldn't be happy if he knew she'd left the house. Not, she thought as she turned onto the pavement, that it was his decision. He was looking out for her, she understood that. But she didn't need wrapping in cotton wool.

–

Behind Hobbs, fifty yards away, a car drew up at the side of the road. She didn't turn her head, didn't register the vehicle was there at all. It was a busy road, people coming and going at all hours.

Inside the car, the driver glanced at his passenger. 'Is it her?'

The second man shifted, nervous and ill at ease. He had a cap pulled down low over his face, but he still felt exposed. If she turned and saw them…

'You know it is,' he muttered. 'Why are you asking?'

'Making certain. When is it happening?'

'Not yet. Tonight? I don't know. Needs to be the right moment. We don't want to start trouble.'

The driver laughed as Hobbs turned the corner at the top of her road and disappeared out of sight. 'You're worried about trouble? That's what we're hoping for, isn't it?'

—

The flat in Rotherhithe was cold and felt unlived in. Caelan turned on the lights as she went into the kitchen and opened the fridge. Everything was as she had left it. Nicky had said she wasn't going to stay here, and when Caelan went into the bedroom, she saw that the bed had been stripped and made up with clean covers. Nicky's bag had gone; there was no trace of her. On the pillow on the right-hand side of the bed, there was a piece of paper with Caelan's name scribbled on it. Caelan stepped closer, picked it up. Her side of the bed, the only one she slept on, as Nicky would know. Caelan's throat closed, tears blurring the writing as she unfolded the note and read what Nicky had written. More apologies, the same explanation. She'd had no choice, there had been no other option. She didn't expect Caelan to understand, or to forgive her, but she hoped eventually they could be friends. Balling the note in her fist, Caelan turned away. She didn't think so.

In the bathroom, she applied dye to her hair, plucking her eyebrows into thin lines while she waited for the dye to take effect. Her oversized hoodies would make her appear thinner. Make-up always helped; with her face as bruised as it currently was, it was essential. She painted her fingernails black, then used a nail file to scuff them. She rinsed the dye out of her hair, watching the red water swirl towards the plughole, and stared at herself in the mirror. Not bad. Caelan Small was beginning to disappear.

After drying her now coppery-coloured hair, she ran some wax through it to make it appear dull and unwashed. Coloured contact lenses changed her eyes from hazel to ice blue. Next, clothes. Skinny jeans, a vest top. The gaudy pink and purple trainers. A baggy navy hoody. A couple of fake piercings through the tops of her ears. Her teeth might be a giveaway, but they'd have to do. This wasn't about deep cover; this was information-gathering. Thick foundation, mascara and black eyeliner. Done.

When she was satisfied, Caelan made herself a cup of tea and settled down to wait. She turned on the TV but left the sound muted as she checked her emails. Nothing new, except for the usual junk. She knew she should let her parents know she would be off the grid for a while, but she hadn't spoken to them since she had agreed to come back to work, and wasn't looking forward to the conversation when she did. They wouldn't be happy to hear she was a serving police officer again, especially if they found out about her injuries. Instead, she sent a text to her brother, asking him to fill their mum and dad in. Within seconds, he was calling her.

'Caelan? I thought you'd resigned from the Met?'

'Hello, Andrew. Fine thanks, how are you?'

He ignored her. 'You know how Mum and Dad are going to react, don't you? They worry about you, it's not fair. Every time the phone rings, we think it's going to be about you being hurt or—'

'I know, I get that. Good thing you have such a safe, boring job doing sums all day, isn't it?'

'Not funny. Why can't you tell them yourself?'

'Because they'll react like you have. There's no risk.'

He snorted. 'We've all heard that before.'

'Come on, Andy—'

'What? This job will kill you, you know that, don't you?'

'Don't be ridiculous. There's no danger at all.' She raised a hand to her bruised face. Lucky he couldn't see her, that he didn't know what she was really going to be doing. 'Just tell them, Andrew, please?'

A sigh. 'All right. Be careful, that's all we ask.'

'I know. I will be.' She coughed, cleared her throat. 'How is everyone?'

After diverting Andrew's attention onto his wife and two daughters, Caelan managed to get him off the phone. Immediately, it rang again. Ian Penrith didn't bother with a greeting either.

'Ready?'

'Where am I going?'

He gave her an address. 'It's the flat Nicky stayed in before. It's owned by the local authority but they're generously letting us rent it for a while.'

'Who am I supposed to be?'

'Use Kay Summers again.'

'That'll be the fourth time...'

'And?'

Caelan stood, went over to the window. Far below, the Thames surged past. 'Just seems risky, that's all.'

'Nonsense. Kay's never been to Edmonton, has she?'

'Apart from earlier today.'

'Fine then.'

'What about Nicky and Richard? Am I to make contact?'

'Up to you. They know you're coming.'

'Who are they?'

'No one to you. If you meet them, it'll be for the first time. Let them introduce themselves.'

'Okay. Anyone else I need to look out for?'

'Remember Frankie Hamilton? We'll have someone follow him to Edmonton, then it's up to you. We'll be in touch about that. We've left a phone and your ID in the flat.'

'How do I get in?' Even as she said the words, Caelan heard the entryphone buzz. Someone delivering the keys. 'Never mind.'

'We'll speak soon.' He was gone. Caelan turned off her mobile, picked up the entryphone.

Time to go.

13

Mealtimes had always been something to look forward to, especially when he had been a child. His mum and dad both loved cooking, and sitting down to plates piled high with curry or stew, rice and vegetables was a memorable part of his childhood. Time to sit with the family, chat about their day. Important times. He had a brother and a sister, and they had always got along well. They'd argued, of course, but stuck up for each other when it mattered. Now, though... He shook his head. They had both let him down. He was alone, and mealtimes were to be endured, not enjoyed. The slop they doled out here didn't deserve to be called food.

And he had sixteen years of it to come.

Jackson swung his legs off the bed, got to his feet, straightened the covers on his bunk. He picked up his plastic plate, mug and cutlery from the table and stood by the locked door. He'd been allowed out of his cell to collect his breakfast, but then had been banged up again. Nothing but a few battered paperbacks and mindless daytime TV to keep him occupied. They didn't seem to know what to do with him. He wasn't an escape risk, had no convictions for violence, whatever he might or might not have done in the past, so what was their problem? He didn't need to ask. No staff, no morale and too many prisoners. Well, boo-fucking-hoo. At least the screws went home at night, saw their families, slept in their own beds.

Jackson clenched his fists. He'd been inside before, served his time, and it had been a breeze. This time, though... this time, he had his business to consider. He'd lose the lot, if it hadn't happened already. He'd built an empire, and it was crashing down around his ears. He stood on tiptoes, stretching his back. If he spread his arms, his fingertips touched the walls on either side. He'd done it often enough, especially the first night. Those first few hours, when Jackson Hobbs, feared and respected throughout west London, had sat with his head in his hands and sobbed at the thought of sixteen years in a concrete cage. It had been his lowest point. Now, though, now he was looking to the future. He had to keep his nose clean, and his hand in. There were ways. They'd never find his money, and there were people he still trusted.

His lip curled as he thought of his sister, working away to bring people like him down. Well, good luck to her. He knew which side of the fence he'd rather be on. When Liv had joined the police, she'd started a prison sentence of her own. Bound by rules, trapped by regulations. The straight and fucking narrow.

Good for her.

The door opened.

'Come on, Hobbs. Egg and chips today, you lucky bastards.'

Jackson left his cell without a backwards glance, pushing his sister out of his mind. He'd had plenty of practice. She was part of his past, and there was no room for her in his future.

14

The flat looked like a shithole. Big surprise. It was on the third floor of a four-storey building, beside a row of terraced houses and hemmed in by several taller blocks. Cars were parked or abandoned everywhere, and the flat below had a boarded-up window. Music echoed around the stairwell, and as Caelan locked the front door behind her, she heard voices raised in argument. There was a thud, more shouting. She closed her eyes, reminded herself why she was here. Opened them and kept walking.

The living room was square, clean and clinical. A scuffed two-seater fake-leather sofa and a coffee table were the only furniture. In the kitchen, a free-standing cooker, a small fridge and a microwave waited. There was a new kettle, still in its box, and cutlery and crockery in a cupboard. In the bedroom, a divan bed, unmade. She dumped her rucksack on it, decided to leave her clothes inside. There would be laundry facilities somewhere in the block where she could wash bedding, but she resolved to buy a sleeping bag instead. Hopefully she wouldn't be hanging around for long. The bathroom was tiny, but clean and functional. She'd lived in worse places. In the single bedside cabinet she found her Kay Summers ID, debit and credit cards, and the mobile phone Penrith had promised her. She slipped it into her pocket. There was also a phone charger and an envelope containing cash.

In the flat below, the argument was still raging. A female voice, then a bang and a clatter. A man yelled back over the pounding music – something about missing money. Caelan tuned them out. She wasn't here to get involved in domestics.

Back in the living room, she paced over to the window, which opened onto a tiny balcony, and looked out at the scrubby grass behind the block. More cars, parked impossibly close together, battered concrete. A children's playground, hooded teenagers riding bikes around it. A couple of trees doing their best. Caelan turned away, slumped on the sofa. Took out the phone, scrolled through the contacts. There were enough to be convincing, but most would ring and never connect. Fake names, fake numbers. All part of the smokescreen. She wondered which name Penrith was hiding behind. No doubt she'd know soon enough. And where were Nicky and Richard? Would they be informed she was here? Would they find her? She didn't know, and she ought to. She knew Penrith would be in touch, but when? And what was she supposed to do until then?

She needed food, other supplies. She slid the bank cards into the empty purse she'd brought, along with some of the cash.

As she jogged down the concrete stairs, the front door of the flat below opened, and a man stuck his head out. Thin and pale, he wore a grubby grey T-shirt and jogging bottoms. The music had been turned down.

'You new upstairs?' he demanded. Caelan looked at him, noted his blackened teeth.

'Might be.'

'Sorry about the noise, yeah? You know how it is. Didn't realise you were up there.'

So how did you know I was? Caelan wanted to ask. They couldn't have heard her moving around, not with the row they'd been making.

'Mate of mine in the block opposite saw the lights go on,' the man continued. Caelan smiled, nodded.

And immediately contacted you. Interesting. 'Just got the keys,' she said.

Behind him, a young woman appeared, her long dark hair hanging lank. 'You must be fucking desperate.' She began to cough, stumbled away with her hands over her mouth. The man grinned, called after her.

'Keep telling you to cut down on the fags, April. Ignore her. I'm Leon.'

Caelan nodded, relieved he hadn't tried to shake hands. 'Good to meet you.'

'If you need any help settling in...' He raised his eyebrows, even winked. The woman reappeared.

'Give it up, Leon. Why would she want a scrawny bastard like you?' She elbowed him out of the way and gave Caelan a long stare. Not aggressive, just appraising.

Caelan shifted her feet, pointed downstairs. 'Need to get to the shops before they close, so...'

'Yeah, see you.' April was already closing the door, and Caelan hurried away.

The look the woman had given her lingered in her mind as she made her way to the Tesco Express she knew was nearby. It had been... knowing, as though April could see exactly who Caelan was. She told herself she was being ridiculous as she dropped tea bags, milk, bread and butter into a basket. She found bananas and apples, jam, yoghurt and cheese. Enough for a few days.

Back in the flat, the music downstairs quieter though still audible, Caelan made herself a cheese sandwich, then stood at the window with a mug of tea, clearly visible to anyone who might be watching. Why had her presence been noticed? What difference did it make to Leon and April if the flat above them was occupied? And why had Leon mentioned that he had been told she was there? Was it a warning, or was it supposed to reassure her? Either way, Caelan knew she had to bring it up when she next spoke to Ian Penrith. He could find out about her new neighbours, if it hadn't already been done. It should have been, but Caelan knew tenants changed quickly. Places were let and sublet. Leon and April weren't necessarily the people whose names were on the rent book.

The phone rang as she was washing her cup and plate at the kitchen sink.

'Kay?' It was Penrith. 'Where are you?'

'At home.' She turned off the tap.

'Nice place? Have you settled in?'

'It'll do. I've been meeting the neighbours.'

A tiny pause, then, 'And?'

'The couple in the flat below seem nice. Leon and April.'

'I see.'

'Someone told them I was here. Saw the lights come on, apparently.'

'What?' Penrith took a breath. 'Seems strange.'

'You're telling me.'

'But you're all right?'

'For now. Not sure how I'm going to keep myself busy, but...'

He cleared his throat. 'Mate of mine told me about a pub.'

'Oh yeah?'

'The Red Lion.'

'Original name.'

'Near the shopping centre. Thought I'd mention it.'

'Thanks.'

'Speak soon, then.'

He was gone. Caelan smiled to herself as she picked up her handbag.

–

She found the pub easily enough, hearing the shouts and laughter of the people smoking outside as she approached it. They were in a plastic shelter by the pub's main entrance. As she approached, a man nudged the person next to him.

'All right, darling? Are you lost?'

Caelan smiled and kept walking. 'Just looking for somewhere to have a drink.'

'Oh yeah? New around here?' He stepped forward, shoving his hands into the pockets of his jeans.

'Fairly.'

He saw she wasn't going to stop, and laughed. 'Maybe see you around, then.'

She didn't reply as she pushed open the door. The smell of the cigarettes followed her, mingling with the scent of beer and cheap aftershave. There were a few people inside, some eating burgers or lasagne and chips, most just drinking. In one corner, a group of men gathered around a fruit machine. No one noticed Caelan as she hesitated in the doorway and glanced around. The bar was in the centre of the room, and she headed for it to order a beer. Ideally she wouldn't drink while she was working, but in a pub, being the only person on lemonade, especially when you hadn't arrived in a car, might be noticed.

The barman passed over the bottle and her change without making eye contact. Caelan swallowed a mouthful before turning and scanning the crowd. She took out her phone and studied it as though checking for texts, not wanting people to think she was here alone. She wasn't worried, but some company would have been good. She thought of Ewan, sitting at his sister's house with his battered ribs, considered giving him a call, but knew she couldn't. Penrith had wanted her to come here tonight, and she needed to figure out why.

As she crossed to sit a table, the reason became obvious.

Frankie Hamilton, the man Spencer Reid from the NCA had first mentioned, was sitting near the bar. He had a pint of lager in his hand, two more lined up in front of him. Beside him sat a man who could only be his brother, such was the resemblance between them. As Caelan set her drink down and pulled out a chair, another man approached Hamilton and they bumped fists. Hamilton waved his friend into the seat opposite him with a grin. Caelan picked up her beer, considering her next move. Someone had clearly followed Hamilton here, and informed Penrith, as he had told Caelan they would. He hadn't been clear about what he wanted her to do, no doubt intentionally. They would know where Hamilton was going to be living now he'd been released from prison, but Reid had hoped he would lead them to his dealer.

Caelan drank some more beer, thinking about it. Reid had suggested that Hamilton hadn't known about his girlfriend moving in with his brother. Looking at them now, laughing and joking together, Caelan found it difficult to believe there was a problem between them. Either Frankie didn't care, or he didn't know yet – or there was another brother. Reid hadn't said so, but it wouldn't have been the first time the intelligence they were given to work with had been wrong.

Hamilton finished his drink and picked up the next. Caelan wasn't sitting close enough to hear what the men were talking about, and decided a visit to the toilets would give her the cover she needed to move closer. She picked up her beer bottle and strolled across the room. As she neared Hamilton's table, she pulled out her phone, silenced the camera, and took a quick photograph. It was risky, but she had held the phone close to her face, as though looking at the screen. Neither Hamilton nor his brother had seen her, and their friend had his back to her. She doubted anyone else had noticed, though she could feel eyes on her back.

Nicky.

She and Richard Adamson were sitting together at the back of the room, pretending to be absorbed in the large-screen TV that was bolted to the far wall. Caelan had seen them immediately, had been careful not to display a reaction. Nicky's eyes had met hers for a second before sliding away. Caelan refused to allow their presence to distract her. She was a professional. It wasn't a huge surprise to see them; perhaps it was even a relief. She dismissed the thought. She didn't want Nicky anywhere near her.

She kept walking, leaving the beer bottle on the bar as she passed. Following the smell of pine disinfectant, she went into the ladies' and checked her appearance in the mirrors over the sinks, though she wasn't concerned about raising suspicion. Hamilton had never met her, and with the dyed hair, thick make-up and coloured contact lenses, she barely recognised herself. She counted slowly to thirty, then headed back out into the pub.

The people who had been smoking outside had come inside, gathering around the bar. The barman had been joined by a surly-looking woman who was doling out packets of crisps. Caelan saw the man who had spoken to her, turned away from him. Frankie Hamilton had one pint left. Maybe he fancied another. She made up her mind, strode over. Hamilton looked up as she stopped by his chair. Caelan smiled.

'All right? Don't I know you?'

Hamilton smirked, looking her up and down. He licked his lips. 'Nah. Think I'd remember you.'

His companions sniggered. Caelan raised her hands. 'Sorry, thought you were Frankie. My mistake.' She made to turn away, and Hamilton's brother nudged him, his eyebrows raised.

'Hey, wait. Where did you say you knew me from?'

Caelan shrugged. 'Can't remember. Just know your face.'

Hamilton laughed, puffed out his chest. 'Once seen, never forgotten, that's Frankie.'

'Yeah, bullshit,' his brother scoffed.

'Good to see you, anyway.' Caelan pointed back towards the bar with her thumb. 'Can I buy you a drink? Looks like you're celebrating.'

Hamilton grinned. 'I am. I've been away, and it's good to be home.'

Caelan couldn't help it. 'Anywhere nice?'

He laughed. 'Yeah, beautiful. Mine's a pint.'

As she went back to the bar, Caelan glanced at Nicky and Richard. Richard wore glasses with wire frames, and hadn't shaved. A sweatshirt under a woollen sweater made him appear bulkier than he was. Simple, but effective enough. Nicky's hair was pulled back into a ponytail, her eyes a deep blue. Coloured contact lenses, a different shade to Caelan's. She wore a T-shirt under a hoody, held an e-cigarette that she was turning and twisting in her hand. Caelan felt a jolt in her chest as their eyes met again, but didn't break her stride. Let them observe. She knew they would follow Hamilton when he eventually staggered out of the door. She was free to muscle in on his evening.

She ordered another beer for herself, and carried it and Hamilton's pint of lager back to the table. He took it with a wink, allowed his eyes to roam over her body again.

'What did you say your name was?' He drank deeply, smacked his lips.

'Kay,' said Caelan. Hamilton nodded.

'Want to sit down?' He pointed an unsteady finger at the man sitting opposite him. 'Move up. I'd rather look at her face than yours.'

Hamilton's friend scowled, but scooted over to the next chair. Caelan sat, leant forward.

'This your local then, Frankie?'

He wiped his mouth with the back of his hand, a thick gold bracelet glinting with the movement. 'Yeah, you could say that. Though like I said, I've been away.'

'Away?'

He grinned. 'Inside. Jail. Sent down.' He folded his arms and stuck out his chin, clearly expecting her to be impressed.

Caelan sipped her beer. 'Yeah?'

'Yeah. It's been a long time, and it's good to see a friendly face, know what I'm saying?' He leered at her, looked at her hand. 'You married?'

'Nah. My bloke's just started a stretch himself.'

Hamilton laughed. 'Unlucky. What for?'

'Drugs.'

'Same as me. Not any more, though. I'm clean, looking for a job.'

'I'm hoping he'll do the same. Stick to selling, not using.'

'Selling? What's his name?' Hamilton sniffed, cleared his throat. His eyes were glazed, his hand trembling as he held his beer glass. Caelan knew she had to keep him talking.

'We're not from around here,' she told him. 'I moved when he was arrested. New start.'

'I can understand that. Things change when someone goes to prison. Feelings change.' He drank deeply again, glanced at his brother. 'Don't they, Jermaine?'

Jermaine held up his hands. 'I was looking after her, Frankie, you know that.'

'Yeah. Two fucking kids are proof of that, you bastard.' Hamilton spoke calmly, and Caelan waited.

Jermaine shuffled in his seat. 'She was already pregnant when you went inside...'

Hamilton laughed. 'By you. Keep talking. You're welcome to her, brother, her and the kids. She's nothing to me, she never was.' He leaned towards Caelan. 'New start for me too, know what I'm saying?'

She smiled. 'Maybe I do.'

'What happened to this boyfriend of yours' business?'

'His business? I don't know. Like I said, I moved. Sick of people knocking on the door at all hours.'

Hamilton laughed, rubbing his jaw. 'When you need a smoke, you need a smoke. Can't blame the poor bastards for trying.'

'Yeah, well, I wasn't selling. Not interested.'

He sat up straight. 'Me neither. Someone else on my turf now anyway.'

Caelan kept her gaze on her drink. 'Yeah?'

'You go away for a couple of years, and the whole area goes to shit.' Hamilton finished his drink, looked at his brother and waved the empty glass at him. Jermaine sighed and got to his feet. 'Had to tell the parole board I wanted to find legit work, but I've no real choice. Fucking kids on my patch now, selling anything you want.'

'Like what?'

'All sorts of shit, stuff I've never touched.' He paused, staring at her, his eyes half closed. 'Why? Are you buying?'

'Me? Nah. Force of habit. When you live with someone who's in the game, you get used to hearing things.'

He tipped his head to the side, still watching her. Caelan felt a chill creep down the back of her neck. 'The important thing is not to hear too much,' he said softly. 'And to know when to keep your mouth shut.'

She forced a laugh. 'Goes without saying.'

'What did your boyfriend sell?' He glanced around, flashed another wink. 'You can tell me.'

'Weed, mainly. He had some tabs on him when he was arrested. Bit of spice...'

Hamilton pointed an unsteady figure at her. 'See, that's what I mean. Fucking spice. Synthetic shit.'

Caelan shrugged. 'It's what people want. Got to follow the market.'

Jermaine returned, thumped another pint down in front of his brother. 'I'm going,' he said.

Frankie Hamilton laughed at him. 'Been on the phone, has she? Wanting you home to tuck the kids in? It's worse than being tagged.'

Jermaine said nothing. The friend, who had been silent since Caelan had approached them, also pushed back his chair.

'See you, Frankie.' He didn't look at Caelan.

Hamilton watched them go, unconcerned. 'Yeah, yeah, walk away. Good to know I've been missed.'

'What's their problem?' Caelan asked.

'Problem? There's no problem. They can see we're getting on, and they're jealous.'

'Want to keep you to themselves, do they?'

He laughed, patted the chair beside him. 'Why don't you come and sit next to me?'

Caelan shook her head. 'I told you, my boyfriend's inside.'

'What, and you're going to wait for him? It's a long time, gorgeous. You'll be lonely.'

'Yeah, well, he knows people. I told him I'd be here when he got out, and I will.'

'But in the meantime...' He grinned. 'I could keep you company.'

She glanced around, making a show of checking whether anyone was watching. 'Listen, give me your number. I'm not saying... Well, I'll think about it.'

He took out a cheap phone, read out the number. 'Can't remember it yet. Had to get a new one this afternoon. Sold the one I had in prison before I came out. You know how it is.'

'I'll give you a call sometime.'

'Make sure you do.' He leaned closer, lowered his voice. 'And if I can help you out, you only need to ask. If you need something to take the edge off, know what I'm saying?'

'I thought you were out of the game?'

He frowned, mock-offended. 'I am, but if I want to do favours for a friend, that's my business, isn't it?'

'I suppose it is.'

'This boyfriend of yours...'

'What about him?'

'Name wouldn't be Jackson Hobbs, would it?'

Caelan froze, but controlled the reaction. 'Hobbs? No. Anyway, he's gone down for a lot longer than four years.'

Hamilton was swallowing more lager. 'I know. Fucking hilarious.' He half turned, looked around. 'Not that I'd say it to his face. You know him, then?'

'Heard of him.'

'Lot of people have. Even more stay out of his way.'

'What I've heard, that sounds sensible.'

'Yeah, he can be a nasty bastard. He ended up in the same prison as me, but a different wing. I was hoping we'd be neighbours. Would have liked to have given him a wave as I headed out the door.' He smirked. 'Nice to see the cocky bastard brought down a peg or two.'

'His business will be fucked as well.'

'He'll be keeping an eye on things.'

'Thought you said there were new people around?'

Hamilton's eyes narrowed for a second. 'On my patch, yeah. I don't know about where Hobbs did his trading.'

'I didn't say—'

'Listen, if you're going to fit in around here, you need to understand something.' Hamilton leaned over the table, held a finger in the air. 'In Edmonton, we keep our mouths shut. We don't ask questions, we hear nothing, see nothing.'

'Yeah, I get that.'

'Jackson Hobbs still has mates here. Don't want to be making enemies, do you?'

Caelan studied the table. 'No.'

'So, any ideas you have about picking up where your boyfriend left off wherever it is you came from, forget them.'

'I never said—'

'Come on, admit it. He left a stash somewhere, and you want to get rid of it. Short of cash, are you?'

'No. I'm not looking to sell.'

'Buy, then?'

She glanced around. No one was near enough to overhear their conversation. 'I don't know. Who would I need to speak to?'

He laughed. 'You reckon you know me, know the game, and you ask questions like that? Think you've said enough, don't you?'

'All right, I'm sorry. It's just... Look, Frankie, I'm terrified. I'm used to having money, cash stashed all over the place. They found it when they raided our flat, took the lot.'

Hamilton gave a slow shake of his head. 'Fucking amateurs.'

Caelan glared. 'We were set up. Some fucker grassed.'

'Then why aren't you inside yourself?'

'He made sure I was kept out of it. I never touched the money, or anything else.'

'He didn't trust you.'

'Yeah, he did. He wanted me on the outside if he ever went down.'

'Keep telling yourself that.' Hamilton's attention was wandering. He pulled out his phone, tried to focus on the screen. 'I'm starving. Fancy a kebab?'

'Are you buying?'

'Joking, aren't you? Thought you might be feeling generous.'

'No money for takeaways.'

He spread his hands on the table, pushed himself to his feet and stood swaying. 'Come on. I've got a mate who runs a chippy. Let's see if he's still in business.'

Caelan nodded, followed him as he lurched across to the door. Several people spoke to him, and he stopped a few times to exchange a handshake or fist bump. Caelan hung back, head down, smiling as though she was having a great time. Nicky and Richard were finishing their drinks, not hurrying, not even looking Hamilton's way. But they were watching.

As they reached the door, someone called, 'Oi oi, Frankie, company on your first night of freedom? Lucky bastard!'

He held up a hand, not bothering to turn. 'What can I say? She's an old friend.'

Caelan held the door open for him and he stumbled outside. She knew she had to stay alert, keep bringing the conversation around to drugs and see what he might reveal. Luckily, it seemed to be a subject he was fond of.

'You used to be able to get anything you wanted in there,' he said, nodding back towards the pub as they walked.

'Like what?' Caelan asked.

'Anything.' He held up his hands. 'Guns, drugs, DVDs – and I'm not talking about Disney films. Proper fucked-up shit.'

Caelan's mind flashed back to the girls from the previous evening. She resolved to call Penrith for an update when she was alone. 'Not interested,' she said.

'Not saying you are. No use if you were. It's all above board now. No cheap booze, no lock-ins. Just a load of dickheads chatting shit.'

'Thought it was your local?'

'It is. You can get a decent pint, but then you can at the supermarket. Don't think I'll be going back there again.' He paused at the kerb, then staggered out into the road.

Caelan hesitated, held back as she heard an engine roar. A car shot out of a side street, heading straight for them. Frankie Hamilton turned, holding up a hand to shield his eyes as the vehicle hurtled towards him, its headlights blinding. Caelan screamed at him to move, but he stood as though frozen. She reached for him, grabbed his arm, and the movement seemed to break the spell. He tumbled towards her, the car speeding past, the two of them ending up in a heap on the pavement as its rear lights disappeared. Caelan pushed Hamilton away from her and sat up.

'Are you okay?'

He was lying still, groaning. 'Fuck, what was that? Crazy bastard could have killed me.'

Caelan heaved herself to her feet, her body aching, her older injuries screaming. She glanced around, but Nicky and Richard were nowhere to be seen. Where were they? Staying out of sight? 'Did you see the driver?'

'Are you joking? I saw the lights, that was all.' Hamilton was on his feet now, bending and rolling up a trouser leg. 'My knees are shredded.' He raised his hands, examined his palms. 'Hands, too. Fuck.' He stared at her, eyes wide. 'You saved my life, you know?'

She shook her head, reminding herself who she was supposed to be. 'Forget it. That was... Do you know anyone who drives a black estate?'

'Is that what it was? Do you think they were trying to hit me?'

'Don't you? We should call the police.'

'No way, I'm not getting those bastards involved. They'll probably tell whoever it was to come back and have another go. I'll call my brother, he'll ask around.'

'Frankie—'

'Listen, I'm going to shoot off.' He grinned at her. 'Thanks again for... you know. I'd have been dead. Make sure you give me a call, yeah?' He leant closer, kissed her cheek.

Caelan resisted the urge to wipe her face with her sleeve as Hamilton jogged away. She noted the direction he took, turned, gave herself a second. Her heart was still hammering. She looked around, saw a bus shelter on the other side of the road and headed towards it. With her back against the cold brickwork, she pulled out her phone. Penrith answered on the second ring.

'Someone's just tried to run over Frankie Hamilton,' she told him.

Penrith paused. 'I assume they missed?'

'Only because I managed to pull him out of the way.'

'Give me your location, we'll get onto it. Not what we were expecting.'

'Really?' Caelan stepped onto the pavement, her eyes searching the shadows. She was taking a risk making the call, but she had no choice. They needed to find the vehicle, and quickly. It hadn't returned, but if it did, she would be vulnerable. 'I need to get out of here. They must have seen my face.'

'Did you see theirs?'

'No. I don't even know how many of them there were.' She described the car, not that there was much to tell. 'The number plate was filthy. This was planned.'

He gave a deep sigh. 'Of course it was. And why? What does Hamilton know?'

'Beats me. He seemed stunned.'

'You're sure they weren't aiming for you?'

Caelan blinked. 'Why should they be?'

'It hadn't crossed your mind?'

'I've only been here a couple of hours.'

'Enough time to make some enemies.'

'You're paranoid.'

'Isn't that my line? Let's be cautious. Go home. Lock the door. I'll be in touch.'

Caelan looked up and down the street again. Deserted. She began to walk back towards the flat, her thoughts tumbling. Had it been coincidence? The car had seemed to accelerate towards Hamilton, but he had walked out into the street without looking, drunk and staggering. It was impossible to say, but considering the collision Liv Hobbs had been involved in, questions had to be asked.

Most of the houses she passed were in darkness. There were a few cars around, but most people seemed to be settling down for the night. She turned onto a side street, passed a row of shops, some boarded up. She hoped Nicky and Richard had followed them, seen the car speed towards Hamilton, and were still following him. She could have gone after him herself, but given the conversation she'd had with him, she didn't want to give him any clue that she wasn't who she had pretended to be. She had to hurry back to the flat, just as the woman she was pretending to be would do.

She walked quickly, keeping her hands free, her eyes scanning the street in front of her, her senses hyper-alert after the attempted attack on Hamilton. The street was well lit, but there were patches of gloom, and she noted a broken street light twenty-five yards or so ahead of her. There was a gap between two buildings there, an alleyway, and as she approached, she heard the slightest movement. She tensed, swallowed, felt her heart rate rocket again. It wasn't fear; more anticipation. If there was someone waiting there, she would be ready for them.

As she drew level with the alley, a black cat leapt out in front of her, causing her to gasp. It gave her a disdainful stare, then trotted across the road and out of sight. She shook her head, laughing at herself, and kept walking.

A quick movement, an arm snaking around her throat, before a hand was clamped over her mouth. Her left arm was seized at the elbow, large fingers digging in painfully.

She froze, furious at herself. So much for being ready. The cat had obviously been a distraction. She had no idea who had grabbed her, but they were pulling her back, trying to drag her into the alley, and she couldn't allow that to happen.

'Don't make a fucking sound,' her attacker hissed. 'I want to talk to you.' His mouth was close to her left ear, his breath hot against her skin. Automatically Caelan assessed his position, and the action she needed to take. Sometimes, retaining your cover meant not fighting back. She was in a deserted alley, being dragged into the darkness by someone who felt taller and was no doubt stronger than she was. This was not one of those times.

The hand over her mouth smelt of cigarette smoke. Caelan filed the fact away as she raised her right hand, turned it towards her body and curled her fingertips over at the first knuckle. She brought her hand down hard and fast onto her captor's wrist, trying to break his grip. He grunted as he was forced to drop his hand and readjust his feet. As he did so, Caelan whipped the same hand down and back, driving her fist into his now exposed groin. He crumpled with a squeak, allowed her to pivot away from him. She turned, wanting to see his face, ready to launch a kick, but he was bent double, wheezing and choking. As she did so, she saw a movement in the shadows. Another man stepped out, dressed in black jeans and a leather jacket, his face concealed by a scarf, black baseball cap pulled low. He held up his hands.

'What are you, some kind of ninja?'

He had a slight accent, but nothing Caelan could pinpoint. She moved backwards, keeping them both in sight. 'I took a few self-defence lessons when I was a kid.'

'Yeah? From who, Jackie Chan?'

Caelan said nothing, stayed on her toes, ready to attack again if necessary. The first man tried to raise his head.

'My fucking balls. Jesus…'

The second man laughed. 'You got what you deserved. No manners.' He turned back to Caelan. 'We want you to pass a message on to Frankie Hamilton.'

'Someone just tried to run him over. Know anything about that?'

He frowned, lifting his shoulder. 'Why should we? When are you seeing Frankie again?'

'I barely know him.'

'You looked like good friends in the pub.'

He was lying. Caelan knew the two of them hadn't been in the pub. They were both over six feet tall, muscular. She would have noticed them, and she hadn't seen them outside either. They must have been watching out of sight.

She lifted her chin, glaring but not wanting to provoke him. 'Give me one reason why I shouldn't call the police.'

He took a step closer. 'Because there's two of us.' Another step. 'And because I have a knife.'

Caelan pretended to consider it. A knife would complicate matters, but she was confident she could still escape if she had to. Still, there was no need to fight if she could run, and it seemed she was being given the chance to.

'What's the message?'

'There isn't one.'

'What?'

He was already walking away. He grabbed his friend, still moaning and cursing, and pushed him in front of him. 'Tell Frankie what happened. He'll understand.'

15

Ryan stood in the shadows, his arms wrapped around his body, looking up at Mulligan's flat. There was a light on, and he wondered if Mulligan was cooking again. He shuddered, wanting desperately to make his way up the stairs and buy some of Mulligan's wares, but knowing he couldn't. He had to stay away. He should have made the delivery hours ago, and whoever Mulligan's customer was, they would have contacted him by now, demanding to know where their goods were. They'd paid up front, Mulligan had told him. That meant they were now seriously out of pocket, and Mulligan would have to find a way to placate them. However he chose to do it, there would only be one outcome for Ryan – pain. Mulligan enjoyed hurting people, especially those who had crossed or wronged him. And Ryan had let him down in the worst way possible.

The light went out.

Down on the pavement, Ryan gasped, tried to take a step backwards. He bumped into the wall behind him, and slid down it so he squatted close to the ground. What was he going to do? What the fuck was he supposed to do? He couldn't run, and he couldn't hide. Mulligan would never believe the ruck-sack had been stolen. He'd think Ryan had taken the contents for himself. Ryan almost smiled at the thought of it. Wouldn't that have been something? It would have been like Christmas morning when he was a kid, but with the best present of all. He'd probably be dead by now.

He gazed up at the window again. He would have to go up there, tell Mulligan what had happened. His mother had always drummed into him that it was best to tell the truth no matter how much trouble you knew you'd be in.

But then she'd never met Mulligan.

He trudged over to the building's entrance, knowing he had no choice. Mulligan knew people. They'd find him. His only option was to go up there now and face the music. And if Mulligan killed him, well, who would care? Ryan rubbed his eyes. No one. He didn't even care himself.

Mulligan's door opened as Ryan climbed the last stairs and reached the landing. He was watching, then. Had the cameras on. Maybe he was expecting his disgruntled customer to pay him a visit.

Mulligan stood in the doorway, arms folded, his expression unreadable. Ryan's hands were shaking, his stomach feeling as though it had liquidised. He stopped on the last step, watching Mulligan's face.

'Where have you been?' Mulligan asked. His voice was as gentle as Ryan had ever heard it. He tried to swallow, but his throat felt choked. Mulligan uncrossed his arms, took a step forward. 'Well?'

'Around,' Ryan managed to whisper. Mulligan cocked his head.

'Around? Anywhere but here, do you mean?'

'I'm sorry.'

Mulligan scrunched up his face. 'Sorry? I ask you to make a delivery, you don't do it, then disappear for hours, and you're sorry?'

'Someone stole it...'

Now Mulligan stormed towards him, all pretence gone. He grabbed Ryan's hair in his fist, shoved his face close. 'Stole it?

Fucking stole it?' Keeping hold of Ryan, he marched him into the flat and threw him onto the floor. 'Who took it?'

Ryan curled up, desperately trying to retain control of his bladder. 'I don't know, I didn't see. A man...'

'A man?' Mulligan's face contorted into a snarl as he drew back his foot and aimed a kick at Ryan's shins. 'A man? Which man?'

'I don't know. He didn't speak. He hit me, took the rucksack. I'm sorry, Mulligan. I'll make it up to you.' As he babbled the words, Ryan tried to scoot backwards, out of range of Mulligan's boots.

'What did you say?'

'I said, I'll repay you.'

Mulligan stopped, put his hands on his hips. Smiled. Warily, Ryan waited. Mulligan was unpredictable, his mood changing as rapidly as the seconds ticking past.

'And how do you think you're going to do that?' Mulligan's voice was gentle again. 'Do you have any idea how much that stuff was worth?'

Ryan ducked his head. 'No.'

'No. You don't have a fucking clue. How are you, a homeless, jobless junkie going to repay me thousands of pounds?'

'Thousands?' Ryan's guts heaved, and he coughed.

'That's right, thousands. Tens of thousands. What did you think I get paid in, fucking chocolate coins? You owe me, and you're going to work for me for as long as it takes to repay your debt. Do you understand?'

'But—'

'I gave you a chance, and you fucked up. You're lucky I'm not chucking you in the Thames. You'll get food, and something to smoke now and then. But other than that, I own you, and I'm talking months, if not years. You do as you're told, no argument. Are we clear?'

Ryan lifted his head, stared at the other man, hating him. He would get out of this somehow, he promised himself. Play along for now, then make some plans. 'Yes. I understand.'

'Good boy. Now get up. Here, I'll help you.' Mulligan stuck out a hand, grabbed Ryan's forearm. 'Come on, we need to shake on it, seal the deal.'

Staggering, Ryan steadied himself against the wall, eventually held out his hand. It wouldn't be for long, not if he got out of London. 'All right.'

Mulligan shook it enthusiastically. Then he bared his teeth in a grin, dropped Ryan's hand and pivoted, his fist crashing into Ryan's jaw with enough force that all he saw was white light exploding as he tumbled across the floor.

Mulligan stood over him, breathing hard, cradling his bruised hand. 'Remember, wee man. I own you now.'

16

Jackson Hobbs always began his day in the same way – with fifty press-ups. In the confines of his single-occupancy cell, it wasn't easy to maintain his routine, but he knew he had to stay sharp, keep his discipline. Sometimes, when he couldn't sleep, when the walls were closing in and the night seemed endless, he exercised in the darkness, until his mind finally stilled and his body tired.

He got to his feet, stretched his back and shoulders. He had already eaten his cereal, which he'd collected the previous night, and had a cup of tea. Nothing to do now but wait for the door to be unlocked. Maybe he'd get a shower today, but there was no guarantee.

He heard feet in the corridor outside, inmates shouting to each other. The door opened, and he stepped outside. Clay, who had the cell next door, nodded to him, crossing his arms over his massive chest. Jackson acknowledged the greeting, but kept his distance. It was too soon to know who he could trust, who would have his back if he needed them. He didn't know anyone in here. When his house had been raided, four of his employees had been there with him, and they were all arrested together. They'd been sent to different prisons, though Jackson knew they would be in touch, one way or another. They were all looking at five years or more, but he'd been handed the longest sentence. Sixteen years. He'd strutted out of the dock, grinning at the judge, but inside he'd been screaming. What was he supposed to do with himself? Take some classes, learn to paint? No chance, not in here. Banged up twelve hours a day, if not longer. Televisions in every cell so they didn't have to pay more guards to keep order.

As they walked, the man beside him, young and scrawny, jostled Jackson's arm. Jackson looked down at him, eyes narrowed. The kid kept his eyes to the front, though his cheeks had reddened. Jackson stuck out his elbow and caught him in the ribs, not hard, but enough for it to be a warning. The kid didn't react, kept walking.

'Problem?' Jackson muttered. Ahead of them, a prison officer stood back, watching the men file past. They were heading for the exercise yard, Jackson's least favourite part of the long and monotonous prison day. The food was shit, the work was boring, but at least people had something to occupy them. During exercise and, later, association, prisoners eyeballed each other, made threats, made deals.

'No. Sorry.'

'Watch where you're fucking going, all right?'

'Yeah, mate. Sorry.'

They marched past the screw, who ignored them, and out into the yard. As Jackson walked, he was shoved in the back, hard, and stumbled, almost fell. As he regained his balance, he whipped around to see who had pushed him, but there was no one nearby. The scrawny kid had disappeared. No one was even looking at him. Jackson felt a coil of fear in his stomach, and stamped it down. Who the fuck did they think they were, trying to push him around? Intimidate him? Not long ago, he had owned Edmonton. People had respected him, and now? Now they thought he was finished. At the beginning of a sixteen stretch, who could blame them? He bunched his fists, held his head high. He needed to earn some respect, and fast.

Otherwise, he was in danger of disappearing, being forgotten about. He still had friends outside, but how long would they stay loyal? Then there was Liv... He clenched his jaw, the betrayal of her joining the other side still fresh, all these years later. She was a Hobbs. She should have known better.

He walked around for a while, always alert, then stood with his back against the fence and watched. Prisoners chatted, laughed together. No one even looked at him. No mates, no one willing to speak to him. He was tainted. It never bothered his friends outside, because they knew they could trust him. In here, though... Maybe they thought he was a grass. Maybe they expected him to go running to his sister with information, try to get a few years knocked off his sentence. Fat chance. He couldn't remember the last time he'd spoken to Liv. Wouldn't do much for her precious career, having him around. Her dead-beat, drug-dealing jailbird brother.

Jackson pushed away from the fence as one of the screws yelled at them to line up. Back to their cells, kicking their heels until feed time. He closed his eyes, just for a second. How would he cope? How would he stand it? He'd never tried his own merchandise, hadn't even smoked for years. Now, though... now, he could see the temptation. Who wouldn't jump at the chance of a few minutes' oblivion?

As they made their way back down the corridor, the kid was at his side once more. Jackson turned his head, opened his mouth. Didn't get the chance to speak before the kid rammed a shiv into his throat, moving so quickly no one saw it happen. If Jackson hadn't felt the blade pierce his skin, he wouldn't have believed it possible. He fell to the ground, his vision already dimming, shouts erupting all around him. The last thing he saw was the face of one of the screws, lurching and swimming before his eyes.

17

Ian Penrith's office was warm, the press of too many bodies in the small space stifling.

Penrith sat behind his desk, hands folded over his gut. As Caelan squeezed through the door, he picked up a grubby coffee mug and peered into it.

'Not sure how long this had been here, but the mould's growing mould.' He looked at her, grinning. 'Will you get someone to send some in?'

She raised an eyebrow at him. 'Who am I supposed to ask?'

'Isn't your faithful assistant with you?'

'If you mean Ewan Davies, you know he isn't.'

He nodded. 'Not yet, anyway. He's on his way here.'

'He told me you were having a meeting.'

Penrith picked up the phone on his desk, murmured into it. Caelan heard biscuits mentioned. He replaced the receiver. 'Perhaps my new office will have a coffee machine. Of course Davies told you. Confidantes, aren't you?'

Caelan ignored him, moving to stand with her back against the wall. She glanced around the room, seeing who else had been summoned here.

Nicky Sturgess and Richard Adamson sat in the two chairs in front of Penrith's desk, their backs to Caelan. Richard turned his head, offered a smile of greeting, but Nicky didn't move. To their left, Tim Achebe stood with his arms folded, staring at the floor. Beside him, Jen Somerfield frowned at her phone. Caelan stepped over to them.

'What's going on?' she asked Somerville in an undertone. Somerville slid the phone into her jacket pocket.

'You don't know?'

'I was told to come over here for a briefing. I wasn't given a reason.'

Somerville's face twisted. Achebe uncrossed his arms, ran a hand over his mouth.

'There's an issue.'

Caelan snorted. 'Isn't there always?'

'Well, this is a little more than a run-of-the-mill problem.' Penrith straightened his cuffs. Caelan stared at him. How had he overheard what they had said?

A uniformed officer appeared in the doorway with a tray of coffee cups, and Penrith beamed at him. 'On the desk here. Thank you, Constable.' He watched the door close before speaking again. 'Jackson Hobbs is dead.'

Caelan blinked, her mind scrambling to take in what she was hearing. 'DI Hobbs's brother? But isn't he—'

'In prison? He is, or at least he was.' Penrith nodded. 'Someone stuck a home-made knife into his throat. Knew just where to aim to kill him quickly. Hobbs bled out before they could get an ambulance to him.'

'Who did it?'

Penrith spread his hands. 'The investigation's ongoing.'

'You mean they don't know? He was killed in prison, and they don't know who it was?'

'I didn't say that. You know how understaffed these places are. There was probably one prison officer supervising a hundred men.' Penrith reached for a mug of coffee from the tray. 'Help yourselves. It'll be awful, but you might as well.'

Caelan looked at Achebe, at Somerville. Both were solemn-faced, watching Penrith, who was already happily slurping coffee. 'Has DI Hobbs been informed?'

Achebe licked his lips. 'Yes. We went to speak to her as soon as we heard.'

'How is she?' As Caelan asked the question, she saw Nicky's shoulders stiffen, though she didn't speak. She still hadn't acknowledged Caelan's presence in the room.

'She was quiet, calm.' Jen Somerville cleared her throat. 'But as we were leaving...'

She paused, bowed her head. Achebe looked at her.

'She made that sound,' he said. 'You'll all have heard it, when you've given terrible news. It's involuntary. Moaning, keening... I don't know how to describe it.'

'You don't need to.' Assistant Commissioner Elizabeth Beckett stood in the doorway, wearing a dark suit and a scowl.

'More coffee.' Penrith reached for his phone again.

'Don't trouble yourself, Ian.' Beckett strode into the room and stood by his desk. Richard Adamson scrambled out of his seat.

'Sit down, ma'am, please.'

Beckett waved him away. 'Thank you, Richard, but I'm not staying, I have a meeting upstairs.' She gave Penrith a hard glare. 'I need an update.'

Unperturbed, he leaned back in his chair, which gave an ominous creak. 'When?'

'Now.'

'What do you want to know? We've a dead drugs baron, a dead police officer, a dead user. Three undercover officers nosing around, nothing yet to show for their efforts.'

Beckett exhaled. 'And Frankie Hamilton?'

'Caelan spent last night cosying up to him, didn't you?'

Caelan stood up straight as Beckett's gaze landed on her. 'Ma'am.'

'What did you discover?'

'It was more what happened afterwards.' She explained about the attack on her, the warning she had been given. Beckett's face flushed.

'And you didn't think to report this immediately?'

'I did, ma'am.' Caelan spoke calmly, though Beckett's manner was beginning to grate.

'Did you? To whom?'

'To me.' Penrith reached his arms above his head and stretched. 'I sent you an email detailing what happened late last night.'

Beckett was unapologetic. 'I haven't seen it yet.' She frowned, pursed her lips. 'Did these men suspect you were anything other than Frankie Hamilton's new girlfriend?'

'I don't think so,' Caelan said.

'You said you fought them off?'

'Not exactly. I was grabbed from behind, so I freed myself.'

'How?'

'I broke his hold, then hit him in the balls.'

'That was all?'

'The second bloke didn't touch me.'

'Can't blame him really,' said Penrith.

'So, you used basic self-defence?'

'Yes.'

'It could still raise eyebrows.' Nicky spoke for the first time. She looked at Beckett, not Caelan. 'I don't think many civilians could fight off two men.'

Caelan took a breath, told herself not to bite. 'I didn't. Anyway, what was I supposed to do? They were dragging me into an alley.'

Nicky said, 'You should have let them.'

'Let them? That's your answer?' Caelan laughed. 'I didn't pull a gun, didn't break any limbs.' *This time*, she added silently, remembering other incidents.

'Why did you approach Frankie Hamilton in the first place?' Nicky wasn't going to let it lie. 'Our brief was to observe him, not become best friends with him.'

Again, Caelan forced herself to speak calmly. 'I knew you and Richard were there watching. I thought approaching him directly was worth a try.'

'You could have compromised the operation.' Nicky finally turned in her seat to look Caelan in the eye.

'But I didn't.' Caelan stared back, unflinching. She had done nothing wrong, and for Nicky to suggest she had was unfair.

Nicky snorted. 'As far as we know.'

'But what did we learn from your actions, Caelan?' Beckett wanted to know. 'These men said they wanted to talk to you.'

'To pass a message on to Frankie Hamilton. They wanted to frighten me so I'd tell him they'd attacked me.'

Beckett pursed her lips, mulling it over. 'Do you think they were in the car that drove at Hamilton?'

'I'd say it's likely, and we also need to consider the link between that and the incident DI Hobbs was involved in,' said Caelan.

'Okay. All this suggests we're right to have been watching Hamilton. He was released from the same prison Jackson Hobbs has just been murdered in.' Beckett's eyes swept the room. 'Did Hobbs and Hamilton know each other?'

Achebe stepped forward. 'They were on different wings, ma'am. As far as we know, there was no contact between them inside.'

'And outside? They both lived in Edmonton. Hobbs was a dealer, Hamilton a user. It's likely their paths would have crossed, isn't it?'

'And Liv Hobbs said she was at school with Frankie. Her brother must have been too,' said Caelan.

'That's correct,' Achebe said. 'Hamilton was in Liv's class, Jackson the year below. It doesn't sound as though they were close at school, and from what we've heard, Jackson Hobbs was too big a player in recent years to deal directly with bottom-of-the-pile users like Hamilton. He employed people to sell on the street for him.'

'Weren't they arrested when he was?' Beckett checked her watch.

Achebe nodded. 'The main men, yes. The footmen we left alone.'

'Because we wanted to watch them? See who they went to for their next employment opportunity?'

'Yes.'

Beckett sniffed. 'Seems to be going well so far. Have we traced the car that drove at Frankie Hamilton? Found the two men Caelan was sparring with?'

'I wasn't—' Caelan began to say. Beckett silenced her with a look.

'Well?' Her hands went to her hips, chin jutting. 'Do we know who these men are? Tim?'

Achebe shuffled his feet. 'Not yet.'

'Ian?'

'I'm leaving it to Tim.' Penrith finished his coffee, set the mug back on the tray with a clunk. 'It's his case.'

'Which one? The murdered police officer, the tortured informer, or the dead prisoner? You're supposed to be working on this together.' Beckett spat the words out.

Penrith raised his eyebrows, smiling. '"You're", ma'am?'

She looked down her nose at him. 'We're. This is showing all the signs of snowballing. We don't need another disaster. We don't need any more scandal. We've been lucky so far that the press has kept their noses out, but it can't last. Find these men. Bring Frankie Hamilton in and ask him about Jackson Hobbs. I want another update this evening.'

She turned and marched out of the room, allowing the door to slam behind her. Penrith rubbed his chin as he looked at each of them in turn.

'Well, Her Majesty has spoken. Better hop to it.'

Achebe said, 'Jen, will you have Frankie Hamilton brought in and interviewed, please? Nice and friendly for now.'

Caelan said, 'Won't it look obvious? I spoke to him last night about Jackson Hobbs, then he's dragged in for questioning? Can't I talk to him again first?'

Achebe pursed his lips, considering it.

'That seems sensible,' Penrith said. 'Assistant Commissioner Beckett doesn't need to know.'

Somerville brushed her hair from her eyes. 'What about Liv? It doesn't seem fair to disturb her again.'

'I know, but we have no choice.' Achebe was grave. There was a silence, everyone studying the carpet tiles or their shoes.

'Can we establish a few facts?' Nicky asked at last. 'I'm not sure about anyone else, but I'm confused. We're assuming there's a link between Ben Rainey's murder, the death of Anthony Bryce, and now the murder of Jackson Hobbs?'

'And the deliberate collision involving DI Hobbs, plus Frankie Hamilton almost being run over last night, and the attack on me,' said Caelan. Nicky narrowed her eyes.

'We don't know for sure that DI Hobbs's car was crashed into deliberately, and you said yourself you weren't certain if the car meant to hit Hamilton or not.'

'Okay, and I imagined a bloke grabbing me from behind too, I suppose?' Again, Caelan fought to keep the anger from her tone. Nicky held up her hands.

'Not what I'm saying. I'm trying to see what links all these events together, if anything. Why would someone kill Jackson Hobbs? He was in prison, out of the way for the foreseeable future.'

Achebe stepped forward. 'I'm going to the prison when we've finished here. We might find Jackson Hobbs was killed after a dispute with another inmate, or on the orders of a business rival. We believe a new player is moving into Edmonton. Maybe whoever it is thought putting Hobbs out of business permanently was in their best interests.'

'They must have an idea who killed him. There had to be witnesses, not to mention at least one prisoner covered in blood. What about fingerprints on the knife?' Caelan said. Achebe exchanged a glance with Penrith.

'They're still collecting evidence,' he said. 'The entire wing's been shut down. All the prisoners are locked in their cells, including the suspect. They're bringing him to South Harrow this afternoon for interview.'

'Aren't you going to see him when you visit the prison?' Caelan asked. It seemed to make sense. 'Why bother to bring him across London?'

'Because, as you can imagine, the prison is a pretty volatile place just now – even more so than usual. The prisoners aren't happy about the prospect of being banged up all day as well as all night. We don't want a riot on our hands.' Penrith rubbed his eyes. 'If this man's guilty, as it seems certain he is, he'll be moved anyway. He can't go back there.'

Richard Adamson spoke up. 'So who is he?'

'Aaron Jacob. He's from Forest Hill, in for GBH,' Achebe told them.

'Not close to Edmonton then, or Northolt or Hounslow, where Ben Rainey and Anthony Bryce were from,' Caelan pointed out.

'No, but he's twenty-three, like Rainey and Bryce. They're all more than ten years younger than Jackson Hobbs.' Achebe raised his eyebrows. 'I don't know if it's relevant, but...'

'What about the possibility that Rainey and Bryce knew each other through church?' Caelan asked. Somerville shook her head.

'Dead end. The woman I saw was the pastor at the church for fifteen years before retiring. She remembered Rainey and his family, but not Anthony Bryce. She'd never heard of Jackson Hobbs either.'

Caelan chewed on her bottom lip. It had been a long shot, but worth pursuing. She was beginning to see why the investigation into Ben Rainey's death had stalled.

A phone rang, and Achebe stepped out into the corridor. Penrith looked at Richard Adamson.

'How do you feel about serving some jail time, Richard?'

Adamson groaned. 'I thought we knew who'd killed Jackson Hobbs?'

'But we don't know why. We don't know how he was contacted, or persuaded. You could ask around. You've done it before.'

'Yeah, and I was lucky to get out alive.'

'Aaron Jacob's cellmate will be lonely. Maybe he'll feel like talking. He's got eighteen years to kill, after all. I won't tell you what he's done.'

Adamson snorted. 'No, *he* probably will when he's stamping on my throat.'

Penrith pointed a chunky finger at him. 'So you *do* know him.'

'Piss off, Ian.'

Penrith laughed, his jowls wobbling. 'It won't be for long. We'll ghost you in, give you forty-eight hours, then bring you out. You'll barely have time for a shower. Probably a good thing.'

'What about me?' asked Nicky. Penrith glanced at her.

'You're going back to Edmonton. You and Caelan still have work to do.'

Nicky shot Caelan a look, her expression impossible to read. Frustration? Anger? Both, Caelan decided, as Achebe came back into the room.

'That was a DC Bailey, from Stoke Newington. You've worked with him, Caelan?'

She frowned at him. What now? 'Yeah, briefly. What did he want?'

Achebe slid his phone into his jacket pocket, took his time replying. 'You went to a brothel with him? One specialising in underage girls, forced prostitution?' His disgust was clear in his voice.

Caelan swallowed, seeing the face of the girl, Ardiola, again. 'I did, and Bailey's team closed it down.'

'They found plenty of fingerprints, as you'd expect.' Achebe's lips thinned. 'A match flagged up.'

'To whom?' Penrith demanded, as all eyes turned to Achebe.

'Ben Rainey.'

There was silence. Caelan was stunned for a second. 'What are you saying?' she asked.

Achebe lifted his shoulders, let them fall. 'I don't know. Either Rainey had a thing for young girls, or...'

'Or he was poking around there, the same as we were.' Caelan was frowning, trying to make sense of what she was hearing. 'Where were the prints found?'

'The bedroom you went in, Bailey said.' Achebe met Caelan's eyes, his face grim. 'Rainey's prints were discovered on the top of the headboard. His right hand. They're surmising he was standing by the bed and leant on it.'

'One of the first-floor rooms, not up on the second floor where the girls were.' Caelan pressed her palms to her cheeks. What did this mean? She'd wondered if Rainey had been doing some off-the-record detecting, but was this proof? 'We need to find out what he was doing there,' she said.

Achebe's smile was forced. 'They're already on it. There's CCTV, but it's going to take some time. We've no idea when he was there.'

'Is it worth asking his parents?' Jen Somerville suggested. 'I doubt he told them anything about it, but you never know.'

'Or his younger brother,' Caelan said. 'Remember, he shared a room with Ben. Joseph probably knew more about what he might have been up to than anyone. I think we should speak to Mrs Rainey again too. When I saw her, I thought... Well, it's possible she didn't tell me everything.'

Achebe nodded. 'Jen and I will brief our team.' He checked his watch. 'I need to go.'

'Who's doing the interview with Aaron Jacob?' Caelan asked.

'Not you,' Penrith told her.

'I didn't expect to, but I'd like to observe.'

'Why? How could doing so possibly help you gather information about the drugs trade in Edmonton?' Penrith tipped his head to the side, stuck out his chin.

'I—'

'It couldn't.'

'Come on, Ian. Three men are dead. Wouldn't Nicky and I be more use here, on the investigative team?'

Penrith pushed himself backwards, the wheels of his desk chair clicking, and lumbered to his feet. 'No. Jackson Hobbs being jailed gave someone in Edmonton the opportunity to move into his shoes. Go and find out who it is. When we know, I'm guessing we'll also know the identity of the person who killed Rainey and Bryce, and ordered the murder of Hobbs himself.'

Achebe shot Caelan an apologetic look. 'Have to say, I agree with Ian,' he said. 'If we're going to find answers, Edmonton is the obvious place to look.'

'Apart from at Aaron Jacob? He must know who hired him, if that's what happened.' Caelan folded her arms, knowing she had no choice. They'd never allow her to speak to the Rainey family again, or to Aaron Jacob. Best to let them think they had won for now. 'All right. What about Frankie Hamilton?'

Penrith was in the doorway, straightening his tie. 'What about him?'

'We're agreed I should contact him, tell him about the attack on me last night?'

'Yes, give him a call. Hopefully he'll mention it later in his interview,' said Penrith. 'We'll delay it until this afternoon, tell him we're dragging everyone from Edmonton who knew Hobbs in for questioning. You'll make sure he's asked about Aaron Jacob, Tim, won't you?'

'Jen will be conducting the interview,' Achebe replied. Somerville was already nodding her head.

'Could we be updated this afternoon?' Caelan glanced at Nicky. 'I'd like to know what Frankie Hamilton says about the attempt to run him over. It could be unrelated to our cases, after all. Maybe an old enemy heard he was free and decided to take a potshot at him.'

Penrith was halfway out of the door. 'I'll call you later. You too, Nicky. Now go and get us some answers.'

—

On the pavement outside, Caelan stood for a moment staring across the Thames towards the London Eye, slowly revolving against the murky grey sky. She heard footsteps behind her, and began to turn as a hand was placed on her shoulder.

'Caelan.' Nicky's voice was hesitant. Stepping away, Caelan frowned at her.

'We shouldn't be seen together,' she said.

Nicky screwed up her face. 'Can we talk? Please? Get a coffee?'

'What? You know we can't.' Caelan ignored the ache in her chest when she saw Nicky's forlorn expression. 'We're colleagues, Nicky,' she made herself say. 'That's all.'

Nicky met her eyes. 'I know you're angry, you feel betrayed—'

'Can you blame me?' Caelan fixed her gaze on the traffic crossing Westminster Bridge, deliberately not looking at Nicky. 'You let me believe you were dead. I cried over your body, went to your funeral, and all the time you were hiding in a safe house. How am I supposed to forget that?'

To their right, Big Ben began to chime. Eleven o'clock. Nicky stepped closer, spoke quietly.

'I know. In your place… well, I don't know how I'd feel. I never wanted to lie to you. I had no choice.'

'As you've already said several times, but you did, Nicky. You could have told me. You think I wouldn't have kept your secret? Our whole lives are built on lies and stories. I thought you trusted me.'

A group of schoolchildren were approaching, wearing fluorescent yellow vests over their coats, harried-looking adults scurrying along with them. Caelan and Nicky stepped back against the black metal railings.

'I did. I do.' Nicky's voice was little more than a whisper. 'Please, Caelan.'

Now Caelan did look at her, her face working. She wouldn't cry, not now, not on the street, in front of this woman.

'You said you don't know how you'd feel in my place. Well, let me try to explain. I feel used, lied to, and yes, betrayed. I respected you as a colleague, then as a friend. When our relationship moved beyond that, I thought I'd found the person I could trust with anything. With my life.'

Nicky's lips trembled. 'And you had.'

Caelan's laugh was bitter. 'No. When you were asked to go into hiding, you were thinking of yourself. Not your parents, your family, who also thought you were dead. How could you do it to them? I saw them at the funeral…' She shook her head, the memories appalling her all over again. 'They were destroyed. Then they were told you'd magically, miraculously been resurrected and were expecting to be welcomed with open arms? How's your relationship with them now, Nicky?'

She blinked. 'We barely have one.'

'Can't say I'm surprised. What did you expect? If I were them, I wouldn't be able to forgive you either. What you did to them was worse than if you really had died. You devastated them twice.'

Nicky's face was red as she took another step towards Caelan, her voice hard and low. 'Don't you think I know that? Don't you think I sat day after day in that fucking place hating myself? You've no idea what it was like, imaging my parents hearing the news, how they would react. The pain I was causing. Do you think I can forget that? I thought it was safer if I was out of the way.'

'Safer for you, maybe.'

'No, Caelan, safer for everyone. Nasenby was killing anyone linked to the Charlie Flynn case. I was terrified for my parents, for you. I knew too much, and I thought if I was dead... well, my knowledge would die with me.'

Caelan sneered. 'Really? How noble of you. Maybe if you'd actually died, that might be more believable. As it is, you just sound pathetic.'

'And you don't?' Nicky shook her head. 'I'm not asking if we can pick up where we left off. You know better than anyone that the job comes first. I did what I was told, as we all do. You're no different. What would you have done in my position? Would you have told me the truth? That you were disappearing for a while, playing dead, while everyone else got on with the job?'

'Yes.'

'What?'

'I'd have told you.' Caelan ran a hand over her eyes. 'I'd have trusted you. Not any more.'

'Bullshit. You'd have disappeared like I did. Allowed yourself to be carried out on a stretcher, taken to a house fuck knows where in the middle of the night and left there.'

'You're expecting sympathy?' Caelan drew her eyebrows together, tipped her head to the side. 'Poor you, Nicky. It must have been awful.'

Nicky blushed. 'You don't have to be sarcastic. I get it.'

'You clearly don't, because if you did, you wouldn't still be trying to justify your decision.'

'I'm trying to explain.' Nicky scrubbed at her cheeks with both hands.

'You don't need to. I told Elizabeth Beckett I'd work with you, and I will. But what we had is gone.'

Nodding, Nicky wrapped her arms around her body. Caelan waited, her throat choked. Saying those words had been more difficult than she had expected.

'I told Assistant Commissioner Beckett that you'd find out what was going on,' Nicky said eventually. 'I knew you'd find out who was dirty in the department if she gave you the chance.'

'But I didn't. Penrith did.'

'Come on, Caelan, I know what happened. It was you who went to Nasenby to confront him, not Ian.' Nicky raised a hand, about to touch the bruising on Caelan's face, then thought better of it. 'Did Nasenby do that?'

'Can you see it? Shit. I thought I'd covered it up.'

'You rubbed some of the make-up off when you touched your face before. Did he?'

Caelan sighed. 'Yeah. Hit me with a gun, gave me a few slaps and kicks.'

Nicky's face tightened. 'Bastard.'

'At least he didn't shoot me.'

'But he did shoot the man who was with you.'

'You know.'

'Who is he?'

171

'Long story. Why don't you ask Beckett? She seems to have told you everything else.'

Nicky scowled. 'I'm part of this team. Why wouldn't she?'

'Forget it. Look, I've got to go. I've a phone call to make, and I can't do it here.'

'What are your plans?'

'It's not as though we've been given specific instructions. I'll speak to Hamilton. Maybe meet him again.' Caelan shrugged.

'Do you want me to…?'

'What?'

'Back you up.' Nicky glanced at Caelan, then away. 'We're both working alone now…'

Caelan was unmoved. 'And that's how we've been told to approach this.'

Bowing her head, Nicky hunched her shoulders. 'All right. Do you want to take my phone number?'

'Nicky, what are you doing? No, I don't. We don't know each other. If I see you around, I'll ignore you. You know how this works.'

Nicky held up her hands. 'Fine. I just… Okay. Goodbye, Caelan.' She turned and walked away.

Caelan watched until she was lost amongst the crowds. Only then did she pull a tissue from her bag and wipe her eyes.

'Do you think she's up to the job?' The voice came from behind her. Caelan turned. Elizabeth Beckett stood there, hands in the pockets of her long black coat. 'Don't pretend you knew I was here.'

'You've made your point, ma'am. I was distracted. It won't happen again.' Caelan straightened her back, lifted her chin.

'I should hope not.' Beckett's eyes strayed over Caelan's shoulder, then focused on her face. 'I asked you a question.'

'Is Nicky up to the job? What do you mean?'

'What I've just seen was unprofessional. I didn't hear what was said, but it was clear you know each other. It's unacceptable. This isn't a game.'

'As I'm aware.' Pressing her lips together, Caelan swallowed what she really wanted to say. Beckett was right: she had been careless, allowing Nicky to drag her into a conversation they should not have been having.

'And yet here you are.' Beckett paused. 'I told you before, if you can't work with Nicky, you'll both be transferred.'

'I remember.'

'I'd like you to keep an eye on her, though.'

'An eye? Difficult to do when I'm not supposed to be in contact with her.'

'Richard agreed to report back to me, but we need him elsewhere now.' Beckett continued as though Caelan hadn't spoken.

'You had Richard spying on Nicky for you? Good to know you trust us.'

Beckett shook her head. 'It's not about trust, you know that. I'm concerned.'

'Really? Why don't you pack her off to a safe house again if you're so worried about her?' Caelan knew she was on dangerous ground, but she couldn't help herself. Beckett was the reason Nicky had disappeared, had hidden away. Had allowed those who cared about her to believe she was dead.

Beckett's expression warned her not to push further. 'I want you to report back to me if Nicky seems to be struggling. She's feeling guilty, and I can't risk her decisions being compromised while she's on active duty.'

'Heaven forbid.'

'Caelan, you might think you're being clever acting like a sulky schoolgirl, but I'll warn you once more. Carry on like this and you'll be transferred, or dismissed. I can't have people in my unit who don't respect me or the work they're involved in.'

'I do respect you, ma'am. That doesn't mean I agree with every decision you make.'

'Understood. But *I* don't agree with people who are romantically involved with each other working closely together.'

'We're not involved. We won't ever be again. You made sure of that.' Caelan stopped, the truth of what she had just said hitting her like a punch.

Beckett held up a finger. 'Don't.'

Caelan stared at her, appalled, the pieces fitting together. 'That's why you sent her away, wasn't it? You guessed how I'd react. Our relationship would be shattered, and I'd be free to find out who was corrupt in our department.'

Beckett's face was unreadable. 'No. Your relationship was irrelevant. I acted in the best interests of my officer's safety.'

It was Caelan's turn to curl her lip. 'Really.'

Beckett was already turning away. 'Go to Edmonton. Do your job. If you'd rather not, let me know and I'll send someone else.'

18

Buttoning her coat as she jogged down the stairs, Jen Somerville almost stumbled, and grabbed the banister for support. Slow down, she told herself. Falling and ending up in hospital wouldn't help her complete her list of tasks. Behind her, DC Gill hesitated.

'Okay?'

'Fine.' Somerville's tone was more abrupt than she had intended, and she moderated it. 'Let's go.'

In the car park, Gill unlocked a dark-blue Ford Focus. Somerville opened the passenger door and climbed in, pushing plastic bottles and fast-food wrappers to the side of the footwell with her toes.

'I've seen cleaner pigsties,' she muttered. Gill grinned at her as he reversed out of the parking space.

'My mum used to say that about my bedroom.'

Somerville cocked an eyebrow. 'Used to?'

'Hey, I've moved out.' He stuck out his bottom lip, mock-offended.

'And you're only just forty-five.'

'Funny.' Gill brought the car to a halt at a red light. 'I'm in a house share. You ever tried renting around here when you're single, have only one income?' He shook his head. 'It's impossible.'

Somerville considered telling him how she had struggled to make ends meet since her husband had walked out, but decided against it. No one at work knew he had gone. She still wore her wedding ring, and avoided talking about him, about home. After overhearing a conversation in the loos one day, she knew she had a reputation amongst her colleagues for being reserved, and a workaholic. Let them think what they wanted. It was less painful that way. She pulled out her phone, checked her emails. 'Maybe if you spent less on takeaways and fancy suits...'

Gill looked down at himself. 'Got to look sharp in this job, Sarge.'

'That's why I brought you.'

He glanced at her. 'How do you mean?'

'We're going to talk to a teenage boy. I'm old enough to be his mum, maybe even his nan. I want someone he's going to connect with.'

'And that's my job?'

'I'll be there too, but I want you to do the talking.'

Gill blew out his cheeks. 'What do we want to know?'

Somerville explained, watching Gill nod and a smile lift the corner of his lips. He was a good officer, but he could be cocky. This was his chance to prove there was more to him than a smart haircut and a wide-boy grin.

—

Caelan watched Jen Somerville stomp across the pavement. Somerville was scowling, stabbing at the screen of her phone as she walked. Behind her scurried a young man, gathering his suit jacket around his body as it was blown open by the wind. Caelan stepped further back into the bus shelter where she had been waiting, and watched them drive away. When the car had disappeared, she moved out onto the pavement, huddling inside her jacket as drizzle began to fall. After a minute or so, Joseph

Rainey appeared, wearing a hooded sweatshirt over his school uniform.

'They're clueless,' he said as he approached her.

Caelan shrugged. 'They want to help.'

His laugh was scornful. 'You should have heard him. Calling me bruv, trying to be my mate. Talking about going down Stamford Bridge.' He shook his head. 'Like I've ever been there.'

'Don't you like football?' Caelan teased.

He gave her a sideways glance. 'You've dyed your hair.'

She thought quickly. 'I fancied a change.'

Keeping her eyes on the pavement, Caelan hoped he would forget about it. He had recognised her easily, but he had been expecting to see her, and the changes she had made to her appearance since they had first met weren't designed to be total disguise.

'Shall we walk?' he asked.

Caelan nodded. 'We can get a drink and some food if you like.'

'There's a McDonald's around the corner.' He pointed with his thumb.

'Handy.'

He managed a smile. 'Mum and Dad don't like us going there for lunch, but...'

'Better than the food at school?'

'Isn't everything?'

'How did you get out of lessons?'

'Told them I'd had enough, I wanted to go home.' He cleared his throat. 'And I had. Those two officers that came...'

'What?'

'Do you know them?'

Caelan hesitated. 'Not really. I've met DS Somerville before.'

'She was all right, but him… It was like he was trying to wind me up.'

'How?'

'Like I said, pretending we were friends. Talking about music, clothes, all sorts of shit.' Joseph glanced at her, as if checking whether she was going to reprimand him for his language. When she didn't comment, he continued. 'He said he'd been mates with Ben, but I didn't believe him. Did he know him?'

'I don't know,' Caelan said truthfully.

'I didn't trust them, *him*. So I said I needed a break, and sent you the text.'

Caelan had received it as she had entered Westminster Underground station. Joseph had asked her to meet him, said he wanted to talk. She had hurried to Northolt before he had changed his mind. She'd inform Achebe and Somerville later.

'What did they want?' she asked him.

'Don't you know? I thought you worked with them.'

'Not exactly. Different departments.'

He shot her a glance, but didn't comment. After a few seconds he said, 'They were asking about some dodgy place. Wanted to know if Ben had talked to me about it.'

'Did they say where?'

'A hotel.' He nodded left as they reached the end of the road. 'This way.'

When they were settled at a table at the back of the restaurant, Joseph tucking into a double cheeseburger and fries, Caelan tried again.

'About this hotel…'

He chewed, swallowed. 'I told them I didn't know what they were talking about.'

Caelan took a drink of her strawberry milkshake, wincing at the ache in her bruised cheek as she sucked on the straw. 'Was that the truth?'

Joseph picked up a few fries, pushed the carton towards Caelan. 'Have some. It was, and it wasn't.'

'Meaning?'

'Meaning, I knew Ben had been going out late, staying out all night sometimes, but I didn't think anything of it. He's... He was twenty-three. I thought he had a girlfriend and he was staying at hers.'

Caelan ate some fries. 'Did you ask him about it?'

'Nah. Well, I teased him, you know. Asked who she was, if I could see a photo. He just smiled.'

'He didn't say any more?'

'No. And I left it. None of my business, I thought.' Joseph bent his head to his burger again, didn't look up until he'd finished the last mouthful. 'Seems I was wrong.'

'Wrong?'

'Well, he's dead, isn't he?' He stared at her, and she saw the tears in his eyes. 'And then you started asking if he talked to me about his work.'

Here it comes, Caelan thought. 'And did he?'

'No. I told you, he knew he couldn't. Even if we asked him about it, he didn't say much.' Joseph shifted in his seat. 'You remember I said they came and searched our room?'

'Yes. It's standard procedure in a—'

'Murder inquiry,' he interrupted. 'I know. That's what they kept telling me.' He bent down, picked up his school bag. He unzipped a pocket, removed something. 'Here. I've kept this with me since Ben died. I didn't know... I wasn't sure what to do.' He reached over the table. Caelan held out her hand and he dropped a mobile phone into it.

'What's this?'

He shrugged, not stating the obvious. 'It was Ben's. He kept it under his pillow; it wasn't the one he normally used. I caught him looking at it one night, and he didn't want to talk about it. That's when I thought he had a girlfriend, something private.'

Caelan turned the phone over. It was a basic smartphone, turned off. 'Have you looked at it, read the texts or call log?'

Joseph shook his head. 'It's password-protected. The battery's dead now too. You have people who'll be able to get into it, don't you?'

'Yeah, shouldn't be a problem. Thank you, Joseph.' She put the handset down on the table, wrapped it in a couple of napkins. 'Why did you hide it? I assume you took it before your room was searched?' She hid her anger, knowing he had done what he thought was right. She didn't tell him he had withheld potentially crucial evidence. She could see from his expression that he knew he had been wrong.

'Yeah, I'm sorry.' He dipped his head, looking embarrassed. 'I thought... Well, I suppose I was protecting Ben. I didn't want anyone poking around in his private stuff.' He looked up, rubbed his eyes. Picked up his drink. 'I know I should have told you before, but Dad was there, and... well, I didn't want to upset him.'

'Why? This phone could be vital, Joseph. It might help us find the person who killed Ben.' She spoke quietly, but there was no mistaking her tone. He chewed his bottom lip, and she was reminded how young he was.

'Yeah, I get that. I'm sorry.'

'Did Ben speak to you about a place in Hackney?'

He was frowning. 'What place?'

'The hotel. You mentioned it before?'

'No. Why would Ben be in Hackney?'

She could see he knew nothing about the brothel. She took out her phone, thumbed a text to Achebe. Joseph watched her.

'What are you doing?' he asked.

'Asking someone to come and collect the phone. We need to get to work on it.'

He pushed back his chair, began to stand. 'Then I'm leaving. I'm going to be in the shit about this, aren't I?'

'No. When did you take the phone?'

He picked up his rucksack, slung it over his shoulder. 'As soon as I knew Ben... wasn't coming home.'

'Then he can't have taken it with him on the night he died?'

Joseph stared at her, tears beginning to fall. He wiped an impatient hand across his cheeks. 'No. Otherwise it would have been found on his body, wouldn't it?'

'And it wasn't, because you had it.' She watched him, wondering if he would make the connection. Whoever had killed Ben Rainey might have been looking for this phone.

Joseph shifted from foot to foot. 'Listen, I'm going to head off, yeah?'

She leaned back in her chair. 'You're sure there's no more you can tell me?'

'No, I swear.'

'Joseph, listen. You've done the right thing giving this to me. Remember, if you see anything that concerns you, worries you, call me.'

He hesitated. 'You think I'm in danger?'

'Whoever killed Ben didn't stop there. Another man is dead, someone we think could be linked to your brother. I'm asking you to be careful. Tell your sister too.'

His eyes widened as realisation dawned. 'You think they were looking for the phone?'

'I don't know. It might be coincidence, totally irrelevant. Maybe your brother really did have a secret girlfriend. Until we see what information the phone can give us, I don't know.'

'All right, I hear you. I get it.'

He walked away, lifting his hand as he reached the door. As it swung closed behind him, Caelan's phone began to ring. Achebe didn't bother with a greeting.

'Jen Somerville's on her way. Why didn't you call her? You knew she was in the area.'

'Because Joseph asked me not to. He didn't want to speak to the DC she had with her again.'

'Jesus. All right. Let's hope the phone gives us something. God knows we've nothing else to go on.'

'Are you at the prison?' Caelan could hear shouting in the background.

'Yeah, though coming here's been a waste of time. You're heading back to Edmonton?'

'When I've spoken to DS Somerville.'

'Okay. Thanks, Caelan.'

Achebe ended the call, and Caelan picked up her milkshake again. He had sounded pissed off, and she couldn't blame him. Joseph Rainey had held onto the phone for three weeks, and Achebe's officers had missed that he was hiding something when they interviewed him. If Ben's murderers had been so determined to find the phone, though, wouldn't they have tried again? Broken into the Raineys' house, grabbed Joseph or Miriam? Or perhaps they had gone to Anthony Bryce instead, aware of a link between him and Ben Rainey the police still didn't know about. Caelan slurped the last of her milkshake, a headache beginning to creep around her temples.

'Didn't you get me a burger?' Jen Somerville strode over, dropped into the chair Joseph Rainey had sat in.

'Do you want one?' Caelan began to stand, but Somerville waved her away.

'I'm joking,' she said. 'Have you got the phone?' Caelan pointed to it, bundled in the napkins on the table. 'Good. Achebe's going mental. Says we should have found it weeks ago.' She ran a hand through her hair, frowning. 'Not sure how we could have done when the brother hid it and didn't say a word.' She grabbed the phone, shoved it into an evidence bag. 'Whole case is a bloody nightmare.'

'I doubt the phone will tell us much,' said Caelan. Somerville leaned forward, elbows on the table.

'Me neither, but we need to check it out, tick the box. If the phone was so important, why did the brother still have it? Why didn't whoever killed Rainey find him and take it? He's only a kid; it wouldn't have taken much to persuade him to part with it.'

'I don't know,' said Caelan, though Somerville was echoing her own thoughts. 'Maybe they didn't know, or it wasn't what they wanted. Or it could be Ben Rainey didn't tell them anything, despite the torture. None of it makes sense.'

Somerville stared at her. 'Or maybe it does.'

'What do you mean?'

'Anthony Bryce was strangled, Ben Rainey was stabbed with a screwdriver. I've been wondering why they weren't killed in the same way.'

'Should they have been?'

'No, but… Think about it. If someone had been torturing Rainey,' Somerville winced as she said the word, 'and he hadn't given them what they wanted, maybe they lost their rag and stabbed him in frustration, in anger.'

Caelan was nodding. 'Whereas Bryce could have given them what they wanted quickly. Or they throttled him until he did, then finished the job.'

'I'll mention it to DCI Achebe. It's supposition, of course, but...' Somerville's phone beeped and she checked the screen. 'I need to go.'

'Me too. I'm going to send Frankie Hamilton a text, see if he wants to meet up later.'

'Before his interview with us?' Somerville bared her teeth. 'That'll be nice.'

'Gives me something to look forward to.' Caelan smiled.

Somerville got to her feet. 'I didn't see you, you know.'

'What?'

'You were there, weren't you? When we left Joseph Rainey's school?'

'In the bus shelter,' Caelan felt obliged to admit. 'I saw you drive away.'

Somerville nodded, her face tightening.

'Must give you a kick, being able to do whatever you want.' There was a bite in her tone Caelan hadn't heard before.

'What do you mean?' she asked.

'You could have told us you were there, that Joseph Rainey had contacted you. You chose not to.' Somerville tossed her head. 'Not a team player, are you?'

'Wait a second. Joseph trusted me. Your DC patronised him, and he didn't want to talk. He had my number, decided to give me a call instead.'

'Whatever you say.'

'We have the phone now. Does it matter how we got it?'

Somerville's cheeks were red. 'Apparently not. See you around.'

19

Was it the fourth cup of tea Adam had brought her, or the fifth? Liv Hobbs had lost count. He didn't seem to know what else to do. She curled on the sofa, her ribs still sore, her head thumping. Her brother was dead. Since she had first heard the news, she had kept repeating the words in her mind as she attempted to make sense of it. It wasn't working. She and Jackson hadn't seen or spoken to each other for years, and if anyone had asked, she would have said she rarely even thought about him. But the news of his murder had hit her like a body blow. She had crumpled, her arms wrapped around her body, blindly stumbling towards a chair. She'd asked them to repeat what they had said. Tim Achebe and Jen Somerville, her colleagues and her friends, breaking the news as gently as they could. She remembered a moan escaping her lips, Tim's arm around her shoulders, Jen's hand clutching hers. Adam had been at work, but he had soon appeared, his face bewildered. She'd reached for him and he'd held her, rocking her in his arms until she was able to speak. Tim and Jen had explained what little they knew, then left with promises to keep her updated. Now she and Adam sat together, drinking tea and wondering what the hell was going on. She looked at her husband: the tired eyes, the pale cheeks.

'Why don't you go to bed?' she said.

He stared. 'What? I'm not leaving you, Liv.'

'You must be exhausted.'

He shook his head, attempted a smile. Jackson had been at their wedding, but Adam had never known him well. When Liv had joined the police and her family had made their feelings about her decision clear, Adam had been there to support her. He'd told her it was her life, and if her family didn't like her choices, it was their loss. Now, imagining her parents holding each other, comforting each other, she wasn't sure.

Adam kissed her cheek. 'You okay?'

She wasn't, and he knew it, but what else was there to say? Her body felt as though it was floating, her limbs heavy and light at the same time. She lifted the tea to her lips, though she didn't want to drink it. Took a tiny sip.

'I feel I should be with my mum and dad,' she said softly.

Adam frowned. 'Really? Why? You think they'll want to see you?'

'I don't know.' She looked at him, saw the hurt in his eyes. 'You're being amazing, Ad, but… I don't know. I always told Jackson he'd end up dead because of the way he lived his life. I didn't expect to be right.' She scrubbed at her face.

Adam pulled away from her, got to his feet. 'You want me to come with you? I'll drive, wait outside the house if you like.'

He thought she was making a mistake, she could hear it in his voice. He was probably right, but she knew she had to try.

'No, it's okay. I'll get the Tube.'

'Sure?' He looked down at her. 'Are you going to tell them…?'

Despite it all, she managed a smile. 'No. Not now.'

'Be careful. They might slam the door in your face.'

'If they even open it. I know. I'll be okay.'

He held out a hand, helped her off the sofa. Liv held him close, her head against his chest.

'Are you certain you want to go alone?' he said into her hair.

She pulled away. 'I think I have to.'

He nodded, followed her up the stairs. Liv washed her face, bathed her swollen eyes. She didn't bother to change out of her jeans and washed-out T-shirt. Didn't check her hair or apply make-up. She put on her coat and picked up her bag, knowing she had to leave the house before her courage failed her.

20

Caelan stood on the train beside an elderly man who kept sneezing into a crumpled tissue. In front of her, a younger man appeared to be asleep on his feet. He had a rucksack on his back, which kept digging into Caelan's body as the train lurched and jolted. She closed her eyes, willing the journey to be over, though she knew she wouldn't arrive at Edmonton Green station for at least forty minutes. She would have to speak to Frankie Hamilton again, meet him if she could. She suppressed a groan as she remembered his lascivious gaze and his wet lips on her cheek. They needed information about the Edmonton drug scene, and Hamilton was the best lead they had. Speaking to him could be vital, but she had reservations, and resolved to call Penrith when she could to discuss it again.

At Seven Sisters, she got off the train and walked until she had a phone signal. Penrith answered immediately.

'Problem?'

'Maybe.' Caelan glanced around, making sure she couldn't be overheard. 'The interview with Hamilton – can it be postponed?'

She heard Penrith sucking his teeth. 'Why?'

'The reason I gave before.'

'You think he'll realise that him being interviewed is linked to yesterday evening's hot date with you?'

'It's a possibility.'

'I don't think we need to be concerned. If you're right about someone trying to run him over last night, he won't be surprised if some friendly coppers turn up wanting a chat.'

'Are you serious? I was the only person who saw it happen. I told him to report it, but there was no way he was going to. It's another link to me. He can't be interviewed today.'

'Then when do you suggest we do it? In a week? A month? When you've retired?' Penrith took a breath, and when he spoke again, it was with authority. 'You've been given your instructions. Contact Hamilton, speak to him. Find out what he knows, then call me. We'll make the decision about him being interviewed then. I'll speak to Achebe.'

He was gone. Reluctantly, Caelan found Hamilton's number and sent him a text suggesting they meet for a drink. She didn't want to go back to the Red Lion, but she had no idea where else to suggest.

As she arrived at Edmonton Green station, her phone pinged with a reply. Hamilton said he was at a snooker club and she was welcome to join him. Caelan typed the name of the place into her phone and discovered it was a five-minute walk away. She found it without difficulty, though from the outside it looked about as welcoming as she had expected. She stood on the opposite side of the road, watching a group of four men smoking and talking outside. Hamilton wasn't one of them. She pretended to tie her shoelace, checking the lie of the land. An old trick, but effective. The entrance, a battered wooden door, was behind the group of men, between a dry cleaner's shop and a bookmaker's. The snooker hall was on the first floor, its windows shuttered. There might be another way out, a fire escape at the back, but she doubted it. She didn't like places with only one escape route.

Two of the four men she had been watching walked away, wandered off down the street. The other two disappeared through the wooden door, heading for the club. Caelan took a breath, let it out slowly. The familiar charge of adrenalin hummed through her veins. This wasn't dangerous as assignments went, and she had enjoyed stringing Hamilton along the previous evening. Looking at the dingy building, the peeling paintwork and the dark windows, she pushed her concerns aside. She had raised her issue with Penrith, been told to forget about it. She marched across the road, pushed open the door.

Inside, concrete stairs, the smell of spilt beer and dirty carpets. Caelan went up the steps, one hand on the sticky metal banister, the other on her shoulder bag. She could hear muted music, male voices. At the top of the stairs was a landing, opening onto a room containing three full-sized snooker tables. Each table was illuminated by a strip light, but the rest of the room was dingy. Navy-blue walls and charcoal carpet tiles added to the gloom. At the far end was a small bar, surrounded by a few white plastic garden tables and assorted chairs. Caelan counted nine men, including Hamilton, who sat alone at one of the tables, a pint of lager in front of him. The only other woman in the room was behind the bar, eating crisps and fiddling with her phone.

Hamilton spotted Caelan, and raised a hand. Reluctant, but forcing a smile, she headed towards him. From his vacant grin and unfocused gaze, she realised the pint he now reached for was far from his first of the afternoon. He took a mouthful of beer, patting the chair beside him with his free hand. Caelan sat.

'Good to see you, gorgeous.' He leaned towards her, grabbed her hand and planted a kiss on the back of it. 'Looking good.'

Caelan reclaimed her hand, resisting wiping it on her trousers. 'You too, Frankie.' She hoped she sounded more enthusiastic than she felt.

'Can I get you a drink?' He pulled a wad of notes from the inside pocket of his jacket, shooting a glance at Caelan to make sure she had noticed. 'I've been doing some business.'

'Yeah? That was quick. I'll have a beer, thanks.'

Hamilton nodded, made his way to the bar. Caelan was aware of several of the men in the room looking her way, some discreetly, some openly staring. She sat back, crossed her legs, making a show of being relaxed. Let them look. She was in control here.

Hamilton plonked the bottle of lager on the table, caressed the back of Caelan's neck for a second as he sat down. She forced her shoulders to relax as his damp fingers touched her skin. He was clearly under the impression that this was a date. She gave him a teasing smile.

'Nice place,' she said. He laughed, missing the sarcasm.

'Yeah, it's not bad. I used to come here a lot, to play a few frames of snooker, have a beer. Wasn't sure if it would still be here.' Casually he slid an arm across the back of Caelan's chair. He was relaxed, smiling.

Caelan lifted her drink, her eyes scanning the room. Most of those playing snooker had gone back to their games. For now, she could concentrate on Frankie. Lucky her. 'Why wouldn't it still be here?'

He leaned closer. She smelt garlic, coffee. His touch was making her skin itch. 'It's been raided a few times,' he said, his mouth close to her ear.

'Why?'

'Employing illegals, licensing stuff. Drugs. The usual. It's okay, they could never prove any of it. Bloke who owns the place is a mate of mine.'

Caelan leaned forward to put her bottle back on the table, taking the opportunity to inch away from Hamilton. 'Talking of mates, have you heard about Jackson Hobbs?'

Hamilton frowned, removing his arm from her chair. 'Heard what?'

Caelan kept her eyes on his face. 'He's dead.'

His mouth opened, eyes widening. He blinked, and Caelan was certain he hadn't known before. 'Dead? What do you mean?'

She picked up the bottle, had another mouthful of beer before replying. 'Murdered. Someone shanked him in prison.'

Hamilton was still staring at her. 'Fuck. I don't... Fuck.'

'Yeah.' Caelan cradled the bottle. 'You didn't know?'

He swallowed. 'No. Who told you?'

'Mate of my boyfriend's called me,' Caelan lied smoothly. Possibly unwise, but necessary.

'Who told him?'

'Don't know. I didn't ask.' She waited, knowing she was on shaky ground if he demanded to know. Hobbs's murder might make the news, the problems facing prisons being well publicised, but there was no guarantee. What was one dead prisoner? One fewer for taxpayers to keep, some would say.

Hamilton was out of his chair. 'Listen, princess, I'm going to have to shoot off.'

She pouted. 'But I've only just got here.'

'I know, but this... Well, there are people who should know about it. I'll call you, yeah?'

He hurried across the floor, attracting curious glances. Caelan watched him leave, wishing she had taken Nicky up on her offer of backup. Hamilton was spooked. Where was he going? Who was he so eager to speak to? He needed to be followed, but she couldn't do it herself. She got to her feet, went over to the bar.

'You got a ladies' in here?' she asked.

The woman behind the bar, now painting her fingernails, nodded towards the far end of the room. 'Sort of. Back there.'

'Cheers.'

Caelan wandered across the room, hoping the men around her were too absorbed in their games to notice.

No chance.

'Looking for some company, darling?' He was young, skinny, wearing tracksuit bottoms, the hood of his sweatshirt up even inside. He stepped towards her, grinning. 'Frankie had to rush off, did he? Why don't you join us? I'll show you how to play.'

He licked his lips, making sure she didn't miss the innuendo. Caelan forced a smile, kept walking.

'What would Frankie say if I did?' She kept her voice light, teasing, playing to his assumption that she was Hamilton's property, though the idea stuck in her throat.

He scowled. 'Like I give a fuck. He's no one now, man.'

She saw the door marked *Toilet*, headed for it, hoping he would take the hint. She pushed open the door, looked around, knowing she was taking a risk. The room was small, just one cubicle, a urinal and a stained sink. A window was open in the corner, but she knew it was useless. She couldn't fit through, and even if she could, climbing out would draw far too much attention. She sent Penrith a brief text explaining where she was and what had happened. Nicky might be nearby, but it was unlikely. Hamilton would be miles away, and they would never know who he was going to see. Fuck. She should have followed him, tagged along.

Her friend in the tracksuit bottoms was waiting for her outside the door.

'What's your name?' he demanded.

'Kay. Look, I've got to go.' Caelan tried to push past, but he held her wrist.

'Not seen you in here before.' He smiled. 'And I'd have remembered.'

'I wanted to see Frankie. He was here.' Caelan glared, not having to pretend to be irritated. 'Didn't know I'd be interrogated about it.'

He let her arm go. 'Just being friendly. I'm Marcus.' He watched her, and Caelan knew he was waiting for a reaction.

'Marcus. I'll remember that.'

'Make sure you do. What did you say to Frankie?'

'What?'

'He went out of here like his balls were on fire. You tell him you're pregnant?'

Caelan had to laugh. 'Nah, nothing like that.'

'What then?'

'Heard some news. Thought Frankie should too.'

He smirked. 'That Jackson Hobbs is dead?'

'How do you know?'

'Everyone does. How do you?'

'Like you said, it's not a secret.'

'Except Frankie hadn't heard. Shows how far out of the loop he is.' He stepped closer, lowered his voice. 'What are you doing with him anyway?'

'I'm not *with* him.'

Marcus laughed. 'Yeah, does he know that? Because before you came in, he was telling us all about this new girl of his.'

194

Caelan hesitated, taking in the confident stance, the smile. 'Here's the thing. I heard Frankie might be able to help me out.'

'With?'

'Doesn't matter. I thought I'd make myself known to him.'

'He said you knew his name, you remembered him.'

'Had to say something, didn't I?' Caelan risked a smile. 'He heard what he wanted to hear.'

Marcus tipped his head back, thinking about it. 'Frankie's out of the game.'

'Yet he has a roll of paper in his pocket.'

A laugh. 'Probably mugged his granny. What's your business?'

'I'm not saying.' Caelan glanced over his shoulder. She had to get out of here. Frankie could be streets away by now.

Marcus shrugged, turning away. 'Then I can't help you.'

'Fine. I'll be on my way.'

She gave him ten seconds. In the end, it was more like five.

'Kay.' He said it quietly. She stopped, waited.

'What's your surname?'

'Summers.'

'Give me your number.'

Facing him, she put her hands on her hips. 'Thought you said you couldn't help?'

'I'll ask around. I'll need to check you out first.'

'Do that.'

Her stomach dropping, she gave him the number of the mobile she was carrying. He tapped it into his phone. She flicked her hair, turned away.

'No promises,' he called.

She kept walking.

Once outside, Caelan moved quickly, her heart thumping. As she had expected, there was no sign of Frankie. Who the hell was Marcus? She needed to get out of the area, then call Penrith and ask him. Though she hadn't given any details about her 'business', he had assumed drugs were involved. Why wouldn't he? That was Frankie Hamilton's line of work, after all. And he was going to check her out. What did that mean? She had used the Kay Summers legend more than once, and now it would have to be altered. Whoever Marcus was, he would have contacts. His involvement could be dangerous, but what choice had she had? There had been no way of avoiding the discussion without arousing his suspicion.

She took a roundabout route towards the station, planning to catch a bus back to the flat she had been sent to. Once there, with the door locked, she would call Penrith.

That was when she saw Liv Hobbs.

The detective inspector was walking towards her, bundled into a thick coat. Her face was drawn, her eyes shadowed. Understandably, she looked ill. Caelan hesitated, knowing she couldn't allow Hobbs to see her. What the hell was she doing here? She'd mentioned having friends here, but why would she be coming to visit them on the day her brother was murdered?

Caelan stepped into a newsagent's, stood by a rack of tabloids until she saw Hobbs pass by the open shop door. She counted to five, stepped back outside, saw her disappear around the corner. She followed. Hobbs was heading for the bus station, walking slowly, her head down. She and her brother might have been estranged, but the news of his death had clearly affected her deeply. She waited for the lights to change before crossing the road, and Caelan was reminded of her car crash. What was Hobbs thinking now? Had the deliberate collision been a warning to her brother, or to Liv herself? Without knowing who had spoken to Jackson Hobbs in prison, or who might have visited him, Caelan had no idea. What would anyone want to warn Liv Hobbs about? Her involvement in the Edmonton drugs investigation? But that would mean someone knew the operation was ongoing. Was Caelan's own position at risk? Was Nicky's? It made more sense that the collision was a warning to Jackson Hobbs, but why use the sister he hadn't spoken to for years to attract his attention? Caelan frowned as she walked, puzzling it over. Another aspect of the situation that made no sense.

Hobbs was boarding a bus, but Caelan knew she couldn't follow. She had altered her appearance since visiting Hobbs at her home, but not enough. Hobbs was sharp. She would realise. Best to let her go and pass the information on.

In fifteen minutes, Caelan was back in the flat, filling the kettle. The place was as she had left it, but she checked it over just the same. Downstairs, the music was thumping again, though not quite as loudly as before. At least she didn't have to worry about being overheard. When she had a cup of tea, she made the call. Penrith began to talk before she could speak.

'Firstly, your pal Frankie Hamilton has just been picked up from his address in Edmonton for questioning,' he told her. 'He didn't seem surprised to find two police officers at his front door.'

'He's probably used to it. Did he mention me?' Caelan sipped her tea.

'He's still en route. I'll let you know. Next, the phone Joseph Rainey gave you.' Penrith coughed. 'Why didn't you tell me about it first?'

'Why? Because Somerville had just spoken to Joseph and I knew she was in the area. What have they found?'

'Nothing.'

'What?'

'They haven't unlocked it yet.'

Caelan closed her eyes. 'It's been hours. How hard can it be?'

'Don't ask me, you know I'm a pay-as-you-go Nokia man.'

'Of course you are.' She pictured Penrith in his office, his belly squeezed behind his desk, one arm behind his head. 'I saw Liv Hobbs just now.'

'Where?' Penrith sounded unconcerned.

'I think she'd got off the Tube.'

'Making assumptions? Tut tut.'

'She caught a bus.'

'She's bereaved, on leave. It's none of our business.' He was interested, though. It was almost imperceptible, but his tone had changed.

'Why is she here? I know she has family in Edmonton, but she's estranged from them.'

'I don't know. Grief can have a strange effect on people. I remember a colleague, years ago, who hated his father. He'd been aggressive, abusive. They hadn't seen each other for years, but when the old man died, the son went to pieces.'

'Mourning the relationship they never had.' Caelan drank some more tea, Nicky wandering unbidden into her mind again.

'Exactly.' Penrith sucked his teeth. 'Maybe DI Hobbs has reacted in a similar way. Still, I'll make a note.'

'I also need you to check someone out for me.' Caelan moved into the living room as she spoke, curled up on the sofa.

'Been mingling with the locals again, have we? Who?'

'Name's Marcus. I met him at a snooker hall. Can you find out who owns it?' She gave the address. 'He's going to check me out.'

'Is he now?' Penrith chuckled. 'Good luck to him then.'

'I hinted I'm a drug dealer, or user. Possibly both. Either way, he thinks I want to do business.'

'All right. I'd better invent some convictions, then. Add them to your record.'

'You're assuming he has a way of accessing criminal records? Why?'

'Come on, you know how these things work. If he's a major player—'

'Which we don't know he is,' Caelan put in. 'No one has said so.'

'If he is, he'll have someone in his pocket.'

'Someone like Ben Rainey?' Was that the link? She rubbed her eyes, tired and frustrated.

'It's a possibility we need to consider. It's much more likely he's a small-time gangster, with no power or inside knowledge whatsoever. He probably meant he was going to ask around on the street.'

'Hamilton may have told him I'm not from around here.'

'Maybe. I wonder how Hamilton ended up in Edmonton himself. He's from south London. You'd think there'd be plenty there to keep him busy.'

'Worth finding out.'

'Then do it. I assume you'll see him again?'

'Don't know. Depends what he hears about me, I suppose.'

'It won't be a problem. We'll have a word in the right ears. They'll pass on anything we want them to, you know that. Now, do you want these criminal convictions adding?'

'Not sure. Don't want him to think I'm an amateur, that I make a habit of getting caught.'

'Something minor, then. A possession charge. I'll have it sorted out. Don't worry.'

Caelan stretched out her legs, drank the last of her tea. 'I wasn't.'

'Anything else?' Penrith's tone suggested he hoped not.

'What happened at the prison?'

'As you were told on your previous call, a waste of time.'

'And the suspect?'

Penrith paused. 'He's been interviewed. Didn't say a word. Wouldn't talk about Hobbs, the murder, or who's paying him. He's currently in a cell at South Harrow. They'll have another go at him later. Verbally, I mean.'

'Were you there?'

'At his interview? I observed, yes.'

'And?'

'My impression was...' Penrith broke off to yawn. Caelan told herself not to bite. 'My impression was the man was terrified.'

'Of possible repercussions? He'd been threatened? "Keep your mouth shut or we'll come for your family"?'

'Along those lines, yes. I'm guessing, but it makes sense. He was sweating, couldn't sit still. Clammed up completely. Even at the prison, he wouldn't talk.'

'What about before the murder?'

'Nothing unusual in his behaviour, I'm told. He was quiet, no trouble. Wanted to keep his head down, his nose clean, and all those other clichés. If something kicked off, he didn't get involved.'

Caelan stood, went over to the window. 'He behaved himself in prison, yet he was in for GBH? He never fought?

I can imagine people trying to provoke him, make him scrap for his place in the hierarchy.'

'I was expecting a more… colourful prison record too. Maybe he's a changed man.'

'Or he was keeping his nose clean, waiting for Jackson Hobbs to arrive. He wouldn't want to be moved from the wing or the prison itself if he'd been ordered to get rid of Hobbs.'

'There was no guarantee Hobbs would have started his sentence in that prison, though. He could have been sent anywhere,' Penrith pointed out.

'Maybe Aaron Jacob was told it was a possibility Hobbs would be arriving. Plans would have had to have been made in advance.'

'Goes without saying.' Penrith was impatient. 'You know how we're approaching it.'

She did. Richard Adamson was probably already preparing for his first night behind bars. She didn't envy him. Prison was a place she had no desire to ever be asked to infiltrate.

'Is he safe?'

'Jacob? Safe as you can be locked in a cell in a police station. What do you mean?'

Caelan ran a hand across her mouth. 'Suicide watch?'

'You think…?'

'I don't know, but Aaron Jacob is a loose end. He's looking at spending the rest of his life in prison. Who knows what he'll be pressured into doing next?'

Penrith was typing; she could hear keys clicking. 'Jacob is already on suicide watch. And Marcus, the man you asked me about? Marcus Crowley's a possibility. I'm looking at his record now.'

'And?'

'He's come to our attention a couple of times, but there are no convictions. There's some intel about possible gang activity, but—'

Caelan sat up straight. 'Gang activity?'

'It was never confirmed.'

'But someone was keeping their eye on him?'

Penrith was still typing. 'His name was mentioned in an interview after a fatal stabbing. The victim was a gang member. Crowley was fifteen at the time.'

'How old is he now? Twenty-five?'

'Twenty-four, as of last month.'

'The same age as Ben Rainey and Anthony Bryce.' Caelan swung her feet to the floor and stood.

'Probably a coincidence.'

'Maybe. Where did Marcus Crowley grow up?'

There was a pause. Caelan visualised Penrith peering at his computer screen, running a chunky finger down the text as he read. 'Hounslow, born and bred,' he said eventually.

Caelan was at the living room window, watching two figures on bikes circling the playground. As they neared each other, one reached out to the other. It was difficult to see exactly what had changed hands, but she could guess. 'Like Anthony Bryce,' was all she said.

'And thousands of other people.'

'Come on, Ian. It needs to be looked at.' Their business complete, the pair on the bikes disappeared, heading in different directions.

'Oh, I agree. I'll pass the information on to DCI Achebe. We need to confirm whether Crowley is the man you met.' He didn't wait for her response. 'What are your plans for the rest of the day?'

Caelan was deliberately, provocatively casual. 'I was assuming Frankie Hamilton would be in touch.'

'Not for a while. Like I said, he's not even arrived for interview yet.'

'Then what do you suggest? Why am I here?'

He made a sound of exasperation. 'Don't ask me.'

'Helpful.'

'I try. We'll speak later.'

Caelan pushed the phone into her pocket, sat on the sofa again. Marcus Crowley, a man the same age as Ben Rainey and Anthony Bryce, with a possible gang background. Did it matter? Was it significant? The lack of information provided by Penrith hadn't helped. If she was going to speak to Crowley again, she needed to know more. Had Penrith even found the right man? How would she know? She needed to see a mugshot.

Decision made, she headed out of the door.

21

'What are you doing here?'

DCI Tim Achebe looked tired, and not a little pissed off. Caelan risked a smile.

'I need some information.'

Achebe's hands were on his hips. 'And a phone call wouldn't have done? We have Frankie Hamilton downstairs. What if he'd seen you?'

'He didn't. He won't.' Caelan tried to look over Achebe's shoulder into the incident room, hoping to see Jen Somerville.

'You shouldn't be here. I suppose you're expecting to watch his interview?' Achebe checked his watch.

'Well, I wasn't, but if you're offering...'

'I'm not. What do you want to know?' Achebe had obviously decided to control his irritation and let her have her say.

'Marcus Crowley.'

Achebe stared, uncomprehending. 'Who's he?'

'Possibly no one, possibly a dealer in Edmonton our intel didn't mention. Have you heard of him? Have the NCA listed his name?'

'No.' Achebe turned, waved to one of the uniformed officers busy in the room behind him. 'Can you find DS Somerville for me, please?'

'Isn't she interviewing Hamilton?' Caelan asked. Achebe gave a grim smile.

'Not yet. He's shit-faced. We can't question him until he sobers up.'

'He was well on his way when I saw him. I want to know where he went when he left me.'

'We found him at home, which I'd guess is about a twenty-minute walk from the snooker hall. Would he have had time to go anywhere else in between?'

Caelan pursed her lips. 'Probably not. He spoke to someone then. Do we have his phone?'

Achebe nodded. 'But no reason to poke around in his texts or call records – yet.'

She knew he was right, but it was frustrating. 'He wanted to make sure someone knew about Jackson Hobbs's death. Could be important.'

'Could be vital, but we can't question him yet. There's no point until he knows what he's saying.'

'He's that drunk?' Caelan found it hard to believe. Hamilton had clearly had a few drinks when she had spoken to him, but she wouldn't have described him as drunk.

'He appears to be.' Achebe didn't seem convinced. 'I don't want to risk him claiming later down the line that he was incapable, if he gives us information we end up relying on. You know how crap like that can come back to haunt us.'

'Unless he downed a bottle of vodka when he left the snooker club, I don't see how he can be paralytic now.'

'Maybe he smoked something on his way home. I don't know. All I can say is, he's off his face on something.'

'It seems convenient.'

'I know, but I doubt he could fake being sick.'

'He's vomited?'

Achebe screwed up his face. 'Several times.'

'Okay. Can we talk about Crowley?'

'Why not.'

'Why didn't we know about him?'

He held up his hands. 'Tell me what you've found out.'

She filled him in about their meeting. 'He was cocky, confident. He's also the same age as Rainey and Bryce.'

'And he's originally from Hounslow.' Achebe clicked his fingers. 'All right. Let's see what we can find out.' He stepped backwards, moving away from the door, and Caelan followed him inside. Achebe sat at a free computer, nodded Caelan into the chair beside him. Jen Somerville appeared in the doorway, frowning as she saw them.

'What's going on, boss?' she asked.

Achebe filled her in on what Caelan had told him. 'Have we heard anything about Ben Rainey's phone yet?'

'No. I was going to chase them again after the interview.'

'Which has been postponed. Do it now.' Achebe turned his attention to the keyboard, leaving Somerville open-mouthed. She shot Caelan a glare as she marched away.

'Any need?' Caelan said.

Achebe exhaled sharply. 'Probably not. I'll apologise later.' He snatched at the mouse. 'This case has been going on too long. I'm getting grief from above.' He tapped on the keyboard, waited, jabbed a finger at the monitor. 'This the man you met?'

Caelan took in the cropped hair, the defiant brown eyes. 'Yep.'

'Marcus Marvin Crowley.' Achebe skimmed his record, then squinted at her. 'You know how to pick them.'

'He approached me.'

'On the off chance you wanted to do business? Someone he'd never heard of or met before?' He tapped out a rhythm on the desk. 'Bit of a coincidence.'

'Yeah, another one.'

'Meaning?'

'I don't know. He didn't say anything incriminating, and he's going to ask around about me.'

Achebe shifted in his chair. 'I'm not sure Hamilton being brought in so soon after you saw him is a good idea.'

'I raised concerns myself, but...'

'You were overruled?' he asked.

'I've been wrong before. Penrith thinks I'm complicating matters, seeing links that aren't there.' She smiled. 'Again.'

Achebe was silent, clearly considering what to do next. 'All right. Stay for Hamilton's interview.'

'How long until you can do it?'

'He was singing when they brought him in, then, like I said, he started puking. No idea.'

'Lovely. Can we check something else?'

'The snooker hall?' Achebe's hands moved over the keyboard again, opening up another search. 'It's owned by...' They waited as the computer whirred and clicked. 'Still steam-powered,' he muttered. Under the desk, his knee was bouncing. Caelan blinked when she saw the name appear.

'Shit,' she said. 'What do we do?'

Achebe was already pushing back his chair. 'We bring Crowley in.' His jaw was set, his face grim. Caelan stepped in front of him.

'Tim, wait. We can't. Frankie Hamilton told me his mate owned the place, but he didn't give me a name. If we bring Crowley in now, it'll be obvious I've been poking around.'

'And?'

'As far as Crowley knows, I'm some woman he wants to impress, someone who's looking to do business. He doesn't trust me yet, but if Ian's done his job properly, he soon will. We can use Crowley. *I* can use him.'

Achebe shifted his feet, clearly not liking what he was hearing. 'Don't want to blow your cover, is that it?'

Caelan lifted her shoulders. 'It makes sense. We don't know for sure that Crowley's involved in the murders of Rainey and Bryce, but we're pretty sure he's in the drugs game. We could send him down for the rest of his life if we do this properly.'

He was shaking his head. 'It's too risky.'

'Not your problem. If we bring Crowley in now, we'll expose the whole Edmonton operation. I'm here, but Richard's in jail, Nicky's still out there. We'll be putting them both at risk. These aren't people that piss around with warnings, Tim.' Caelan spoke urgently. This could be huge.

'That's your worry, Nicky and Richard's safety?' He shook his head. 'We'll call them in.'

'Not without Assistant Commissioner Beckett's say-so, and she won't like it. It's too early, we don't know enough. There's no evidence. Not yet.'

'We now know Marcus Crowley owns the snooker hall himself. We could guess he's got cash he needs to wash through a legit business.' Achebe narrowed his eyes at her. 'Plus the money he'd have needed to buy the place. Wonder where that could be coming from, especially considering his age.'

'He'll have some bullshit story about an inheritance or a gambling win. We've nothing concrete, and Crowley will know it. We can't touch him, not yet.' She took a step towards Achebe, willing him to understand.

He said, 'What about the NCA? Reid and Webster? We'll have to speak to them.'

'They were supposed to have identified the drug dealers in Edmonton, so why didn't they know about Crowley?'

'They couldn't have been aware of all of them, it's impossible.'

'They were half-hearted, half-arsed,' Caelan said. 'They didn't seem to understand that in our game, the wrong information can get people killed.'

'They didn't care.' Achebe was firm. 'What you said about Ben Rainey doing some investigating of his own, playing at being a detective while he was still a PC – were you serious?'

'It's possible, isn't it?'

'Yeah, but...' Achebe bunched his fists. 'None of this makes sense. Rainey and Bryce grew up a few miles apart; they're both dead, both tortured, bodies found in the same area, but they didn't know each other.'

Caelan pursed her lips, thinking about it. 'Are we sure?'

Achebe stared. 'What do you mean?'

'You said Bryce was questioned after Rainey's death. Why?'

'Because he'd given us information about a new dealer in Edmonton. We had your colleague Nicky on the street, and then a dead copper turns up. We panicked, wanted to see what Bryce knew.'

'But he couldn't help?' Caelan watched Achebe's face.

'No. He didn't recognise Rainey, said he'd never seen him before.'

'And this was after Jackson Hobbs was sentenced?'

'Yeah, a couple of months after, I think.'

'Okay.' Caelan began to pace. 'So Bryce came to you with the information about a new dealer being in Edmonton after Jackson Hobbs was arrested?'

Achebe licked his lips. 'Yes.'

'After Liv Hobbs transferred onto your team?'

'What are you suggesting?' His voice was quiet, but there was no mistaking his tone.

Caelan shrugged. 'You think it's a coincidence?'

'Is there another possibility? Are you suggesting Liv is somehow involved in her brother's schemes? You're on dangerous ground.'

'Not what I said. I'm trying to figure out a timeline. I don't understand why someone would crash into Liv Hobbs, then have her brother killed. If it was a warning to Jackson, what were they asking him to do?'

'If he still had people selling for him in Edmonton, maybe he was being asked to call them off, or move them on.'

Caelan considered it. 'Makes sense. But why use his sister, someone he's estranged from?'

'I don't know. Maybe because she's a copper? Maybe whoever this new dealer is was making a point, saying no one is untouchable?'

'And Jackson Hobbs didn't do what they wanted, so they killed him?'

Achebe glanced at his watch again. 'Like I said, no one's untouchable. We need Aaron Jacob to start talking.'

'You think he will?'

'Who knows? He's no doubt been warned what will happen to him, or more likely to his family, if he does.'

'What about a possible gang link?' Caelan held up her hands as Achebe exhaled. 'Hear me out. Rainey, Bryce and Crowley are the same age, and they grew up near each other. Crowley's name was linked with a gang killing ten years ago.'

'And what, since then he's stayed out of trouble?' Achebe's voice was tight. 'Yes, the three of them were or are young, black, and male. Does it automatically follow they were members of a gang?'

'Of course not.'

'No. I get we have to consider the possibility, but... Listen, they lived in different areas, had different postcodes. Why the fuck would they have been in the same gang?' He took a deep breath. 'Sorry. It's just…'

'I know. But isn't it possible?'

'Rainey was a copper. Don't you think it would have come up before, during recruitment?'

'Not necessarily, if it was years before. Not if he stayed quiet about it.'

Achebe chewed on his bottom lip. 'His mum and dad would have known.'

'Would they? Did your parents know everything about you when you were growing up? Mine didn't.'

'No, but… I don't buy it, Caelan.'

'I'm just looking for a link.'

'And that's the conclusion you jump to?'

Caelan held in a scream. '*No*. I'm suggesting it as a possibility. When I first heard Anthony Bryce's name, I thought I recognised it.'

'And?'

'I don't know. Maybe I've read it somewhere.'

Achebe threw up his hands. 'Well, get back to me when you've got a clue.'

Caelan said nothing, and he stepped towards her, touched her arm.

'Apologies,' he said softly. 'It's—'

'The case. I get it.' Caelan raised her eyes to the ceiling, trying to focus. Let Achebe ignore the possibility, but she knew she had been right to mention it. She didn't think Rainey had ever been in a gang either, but maybe Bryce had. 'We're missing something,' was all she said.

Achebe forced a laugh. 'That we can agree on.'

Jen Somerville pushed the door open, walked towards them. From her expression, it was impossible to tell whether she had anything to report. Achebe raised his eyebrows.

'Well?'

She grinned. 'They were about to ring me. They've accessed Ben Rainey's phone.'

'And?' Achebe demanded.

'No calls or texts received. No contacts stored in the memory, but it was used to make some calls to a number.'

'One number?' Caelan wanted to be sure. Somerville nodded.

'Just one – the same pay-as-you-go SIM Anthony Bryce called us from to set up the meeting where he gave the information about the new dealer in Edmonton.'

There was a pause, Caelan trying to figure out what this meant, Achebe no doubt doing the same.

'Then Bryce lied when he said he didn't know Rainey.' Achebe looked furious. 'Who spoke to him about Ben Rainey, Jen?'

Somerville blinked. 'I'm not sure.'

'Find out, please.'

'What, so you can give them a bollocking?' Somerville stood her ground. 'Is that necessary?'

Caelan waited for Achebe to explode, but instead he gave a slow shake of his head. 'No. No, the last thing we need is to piss our team off even more after three weeks, no leads, and no paid overtime.'

'So, we have evidence that Bryce knew Rainey, or at least had spoken to him. How many calls were made, Jen?' Caelan asked. Somerville looked her up and down before replying.

'Four, the last about three hours before Ben Rainey died.'

'Then we can assume—'

'No, we can't,' Somerville put in.

'All right, it's *possible* Bryce lured Rainey to his death, whether intentionally or not. Maybe he set up a meeting.'

'Bit of a leap, isn't it?' Somerville looked sceptical.

'Maybe, but it makes sense,' Achebe said.

'Do we know where Rainey was when he made the call?' Caelan asked.

'Only just. He was at home in Northolt, or in the area, anyway,' Somerville told her.

'And Bryce?' Achebe wanted to know.

'Also at home. Hounslow. Bryce's SIM wasn't used again after that call either. He probably changed them regularly, if he was up to something dodgy,' said Somerville

'What if Bryce was told to come to us, to say there was a new dealer on the scene?' Achebe suggested.

Caelan frowned at him. 'Why?'

'Don't know. When you think about it, though, why would he do it otherwise? What was in it for him? We didn't pay him for the information. He wasn't trying to win Brownie points with us; he had no need to. Why bother?'

'You're giving me a headache.' Somerville rubbed her eyes. 'We have evidence proving Bryce talked to Rainey then denied knowing him, and no more.'

There was another silence, broken by Caelan.

'Then we need to go back to Ben Rainey's family and ask them why they lied about Ben and Bryce knowing each other.'

'Haven't you just said yourself parents don't know everything about their children's lives?' Achebe reminded her.

'Why don't you speak to Joseph Rainey again?' Somerville nodded at Caelan. 'You seem to get on well with him.' There was no bite in her tone, but Achebe shot her a look anyway.

Caelan smiled. 'Worth a try. I'll give him a call.'

'And I'll send someone to talk to Mrs Rainey. Maybe we should bring her in? She might be more open to talking if her husband's not there.' Achebe looked from Somerville to Caelan, then made the decision. 'No. I'll go and speak to her myself.'

Caelan listened to Joseph Rainey's phone ring, then his voicemail message. 'Joseph's not answering.' Unease stirred in her belly. Achebe picked up on it in her voice.

'He'll be okay,' he said. 'I'll head out there now, give him a nudge if he's there. Get him to call you back. Aaron Jacob and Frankie Hamilton will have to wait their turn.'

—

As Caelan stepped off the bus, she saw Joseph Rainey walking towards her, his hands tucked into the front pocket of his hoody.

'You're back.'

He said it without inflection, not sounding pleased to see her, but not irritated either.

'I am,' she agreed. 'Is there somewhere we can walk?'

He glanced left and right. 'It's just houses, maisonettes. It's not the Lake District.'

She laughed. 'Thought you might want to avoid being seen with me.'

Joseph smirked. 'By my crew?'

'Your crew?' She smiled, realising he was laughing at her, and possibly at himself. 'Your mates, I meant.'

She moved away, began to walk back towards the main road, hoping he would follow. After a second, he did.

'He send you?' Joseph asked.

'Who?'

Joseph tilted his head backwards, indicating the direction he had come from. 'The bloke who's sitting in our living room, chatting with my mum and eating my favourite biscuits.'

'DCI Achebe?'

'That his name?' He sniffed. 'What does he want?'

'It's about the phone, Joseph.'

He closed his eyes for a second, as if the words caused him pain. 'Shit. I knew it. Mum's going to kill me.' Realising what he'd said, he coughed. 'You know what I mean. You found something on it, then?'

Caelan stopped walking, ignoring the question, waiting until he met her eyes. 'Have you heard of someone called Marcus Crowley?'

Joseph drew his eyebrows together. 'No. Who's he?'

'Ben never mentioned him?'

'No, like I said. I've never heard the name.'

Caelan watched him closely as he spoke, detecting no hint of a lie, or omission.

'Okay,' she said.

Joseph ran a hand over his hair. 'That's all you wanted, to give me a name? See if I lied to you?' He pulled up his hood, scowling. 'If I knew it, I'd say so. This is my brother we're talking about. I knew anything, I'd tell you.'

'Like you did with the phone?' Caelan couldn't help saying. She began to walk again.

'Yeah, all right. I explained about that. So who's Marcus Crowley?'

'He's from north London.'

Joseph shot her a glance. 'Edmonton?'

'Why do you say that?'

'Because that's where Ben was found,' he answered immediately.

'Do you know anyone there?'

'No, I don't.' His voice was hard, impatient. 'Why would I? I live here, go to school around here. I don't know anyone in north London, the East End, or anywhere else.'

Caelan held up a hand. 'All right, no need to snap. What about your sister?'

'Miriam? You'd have to ask her. Doubt it, though. She spends most of her time in the library. Wants to be a doctor.'

Caelan caught the grudging admiration in his tone. 'And you?'

'Dunno. Something with computers. Police, maybe, like Ben. You always need geeks, don't you?'

'More and more,' Caelan agreed.

'I know one thing, though.' He lifted his chin, gazing around at the blocks of housing, his lip curled. 'I won't be staying around here once I'm working.'

'You don't like it?'

'It's a shithole, isn't it? No opportunities, not enough houses, no space. Traffic. Everyone on top of each other. I know people—'

He caught himself, closed his mouth.

'What were you going to say?' Caelan asked.

Joseph looked around, lowered his voice. 'It's easy to get caught up in stuff, is all I'm saying. Someone was stabbed not far from here last week. A kid from my school was arrested for it. A few days before it happened, he'd shown us the knife. Started carrying when his brother got jumped, beaten up.' He paused, shook his head. 'I'm not stupid. I know there are people around who could offer me opportunities, ways to make money. I'm not going to take them, though.'

'You're talking about a gang?'

His laugh was scornful. 'Have you been speaking to my dad? That's all he bangs on about. I don't need you to… Like, I said, I'm not stupid.'

'Can you give me any names?'

'No.' He quickened his pace. 'No names, no specifics.'

'What about Anthony Bryce?'

He made a noise of exasperation. 'Someone else I've told you I've never heard of. Getting boring now.'

'Your brother knew him. Bryce denied they'd ever spoken after Ben was killed, then was murdered himself. If you know anything about him, Joseph, now's the time to speak up.'

'How do you know they knew each other?' He sounded curious, not worried or concerned.

Caelan explained what they had found on the phone. 'If you can help…'

Joseph said nothing. Caelan allowed the silence to grow, hoping he would fill it, but he stayed quiet. They turned into a street of semi-detached properties, some run-down, most well maintained.

'You know what it's like to grow up somewhere like this?' Joseph spoke in a voice not much above a whisper.

'Well, I lived on a council estate when I was younger, but…'

He smiled. 'But not like ours.'

'No.' Caelan wasn't about to go into details.

'You see, Ben was different. He had a goal, and he went for it. Unusual, around here. It's not bad, not as rough as some places, but still, he was a police officer. A Fed.' Joseph grinned, though again, whether he was poking fun at her or himself, Caelan wasn't sure.

'You've got good parents, a stable home. It helps,' she said.

'But it's not always enough. And if you don't have that, the protection of a family... There are people willing to provide it.' He glanced around again. 'You see the kid in the distance?'

Caelan didn't turn her head. 'On the bike?'

'Yeah. Know what's in his bag?'

'What?' She had a good idea.

'I'm guessing it's not his homework. He's ten, eleven? And he's already running errands for his older brother. Making deliveries, collecting stuff. Passing on information. No one notices a kid on a BMX.'

'Except you.'

'Come on, this isn't news. People on bikes or mopeds have been stealing from people all over London, you know that. Taking stuff, or else delivering it. My mum and dad might think they can protect us. Like we're clever, got our heads on right. We won't get involved. But this shit is all around.'

Caelan nodded. 'What are you saying?'

'I'm saying, sometimes you get caught up in a web, only you don't see it until it's too late.' He ran his palm over his mouth.

'Are you talking about yourself?'

'No. Not me. People I know. I could maybe... ask around, you know? See if anyone knows Anthony Bryce, and the other one, Crowley? If they're so important to you.'

Caelan was already shaking her head.

'I can't allow you to do that, Joseph.'

He scowled. 'Because I'm a kid.'

'Because I'm paid to talk to people, to take risks. You're not.'

'Risks?' A snort. 'What risks?'

Caelan looked at him, taking in the defiant eyes, the set jaw. 'You know what I mean. These aren't people you can approach for a chat. They're willing to kill to get what they want.'

'Which is?'

'If I knew, I wouldn't be standing here.'

He scowled again, chewing on his bottom lip. 'You do it.'

'What?'

'Ask questions. Wouldn't matter if it was a harmless old lady or a serial killer, you'd have to talk to them, wouldn't you?'

'Yeah, because it's my—'

'Job?' he sneered. 'Yeah, that's what Ben always said. What a fucking superhero. Doesn't make him any less dead, though, does it?' He turned away, shoulders heaving.

'You want to help, I get that,' Caelan said softly. 'But you're what? Fourteen? Even if you were an adult, this isn't your job. If you can give me information now, please do. Otherwise…'

He turned. 'What? You're leaving? The conversation's over?'

Caelan shrugged. 'Yeah. You've answered my questions.'

'Are you going to our house?'

'No.'

'Why's your boss there?'

'He's not my boss.'

Joseph waved a hand. 'You're a sergeant, aren't you? He's a DCI.'

She smiled. 'Goodbye, Joseph.'

'Wait a second.' He moved towards her. 'Don't go that way.'

'What?' She looked at him, watching him wrap his arms around his body.

'Trust me. If anyone's seen you talking to me, if you were followed here…'

He was alert, ready to bolt away.

'What are you talking about? What have you seen?' Caelan demanded. 'No one followed me.'

'How do you know?'

'I do. Part of my training.'

His face relaxed, his smile smug. 'I knew it. You're not an ordinary copper, are you? You're Special Branch or something. That's what changing your hair and stuff was about. You're sniffing around, and you don't want people to know who you are.'

Caelan's stomach lurched. He'd tricked her, and she'd fallen for it like an amateur. 'I'm a detective, that's why I'm in plain clothes. It helps if we don't stand out a mile when we're working.'

'Yeah, yeah. Maybe you should have left your hair brown then.'

'Joseph...'

He grinned. 'Don't worry, I'll keep my mouth shut about you. But I'll ask around.'

Caelan stepped close, touched his arm. Lowering her voice, she made a last attempt to reason with him. 'Come on, Joseph. People have already died.'

'Yeah, I remember.' He blinked rapidly, refusing to look at her. 'Wonder why? I'll be discreet.'

'Don't. Please.'

'What are you going to do, arrest me?'

He sauntered away, clearly pleased with himself. Caelan thought about calling him back; decided there was no point. She would speak to Achebe, and hope Joseph had the sense to leave the whole mess alone.

–

Back at South Harrow police station, Tim Achebe and Jen Somerville were waiting in the incident room when Caelan arrived back.

'Mrs Rainey couldn't tell me anything,' said Achebe.

'Neither could Joseph.'

Achebe exhaled sharply, as though he'd been punched. 'Great. So we've totally wasted a couple of hours.'

'And Joseph is now threatening to play detective,' Caelan said.

Achebe stared. 'What?'

She told him.

'Where did he get Special Branch from?'

'I've no idea, but it's potentially a problem. He knows my real name. If he mentions this to anyone with connections in Edmonton…'

Achebe groaned. 'Fuck. What do we do?'

'Other than lock him up?'

'We could ask his parents to ground him,' Somerville said.

'Or we could solve the fucking case and get whoever killed his brother behind bars.' Achebe looked at Somerville. 'You ready to talk to Aaron Jacob again?'

She bared her teeth. 'Let's go.'

—

Caelan followed Achebe into the observation room adjacent to the interview suite where Aaron Jacob was waiting. He sat at the small, grimy table with his head bowed. In his threadbare grey sweatshirt and jogging bottoms, cheap plimsolls on his feet, he looked like a schoolboy. It was difficult to believe he had ever been in a fight at all, much less been convicted of GBH. Beside him sat another man, wearing a suit and scrolling on his phone. His solicitor, Caelan assumed. Eventually Jacob looked up at the camera high in the corner, wiping his face with his sleeve. He was slim, pale, looked exhausted and feeble. Under the harsh light, sweat was already beading along his upper lip, Caelan noted.

Achebe settled in a chair, and she sat beside him.

'Did we hear any more about Ben Rainey's fingerprints being found in the hotel in Hackney? Any clue why he was there?' she asked, keeping her voice low.

Achebe shook his head. 'Not yet. Something else that makes no sense.' He looked at her. 'Maybe he just liked paying for it.'

'Has Liv Hobbs been asked about it?'

'Liv? Why?'

'She worked at the same station as Rainey, didn't she? Limehouse? If Rainey was into prostitutes, someone would have known.'

'Not something you chat about on your tea break, though, is it?'

'But you know what police stations are like. There are no secrets.'

'No one's mentioned it to Liv, and we can't now, not after the news we gave her this morning.' Achebe sat up, gesturing at the monitors. 'Here we go.'

They watched Jen Somerville clatter into the interview room, followed by the male officer Caelan had seen her with earlier, the one Joseph Rainey had taken a dislike to. The solicitor checked his watch, put his phone away. Somerville threw herself into the nearest chair, while her colleague straightened his jacket and brushed off his trousers before taking his own seat. They started the recording equipment, asked Aaron Jacob to confirm his name, address and date of birth before introducing themselves. Somerville's colleague was DC Sebastian Gill. Caelan watched him run a hand over his hair as Somerville leaned towards Jacob.

'Afternoon, Aaron.' Somerville gave an insincere smile. 'How are you doing?'

'Fine,' he mumbled.

'Ready to talk to us yet?'

'No comment.'

Somerville blew out her cheeks. 'Still like that, is it?'

'Come on, Aaron.' Gill leaned forward, elbows on the table. 'Talk to us. What happened between you and Jackson Hobbs?'

Aaron Jacob sniffed. 'Nothing.'

'Nothing? Were you friends?' Gill waited. 'Aaron?'

'No. I'd never spoken to him.' Jacob glanced at his solicitor, who nodded.

'Are those your clothes?' Gill nodded towards Jacob. He scowled.

'You know they're not. Nothing's your own in prison.'

'But they're not the clothes you put on when you got up this morning, are they?' Gill tapped a fingernail on the table. 'What happened to those?'

Jacob sneered. 'Like you don't know. You've got them.'

'Correct. See, it's not so difficult, is it? We ask the questions, you give us the answers, and we'll all be home by dinner time. Oh.' Gill feigned a look of embarrassment. 'Some of us will. You'll be going back to prison – for the rest your life this time.'

Caelan saw Jacob's Adam's apple bob as he swallowed, but there was no other reaction.

'Your clothes from earlier today are covered in blood, Aaron,' Gill continued. 'Whose is it?'

'No comment.'

'Is it yours? Did you cut yourself shaving? Must have been a nasty nick.' Pausing, Gill narrowed his eyes. 'A man stabbed to death on your wing, and your clothes are soaked in blood. Doesn't take Hercule Poirot to figure out what happened, does it?'

'I wouldn't know.' Jacob sat up straighter, his eyes fixed on a spot above Gill's head.

'We're running tests on it. Shouldn't be long before we're able to confirm it came from Jackson Hobbs.'

Jacob didn't react.

'Who told you to do it, Aaron?' Jen Somerville spoke gently. She was ignored.

'We'll find out anyway,' said Gill. 'We're talking to every lowlife in the prison. Funny what people will tell you if there's something in it for them.'

'Is that what happened? Were you offered something in return for killing Jackson Hobbs?'

'No comment.'

Gill grinned. 'Or maybe a threat was made. You've a GBH conviction; you know about violence, don't you?'

The solicitor frowned. 'Is this relevant?'

'I'd say so. I'd say it proves your client is a man who's prone to vicious assaults when crossed. Just the sort of person you'd want to take an enemy out for you,' said Gill.

'The GBH was... The bloke hit me first. I pushed him, swung a punch... Next thing I knew, he was on the ground, and I kicked him. I don't...' Jacob's voice was choked. 'I lost it. I'd never done anything like it before, never even been in a fight. I still can't believe I did it.'

'And yet you did.' Gill stared at Jacob again. 'Who is it? Who are you willing to shoulder a life sentence for?'

'What did they promise you?' Somerville asked again.

'Or who did they threaten?' Gill paused. 'You've got a young daughter, haven't you? Did they say they'd come after her?'

Jacob blinked, but didn't speak. Caelan could see the indecision in his face, the urge to confess fighting the fear of what would happen if he did.

'Who else?' Gill went on. 'Did they say they'd kill your mum? Your nan? Your dog?'

'We can protect them, Aaron. We can protect *you*.' Somerville met Jacob's eyes. 'Help us understand what happened. Your family will be safe, there'll be no repercussions.'

'I really think—' the solicitor began.

'You don't know what you're talking about.' Jacob's chin was up, defiance, fear and tears in his eyes.

'Then tell us,' Somerville urged.

'Who are you working for?' Gill had softened his tone, his eyes on Jacob's.

'I can't tell you.' It was a whimper.

'Let me remind you that you're looking at the rest of your life in jail, Aaron. This is your chance to do yourself a favour. You were coerced, forced to kill Hobbs. Tell us what happened, and we can help.'

Gill didn't move. Somerville was silent. In the observation room, Achebe folded his arms.

'Keep pushing,' he muttered. 'It was the mention of his daughter that got to him. Use it.'

Aaron Jacob's hands were over his face, sobs choking him.

'I can't tell you, because I don't know,' he managed to say. Somerville and Gill stared at him, uncomprehending. Sitting beside Caelan, Achebe groaned.

'What do you mean?' Gill demanded.

Jacob stared at them, his cheeks wet, his eyes puffy. 'I spoke to my girlfriend on the phone, and she said my cousin wanted to talk to me urgently. I called him. He said someone had pushed an envelope through his door. Inside was a photo of my daughter in her paddling pool.' He gulped. 'There was a note. It said... it said I had to get rid of Jackson Hobbs, otherwise they'd take her and sell her. Said they knew people who'd pay thousands for a pretty little blonde girl.'

In the observation room, Achebe said, 'Jesus. Fuckers.'

'If anything was going to work…' Caelan felt sick. Whoever was behind this, they had chosen their target with hideous efficiency. Aaron Jacob, locked away, powerless, would have felt he had no choice but to do as he was ordered. Caelan knew only too well that there were people around who would follow up such a threat without thinking twice.

'I knew I had to do it,' Jacob whispered. 'I wasn't going to be there to protect her. She's three, for fuck's sake. A baby. I had no choice.'

'You had this conversation on the phone, while you were in prison?' said Gill, showing no emotion. 'No one heard you, none of the staff were listening in?'

Jacob snorted. 'You think they've the time? That place has half the staff it should have. Listening to our calls isn't exactly a priority.'

Gill said, 'The conversation wasn't recorded either, then? Handy for you.'

Jacob pressed his lips together, ignoring the comment, though his eyes were blazing.

'All right, Aaron.' Somerville exchanged a glance with Gill. 'Thank you for telling us. I assume your cousin was told to destroy the note and the photograph?'

A nod. 'He had to burn them as soon as he'd read the note. And he did, or so he said.'

'What's your cousin's name?' Achebe prompted his officers. He was becoming restless. 'We can find out, but it'll be quicker if he tells us.'

Somerville asked the question. Jacob froze, pressing his lips together.

'Come on, Aaron, you must have realised we'd want to talk to him,' Gill said. 'You need to give us a name. How do we know you're not making all this up to save your own skin?'

Fury darkened Jacob's pale blue eyes. 'How fucking dare you? You think I'd make up twisted shit like that involving my own daughter?'

Gill shrugged. 'I don't know what you'd do, or what you'd say. You know we'll be able to track this cousin down anyway. It'll be something else the judge might look on in your favour, if you help us out again.'

Jacob looked mutinous. The solicitor cleared his throat, spoke into his client's ear. Jacob blew out his cheeks.

'All right. First, though, I want you to promise he won't face any charges.'

Gill touched his index finger to his lips, looked at Somerville. She was stony-faced. 'Tell us his name, Aaron. Last chance.'

'Fine. Might as well. I'm fucked anyway.' He pressed his hands to his cheeks. 'Ryan Glennister.'

'Where does he live?' Somerville asked.

'Don't know. He moves around a lot. What do they call it? No fixed address.'

'So which letter box did this mysterious envelope get pushed through?' Gill placed his hands palms down on the table, leaning towards Jacob. 'If you're lying to us...'

'I don't know, I'm just telling you what he told me.' Jacob's eyes were panicked; he clearly hadn't thought about the discrepancy with his cousin's address. 'Maybe he has a regular doss house. Like I said, I don't know.'

'But he does live in London?' Gill pressed.

Jacob blinked at him. 'Yeah, course he does.'

Somerville held up a hand. 'We'll find him, see if his story matches yours.

In the observation room, Achebe stood. 'I think we've heard enough.'

'Do you believe his story?' Caelan followed Achebe out of the room.

'Yeah, I think so. He caved pretty quickly in the end.' He rubbed his jaw. 'You think that could be significant?'

'I think he was telling the truth.'

Achebe logged into the nearest computer. 'Let's see if this Ryan Glennister has a record.'

As they waited, a uniformed officer approached.

'Sir, I'm sorry to interrupt, but I've just had a call...' She hesitated. Achebe looked up, smiled.

'No problem. What is it?'

'DI Hobbs's husband is at the front desk, sir. I'm told he's demanding to see you.'

Now Achebe was frowning. 'Adam? What does he want?'

'Don't know, sir, but I'm told he's insistent.'

'Okay. Will you ask them to take him to my office, please?' The officer nodded, scurried away. Achebe turned back to the computer screen and scanned it. 'We've nothing on this Ryan Glennister anyway. Jen Somerville will be straight on to the search for him when the interview's over. We need to find him fast.'

Caelan understood. 'And not only because he might be able to help us. Because he's potentially at risk now Jackson Hobbs is dead.'

'Exactly. He's a loose end, and we know how they've been dealt with so far.'

She was following Achebe towards his office, wondering why Adam Waits was here, half expecting Achebe to tell her it was none of her business. In the end, though, Waits rounded a corner in front of them, closely pursued by another uniform.

'Where's my wife?' he bellowed, barrelling towards them.

Achebe stopped, held up both hands. 'What are you talking about, Adam?'

Waits stood glaring at them. 'If she's back at work...'

Achebe's face showed his incomprehension. 'Listen, mate, there's been a misunderstanding. I haven't seen Liv since we came to tell her about Jackson this morning. I haven't even spoken to her on the phone. I planned to give her a call this evening, see how she was doing, but...' Waits was shaking his head, clearly not believing a word of it. 'Look, let's go into my office and talk about this, shall we?' Achebe tried to take Waits's arm, but the other man shrugged him off.

'I just want to know where she is, that she's safe.' He folded his arms.

Fear clutched at Caelan's gut. Edmonton, she thought. Liv Hobbs had been in Edmonton.

Waits pointed a finger at her. 'She hasn't been the same since you came to the house, telling her the accident was deliberate. Do you have any idea how worried she's been? No, of course not. You just breeze in and fill her head full of nonsense, then go back to playing cops and robbers.' He stared at Caelan as if seeing her for the first time. 'Who are you, anyway?'

Achebe had reached his office and was beckoning them inside. Waits glared at him as he stalked down the corridor.

'This job is her life, you know. I know she hates being off work, and I thought...' All at once, as he reached Achebe's office door, Waits looked defeated. 'I don't know where else she would go.' He slumped into a chair. 'She was going to see her parents, wanted to find out if they would talk to her. According to them, she never arrived. She's not answering her phone, none of her friends have heard from her...'

Achebe had his mobile in his hand. 'When did you last see her?'

'This morning.' Waits glanced at his watch. 'Hours ago. Shit...' He groaned. 'Where the hell is she?'

'Let's not panic.' Achebe sounded as if he was trying to reassure himself. 'I'll get an alert put out.'

'She's pregnant,' said Waits softly. He rubbed his eyes. 'I should have gone with her, but she didn't want me to. I should have insisted, stayed with her.'

Caelan realised why he had been so protective when she had visited their house. Not just because his wife had been involved in a car accident, but because of their unborn child.

'Liv's expecting a baby?' Achebe was staring at Waits.

'We only did the test at the weekend, had it confirmed by the doctor. Six weeks. I wanted her to tell you, then she had the accident, and we were so worried... We couldn't believe it; we've been trying for years, had given up hope, and now...' He swallowed, staring up at Achebe. 'Find her. Please.'

Caelan moved towards the door, knowing she should be out on the streets. Jackson Hobbs was dead, and now his sister was missing. It couldn't be a coincidence.

Her eyes met Achebe's, and she didn't need to say where she was going to start the search.

Edmonton.

22

Ryan opened his eyes, lifted his head. As agony rocketed along his battered jaw, he wished he hadn't bothered. Where the hell was he? Someone's living room, lying on his back on a sofa. He sat, looked around. Nice place. Huge TV hanging above the fireplace. Wooden flooring, and not cheap laminate either. Proper stuff. Not the kind of house his mates could usually afford. He had no idea how he'd come to be here, but for now, he wasn't complaining. After Mulligan had thrown him out, he'd wandered around for a while, then met up with some friends and borrowed enough money to buy a couple of rocks. They'd ended up in a pub, then a squat with a few bottles of vodka. Then his memories of the previous evening became hazy.

He got to his feet, head aching, mouth dry, and tottered over to the window. No clues out there; just grey sky, parked cars, and a row of terraced houses across the street.

The house was silent. He crossed the room, stuck his head into the hallway. Nothing. In the kitchen, a similar story. He opened a couple of cupboards, all well stocked, filling his pockets with chocolate bars and crisps. He ran the tap and took a few gulps of water, then stood and listened.

Silence.

He swallowed, his throat still parched despite the water. Where was he? Who had brought him here? He stepped over to the back door, tried the handle. Locked, and there was no sign of the key. An ache in his stomach, damp palms. He hurried into the hallway, tried the front door. Locked.

A thud from upstairs.

Ryan heard himself gulp. Someone was up there, and he didn't want to hang around to find out who it was. He moved quickly, quietly, and tried to open the nearest living room window. Locked. He let out a hiss of frustration between his teeth. Upstairs, a door opened. He heard footsteps on the landing. He ran to the second window. Locked, and no sign of the key.

'Ryan?'

It was Mulligan. Ryan froze as he strode into the living room wearing a navy towelling dressing gown.

'You're awake then. Make us a cup of tea, would you? I've been awake all night, entertaining one of the new girls. Punters are going to love her. She's still upstairs, if you fancy a go.' Mulligan began to cough, fumbling in the pocket of his robe and bringing out a packet of cigarettes. He lit one, watching Ryan as he did so. 'What?'

Ryan took a step backwards, sensing a trick. 'I didn't know where I was.'

Mulligan snorted. 'Nothing new there then, wee man. Pal of mine saw you last night, said you were barely standing. I thought it best to have you brought here, where I could keep an eye on you.'

Blinking, Ryan tried to make sense of this. Mulligan wouldn't have done it out of concern for his welfare. And offering him a girl? What was his game? 'I thought you weren't happy with me.'

Mulligan nodded towards Ryan's face. 'You mean that? You pissed me off, I lashed out. All forgotten now, though, eh?'

Except my jaw's killing me, Ryan thought. 'Okay.'

'Anyway, you did something right for a change. Happy days.' Mulligan smiled. 'Where's my tea?'

In the kitchen, out of sight and under the noise of the kettle coming to the boil, Ryan hurriedly shoved all the food he'd taken back into the cupboards, praying Mulligan would stay where he was. He had seen him in this mood before, and it was no less dangerous than one of his rages. Best to make his tea, and try to get out of here. Was this Mulligan's house? He boasted of owning different properties, but Ryan had never visited any of them.

A bellow from the other room. 'Come on, man, I'm gasping here!'

Ryan slopped milk into the mug. Mulligan had his phone out, jabbing at the screen. Ryan waited, holding the handle out towards Mulligan, trying to ignore the scalding heat assaulting his fingertips. Mulligan looked up, saw what was happening, and went back to his phone with a smile. Ryan swallowed. Two more seconds, he told himself. Finally, Mulligan reached out and took the cup.

'Cheers, pal.' He took a slurp. 'Not made one for yourself?'

'No. I didn't...'

'What? Didn't dare?' Mulligan grinned.

'Didn't like to.'

'Wise man.' They heard a knock, and Mulligan inclined his head. 'Here's your lift.'

Ryan stared. 'What?'

'I've given you a bed for the night; now it's time for you to leave.' Mulligan raised his mug in a mock toast. 'Safe travels.'

23

She saw him as she stepped into South Harrow Underground station. He was leaning against the wall, wearing a dark overcoat and a pair of black-framed glasses. At least he wasn't hiding behind a newspaper with eyeholes cut into it, Caelan thought as he came towards her. She allowed him to lead her out back outside as though their meeting had been planned, neither of them speaking until they were away from the station, standing outside an estate agent's premises. Penrith leaned towards the window as if viewing the properties on display, while Caelan half turned, keeping an eye on the street.

'We need to talk,' Penrith said.

'There's me thinking you were going to buy me a coffee.'

He rounded on her. 'I've been told to bring you in.'

Whatever Caelan had been expecting, it wasn't this. Taking her off the case, reassigning her? 'What are you talking about?'

'Come on, Caelan. You've ruffled feathers, stuck your nose in. Stepped out of line.'

'Are you going to get to the point, or keep spouting clichés at me?' She folded her arms, her mind working. Had he been told already that Joseph Rainey was planning to do some digging? 'Let me guess. You've spoken to Tim Achebe?'

'I've heard DI Hobbs has gone AWOL, yes. Last seen in Edmonton.' Penrith turned his head, meeting Caelan's eyes. 'Who told you to contact the young lad again? Rainey's brother?'

'No one *told* me to. Jen Somerville suggested it, but…'

Penrith looked away, giving a sharp nod as though she had confirmed what he already knew. 'We've handled this badly. *You've* handled this badly. Breezing into police stations, into the homes of people related to the case, dressed like someone who's off to the pub. Unprofessional. Some would say downright stupid. People have noticed you.' He tipped back his head, looking up at the sky. 'We don't know what's happened to DI Hobbs, but if her disappearance is linked to your disregard for procedure, I'm not sure I'll be able to save you.'

Caelan forced herself to remain calm. 'What are you talking about? Save me from what?'

'You think Assistant Commissioner Beckett isn't aware of what's going on? She's watching us more closely than ever. None of us is indispensable, even you, the officer she's dragged back from leave twice when only you could save the world.' He sniffed. 'Didn't work, did it? You've raised lots more questions, but not answered any, and now you've dragged a teenage boy into the mess.'

'I think Joseph was dragged in when his brother was murdered, don't you?'

'And when he concealed evidence.'

'Which he gave to me because he trusted me, and not DCI Achebe's officers.'

'It's not a point-scoring exercise, Caelan.'

'Considering that Nicky, Richard and I were sent in with no real brief or direction, I think we've done okay. We've brought you names, leads. How's Richard doing?'

Penrith was rummaging in his coat pocket. He brought out a handkerchief and blew his nose. 'He's banged up with the former cellmate of Aaron Jacob.'

'Has he heard anything?'

'Give him a chance, he's only just arrived. Apart from a lot of farting and shouting, I doubt it.'

'What's being done to find Liv Hobbs? How do we know she hasn't just gone to see a friend or decided to do some shopping?'

'We don't, but her husband's insistent she wouldn't have changed her plans without at least sending him a text. She never arrived at her parents' house. Achebe's got a full-scale search in progress.' Penrith raised his eyebrows. 'After Rainey and Bryce, let's hope she's in one piece when she turns up.'

'If someone wants information from her...' Caelan didn't give her brain the time to imagine the scene. 'You know she's pregnant?'

'Achebe said.'

'I saw her this morning.' Caelan explained, and Penrith gave an exaggerated roll of his eyes.

'Did she see you?' he asked.

'I made sure she didn't. Does she know about the operation continuing in Edmonton? I know she was involved in the early stages.'

'She shouldn't.' Penrith paused. 'She knew Rainey, didn't she?'

'To say hello to, I was told.'

'She's Jackson Hobbs' sister, she knew Ben Rainey, and she was involved in the drugs op in Edmonton. Now she's disappeared.' He clicked his tongue. 'I don't like it.'

'Me neither, and DCI Achebe was horrified.'

'Well he might be. They're trying to trace her phone. I'll let you know if they find pieces of her body next to it.' Penrith turned to face her. 'Go to Edmonton. I'm trusting you here, going against explicit orders to take you off the case. I want Liv Hobbs home in time for cocoa.'

'Right. Are we being issued with magic wands now?'

Penrith wasn't amused. 'You're supposed to be the best we have. Prove it. Achebe's officers are talking to your boyfriend, Frankie Hamilton. He'll be on his way back to Edmonton soon enough. I want to know what he's up to.'

'Has he told us anything?'

'Not yet, and I doubt he will, since we don't know what questions to ask. We'll ask him about DI Hobbs, but we don't want a missing police officer to be lead story on tonight's news.' Penrith glanced at his watch.

'What about Nicky? Have you spoken to her?' Caelan didn't want to have to talk to Nicky herself. The current situation was complicated enough.

'She's been informed. She's watching Marcus Crowley's snooker club.'

Caelan pounced. 'Then you do think he's involved?'

'Not necessarily, but he's worth keeping on the radar because of his potential drug interests, and the possibility of gang involvement, even if it was a while ago. Sounds like he's shady enough to justify our time.'

'Has Crowley spoken to anyone about me yet?'

'I don't know. If he does, he'll be told what he wants to hear.'

Penrith's phone began to ring. He pulled it from his coat pocket, checked the screen. 'Achebe,' he told Caelan, then spoke into the phone. 'Tim? Any news?'

Caelan watched his face, though she could tell nothing from his expression. When he put the phone away, she said, 'Well?'

'They traced DI Hobbs's phone to an area of Edmonton, and have just had a vanload of uniforms out searching. They found it in a skip.'

Caelan blinked at him. This was not good news. 'A skip?'

'Outside a house, on top of a roll of carpet. Seventeen missed calls from her husband, several from Tim Achebe and Jen Somerville, but no sign of DI Hobbs herself. They're pulling whatever CCTV they can from the surrounding area, but it's mainly residential. There won't be much.'

'Didn't any of the locals see anything?'

'Door-to-door's ongoing, but most of them are out, probably at work.' Penrith pursed his lips. 'I think we have to assume she got into a vehicle, either of her own free will, or she was forced to.'

Caelan nodded. Horrible though the thought was, it made sense. 'Or she's in one of the houses. I was hoping she'd gone to see a friend, forgotten the time and not charged her phone, but now that it's been found…'

'You don't leave your phone behind unless you're forced to.' Penrith looked grim. 'Hobbs is an adult, not to mention a police officer. She knows better than to go off with strangers.'

'But if it were someone she recognised, or they seemed to recognise her…' Caelan thought about it. 'No, I think she must have been forced. She would have done as she was told to protect the baby.'

Penrith rocked back on his heels. 'We're wasting time. Extra officers have been drafted in to look for Liv Hobbs, and the tech people are seeing if there's anything on her phone or computer that could help us. We're questioning her parents, her other brother, and anyone her husband can remember her mentioning from Edmonton. I don't have to remind you what happened to Ben Rainey and Anthony Bryce. We don't want a repeat performance.'

'If they know she's a police officer, which they no doubt do, they must think she can tell them something, especially considering the link to her brother.'

Frowning, Penrith checked his watch again. 'They'll probably use Jackson's death as a warning; point out how even locked away in prison they were able to get to him.' He sucked his teeth. 'This is a nightmare. Go and see what you can do. I'll phone when I know more.'

–

Nicky Sturgess was tired and cold, the brick wall she was leaning against leeching the warmth from her bones. She dug her hands deeper into her jacket pockets, hunching her shoulders and tucking her chin into her collar. She had been waiting for a couple of hours in an alley opposite the snooker hall Penrith had ordered her to watch, and no one had left or entered. Why she was here, she'd no idea, but Penrith had been insistent. Something to do with Caelan, he'd said. The familiar ache echoed around Nicky's chest as she thought about her colleague, her former lover. She had hurt Caelan, and damaged their relationship beyond repair, and she couldn't forgive herself. It was true that when she had gone into hiding she had been following the commands she had been given, but she knew Caelan was right. She should have told her, trusted her. Caelan would not have let her down. Nicky had spent long hours berating herself for her stupidity, for allowing her ambition and concern for her career to blind her to what was truly important. If the situation had been reversed, if Beckett had told Caelan she was being removed to a safe house for her own safety, that her family and friends would be informed of her death, Caelan would have told the Assistant Commissioner where to go. But Nicky had taken a familiar route – passivity. As she had so often in her life, she had simply done as she was told.

After the attack that had supposedly ended Nicky's life, Caelan had run to her, bloodied and battered, cradling what she had believed to be Nicky's dead body. And Nicky had lain there, played dead, allowing Caelan to be dragged away, weeping, by their colleagues. Caelan was the only person who had ever seen past the persona Nicky had worn at work, the one she had always worn for her family, and loved her – the *real* her.

And she, Nicky, had destroyed everything.

She wasn't stupid. She knew she had betrayed Caelan in the most devastating way possible. They could never go back, not now, and Nicky had begun to accept it. She had offered her resignation to Ian Penrith, then to Assistant Commissioner Beckett. Both had refused to even read the letter. Her request for a transfer had been ignored. She rubbed her eyes with chilly fingers. She was beginning to hate the job. Having realised who she really was, becoming someone else during working hours was increasingly impossible. And it wasn't just a job, as she knew only too well. It was a way of life, one that devoured every other interest, hobby or even relationship. In Caelan she had found someone who truly understood. Now she had wrecked their chance, and she was coping in the only way she knew – by working, and not thinking.

Movement across the street. Two men, walking in her direction with purpose. Remembering Caelan's description of the men who had grabbed her, Nicky slid her hands from her pockets, adjusting her position so she was ready to move if necessary. She had chosen her vantage point carefully, and she knew she could back along the alley and join a busier street if she judged it necessary. The men weren't chatting or laughing, and the skin on her forearms tingled. She stepped back, no longer able to see them, turned, and moved quickly. She was probably being ridiculous, but the news about the disappearance of Liv Hobbs had rattled her even more than the attack on Caelan had. She felt like an amateur, as though she had never been out in the field alone before.

She darted silently down the alley and walked to the bottom of the adjoining street. Approaching the corner nearest the snooker club with caution, she leaned forward just enough to be able to see around it. The men were standing outside, one smoking, the other concentrating on his mobile. Nicky slid her own phone out of her pocket, made certain the flash was turned off, and took a photograph. Stepping back, she sent it to Penrith so he could forward it to Caelan, then deleted the picture. It wasn't the best quality, but it was good enough to make out their faces. They were probably just going for a game of snooker, but Penrith had wanted to know about everyone who went into the place.

Back at her post in the alley, she watched as the smoker flicked his cigarette butt into the gutter. As they disappeared through the hall's entry door, Nicky wondered whether she should follow them inside. Her phone was still in her hand, and she decided to request instructions.

'No,' Penrith told her immediately. 'Why would a woman go into a place like that alone? You'd arouse suspicion.'

'But Caelan didn't?' Nicky didn't care if he heard her irritation.

'She was invited there. You haven't been.'

'Would you say the same to Richard?'

He ignored the question. 'I asked you to watch the place, not go barging in. Hang around for a while longer. I want to know if Marcus Crowley arrives.'

He ended the call, leaving Nicky furious. She didn't have Caelan's number, or she would have called her, demanded to know if she recognised the men. There was no reason why they should be the same people who had grabbed Caelan, but the descriptions fitted, they were here in Edmonton, and they weren't carrying snooker cues.

Hunching her shoulders, Nicky blew on her hands, promising herself she would only wait for another hour.

—

Liv Hobbs opened her eyes to darkness, the pain in her head excruciating. She was quiet, listening, fear choking her throat, her heartbeat rocketing. She tried to remember where she was, what had happened, but came up blank. A hazy wisp of memory, walking down a street, familiar but blurred. Footsteps close behind her. Had she stumbled? She didn't know. Then, with startling clarity, she remembered.

The baby.

She tried to move her right arm, but it was restrained, as was her left. Her feet wouldn't move either, and she realised she had been bound to a chair. She tried to call out, but her mouth was taped. Panic filled her mind, flooded her body. She braced her feet and bucked. The chair screeched against the floor, but she was stuck, and she knew that if she tipped the chair over, if she fell, she wouldn't be able to get up again. And – the same thought that had been a constant in her mind since they had found out for sure she was pregnant – she might harm the baby. Maybe whatever she had been drugged with had already done so.

She closed her eyes, then opened them wide and told herself to focus. Fighting the restraints was not going to help. She had to think, to figure out who had brought her here, and why. Ben Rainey and Anthony Bryce had been bound to chairs, she knew, and she had no intention of ending up like them. She owed it to her unborn child to get out of this alive.

Concentrating on breathing as evenly as possible through her nose, she looked around. The room was dark, but not completely. Her eyes were quickly adjusting, and she could make out shapes in the gloom. Where was she? She could smell petrol. A garage? A workshop? Or just a building by a road? She could hear the low hum of traffic, but it didn't sound close. Was she still in Edmonton? There was no way of knowing.

She sniffed, tears gathering in her eyes. She blinked them away. Crying wouldn't help either. She needed to be strong, for the baby she carried, and for herself. If the people who had brought her here were the same ones who had tortured and killed Ben Rainey and Anthony Bryce, her chances of leaving this place alive seemed slim. But she couldn't allow her thoughts to rampage out of control. She was the sister of Jackson Hobbs, and though she was a police officer, she knew more than she had admitted about his business activities. It wasn't much, but might it be enough?

Perhaps now was the time to begin to share her knowledge. Jackson was dead, and if spilling her guts meant she would live, then she would share what she knew with whoever was asking the questions.

The time for loyalty was over.

She remained still, hearing the rattle and clink of a metal chain, possibly a padlock being unlocked. Terror grabbed her gut again, but she lifted her chin. Whoever was about to confront her, they would be expecting a cowed and frightened prisoner. They were in for a surprise.

There were two of them. Though the room was still in darkness, she could tell from the footsteps, from the sniffs and shuffling. Then a torch was clicked on, the sudden light shockingly bright, cutting through the gloom, blinding Liv for a second. She couldn't see the person who was wielding the torch, just their hand, wearing a black leather glove.

'You're awake.' A male voice, the accent local. Confused, Liv realised he sounded nervous. The beam of the torch was pointed to the ground and she heard him step towards her. 'I'm going to take the tape off your mouth. If you scream, or speak other than to answer my questions, you'll be drugged again, and this time you won't wake up.' He swallowed audibly. 'Understood?' The torch played over Liv's face, and she nodded. 'Remember what I told you,' he said.

Liv braced herself, but he was gentle, peeling the tape away as though removing a plaster from a child's grazed knee. The beam of the torch was in her eyes, still blinding, and she closed them. 'You know you're making a—' she began.

The slap stung her cheek, though it wasn't hard, more of a warning. Liv pressed her lips together, furious.

'You were told not to speak. Last chance. You're Liv Hobbs, yeah?'

'You know I am.' To Liv's satisfaction, her voice was strong, almost defiant. She would not allow them to see how frightened she was.

'And you're a police officer?'

'Detective inspector, as you'll be aware if you've done your homework.' Liv resisted the temptation to say more. If they wanted answers, let them work for them. She narrowed her eyes, trying to peer past the powerful torch beam. Who was the second person? She could see a vague outline, but no more.

'You know your brother's dead?' The voice didn't change. There was no triumph, no gloating. Just a simple statement of fact.

Liv swallowed, forced herself to reply. 'I've been informed.'

'Want to know who killed him?'

'It's no secret. Geezer on his wing.' Keeping her tone casual, conversational cost Liv dearly. She wanted to scream at them, demand to know what they thought they were doing, what they wanted. She wondered what they knew. What did they expect *her* to know? And if they brought out an iron, or a kettle of boiling water, what was she supposed to do?

24

Caelan glanced at her phone as she emerged from Edmonton Green station. With her thumb, she tapped out a reply to Penrith. Whoever the two men Nicky had been watching were, it was possible they were the ones who had grabbed her and told her to give Frankie Hamilton their message. It was difficult to be sure, especially as she hadn't seen their faces, and the photo Nicky had taken wasn't the clearest. Penrith sent another text: *Don't leave the station.* Caelan frowned, stepping to the side of the pavement, out of the stream of hurrying people. Rain was beginning to fall, the air chill and damp. Why had he sent such a cryptic message? It wasn't like him to be coy. In their job, instructions tended to be explicit. Misunderstandings could lead to covers being blown, masks fading away. To injury, even death.

Then she saw him.

Ewan Davies, newest recruit to their unit, wearing a scruffy hoody and jeans, unshaven, walking as though he had just been kicked in the balls. Or as though he needed a fix. Caelan knew that his awkward gait was due to the pain from his damaged ribs, but no one else would. She had to admit, it was effective.

She knew Ewan had seen her, but he gave no indication that he recognised her. She waited, seeing what he would do. He kept walking, head down, shuffling past her and out into the street. Her phone beeped. Penrith again: *Go to your flat and wait.* She deleted the texts and did as she was told.

She had boiled the kettle, made two cups of tea before she heard a tap on the front door. Ewan looked sheepish, as if not sure of his welcome. Caelan decided to play along.

'What do you want?' She said it loud enough for any nosy neighbours to hear. There was no music coming from the flat below now, and Caelan was mindful of the way the occupants, Leon and April, had kept their eye on her. They were probably involved in nothing more than drug-taking, but it never hurt to be cautious.

Ewan smirked. 'Your mum said you had a new place. She soon told me where it was.' He spoke naturally, not attempting an accent. His slight Welsh lilt was barely noticeable after years moving around during his army career.

Caelan's hands were on her hips. 'The stupid bitch. I said not to talk to you.'

There was a silence. Ewan raised his eyebrows slightly, as if asking for her permission to continue. Caelan gave a long, loud sigh. 'Suppose you'd better come in then.'

In the kitchen, she asked him what was happening. 'You're injured; what are you doing back at work?' she whispered.

'I'm here to help.'

'Great, though I don't know what to do myself. How much do you know?'

From what Ewan told her, it was clear Penrith had brought him up to speed on the situation with Liv Hobbs, as well as the floundering investigation into the deaths of Rainey and Bryce. Caelan led him into the living room, and he lowered himself painfully onto the sofa. She remained standing, pacing the room.

'We have a lot of questions, but no real answers,' she said. 'We think the murders are linked to the death of Jackson Hobbs, but how, we've no idea. Then there's Ben Rainey's fingerprints being found in the brothel I went to.'

Ewan blinked. 'Brothel?'

Caelan explained. 'We don't know if Rainey was a john, or if he was poking around for reasons of his own.'

'What do you think?'

'I can't see him having a taste for teenage prostitutes, but I've been wrong before.'

Ewan chewed on his thumbnail, clearly mulling it over. 'You said the girl you met was obviously on something?'

Caelan remembered the scrawny limbs, the faraway gaze. The track marks. 'Definitely.'

'What if that's the link?'

She stared at him. 'I'm not following?'

Ewan spread his hands. 'I just thought… They have to be getting the drugs for the girls from somewhere, don't they? Plenty of smack, a regular, reliable source?'

'You mean this mysterious new dealer in Edmonton could be supplying them?'

He nodded. 'What if that's why Rainey went there?'

Caelan dropped onto the sofa beside him. 'But why go to someone in Edmonton when there'd be any number of lowlifes in Hackney willing and able to deal you anything you liked?'

'I don't know, I…' He flushed. 'Forget it.'

She touched his arm. 'No, I'm not saying you're wrong. We know Ben Rainey was at least speaking on the phone to Anthony Bryce, who came to us about a new dealer in Edmonton. What if he told Rainey first? Maybe Bryce had heard about the brothel. What if Rainey decided to visit it and see what he could find out?'

Ewan shifted uncomfortably, still not sure if his suggestion was nonsense. 'But why go there? Why not pose as a customer, buy a wrap of something? That's what you'd do, isn't it?'

'Yeah, buy some merchandise, make a few visits, gain their trust. But Rainey wasn't one of us. He was young, a new copper. Wanting to make his mark, knowing he had at least another year in uniform to look forward to.' Caelan had wondered about the possibility of Rainey conducting his own enquiries but hadn't seen the truth. Ewan, looking at the case with fresh eyes, might have reached the right conclusion. 'I need to talk to Achebe.'

She made the call, reached his voicemail. Frustrated, she set the handset on the worktop.

'What now?' asked Ewan.

Caelan stared at him, her mind working. Liv Hobbs had disappeared, she couldn't reach Achebe, and Penrith had given her no instructions. She made up her mind, shooting Ewan a grin. 'Fancy a game of snooker?'

–

Achebe sat opposite Frankie Hamilton, the stink of sour alcohol and vomit drifting across the table between them. He wouldn't usually conduct interviews himself, but the fact that his team had failed to find the phone Joseph Rainey had been hiding rankled. He didn't want to miss anything this time. Beside Hamilton, his solicitor was managing to keep her expression neutral, though the smell had to be even worse for her.

'How are you feeling, Frankie?' Achebe asked.

Hamilton managed a grin. 'Yeah, I'm okay. Sober, you know?'

'Sure?'

'Want me to walk in a straight line? Breathalyse me?' Hamilton drummed on the table. 'I just want to get out of here.'

'Answer our questions and we'll see what we can do.' Somerville looked stern, and Hamilton threw her a wink.

'I'm scared, love. Really.' He laughed.

Achebe ignored the performance. 'Have you heard of someone called Jackson Hobbs?'

Hamilton sketched a yawn. 'Who?'

Achebe told himself to be careful. Hamilton couldn't know that Caelan had told them about the conversation she'd had with him. 'He's from Edmonton. So are you. You're telling me you've never heard of him?'

'As I told the officers who insisted I came here with them, I don't know him. I've heard the name, yeah, but then I've heard of the Queen. Doesn't make us best mates, does it?' Hamilton sneered, but his eyes roamed the room.

Achebe leaned forward. 'Hobbs sold drugs. You expect us to believe your paths never crossed?'

Hamilton didn't blink. 'Like I said, I don't know him.'

'And yet you went to the same school,' said Achebe.

Hamilton licked his lips. 'You reckon?'

'We know. One of our officers told us, Frankie. We checked.' Achebe didn't allow himself to dwell on where Liv Hobbs might be, or what she was enduring. Whether she was even still alive.

Hamilton smirked. 'Oh yeah?'

Was he smiling because he knew who had Liv? Where she was? Achebe fought the urge to grab him by the throat and throttle the truth out of him. 'You know who I mean?'

'Liv Hobbs.' Hamilton licked his lips. 'I knew her, yeah.' He leered. 'Very well. Most of my friends did too.'

Achebe felt Somerville stiffen beside him. Hamilton was trying to provoke them, and it was vital they remain calm. 'You remember Liv, but not her brother?'

Hamilton laughed. 'Didn't shag him, did I?'

Achebe's fingernails dug into his palms as he clenched his fists beneath the table. A glance at Somerville and he knew she was doing the same. 'Jackson Hobbs is dead,' was all he said.

Hamilton stared at him. 'You expecting me to burst into tears? Geezer I don't know is murdered and you want me to go into mourning?'

Somerville pounced. 'Who told you Hobbs was murdered? We didn't.'

Hamilton's eyes flicked between them as he realised his mistake. 'It's obvious. How else would he have died?'

'Heart attack? Car accident?' Somerville suggested.

'Nah, he was in prison.'

Achebe smiled. 'You seem to know a lot about a man you say you don't know. Shall we cut the crap?'

Hamilton leaned back in his chair. 'All right, yeah, I know the name, but I haven't spoken to Hobbs in years.'

'Because he was a major dealer and you're just a user? Bottom of the pile?' Somerville raised her eyebrows.

Hamilton bristled. 'What, you think Hobbs was a player? Not clever enough to stay out of jail, was he?'

'Neither were you,' Somerville reminded him.

'Yeah, well, we all make mistakes.'

'Who do you buy from now Jackson Hobbs is off the scene?' said Achebe.

Hamilton wagged a finger. 'Forget it. You think I'm a grass?'

'I think you should answer our questions. We've been told that a new dealer has moved into Edmonton, and we need a name.'

'Better ask your informant then, hadn't you? Sounds like they've given you half a story.' The idea clearly amused Hamilton. Achebe decided to change his approach.

'Where were you drinking earlier today, Frankie?'

'Why?' Instantly suspicious, Hamilton narrowed his eyes. 'What does it matter? I've done nothing wrong.'

'Then you won't mind telling us, will you?'

The solicitor cleared her throat. 'Is my client being accused of something, Chief Inspector?'

Achebe shook his head. 'As you know, we're talking to all known acquaintances of Jackson Hobbs. Your client told us he didn't know Mr Hobbs, which we know is a lie. We just want to know who told him that Hobbs was dead.'

'Why?' Hamilton demanded.

'Because it was supposed to have been kept quiet.' Achebe lowered his voice, making it sound as though he was confiding in Hamilton. 'Someone knew Hobbs had been killed well before they should have done. You're out on parole, aren't you, Frankie?'

'You know I am. And?'

Achebe lifted his shoulders. 'Might be better for you if you help us out.'

'Chief Inspector—' the solicitor began. Achebe held up a hand.

'Frankie? Who told you Jackson Hobbs was dead?'

He looked mutinous. 'Will she know I told you? Will she be in trouble?'

'No. We won't mention you.'

'And I'm supposed to trust you? Good one.' Hamilton shuffled in his seat. 'I don't know her surname.'

'Not an issue.'

'I only know her as Kay.'

Achebe pretended to make a note. 'All right. When did you speak to her?'

Hamilton gave the approximate time. 'She wanted to meet me.'

'Where?'

'The One Four Seven. It's a—'

'Snooker club.' Achebe nodded. 'I've heard of it. Keep going.'

'Not much more to say. We had a beer, she told me about Hobbs.' Hamilton looked up. 'Am I going back to prison?'

'Because you had a few drinks, met a woman?' Achebe quirked an eyebrow. 'Not yet.'

Hamilton scowled. 'You're turning me into a fucking grass, man.'

'Come on, Frankie. It's in your interests to keep your nose clean.'

'When I heard about Hobbs, I knew... Well, I knew there were people who would want to know. People who'd be interested.'

Achebe waited, not wanting to rush him. When Hamilton remained silent, he said, 'Which people?'

Hamilton hugged himself. 'I've said enough.'

'Enough? I need names, Frankie.'

'No. No way.' His eyes darted around the room as though looking for an escape route. 'Put me back in jail if you want. It's better than...'

'Better than what?' Somerville asked softly.

'Grassing.' Hamilton's voice was a whisper.

Achebe pushed back his chair. 'Okay, it's your choice. We'll go and get the CCTV footage from around the snooker club, see where you went. People will notice us doing that, don't you think? They'll wonder what we're up to. Won't take them long to figure out where our information came from.'

Hamilton looked defeated. 'What do you want me to say?'

Achebe stopped, his hand on the back of his chair. 'Have you heard about the two men who were found dead in Edmonton recently, Frankie?'

'What?' Hamilton was frowning, bemused by the change in direction.

'You couldn't have killed them, of course. You were inside. But if you have information…'

Hamilton squirmed. 'What? What are you talking about?'

'Anthony Bryce. Name ring a bell?'

'No, I—'

'Ben Rainey? Ryan Glennister?'

And there it was. Hamilton's eyes widened at the mention of Glennister's name. Slowly Achebe sat back down. Hamilton moistened his lips.

'I know Ryan, all right? Knew him, I should say. Met him through a mate, before I went inside.'

'You've not spoken to him since?'

Hamilton blinked. 'I tried to earlier today, but the number I had for him isn't working. No surprise. I asked around, but no one had seen him.'

'Why were you so keen to talk to him?'

A pause. 'I don't know why I'm telling you all this.'

'Because you're sensible, Frankie. You know what prison's like now. No joke, is it?'

Hamilton shuddered. 'No.'

'So why would you want to go back?'

'I don't. Ever. I want to stay clean, and get my life back.'

The solicitor opened her mouth, then closed it again. Achebe pointed a finger at Hamilton.

'Good man. Tell me about Ryan Glennister.'

'He's a crackhead,' Hamilton sneered. 'A lowlife, pathetic. I've bought a few rocks from him in the past, but not recently. He doesn't sell any more, he's too busy using.'

'He used to deal?'

A nod. 'Most dealers, the serious ones, stay away from the merchandise. Hard to do business when you're off your face. Not Ryan. He's always looking for his next fix. You're not much of a dealer if you smoke all your stock.'

Achebe was silent, joining the dots. Aaron Jacob had been approached by Ryan Glennister with the photograph of his young daughter. If Glennister was as heavy a drug user as Hamilton was saying, he would be desperate, willing to do anything to feed his habit. If he was working for someone else, they would only need offer him a few quid to approach his cousin, and Jackson Hobbs's death warrant would have been signed. It wasn't much of a leap to imagine Glennister telling his cousin Aaron that knifing Jackson Hobbs was the only way to save his daughter. They would need to dig deeper, but as a theory, it hung together well enough for now. 'You're sure Glennister doesn't sell any more?'

Hamilton snorted. 'No way. I'm telling you, most days he doesn't know where he is, or even who he is. Piss-up in a brewery? Not Ryan. Crackhead, smackhead, you name it. I even heard he was a rent boy for a while.' Hamilton shook his head. 'Anything for a few quid.'

Then Glennister had to be working for someone. Who? Achebe knew he had to be careful. He didn't want the solicitor stepping in, or Hamilton clamming up. Softly, softly. 'If Ryan doesn't deal now, how does he make his money?'

'No idea. Maybe he's gone back to selling his arse.'

'Does he work for anyone?'

'No idea.' The reply was instant, and Achebe suspected it was not entirely truthful.

Hamilton shifted in his seat. 'Look, are we done?'

The solicitor stirred. 'I think my client has told you all he knows.'

Achebe exchanged a glance with Somerville. 'All right, get out of here,' he told Hamilton.

Back in the incident room, Achebe opened a bottle of water and gulped down half. Somerville ran her hands through her hair.

'Any news on DI Hobbs?' she bellowed to the room. Shaking heads, blank faces. Somerville turned back to Achebe.

'Shall I follow Hamilton when he leaves here?' she asked.

'You think he knows more than he let on?' Achebe put the bottle down on the nearest desk. 'I agree, but we have to be careful. We're lucky the solicitor didn't call a halt to the interview.'

Somerville sniffed. 'Hamilton was looking out for himself.'

'But we know Caelan told him about Jackson Hobbs. A defence lawyer might have something to say about that.'

'Feels like we're a long way from a prosecution.'

'Ryan Glennister is in this up to his neck. We need to find him.' Achebe scanned the room. He waved a hand, beckoned DC Gill over. Gill had shadows beneath his eyes, and needed a shave. 'Seb, have we located Ryan Glennister?'

Gill shook his head. 'No, sir. Without an address, it's difficult.'

Achebe gave him a hard look. 'I'm aware of that, but it's vital we find him. I want us talking to homeless people, visiting shelters and drop-in centres. Even if Glennister lives on the streets, someone must have seen him.'

'Unless...' Somerville raised her eyebrows.

Achebe didn't believe it. 'Come on, Jen. If he's dead, his body would have been found.'

'Not necessarily. Not if he's in the Thames, or an empty house somewhere.'

Something hovered at the back of Achebe's mind. 'The man who owns the house where Bryce's body was found,' he said slowly. 'We followed up on him and his kids, didn't we? He and his wife were in Turkey, but they should be back by now.'

'They are,' Somerville confirmed.

'I spoke to him earlier – Mr Tabak. Nice bloke,' said Gill.

Achebe glanced at him. 'Anything else?'

Gill looked flustered. 'We checked the movements of his three kids for the day Bryce's body was found, and the days immediately before. Nothing suspicious, sir.'

Achebe gazed at him. 'All right. Thank you, Seb. Get back to finding Glennister.'

A look of relief flashed across the younger man's face. 'Sir.'

Taking Somerville aside, Achebe lowered his voice. 'You remember I asked who it was who spoke to Anthony Bryce when he denied knowing Ben Rainey?'

Somerville flushed. 'Yes.'

'It was Gill, wasn't it?'

'Tim—'

'Why didn't you tell me? He fucked up, Jen.'

'I know.' Somerville looked at her feet, then met Achebe's eyes again. 'He's young, he's learning.'

'Bryce might still be alive if Gill had handled him better.' As Achebe spat out the words, he knew he was being unfair, but he couldn't help himself. 'You should have told me. Instead, Gill's been stomping around pissing people off.'

'I've been supervising him. I'm his sergeant, after all.'

Achebe tipped his head to the side. 'Do you babysit all the DCs, or just your favourites?'

She clenched her jaw. 'That's unfair.'

'Is it the smart haircut or the tight suits that appeal to you?' Achebe knew he was crossing a line, but the frustration of the past few days was boiling up, spilling over.

Somerville said nothing, staring down at her shoes, but her face was thunderous. Achebe took a breath, told himself to calm down. He was aware of curious glances, raised eyebrows. He was in charge here, their leader, and he was letting them all down. 'All right, I'm sorry.'

'Sorry?' Somerville spat out the word. 'You had no right to say what you did. You've no reason to question my professionalism.'

'Let's go and—'

'And what? Discuss it?' She sneered at him. 'You think you're the only one feeling the pressure? The only person imagining what Liv might be going through? She's my colleague too, you know. She's my friend.'

'I know.' Achebe bowed his head, knowing she was right. Somerville was loyal, and he trusted her. He met her eyes. 'I'm sorry, Jen. I really am.'

She nodded, lips pressed into a thin line. 'As DC Gill said, we've no reason to believe there's a link between the owner of the house Bryce was dumped in and our victims.'

'All right.' Achebe ran a hand over his mouth, frowning hard. 'Then we focus on finding Liv.'

'Good.' She turned away. Achebe watched her move through the incident room, offering a smile here, a word there, and mentally kicked himself again. He needed all his officers onside, now more than ever. They liked Jen, and respected her. If he alienated her, he ran the risk of doing the same to the entire team. He had been stupid, allowing his frustration and feeling of helplessness to take over. Unforgivable.

Furious with himself, he sat at the nearest desk to check his messages. When Caelan answered his call, it was clear she was out in the street.

'You wanted to speak to me?' He was never sure how to talk to any of Penrith's team when they were in the field. He knew Caelan was using the name Kay, but it always felt contrived, almost ridiculous, to call her by anything other than her real name.

'I did,' Caelan said. 'Give me a few minutes.'

Achebe waited, hearing the traffic noise and hum of voices recede. A door closed, and then she spoke again. 'Okay. I've been discussing what's happened with a colleague, and he made a suggestion.'

She meant Ewan Davies, Achebe realised, knowing Penrith had sent him to Edmonton. 'Go on,' he said.

'What if our mysterious new dealer in Edmonton is supplying the drugs for the girls in the Hackney brothel?'

He paused, wondering where this was going. 'I don't follow.'

'We're struggling to understand why Ben Rainey was there. Maybe Anthony Bryce told him about it.'

Achebe blinked, thinking it over. 'Which could link to Rainey taking an interest in the place. He wanted to know where the drugs were coming from.'

'Worth considering, do you think?'

He heard a rush of water, and realised Caelan must be hiding in a public toilet somewhere. He smiled to himself. The glamorous side of policing. 'Yeah, I reckon so,' he said. 'Thank you. We'll bear it in mind.'

'What about the interview with Frankie?'

He filled her in on the details.

'Wait a second. Frankie said Ryan Glennister had been a rent boy?' said Caelan.

'Yeah, why?' Achebe frowned, failing to see the relevance.

'Because we've been talking about a brothel. If Glennister worked there, even if he knew someone who did, he could be the link between the brothel and our major dealer, couldn't he?'

Achebe considered it, conceded it was possible. 'We have no idea where Glennister is, though. His last known address is a squat, but no one there could help us. They weren't willing to, anyway.'

'We're on our way to the snooker hall,' Caelan said. 'Maybe we can ask around.'

'Why are you going there?'

'Where else do you suggest?' Caelan sounded tired, and irritable. Achebe could sympathise. 'No one has given us any instructions,' she continued. 'If you've nothing new to tell us…'

'We're looking at the CCTV from the area where you saw Liv. Nothing leaps out so far.'

'We're dealing with people who know what they're doing.' There was a pause, and then Caelan spoke quietly. 'I wish I'd followed her. I considered it.'

'You couldn't have known, any more than her husband could have.'

'Is he still at the station?'

'No, thankfully. We got someone to take him home and stay with him. He was threatening to go out and search himself.' Achebe checked his watch. Liv Hobbs hadn't been seen for almost six hours. The chill he had felt since hearing the news deepened. Why hadn't she told them she was pregnant? 'Listen, I need to go and brief the team on your theory. I'll call if there's any update.'

As he slid the phone into his trouser pocket, Jen Somerville approached him. He tried a smile, but it wasn't returned.

'You need to see this.' She spoke urgently, and Achebe felt his pulse quicken. Somerville led him to one of the computers. On the screen was a frozen image. Achebe glanced at her.

'What are we looking at?'

'This is the footage from inside the bus Liv boarded.'

Achebe bent closer to the screen. 'You're certain?'

Somerville pointed. 'Watch.'

The clarity wasn't great, but it was good enough for Achebe to be sure that the next person to take a seat was DI Liv Hobbs. They watched her fold her hands in her lap and turn to gaze out of the window. 'What happens?'

'She's on the bus for eight minutes. She gets off at the stop closest to her parents' home.'

'This narrows down the area and time she disappeared, then.' Achebe was back on his feet. Jen had watched the rest, so he didn't need to. 'Have the team seen this?'

Somerville shook her head. 'No, but they know what I've just told you. The bus stop is about half a mile from the street where Mr and Mrs Hobbs live. Liv still had a way to walk when she got off the bus. It's an area with lots of housing, traffic. Plenty of opportunity for her to be taken.'

'Does anyone speak to her while she's on the bus? Does she receive a phone call or message?'

Folding her arms, Somerville shifted her feet. 'No. She just sits there staring out of the window. A few more people get on, but Liv doesn't even look at them. If someone snatched her, they didn't approach her on the bus.'

'We need to redirect the officers who are talking to people in the area,' Achebe said. 'I assume you've put the message out?'

'Yeah, for what it's worth.' Somerville sounded frustrated. 'No one so far saw anything. As usual, people seem to have been walking around with their eyes closed.'

'What about CCTV cameras in the area where Liv left the bus?' Achebe held up his hands. 'I know what you're going to say, it takes time to search through the footage. I get that. I just want to know if we're on it.'

'We are.'

'Never doubted it.' Achebe tried to smile, but his face didn't seem to want to play ball. 'I'll be honest, I'm not sure what else we can do. Liv's an adult. We can hardly start a full-scale search, however much noise her husband makes.' He glanced at her. 'Even though we might want to.'

'You said you wanted to concentrate on finding her.' Somerville looked wounded. 'Her disappearance has to be linked to her brother's death.'

'Why? How do we know she doesn't just need some time?' Achebe knew the words sounded hollow as he said them. 'Okay, the phone. I know. But it could have been snatched, then dumped. If someone did grab her, why not switch the phone off, remove the SIM? Leaving it behind just suggests something sinister happened to her.'

'Maybe DI Hobbs threw it into the skip deliberately?' Somerville spoke slowly, as though she was still figuring it out. 'She might have wanted to leave it for us to find?'

Achebe rubbed his jaw. 'She would know we could trace it. You could be right.'

'All the more reason for us to focus on finding her,' said Somerville.

'But she could be miles away by now. In another country even,' Achebe pointed out.

'Her passport's not been used.' Somerville was frowning, hands on hips, increasingly impatient. 'We've no leads, no idea what happened when she left the bus. Going through the CCTV could take hours, even days, which we don't have.'

'What do you suggest?' Achebe knew Somerville was right, but where were they supposed to go from here?

'Think of Ben Rainey, of Anthony Bryce. Imagine what they suffered happening again, but this time to Liv. There must be something we can do.' Somerville turned and marched away, throwing herself into the chair behind the nearest empty desk and hunching over the keyboard.

Achebe ground his teeth together. Jen was right, they were wasting time. When he had updated the Chief Superintendent, he would send Caelan a text, explain that Liv had been spotted close to her parents' house. Nicky Sturgess should be informed too. Maybe one of them could help, turn up a lead the rest of them had missed.

Somehow, though, he doubted it.

25

Ewan Davies looked up at the sign over the door of the snooker club as they approached it.

'The One Four Seven?' He shook his head. 'Original name.'

Caelan smiled. 'What would you have preferred? Pot Black? No Cues?'

He looked at her, eyebrows raised. 'That's actually pretty good.'

She waved the comment away. 'Let's go.'

Inside, only one table was being used. Two men circled it, ignoring Caelan and Ewan. Behind the bar, the same woman was polishing glasses. Caelan asked for two beers. Silently the woman handed them over, took the twenty-pound note Caelan held out to her. As she turned back from the till and deposited the change, all in coins, into Caelan's hand, she managed a surly 'Cheers.'

Surveying the club, Caelan drank from the bottle.

'Marcus not in?'

The woman lifted a shoulder. 'Not unless he's hiding under one of the tables.'

Caelan let it go. 'No Frankie either?'

'Not since he was in here with you earlier. Isn't he company enough?' She looked at Ewan from under her eyelashes with a smirk. 'Better-looking than Frankie, too.'

Ewan flashed her a grin. 'Not difficult, is it?'

Shifting her foot to the side, Caelan gave his shoe a gentle kick. He didn't know Frankie Hamilton, and pretending he did could be risky.

'Doesn't have much luck, does he, Frankie?' The woman shook back her hair. 'I heard he's been arrested.'

Caelan kept drinking, hoping Ewan kept his mouth closed too. Acting surprised or concerned would be the wrong decision. The woman clearly wasn't worried.

'Yeah?' Caelan said eventually, wiping the back of her hands over her lips. 'Shame.'

'It's about Jackson Hobbs,' the woman went on. 'You know he's dead?'

Caelan found her assumption that they would know who Hobbs was interesting. She couldn't have overheard the conversation Caelan had had with Frankie Hamilton earlier. The only reason Caelan could think of was Hobbs's reputation. The woman must have assumed that if they lived in or even frequented Edmonton, they would have heard of him. She nodded, making eye contact.

'Doesn't everyone?' she said.

'Yeah, well now the police want to talk to people who knew him. So, if that includes you, you might want to keep your head down.'

'I've never met him,' Caelan said truthfully.

'He used to come in here, flashing his cash around.' The bartender sniffed. 'I went out with him for a few months, years ago, not long after we left school.'

'Brave woman.' Ewan moved his foot away from Caelan's as he spoke.

She laughed. 'Jackson was always a gentleman with me. Even introduced me to his mum and dad.'

Caelan took another mouthful of beer, not wanting to push. If this woman had known Jackson Hobbs at school, maybe she remembered his sister too. She was aware of Ewan moving closer to the bar, resting his forearms on it.

'Any chance of a couple more drinks?' he asked with another grin.

The woman smirked as she bent to retrieve them from the fridge beneath the bar. Caelan took the opportunity to shoot Ewan a glare. The woman pushed the bottles towards them and held out her hand. Ewan dropped a folded note into it.

'Cheers.' He took a long drink, and Caelan seized the opportunity to speak.

'Isn't Jackson's sister in the police?' It was a risk, and if Liv Hobbs hadn't been missing, Caelan would never have shown her hand so soon. But they needed answers, and quickly. The woman frowned, took her time opening the till and rummaging for Ewan's change.

'Yeah, the silly cow. She could have made a fortune if she'd gone into the family business, but no, it wasn't good enough for her. She wanted to save the world.' A sneer. 'Wonder how that's worked out for her.'

'What did Jackson think?' asked Ewan.

'Of his sister betraying the family? What do you think? He hated it. Not as much as his brother, though.'

Caelan paused. The other brother. She'd forgotten about him, though she assumed Achebe and his team hadn't. The bartender was watching them, waiting for a response. Caelan searched her memory, trying to remember if she had ever heard the other Hobbs brother's name. She didn't think so. Could she talk her way around it? If she knew of Jackson and his sister, shouldn't she know about their brother too? She was on dangerous ground, and knew she had to think quickly.

'I don't think I've met him,' she said.

The bartender tossed back her hair. 'Keep it that way.' She turned her back on them, pulling her phone from her pocket and tapping at the screen. It was clear the conversation was over.

As they moved to one of the tables, far enough from the bar to be able to talk relatively freely, Caelan wondered if the bartender was sending a text. She was confident they had both been convincing enough not to set any alarm bells ringing, but it was hard to be sure. Bar staff heard things, saw everything that went on, especially in a place like this. The woman had made no secret of her link to Jackson Hobbs. They should have asked her name, though it wouldn't be too difficult to find her.

Caelan sat back in her chair, drinking her beer as slowly as possible and watching the bartender over Ewan's shoulder. She was wiping glasses again without much effort, the white cloth barely moving inside the glass before she bent to put it away. She had left her phone on the top of the bar, and Caelan guessed she was waiting for a text or call. Maybe it was innocent – perhaps she had children, was checking up on them, or... There were hundreds of possible reasons. Caelan knew one of them could be her and Ewan's presence and their comments.

Over at the furthest snooker table, the two men who had been playing when she and Ewan had arrived shook hands and moved away from the table. Caelan watched one of them leave the club while the other stopped to speak to the bartender. She couldn't hear their conversation, but almost immediately, the man cast a glance over his shoulder, making no secret of staring at Caelan and Ewan. Caelan saw the movement, though her eyes were fixed on Ewan's face.

'Talk to me,' she said quietly.

'What about?'

'Anything. We need to look as though we're having a conversation. Tell me about the army.'

He flinched. 'Do I have to? Are they watching us?' Ewan had his back to the room, but had realised that only one man had left the building.

'Yep.' Caelan raised her bottle and drank, the beer tasting sour.

'What do you want to do?'

'Nothing. We'll wait and see what happens.'

Ewan smiled. 'Sounds like a plan.'

The snooker player was still at the bar, one hand in his jeans pocket. They heard a phone ring, and Caelan watched the bartender snatch her handset up. She had a short conversation, then came around the side of the bar and disappeared through the door leading to the toilets. The man was still at the bar, as though guarding it. Perhaps he was.

When the bartender emerged, Caelan saw she had applied fresh lipstick. She didn't look at them as she resumed her position behind the bar, but went back to wiping the glasses. The man spoke to her, their heads close together, then he walked away towards the stairs.

'Someone's on their way,' Caelan said softly.

Ewan leaned forward. 'How do you know?'

'She's polishing the glasses properly, she's done her make-up. It's someone she wants to impress.'

'Could be the other Hobbs brother – whatever his name is.'

Caelan pulled out her phone. 'I'll ask.'

'More likely to be the bloke who owns the place, do you think?'

'Maybe.'

Caelan remembered Marcus Crowley – his confidence and the way he had stood too close to her. Making the point that she was on his turf, and he could do what he wanted. He was in charge. Would he have had time to ask his contacts about her, the mysterious Kay Summers who had a conviction for drug possession and was hinting she was on the lookout for someone to offload her boyfriend's unsold stock to?

Caelan shuddered, feeling Crowley's hand on her wrist again. The insistent press of his fingers, the smell of aftershave and, underneath, of his skin. She hoped she was wrong, and she wouldn't have to meet him again. Beneath the grin and the friendly tone, she had glimpsed a coldness in his eyes, one she had seen many times in her career. Crowley was intelligent, unsentimental and brutal. If he discovered she had lied to him, she knew he would react. During their short conversation, she had sensed the man behind the mask, and though he didn't frighten her, she knew he would have to be treated as extremely dangerous. Could he have ordered the torture of Ben Rainey and Anthony Bryce? Even wielded the kettle of boiling water and the iron himself? She doubted he would think twice, but why? Was Crowley the new dealer in Edmonton Bryce had warned them about? Something else she needed to check with Achebe. She looked at Ewan.

'You've stopped talking. How's your nephew?'

He grinned. 'If I ever mention wanting kids, remind me of this morning, when he puked and simultaneously filled his nappy. Never seen anything like it – or smelled it.'

'I'll bear it in mind.' Caelan finished her beer, set the bottle on the table as her phone vibrated. 'The other brother is called Taylor Hobbs.' She deleted the text. It wouldn't disappear completely, of course, but if anyone managed to get hold of her phone, there would be nothing incriminating unless they had the contacts to dig deeper.

'Never heard of him,' said Ewan.

'Me neither, but we should have. He could be important.' Caelan looked over at the bartender, still polishing. 'Do you think we should get out of here?'

'I thought you wanted to see who—'

Her unease growing, Caelan interrupted him. 'I do, but we can do that outside.'

'Won't it look strange? We've not even played a game of snooker.'

'No, but we've bought a couple of drinks, had a chat. Hopefully they'll think I wanted to see Marcus again, then left when I realised he wasn't here.'

They strolled towards the stairs, not speaking, not hurrying. The bartender didn't look up.

As they reached the pavement and began to walk down the street, Caelan touched Ewan's arm.

'I think we should split up.'

'Break it to me like that.' He grinned at her, but Caelan shook her head, refusing to share the joke.

'I want to see who the bartender contacted, but I want to do it alone. They'll be expecting both of us.'

Ewan's mouth turned down at the corners. 'And what am I supposed to do?'

'Hang around, but don't be obvious.'

He glanced around. 'Where?'

'Find a shop, or a café. I don't know.' And I'm not here to babysit you, she added silently. Her irritation with him was unfair, she knew, but bringing him here with her had been a mistake. Penrith should have kept him off active duty until his ribs healed, at least. Caelan was still feeling the occasional twinge from her own injuries, but at least she could walk without wincing. Ewan was clearly struggling, meaning he was likely to be a passenger if she need to run, or worse, to fight.

'There's a coffee shop over there.' He nodded towards it.

'Fine. Give me half an hour. I'll come and find you.'

'I don't like going without you.' He shuffled his feet. 'Never leave a man behind, you know?'

'Come on.' She tried a smile. 'No one's shot at me for at least a day.'

He walked away, reluctant, but not looking back. Caelan ducked into the alleyway opposite the snooker hall, which provided some cover, but also a clear view of the entrance.

'What the hell are you doing?' The voice came from behind her. Caelan turned, knowing who she would see. Nicky, scowling, hands bunched in her jacket pockets. 'I was told to keep a watch on the place until I heard otherwise.'

'You saw us go in?'

Nicky inclined her head. 'Yep. I moved away when I saw you leave, was going to ask for instructions. Then I saw you hiding down here without checking who might be around.'

Caelan felt a blush start in her cheeks. Nicky had a point. 'What was I supposed to do, search every inch of the surrounding area?'

Nicky leant against the wall, pushing her hair out of her eyes. 'That's generally considered a good idea.' She was hiding a smile. The realisation ignited Caelan's fury again, and she turned her back on Nicky, gazing across at the snooker club, ignoring the tension in her shoulders.

'Can you go?' she said.

She heard Nicky snort. 'Sorry, am I in your way?'

'Both of us standing in an alley looks a little conspicuous, wouldn't you say?'

'Not if we're careful. Who are you looking for?'

Nicky had taken a step closer, Caelan realised. If she moved back, she would be in her arms. Not a happy thought. Once more Nicky was acting unprofessionally, placing them both in a situation that could potentially compromise their objective, and their safety.

'Please, Nicky, just leave,' Caelan said.

'Can't. I'm under orders to watch this place.'

'You're being ridiculous. You're going to blow both our covers.'

She heard Nicky's coat rustle as she folded her arms. 'Rubbish. Who are you waiting for?'

'I don't know.' Reluctantly Caelan explained what had happened when she and Ewan had been inside the club.

'You think Marcus Crowley is coming over.' Nicky clicked her tongue softly. 'You're branching out into drug dealing now?'

'I want to talk to him again, if that's what you mean.'

Caelan's mobile beeped, signalling the arrival of a text. She heard Nicky fumble for her own phone. There was a pause as Nicky read the message. 'Looks like I'm leaving after all.'

'What's happened?'

'They've narrowed down the area where Liv Hobbs disappeared, want me to go and have a look around.'

Caelan felt rather than heard Nicky move back. 'Narrowed it down to where?'

Nicky was already a few paces away. 'You'll have to read your text.'

Swallowing a smart reply, Caelan ignored her. It didn't matter. She was going nowhere for now. She gave Nicky thirty seconds to leave the alley, then turned to make sure she had gone. When she focused on the club again, she saw a black car draw up to the kerb in front of it. The car was new, expensive without being ostentatious. It whispered money rather than screamed it. The driver's door opened, and Marcus Crowley got out. Watching him stroll towards the entrance of his club, Caelan wondered if his arrival was a coincidence. What should she do now? If she followed him inside, it would be obvious she had been watching. If she stayed put, she would learn nothing.

As she dithered, another black car slid in behind Crowley's and two men wearing dark padded coats and black beanie hats emerged. They kept their heads down, and Caelan couldn't see their faces. The car's number plate was obscured by a brown paper bag. It looked as though it had blown there by accident and stuck, but Caelan's heart began to thump. Dodgy. Could they be the same two men who had grabbed her and delivered the warning for Frankie Hamilton? The same two they suspected of trying to run him over, the blokes Nicky had seen here earlier? They were the right height, the same build. It was possible. Did they work for Crowley, or were they here for something else?

As they pushed through the entrance to the snooker club, moving with purpose but not so quickly as to draw attention to themselves, Caelan ran to the far end of the alleyway then rounded the corner and walked towards the club, her phone in her hand as though typing a text. She hoped Ewan stayed where he was. She needed backup, but not from an injured, unarmed man. Caelan had been ordered to carry a gun on many occasions throughout her career, but she had never enjoyed the experience. Now, though, she wished she had one at her hip. She had no reason to believe the two men were there to harm Marcus Crowley, but the way they had moved, the lack of conversation between them, had hinted at a mission rather than a meeting. She told herself to remain calm as she raised her phone to her ear. Five yards from the club, Penrith's voicemail ordered her to leave a message. She chewed on her bottom lip, then ended the call and tried Achebe. Same result. Unacceptable when they had officers out in the field.

She was past the club now, approaching the café Ewan had headed to. She kept her face turned away as she went by, hoping he wouldn't see her. There was a Chinese restaurant next door to the café, a menu displayed in its window, and she stopped and waited, pretending to read it. She heard heels clicking towards her, and leaned closer to the glass window. The bartender from the One Four Seven club hurried past, pulling her coat around her. She didn't seem to notice Caelan, much less recognise her. Even more concerned, Caelan checked her phone, confirming what she already knew. Neither Achebe nor Penrith had responded. She didn't have Nicky's contact number, Ewan needed to stay out of the way, and Richard Adamson was banged up.

She was on her own.

She crossed the road, headed back towards the club. Both cars were still parked by the kerb. She walked quickly, hands by her sides, head up. She thought about grabbing a hammer or heavy spanner from a hardware shop she marched past, but decided it would take too long, and look too obvious. Best to go in quickly, quietly, and see what was happening.

Remembering that she had a pair of wire-framed glasses with clear lenses in her jacket pocket, she pulled them out and slipped them on, then scraped her hair back into a ponytail as she walked. Her makeshift disguise probably wouldn't fool anyone, but it might give her a few seconds' advantage if she wasn't recognised instantly.

She approached the car the men had arrived in, checking the rear number plate. It was filthy, and she snapped a quick photo on her phone, sending it to Achebe and Penrith. There was no time to wait until either one called back to tell them what she was doing. She slid the phone on to silent, pushed it back inside her pocket, and approached the entrance, hoping no one was taking any notice of her movements. She was aware she looked suspicious, but there was little she could do. There were times when caution and strict application of procedure was the only way. This was not one of them. Every one of Caelan's senses was screaming at her. Marcus Crowley might be a drug dealer and money launderer, but her job was to protect him regardless. She set her shoulders. Time to act.

As she neared the door, she heard the clatter of footsteps. She kept walking. Ten paces away was a litter bin, and she paused, turning towards it, pretending to drop something inside. The two men emerged and walked towards their car, still unhurried, still not speaking. Caelan's mouth was dry. Crowley wasn't with them. They weren't covered in blood, didn't even look ruffled. They'd spent five minutes at most inside the club, but Caelan knew it was plenty of time. It didn't take long to deliver a threat; it took even less time to kill someone. She turned her head as they drove away, waiting until the car was out of sight before making her next move.

She checked her phone again, sent another text with an update to both Achebe and Penrith. They needed to trace and stop the car as soon as possible. The bartender needed bringing in too. She might have spoken to the men, seen them at least. She could be a vital witness, or she might also be in danger. Caelan exhaled through pursed lips. This case, confused from the beginning, was now threatening to hurtle out of control. What had gone on inside the club? There was only one way to find out.

Pulling the sleeves of her jacket over her hands since she had no gloves, she pushed the door open and stood listening. Nothing. No cries for help, no screams of agony. She sniffed the air. The same as earlier – stale beer. If they had fired a gun, she'd expect to be able to smell it, but there was no guarantee.

Slowly, quietly she climbed the concrete stairs.

Silence.

No blood on the steps. At the top, she paused again, still listening. She crept into the club, her eyes scanning the place. No signs of a disturbance, no upturned tables or smashed chairs.

No Marcus Crowley.

On her toes, moving quickly but with care, she reached the bar. Careful not to touch the polished wooden surface, she peered behind it. No one. The till was closed, nothing had been disturbed. Not that she thought the two men who had just been here were petty thieves, but they might have helped themselves if given the chance.

She stepped back, hands on hips. Where was Crowley? As far as she was aware, there was only the main room and the toilets. Could he be hiding in there? She strode over to the door between them, shoved it open.

'Hello? Anyone serving?' she bellowed.

A definite noise from the toilets – not a reply, more like struggling and shuffling, as though someone was trying to stand. Caelan paused.

'Hello? Anyone here?'

The sound again. She moved closer, stood waiting outside the door to the toilets. It opened slowly, and Marcus Crowley appeared, leaning on the frame, his face pale. He attempted a smile, but his expression was more a grimace.

'Back already?' he managed to say.

'Seems so. You all right?'

He took a step forward, wincing but trying not to show it. 'Yeah, fine. Had a kebab for lunch. Must have been dodgy. My guts feel like they're on a roller coaster.' He spoke haltingly, as though unable to catch his breath. Caelan smiled at him. If that was how he wanted to play it, fine.

'Fancied another drink, but there's no one at the bar,' she said. Crowley allowed the door to swing closed behind him.

'Yeah, Nina had an appointment, so I gave her the afternoon off.' He waved her forward, the movement obviously causing him more pain. Caelan made sure she walked quickly, reaching the bar before he had taken more than a few steps.

'You sure you're okay?'

'I told you, I'm fine. Now, what can I get you?'

'Just a beer, and one for yourself.'

He laughed. 'Thanks for the offer, but I think I'll pass.' He bent slowly, painfully, to the fridge and handed her a bottle.

Caelan took a sip. She didn't want to drink any more after the two bottles she'd had with Ewan, but she needed an excuse to hang around. She watched Crowley limp out from behind the bar and head for the nearest chair.

'Come and sit down,' he said.

Reluctantly, she did as he asked. He'd clearly received at least one punch to the stomach, and she wanted to find out more, but without asking him directly about the two men, it was difficult to see how she was going to discover who they were. She hoped Achebe would have put out an alert for their vehicle, but it was a long shot. In their shoes, she would have stopped, removed the paper bag from the front number plate, cleaned up the back one and gone on her way. Maybe even left the car somewhere and disappeared on the Underground. She looked at Crowley, hunched in the chair, and remembered Liv Hobbs. Fuck it, she thought. The time for caution had passed. She moved her chair closer, leaning towards him.

'Those two blokes seemed in a hurry,' she said.

Crowley's eyebrows bounced. 'Blokes?'

'Went storming out of here as I walked in. Almost knocked me over.'

His eyes darted from left to right. 'Yeah, I'd just taken a couple of frames and fifty quid off them both. Sore losers. What can you do?' He aimed for a casual shrug of the shoulders, his face again betraying the pain the movement caused him.

'What, and they decided to teach you a lesson? Wanted to let you know who should win next time?'

Crowley stared at her, eyes narrowing. He tipped his head back. 'What gives you that idea?'

'Come on, you're hurt. Anyone can see it.'

'Bollocks. Got a stomach ache, that's all.'

'After someone's fist collided with it a few times, yeah.' Caelan shook her head. 'Makes no odds to me. Just a warning: you're fooling no one.'

He leaned forward, his lips parting in a mocking grin. 'Yeah? Well I'll tell you something, sweetheart. Neither are you.'

Caelan's heart seemed to thump the bottom of her throat. She knew she had to stay calm, trust her colleagues and her cover story. There was no way Crowley could know who she really was. He was bluffing, he had to be. Unless... The thought shot into her mind, chilling and horrifying. Unless Liv Hobbs had been talking. Unless she had been persuaded – *forced* – to share what she knew. Caelan took a breath, stared back at Crowley. No. Liv didn't know about the undercover officers in Edmonton, did she? But then she had been involved in the early stages of the operation involving Nicky. She had known Ben Rainey, had spoken to Anthony Bryce. Caelan had visited her home, given Liv her phone number. It was for a pay-as-you-go phone she rarely used, the handset still in the flat in Rotherhithe. She had known Liv would be able to reach her through Achebe and would never give out a number that could be easily linked to her, but if she had saved her name with the number... Liv had seen her ID, knew her rank and real name. They had dumped her phone, but they could have checked her contacts first. Shit.

Crowley was waiting, leaning back in his chair, a knowing smile on his face. Caelan knew she had to respond.

'What do you mean?'

Not her wittiest comeback, but at least she didn't sound rattled.

He tapped his nose. 'You told me you had merchandise to sell. I've heard what it is.'

Caelan licked her lips to give herself another second. It would have helped if Penrith had told her what information he was planning to add to her legend. Crowley seemed still to believe she was legit, which was all that mattered. 'From who?'

'Never mind who told me. I've also heard you're no stranger to the inside of a police station either.'

'Meaning?' She couldn't deny it, but she was usually on the right side of the cell door. Not always, but usually.

'Meaning, you've been caught carrying a smoke or two.' Crowley sat up straight, attempted to cross his arms, then decided against it.

Caelan kept her face blank. 'Not sure what your point is.'

'You've got a record. I don't do business with people who've been in trouble. It's too risky.' He leaned forward, one hand to his stomach. 'So I suggest you get of here, and try to peddle your shit elsewhere.'

Slowly Caelan pushed back her chair, her eyes not leaving Crowley's face. 'Got a better offer, have you?'

A snort. 'Wouldn't take much, would it?'

She stood, her hand on the back of the chair. 'You're making a mistake, Marcus.'

He watched her, sneering. 'No, love, but you will be if you're still standing there in five seconds.'

Caelan's laugh was genuine. 'Going to throw me out, are you? Like to see you try.' She curled her lip. 'I'd heard you were small-time. Maybe I'll go and talk to those two fellas instead.'

'What?'

'You think I didn't speak to them before? Didn't want to know what they'd been up to in here?'

'And they told you?' His turn to laugh. 'Nice try. Now get out.'

She took a step backwards, still watching him. 'Like I said, Marcus, I've been told you've got too big for your boots. You know where I lived before?'

'Northolt. I asked around, like I said I would. Am I supposed to be impressed? I told you to leave.'

'And I will when I've said my piece. You think I'm not worth your time? You know Anthony Bryce?'

His eyes flickered. 'No.'

'Yeah, whatever.' Time to gamble. 'If you don't want to buy, I've others interested. Someone told me about Ryan Glennister.'

He pulled his phone out of his pocket, pretending not to care, but Caelan saw he recognised the name. 'And?'

She shrugged. 'Maybe I'll speak to him instead.'

Crowley began to laugh. 'You must be fucking desperate.'

'Who's he working for now?'

Crowley dropped his phone onto the table with a clatter. Moving with a speed she wouldn't have thought him capable of considering the pain he was obviously in, he stood and stepped forward, grabbing the front of her jacket in his fist. 'You know, you ask too many questions.'

Caelan fought the urge to laugh as she snapped her hand up and broke his grip. 'And you watch too many films.'

'Bitch, that hurt.' He cradled his wrist, glaring at her.

'Fuck off, Marcus.' She turned on her heel, made for the stairs. He made no attempt to follow her, but as she reached the top step, he called her name, her fake name.

Against her better judgement, Caelan stopped. 'What?'

'What are you selling?'

She hesitated, turned to look at him. 'Why?'

He spread his hands. 'I'm interested. And if I help you sell it, then maybe you'll want to buy.'

'You're offering to do business?'

'No, I'm offering to think about it.'

'You liked what you heard about me then?'

A smirk. 'In a way. Like you said, I've had a better offer. I don't want what you're selling, but if I can, what, *facilitate* a deal, I get a cut of the profit with no risk to myself.'

'Who would I actually be selling to?'

'As it stands, you don't need to know. I have contacts.'

Caelan waited. When he didn't continue, she said, 'And?'

'And I need to know what we're talking about.'

'I told you. My boyfriend dealt weed.'

'Bullshit. Tell me the truth.'

'I don't know what you're talking about.'

'I was told that when he was arrested, the police were expecting to find a kilo of white in his garage. And guess what?'

'Surprise me.' Thank you, Ian. Caelan silently lauded Penrith. He had judged the situation perfectly. If anything was going to whet the appetite of someone like Marcus Crowley, it was a kilo of coke.

Crowley smiled. 'I'm sure I don't need to tell you, but it wasn't there.'

'So?'

'I think you have it. I think you're sitting on a kilo of coke, shit scared someone will take it from you. And you know what? If I put the word around, no doubt they will.' He barked out a laugh. 'Try talking your way out of that.'

'You're threatening me. The man who's almost in tears because he got punched in the gut.'

His face hardened. 'They'd destroy you, you know that? A kilo. Shit. You're playing a dangerous game, and you're as green as fucking grass. I can help you.'

'You're all heart, Marcus.'

'Around here, people will rip your face off for a couple of rocks, never mind what you've got stashed away. You're vulnerable.'

'And you're full of shit.'

'For twenty per cent of what you make, I'll get the deal done for you. You stay safe and make a shitload of money, and I'm laughing too. No one gets hurt, and we stay friends. What do you think?'

Caelan gripped the banister, her mind whirling. What could she say? To commit to a deal would be insanity. Then again, she had been involved in similar schemes before and come out unscathed. Penrith must have had plans when he told his contacts the quantity to mention. It depended on how far you were willing to go. She would have to speak to Penrith, see what they wanted to set up. She wasn't concerned about the risk, but about the possibility of making a move too soon, of bringing down Crowley but not the people who were ultimately in charge. And strangely, she didn't have a spare kilo of coke kicking around at home.

'Let me think about it,' she said.

Crowley's smile seemed genuine. 'Don't take too long. If word gets out...'

'Give me a day.'

He pointed at her, making his hand into a gun. 'Twenty-four hours. Then it's game on.'

–

Back in the alley, opposite the club that was beginning to feel more like home than the flat she had been sent to, Caelan called Penrith again. He answered on the first ring.

'What the hell are you playing at?' he demanded. 'Sending me cryptic texts and garbled messages?'

'Listen, I need someone here.' Caelan watched the club, hoping Crowley would stay put. He could be on the phone, though, making plans. She should have planted a microphone. Too late now.

'You've got your little friend. Have you lost him already?'

'He's injured. I need someone fit.'

'Well, then there's only one other option.'

Nicky. Caelan suppressed a sigh. 'Where is she?'

'Not far. I'll send her to you. She's kicking her heels anyway.'

'What's happening?'

'No comment.'

More unnecessary cloak-and-dagger nonsense. Penrith enjoyed it, she was certain. Revelled in the game-playing, the winks and nudges. The smug superciliousness of it all. Not for the first time recently, Caelan was tempted to head for Heathrow and leave them to it. 'I need to speak to you.'

'I've—'

'I'll be there in an hour.'

She ended the call on his spluttering. She needed an update on the Liv Hobbs situation, and she had to speak to him about her conversation with Crowley. It would be better to see him in person, but it would mean trekking across London again.

Her phone was ringing.

'Kay?'

She was beginning to hate the name.

'I didn't know you had my number,' she said. It was Nicky. So much for them not contacting each other.

'I was told you were looking for me.'

Caelan shook her head, irritated. Nicky had always liked the idea of playing James Bond. Secrets and subterfuge had once seemed glamorous to Caelan too. Not any longer. 'I need a chat,' she said.

'Where?'

'The club.'

'On my way.'

Caelan checked the time. Five minutes before Ewan came looking for her. She hoped he would stay put, keep his head down, but then following orders was what he did best. She doubted today would be any different. She left the alleyway at the far end, and trotted around to the café. The club was out of sight for a few seconds, but not long enough to allow Crowley time to leave. Ewan was at the counter, money in hand. Caelan waited outside, grabbing his arm as he limped through the door.

'I've been worried—' he began.

'I'm okay, but I need to run. See you at home.' Ewan opened his mouth, totally bemused. Caelan bent close to his ear, as if kissing his cheek. 'I'm going to Westminster. Stay here, watch the club. You won't be alone, but don't make contact. I'll call you later.'

'But...'

She squeezed his arm and took off. It was a risk leaving him there, but she knew she had no choice. He would slow her down if he came with her, and there would be no point him tagging along. He would have nothing to add to her conversation with Penrith. She hoped Nicky wasn't too far away and Ewan wouldn't need to follow Marcus Crowley. Mentioning Ryan Glennister to him had been a shot in the dark, but it seemed drug-dealing circles in Edmonton were close-knit. If Glennister hadn't been found already, and Caelan didn't expect he had been, perhaps Crowley would lead them to him. Then a decision would have to be made, but by people well above her own pay grade. From what she knew about Glennister, he was unlikely to be a mastermind. But even a puppet needed someone to work the strings. Glennister was tied up in the whole messy web, and he had questions to answer.

26

Liv's stomach was rumbling. She hadn't eaten since the previous evening, which couldn't be good for the baby. She didn't feel hungry, though; she just had the same heavy nausea sitting in her belly that had settled there as she was told the news about her brother's death.

They had left her alone. She tried to move her feet, the pins and needles in them having given way to numbness long before. The man with the torch and his shadowy companion had promised they would return with more questions, and the tape had been stuck back over her mouth before she could muster up a pithy response. She hadn't told them anything – not because she didn't want to, but because they hadn't seemed to know what to ask her. She'd demanded to be released, promised there would be no repercussions if they let her go. When that didn't work, she told them about the baby, pleaded with them, said she needed water, food and rest. No chance. They had backed away, left her with her ribs aching and her mouth parched. Her bladder had released at some point, leaving her smelly and uncomfortable.

Furious, she tried to stamp her foot, but could only manage a feeble tap of her toes on the floor. She clenched her fists, trying to test the strength of the restraints around her wrists. She had never worn cuffs before, but had snapped them over the wrists of more criminals than she could remember. These felt like cable ties, and they weren't going to give. She was stuck, at the mercy of her faceless captors. Surely someone would have noticed her absence by now? She had no idea what time it was, but Adam must have finished his shift. He would be terrified, probably combing the streets. Her colleagues too would rally round, throw everything they had into tracking her down.

Wouldn't they?

She blinked, thinking about it. Her parents hadn't been expecting her, so they wouldn't miss her. If the men who had taken her put Adam out of the picture, no one would be any the wiser until Tim Achebe or Jen Somerville remembered their colleague and contacted her. Since her brother had just been murdered, and she was on sick leave anyway, they might not be in touch for weeks, especially with their current workload. Tears gathered in her eyes again. Where was Adam? Was he safe? He wouldn't know where to look, even if he was able to go out searching. She could be anywhere.

Her cheeks wet with tears, Liv squeezed her eyes closed and tried to think clearly. Whatever happened, she had to get out of this unhurt. For the baby to come to harm was unthinkable. She didn't care about herself, but the child she carried was precious.

Who was she kidding? She was terrified.

What could she tell them? What did they want? She hadn't recognised the voice of the man with the torch, and the other person hadn't spoken. Did that mean she had met him or her before? She frowned, thinking about it. Who was involved? If this was about Jackson and his business activities, she would have no idea, but if it was about the deaths of Ben Rainey and Anthony Bryce...

As a detective inspector, Liv might have been forgiven for barely noticing the uniformed constables around the station, but that wasn't the case. She had always prided herself on treating everyone the same, regardless of rank or what they might be able to do for her career. And Ben Rainey, with his eager smile and obvious enthusiasm for the job, had been a popular figure around Limehouse station. When she had transferred, they hadn't stayed in touch, but Liv knew the fury and outrage she felt about his death would be echoed by everyone who had worked with him. And whoever had tortured and killed him was still walking the streets. As for Anthony Bryce, he had made different choices in his life, but his death was no more deserved. The agony they must both have suffered was unimaginable. She wondered if it had been inflicted in this place, even in this chair. What had they told their captors? Had what they said led to Jackson's death? What was the link?

Liv shook her head, tired, angry and frightened. She had no answers, could think of no reason why she should be here.

Unless…

She sat up straighter, her mind hurtling through the implications, then discarding them. It couldn't be relevant. No one knew, and he would never have admitted it. It couldn't have any bearing on what had happened. It couldn't.

A sound outside. Were they back? She lifted her chin, blinking away the last of her tears.

The torch again. She was ready for it, closing her eyes as he neared her. He smelt musty, unwashed. The tape was removed, his warm skin touching hers for a second as he pulled it away. She recoiled. Another scent lingering as he moved away, one she recognised. Interesting. A clue that this was about Jackson? Perhaps.

'I'm starving,' she said. Her voice rasped on the words, and she coughed, cleared her throat.

'I doubt it.' The rustle of a carrier bag, the torch beam dipping, dancing on the floor. Concrete, oil-stained. A glimpse of his ruined trainers and grubby jeans. The other person was there, but keeping well back, in the shadows.

Liv filed the images away in her memory. They weren't being careful enough. Either they were confident she wouldn't be able to track them down, or she wasn't going to be given the opportunity to do so. She ignored the tightening of her throat. He came closer again, and a bottle of water appeared under her nose. He held it to her lips, and reluctantly she drank a few mouthfuls.

'You stink,' he told her.

Liv wrinkled her nose. 'So do you. I can't move from the chair, what's your excuse?'

A muffled sound from the far corner. A stifled laugh? Liv leaned forward, trying to make out the figure of the other person, but it was impossible. Why come if you were going to be silent? Perhaps he or she was here to keep an eye on the man with the torch. Maybe to boil the kettle, heat up the iron. Dole out the beatings. Liv gulped as the bottle was withdrawn and a sandwich appeared, thin white bread with a slice of processed cheese.

'Here.' His voice had changed; the remark about his hygiene had hit home, offended him. Liv eyed the sandwich, held in his grubby fingers.

'Could have washed your hands,' she said.

'Don't you want it?' He moved it away slightly. 'Thought you were hungry.'

'Didn't say I didn't want it.' Liv thought of the baby as she took a mouthful, keeping her lips well away from his hand. The fact that they were feeding her was a good sign, surely? If they had been going to kill her any time soon, why would they bother giving her something to eat? She chewed, swallowed. 'Mmm. Delicious. Is there any pickle?'

He didn't comment, just moved the sandwich so she could take another bite. She thought about savaging his fingers, but knew it was pointless. She was incredibly vulnerable, and while they were keeping her fed and watered, she might as well play along.

'Will you tell me why I'm here?' she said.

'No.'

She chewed. 'Then what's the point? I can't tell you what you want to know if you don't ask questions.'

'Who says we want to know anything?'

Last mouthful. As she swallowed it, the water bottle reappeared. She drank. 'You've just decided to keep me as an exotic pet, is that it?'

He actually laughed. 'We're doing as we're told.'

'You're just the monkeys? Well I'd worked that out for myself. Is this about Jackson?'

'You haven't figured it out yet?' He held up the bottle again.

'Being tied to a chair isn't doing much for my thought processes. Let me go. I'm pregnant, you bastards.'

A sigh. 'So you keep saying. Makes no difference. Have we hurt you?'

'Well…'

'No, we haven't. Play your cards right, and we won't have to.'

'Is it about Ben Rainey?'

Silence. 'Who? Never heard of him.'

'You're a crap liar, you know that? I can't see your face, and I can still tell that's bullshit. Okay. What about Anthony Bryce?'

He said nothing, but the beam dipped again and the bottle disappeared. Liv snarled. 'My husband will find me, you fuckers. My colleagues will be searching all over London. Let me walk away now, and you'll be forgotten about. I'll pretend I got lost for a while.'

'Your husband? Your colleagues?' Laughter. 'Yeah, okay.' He had the tape in his hand again, ready to cover her mouth.

'Just tell me what you want.' Her voice shook.

'Want?' He leaned closer, his mouth warm, damp against her ear. 'What we want is to keep you out of the way.'

Liv told herself to stay calm, though the urge to scream in his face was overwhelming. 'What do you mean?'

'Don't you know? I was expecting a detective inspector to be cleverer.'

'If you want money...'

Laughter. 'What, you've a few million tucked away? Come on, think about it.'

Liv closed her eyes, exhausted, struggling to give a shit what they did with her as long as she could sleep. 'Mad bastard.'

'You think *I'm* crazy?' His eyes flicked towards the figure in the corner. 'Wait until you meet the boss.'

27

Penrith was eating a crusty ham roll, crumbs decorating his lips and chin before drifting down onto his desk. He held up a finger as Caelan barrelled into the room. 'I'm on my lunch break.'

'Fuck off, Ian. When was the last time any of us had one of those?'

He gave a serene smile. 'If you're asking, I make sure I have one every day. Sit down. Start talking.'

She did as she was told, summarising the conversation with Crowley.

'Don't suppose we found the two men who gave him a kicking?'

'Not yet.' He took another huge bite, spoke with his mouth full. 'London traffic.'

'What about Ryan Glennister?'

'Nothing. We've more chance of finding the Loch Ness monster holidaying in the Thames. He'll be hiding in a doss house somewhere.'

'No news on Liv?'

Penrith shook his head, more crumbs flying. 'No. Nicky found nothing, as expected. Liv's parents weren't helpful; her husband's raging around the house demanding to be allowed to join the search. Achebe's wringing his hands, bleating at Somerville, who's coordinating everything.'

'At least we haven't found a body.'

He pointed a thick finger at her. 'Knew I could rely on you to look on the bright side. Let's talk about Crowley.'

'He thinks I'm sitting on a kilo of coke.'

Penrith grinned, delighted. 'Stupid arse. Some people would believe anything.'

'What are your plans?'

'My plans? You're the one with the drugs to sell.'

'I think he might notice if I turn up with a shitload of talcum powder.'

'It won't come to that. Let him talk to his friends, then lead us to Ryan Glennister.'

Caelan pursed her lips. 'Isn't this all too convenient? I happen to meet Marcus Crowley, who happens to be linked to Ryan Glennister, the man we're desperately trying to find?'

'Maybe. But you met Crowley because of Frankie Hamilton, who we knew had links to dealers in Edmonton. From there, it's not much of a leap.'

'Have we any idea who Ryan Glennister's involved with?'

'No. He doesn't have a criminal record, as you know.'

She slammed her hands down on the arms of her chair. 'This is ridiculous. Why can't we find him?'

'You know why. He lives like a rat, darting from place to place. How do you track down a single rat when the city's full of them?'

'Almost poetic. The two blokes who attacked Crowley then. They can't have vanished.'

'But they have, for now. Achebe's got officers on it. I can't help it if they're not working quickly enough for your liking.'

'One of our officers is missing.'

'As I'm aware.' Penrith ran a hand over his eyes. 'You think I don't care?'

She knew he did, but it wouldn't help Liv Hobbs. 'How do you want me to play it with Crowley?'

'Wait for him to come back to you. Then you set up a deal. You've done it before. Let them suggest a time and place. For now, it's all we have.'

Caelan shook her head. 'They'll want a sample. You know how it works. I won't have one.'

'We'll move in before then. Arrest you too, nice and tidy. Then, when we've got Glennister—'

'You're assuming he'll be there. What if he isn't?'

'I don't know, Caelan. But what else do we have?' He looked exhausted.

'If it goes wrong, if they guess I'm lying...'

'We'll lose Crowley, Glennister, whoever he's working for and the whole shebang. I know. Let's hope Crowley leads Nicky to Glennister instead.'

'Have you heard from her?'

'No, but she's out there alone. Your friend Ewan was wandering around like a lost child. I had to stand him down.'

'What?'

Penrith held up his hands. 'My fault. I should have realised he might jeopardise your position with Crowley.'

Caelan scrambled to her feet. 'I need to get back out there.'

'Let Nicky handle it. If Crowley sees you, realises you're waiting for him to make a move...'

She stood looking down at him, hands on hips, her mind working. 'What if...'

'What?'

'What if Liv Hobbs is involved in this somehow?'

'Caelan—'

'Hear me out. We've only her word for it she was estranged from her brother.'

'What are you suggesting? She was helping him stay out of prison all these years? She ordered him killed herself?' Penrith rolled his eyes. 'Even for you, it's fanciful.'

'We're missing something, Ian. Achebe and his team are chasing their tails. We've no witnesses, forensic evidence is non-existent. Even if Liv Hobbs isn't involved, why snatch her? She has to know something.'

'She would have said so. Her record's exemplary.'

Caelan frowned. 'Why did she transfer to South Harrow station?'

'No idea.'

'It wasn't because of her promotion?'

Penrith didn't have to check. 'No. Does it matter?'

'No idea, but she knew Ben Rainey at Limehouse. Rainey knew Anthony Bryce, whose information set the Edmonton operation in motion.' Caelan pinched her lower lip. Was it relevant? Did it matter? She had no idea, but it had to be worth doing some digging. 'I'll go and speak to Liv's former colleagues at Limehouse station, then her husband again. Maybe he can help.'

'Waste of time.'

'Then give me instructions. You don't want me in Edmonton. What shall I do?'

Penrith closed his eyes. 'All right. But try not to wind Adam Waits any tighter. Hasn't he had a go at you once today already?'

'He was distressed, lashing out.'

'And you think he'll be calmer now?'

Caelan was already opening the door.

–

An hour later, she was sitting in a marked police car beside Adrian Dennis, the officer who had been identified by Achebe's team as the colleague Ben Rainey had been closest to. She had read through what he had said to Jen Somerville when she had broken the news of Rainey's death to him. Apart from his obvious distress and shock, he had mentioned little of note, unable to throw any light on his friend's murder. Looking at him now, his uniform damp from the drizzle that had begun to fall as she had arrived at Limehouse station, Caelan saw the resentment at being forced to face his loss again. She folded her hands in her lap, steadied herself. She was here because she hoped he could help her discover the truth about what had happened to his colleague and friend.

Dennis sat with his hands clenched around the steering wheel of the car, not looking at her. 'I don't know what you want me to say. Ben was a good officer, and he was my mate.' He blinked, swallowed a few times. 'He was well liked here, someone you'd want at your side if things kicked off. Ask anyone. Ben was the last person to deserve what happened to him.'

'I'm not suggesting anything different.' Caelan glanced at him, taking in the hunched shoulders, the set jaw. Why so defensive? 'You must have wondered why he was killed?'

Dennis turned his face away, looking out of the window beside him. 'I haven't wanted to think about it. Ben's gone, and he's not coming back. I'll leave wondering why someone killed him to you lot.'

'Did he ever mention someone called Anthony Bryce?'

'No. I'd never heard of Bryce until he was killed.'

'You were questioned again?'

'Briefly.'

'Do you recognise any of these names: Ryan Glennister? Marcus Crowley? Aaron Jacob?'

Dennis shook his head each time. 'How do you know Ben's death is even related to work? Couldn't he have pissed off the wrong person, stepped in to break up a fight or something?'

Caelan realised Dennis knew nothing of the torture his friend had been subjected to. 'Would he have done that?'

'Yeah, definitely. He may not have been a copper long, but his job was important to him. He said it was like being a doctor – we're never off duty.'

'Never off duty. Right.' Caelan repeated the words, remembering Rainey's presence in the brothel in Hackney. Had he been there because he'd been told about the underage girls, the drugs they were being given? Had he wanted to find evidence to prove they were being kept there against their will? 'Did Ben ever talk about a place in Hackney?'

'Hackney? No. He lived in Northolt.'

'What about drugs?'

'Drugs?' Dennis rounded on her. 'Look, what is this? You're accusing Ben of being a druggie now?'

Caelan held up a hand. 'Calm down. No. I know what caused Constable Rainey's death, and it wasn't an overdose.'

Dennis licked his lips. 'How did he die?'

'You don't know?'

'We weren't given details. They just said suspicious circumstances.'

Should she tell him? Strictly speaking, no. But as Rainey's colleague, his friend, she could understand his need to know. 'Ben was stabbed.'

Silence. Then, 'Stabbed. And you don't know who by?'

'It's… complicated.'

'Is it?' Dennis released the steering wheel, bunching his fists in his lap. 'Why?'

She didn't want to mention the torture. It would conjure images no friend of Rainey should be forced to have in their mind. 'There were no witnesses, no suspects. No forensic evidence.'

'You mean you've still not got a clue what happened?' The scorn was clear in his voice. 'It's been weeks.'

'I know. If you can help, if you know anything…'

'I don't.' Dennis folded his arms. 'If I could help, I would, but it looks to me as though you're clutching at straws.'

You're not wrong, Caelan thought. She decided to change tactics. 'What about Liv Hobbs?'

Now he looked at her. 'Detective Inspector Hobbs?'

'She was based here, wasn't she? Before her transfer?'

'Yeah, but…' Dennis shook his head. 'Why are you asking about her? What does she have to do with Ben's death?'

'Please, humour me. What did you think of her?'

He looked bemused. Caelan could sympathise. 'I barely saw her,' he said eventually. 'She was friendly, always smiled if you passed her in the corridor, but she's a DI, I'm a uniformed bobby. We didn't mix socially. You know how it is.' His mouth twisted. 'Or maybe you don't.'

Caelan ignored the comment. She had done her own stint in uniform, and wondered now if she should have stayed there, climbing the ladder in a different way. 'Do you know who Ben saw socially?'

He hesitated. 'I sometimes had a few beers after work with him. Me and some of the others from our shift. No one in particular. They were all spoken to when we were told Ben had died.'

He was keeping his cards close to his chest. Caelan wondered why. 'What about girlfriends?'

'I'm married.'

'Ben wasn't.'

'Well, he mentioned the odd name. I don't think there was anyone special.' Dennis shuffled. 'I told the other officer all this.'

He had, Caelan knew. All the same, his manner had changed. 'Listen, Adrian.' Was she really going to do this? But he knew something, she was sure. 'You need to keep this to yourself. Before he died, Ben was hurt. Badly hurt.'

He stared at her. 'What do you mean?'

'I mean, we believe he knew something, and whoever killed him was prepared to inflict a lot of pain to find out what it was.' Caelan took a breath, hating herself. It was a low blow, but she had no choice. Adrian Dennis had gone pale. 'And Ben wasn't the only victim.'

'You mean he was tortured?' Caelan didn't answer, and Dennis held his hands to his cheeks. 'The other bloke, what's his name, Bryce too? Fuck.'

'If you know anything, Adrian, please tell me.' Caelan thought of Liv Hobbs, missing and vulnerable.

Dennis's face tightened. 'I don't.'

Caelan said nothing, waiting to see if he would fill the silence. He didn't. He knew her game. 'Is there anyone who might be able to help me?'

'Don't think so.'

She began to open the car door. 'Thanks for your time.'

Dennis turned in his seat. 'Why did you ask about Liv Hobbs?'

'What?' She didn't want to mention Liv being missing, but she would if she had to.

'Isn't her brother some big-time dealer?'

'Yeah, but he's in prison now.'

He nodded. 'It's just, one time, I saw them talking.'

'Who?'

'Ben and DI Hobbs.'

'They were talking together?'

A nod. 'Ben and me, we'd just finished our shift. I'd been to the loo, and when I came out, they were standing by the lockers, having a chinwag. No reason for her to be there; she didn't have a locker, she shared an office. When they saw me, she walked away.'

'Could be meaningless. Maybe she was asking if he had some painkillers, or change for the vending machine.'

'Maybe. But I asked him about it, took the piss — senior officer, older woman and all that. And Ben, he usually played along, he liked a laugh, but not that time. He didn't want to talk about it.'

'And you let it go?'

'Yeah. I actually thought she'd been having a quiet word, giving him a bollocking, and he was pissed off, you know? Embarrassed.'

'Did she have a reason to? Had he done something wrong?'

'Not as far as I know, but he could have. I didn't always work with him.'

Caelan met his eyes. 'You didn't mention this when Ben died.'

He squirmed. 'I didn't think. It was six, seven months ago. The whole thing lasted about five seconds. She left soon after, and I forgot about it until you mentioned her name.'

'But you weren't going to tell me.'

'Well, Ben's dead.' His voice caught, and he coughed. 'I didn't think it was relevant if he got told off six months ago by a woman neither of us has seen since. How could it matter?'

Caelan had no idea, but it was new information. There had been little enough over the past couple of days.

Caelan knocked on the door of the house Liv Hobbs shared with her husband, bracing herself. The door was flung open, and Adam Waits stood glaring at her.

'Have you found her?'

'Not yet. I'm sorry.'

'Then why are you here?' He looked over her head and down the street, as if expecting to see his wife walking towards him. 'Where the hell is she? No one's telling me anything.'

'Mr Waits, could I come in?'

'Why? I've already got a constable in here with me, sitting on his arse when he could be out looking. When *I* could be out looking.'

'You know we can't allow that.'

He lifted his chin. 'You think you could stop me?'

She stared back at him. 'I'd have a go.'

'Got a Taser, have you?' He eyed her. 'You'd need it.'

'I need to ask more questions about Liv.'

Waits scowled. 'Because that'll help.'

Caelan said nothing; just stood her ground and stared him down. He gave in, moved back. She followed him into the living room, where a uniformed constable stood, his face red. Caelan smiled at him.

'Would you mind sticking the kettle on, please?'

'Not more bloody tea.' Waits threw himself down on the sofa, snatching his phone from the arm and staring at it. 'Why isn't she calling me back? I don't understand why you haven't found her yet. The baby...'

'I understand this is upsetting, but—'

'Upsetting? My wife and unborn child are missing. I want to be out there searching for her, not waiting here with a babysitter.' Waits rubbed his eyes. 'What you said to Liv about her accident. Is the crash related to her disappearance?'

Caelan remained standing. 'It's possible.'

'Then... Fucking Jackson. Still ruining her life, even though he's dead.'

'You think this is about Jackson?'

A bark of laughter. 'Isn't it always? Liv turned her back on him, but the name follows you around.'

'Especially if you don't change it when you get married.'

Waits narrowed his eyes. 'It was her choice. Why should she? It was her name as well as his.'

'But if she was so keen to distance herself from her brother, from her family, it was an ideal chance to do so, wasn't it?'

'She said there was no point. Everyone would still know who she was.' Waits clutched his phone tightly, as though having it close might make it ring.

'Let's be honest, the name gave Liv some status, didn't it?' Caelan said. 'Some notoriety? She might be a copper, but she was also a Hobbs from Edmonton. It meant respect, especially amongst people involved in the drug scene. People knew Jackson's name, and once Liv introduced herself – well, it would give her an edge.' She watched Waits, prepared for the inevitable explosion, but he just shook his head.

'Maybe. Maybe you're right. But what does it matter? Not going to help you find her, is it?'

'I don't know. Liv told me she still had friends in Edmonton. Do you know who they were?'

'I gave the names to Achebe and Jen. They're people she knew at school, or old neighbours. Mostly women with young kids. I can't see any of them grabbing Liv off the street.'

'What about their partners?'

'No idea. But Liv…' He screwed up his face. 'She hadn't seen any of them in person for years. She kept in touch by text or on social media, but that was all. She'd never met their husbands, kids or boyfriends. How could any of them be involved? It's got to be about Jackson.'

Caelan wasn't going to say it, but she suspected he was right. 'Did Liv talk to you about Ben Rainey and Anthony Bryce?'

His lips twitched. 'They're the men who were killed? Yeah, she mentioned them, and I've seen it in the news. I didn't want her to think about it, not when she was off sick. Not after the accident, and what you said to her.'

Caelan waited to see if he would work out her concerns about Liv's disappearance being linked to the deaths of Rainey and Bryce, but he kept his gaze on the floor. Should she mention it? It might distress him further, but it was a risk she had to take. As she considered how she would phrase what she had to say, his head jerked up.

'You don't think the bastard who killed Rainey has Liv?'

'We don't know, but we have to consider it.'

Waits groaned. 'He was tortured, wasn't he? The other bloke too? Shit, what if they're doing the same to Liv?' He jumped up, looking around wildly. 'I need to get out of here.'

The constable appeared in the doorway, three mugs in his hand. 'I don't want any more fucking tea,' Waits spat.

'Please sit down, Mr Waits,' said Caelan. She didn't raise her voice, but Waits looked at her, wrapping his arms around himself.

'I can't just sit here, I need to—'

'Drink your tea, and please try to answer my questions. We're doing everything we can to find Liv. Believe me, her colleagues are as worried as you are.'

Waits gave a snort of derision. 'Really? Somehow I doubt it.'

He accepted the cup the constable held out to him with a curt nod. Caelan wrapped her hands around her own drink, took a sip, again formulating what she wanted to say. Waits had focused on Rainey when she had mentioned the two men, but not Bryce. Why? Because he recognised the name? Because Liv had known him?

'Had Liv mentioned Ben Rainey before? When she worked at Limehouse?'

Waits looked at her over the rim of his mug. His eyes cut to the constable, and Caelan read his meaning. 'Could you give us a second?'

The officer nodded, left the room again, closing the door behind him. Waits took another sip of the scalding tea, screwing up his face. 'Who have you been talking to?'

'What do you mean?'

'I didn't think anyone knew about it.' He was frowning, running one hand through his hair. Cradling the mug against his chest, he met Caelan's eyes. 'A while ago, Liv and I were having problems. You know what I mean.'

'Marriage problems?'

'If you like. We'd wanted a baby for so long, but it hadn't happened. We'd been to doctors, given samples, been poked and prodded. Nothing worked. We were both absolutely gutted, possibly even depressed. Liv threw herself into her work, even more than usual, and I...' He gulped. 'I had an affair.'

Caelan waited, watching his mouth work as he struggled to control his tears. When he spoke again, his voice was choked. 'I'm not proud of it. It was stupid and weak, and it almost destroyed our marriage. It only lasted a couple of weeks, then

I told her… I said I couldn't carry on. Coming home to Liv, seeing her so quiet, so exhausted by it all. I knew I was going to lose her, and it gave me a kick up the arse. I realised what a shit I was being.'

'Did Liv find out?'

'I told her. She could see something was wrong, and I knew I had to. No, I wanted to.'

'How did she react?' Caelan couldn't see how it was relevant, but at least Waits was talking rather than snarling at her. He gave a lopsided smile.

'She heard me out, nodded, then left the house. I didn't see her till the next morning.'

'Where did she go?' Caelan thought she could guess.

'To give me a taste of my own medicine.'

'Meaning?'

'The lad you mentioned, the one she worked with – Rainey. She seduced him. Came home the next day to tell me about it.'

Caelan wasn't shocked, but she was surprised. When she had visited Liv Hobbs at home, her relationship with her husband had seemed solid, secure. As she had seen many times in her work, though, outward appearances could conceal totally different truths. She could imagine the strain months and years of trying and failing to have a baby could put on a relationship. 'What happened?' she asked.

Waits read her expression. 'I didn't go out and kill Rainey, if that's what you mean.' He forced a laugh. 'Doesn't look good for me, does it? But I never even met Ben Rainey. This was seven, eight months ago.'

'Before Liv left Limehouse?'

'Yeah. After it happened, we realised we'd both been stupid. Instead of talking about what had happened – the problems we'd had trying to have a family, I mean – we'd both put a brave face on and gone about our lives.' He sniffed. 'And we ended up pushing each other away. It sounds stupid, but the pair of us being unfaithful probably saved our marriage.'

'And Liv asked for a transfer, away from Limehouse.'

'She didn't want to keep seeing Rainey every day. She'd made it clear there was no chance of it being anything more than a one-night stand, even if he wanted it to be, which I don't think he did.'

Caelan wondered, remembering what Adrian Dennis had said. 'And Ben accepted that?'

'A no-strings night with an older woman – why wouldn't he?' Waits spoke lightly, but she could see the thought hurt him more than he wanted to admit.

'How did you feel about it?'

He grimaced. 'At first, I was furious, kept imagining them together, him touching her… But I knew it was payback, my own fault. Tit for tat, if you like. Liv swore it wouldn't happen again, and I believed her. I suppose she used him, but I don't think he was complaining.'

'Well, Ben's dead, so…' Caelan raised her eyebrows, deliberately needling him, but Waits remained calm.

'I know. Makes me feel like shit. I mean, I hated him, but I'd never wish him dead.' He shuddered, and Caelan had to admit the horror appeared genuine.

'And now? How's your relationship with Liv?'

'Now?' Waits met her eyes. 'We're good. Great, in fact. And we're having a baby.' His face closed, the strain of the past few hours showing in the faint lines around his mouth and eyes. 'If anything happens to her, to either of them…'

'It won't.' Caelan sounded more confident than she felt. They would need to check where Adam Waits had been when

Ben Rainey was killed. He couldn't have abducted his wife himself, as they had confirmation that he had been working, hurtling around London in an ambulance, but they'd had no reason before to check if he'd been working on the night Rainey died. She looked at him – the powerful build, the hurt in his eyes.

And she wondered.

28

Marcus Crowley hadn't left his snooker club, and no one had gone inside either. In the alley, Detective Nicky Sturgess stamped her feet and blew on her hands, knowing she was wasting her time. If Crowley was hurt, as Penrith had told her Caelan had reported, why would he leave? He could contact anyone he wanted to using his mobile.

She looked up at the club, assessing her options. Going inside alone would be a risk, but standing out here freezing was pointless. After sending Penrith a quick text to explain, which she immediately deleted, she strode towards the building.

As she crossed the road and stepped onto the pavement, a familiar black car approached. Nicky kept walking. Sure enough, two men got out. From their bulky build and dark clothing, she guessed they were the same two she had seen earlier. She had her back to them now, and knew she had to find an excuse to turn, to see what they were going to do.

In the end, she didn't need one.

She heard the footsteps behind her and spun around, but was too slow. They stood grinning at her, arms folded.

'Help you?' The man who spoke was taller than his friend, but not by much. His features were shadowed by the cap he wore, but Nicky made herself look into his face. Her heart began to thump. They couldn't have seen her watching; she had been careful. She always was. Unless... unless Crowley had spotted her from above, through the window. Caelan had been lurking here before, and perhaps he'd seen her, grown suspicious. Did these two louts work for Crowley? It didn't seem likely if they were the same men Caelan had seen go in and beat him up. Who, then? Ryan Glennister? No one seemed to believe him capable of employing anyone. Nicky knew she had to respond.

'No. Just minding my own business.'

The man laughed at that. 'You're not interested in the club?' His English was perfect, an accent she couldn't place just noticeable.

She looked bemused. 'The club? No.'

'In Marcus, then? You know him?'

'Crowley? I've heard of him. Never met him.'

'Yet you're waiting outside for him? What do you want?'

Nicky took a step back, bumped into the brick wall behind her. Shit. Stay calm. They're fishing. 'What are you talking about? I'm a cleaner, it's my day off. I'm on my way to the off-licence.'

'Oh really? You like a drink?'

'Doesn't everyone?' She assessed the distance between them. No room for her to push past, and they'd be on her if she did. No visible weapons, but she couldn't be certain. Better to try to talk her way out of it.

'We're going into the club for a drink. Why don't you join us?'

Nicky tried a smile. 'No thanks. I've never played snooker.'

'You don't need to.' He moved closer, his face set. 'Come on.'

They were either side of her, blocking off any escape route. The street was deserted, no cars or pedestrians in sight. Nicky slid a hand into her pocket, fumbling for her phone. He spotted the movement, grabbed her wrist.

'What have you got there?'

Without thinking, she swept his hand away, following the movement with a kick to his groin. He let out a roar, his knees buckling.

'Bitch!'

The other man reached for her hair. She twisted her body, blocking him with her forearm, her other hand going for his face. He ducked, his fist hurtling towards her stomach. Nicky tried to turn, but he was too close, and the blow glanced off her ribs. Her vision filled with bright dancing spots, and she clenched her jaw against the pain. She knew she couldn't fall to the ground. If she did, she would be finished. He was moving again, trying to catch her around the waist. The first man, still clutching between his legs with one hand, reached out to grab her with the other. Get away, she told herself. Put them down and run. Another kick was out of the question because of the agony pulsating around her ribcage.

She staggered back, hit the wall again. The man who'd punched her grinned.

'Another woman who can fight.'

Nicky jabbed at his throat, but he pushed her away as though swatting a fly, keeping hold of her forearm and twisting it the wrong way. She gritted her teeth as the pain began to build, knowing he would snap her arm if she didn't break free. The first man was watching, smirking, believing his friend could handle her. The realisation infuriated her, and she ordered herself to act. With her arm twisting between them, reaching her attacker would be impossible, unless... Without warning, she shifted her weight, lifted her foot and booted his shin. He let go of her arm, fury darkening his face. She broke away, tried to run, but every step jolted her ribs, and she was already struggling, panting, her breathing laboured, her vision swimming.

She clutched her ribs, kept going, but she could hear them behind her and she stumbled. Where was everyone? How could she be in one of the most crowded cities in the world with no one in sight?

She remembered the phone and hauled it out of her pocket, her fingers clumsy on the screen. She didn't know if it connected before a hand reached over her shoulder, another snatching at her waist. Hot breath in her ear, a thick arm pulling her off the ground. Something sharp against her neck, tugging on her skin. The sky blurring, darkening.

Disappearing.

29

In his office, Ian Penrith had the receiver of his desk phone jammed under his chin, listening to Chief Superintendent Adele Brady's forthright opinions on where the investigation had gone wrong. He balled the paper bag that had contained his ham roll in his fist and, squinting, lobbed it towards the bin. It bounced off the rim and skittered across the carpet. Penrith pulled a face. The screen of his mobile lit up with an incoming call, darkening again before it had a chance to ring. Penrith frowned, reaching for the handset. Nicky. A missed call. He waited for her to try again, Adele Brady's monologue continuing in his ear. She didn't seem to require much input from him. He was tempted to set the receiver on the desk and let her blather on while he retrieved the paper bag from the floor, but didn't quite dare.

After a couple of minutes, when Nicky hadn't called back, he picked up the phone again and sent her a text, asking if she was okay. No response.

'Ian?' Adele Brady sounded impatient, and he wondered what he'd missed. Nothing important, or at least nowhere near as important as his own team. He might not show it, would never admit it, even to himself, but he thought of them as family.

He blinked. 'Sorry, one of my officers is trying to contact me. She's out in the field and I really should—' He pressed the button to end the call with Brady, their discussion already forgotten.

He listened to Nicky's phone ring, the automated voicemail eventually asking him to leave a message. He stared at the phone, a chill spreading through him. It wasn't unusual for an officer to be interrupted when they were trying to call in, but they usually chose a time and location where they wouldn't be disturbed. Nicky was alone, watching a potential person of interest. If she required backup, he needed to act. What was she playing at? With one officer already missing, he knew he couldn't afford to take chances. He tried again, willing her to answer.

'Come on, Nicky,' he mumbled, tapping his fingers on the desk. Voicemail. 'Shit.' Where the hell was Caelan? Wandering around with no direction when she should have been with her colleague. And Richard Adamson, kicking his heels in prison. Pointless.

Penrith told himself to calm down as he ran a hand across his forehead, feeling sweat beginning to dampen his hairline. There was no evidence that Nicky was in danger, or had been exposed for who she truly was. No proof except the fear crawling across his shoulders and the dread in his belly. He called Caelan, using his landline. She answered immediately, and Penrith, hearing the relief in his own voice, hoped she wouldn't pick up on it.

'Are you okay?'

She sounded bemused. 'Fine. What's the problem?'

Of course she had realised. 'Hopefully nothing,' he told her. 'Can you get back to the club?'

She knew better than to ask. 'On my way. What am I looking for?'

'Who. I can't reach her.'

A pause. Then: 'Shit.'

It was a whisper, and Penrith closed his eyes, silently berating himself. In his hurry, he had forgotten Nicky and Caelan's history. Then he straightened his back, told himself to focus on what mattered – making sure Nicky was safe. Caelan would be nothing but professional, he knew.

'Can you check something for me?' Caelan asked. She was hurrying, he could tell from her breathing. There was traffic noise, the sound of the wind. She was on her way. It would be okay. Backup, looking out for each other. It was what they did best, except he had sent Nicky out alone. He shut the thought down. She was a professional, had worked on her own hundreds of times and in much more perilous situations.

'What do you need?' he asked.

He listened to what Caelan had discovered, picking up his mobile and firing off a text to Achebe as she talked.

'I don't think Waits is involved, but...' The rest of her sentence was lost in the blare of a car horn.

'We need to check.' Penrith was nodding though no one could see him. 'He's a paramedic, he'd have a good idea how much punishment the human body could stand.'

'You're thinking about the torture?'

'A man who'd slept with his wife...' Penrith thought about it. 'No, I don't buy it. Going up to Ben Rainey and thumping him, yes, but prolonged torture? And where would Bryce fit in?'

'Like I said, I don't think he's who we're looking for. He didn't have to tell me about Liv and Rainey. Why would he draw attention to himself? He just wants her found.'

'Don't we all.' Penrith used his mobile to try Nicky's phone again. 'Nicky's still not answering.'

'It'll take me well over an hour to get there. Isn't there someone else nearby?'

Penrith turned to hook his jacket from the back of his chair. 'I'll meet you there.'

–

Caelan jogged towards South Harrow station, her phone in her hand, her body feeling electrified. Penrith sounding even slightly perturbed was unheard of, and for him to show real concern was disconcerting to say the least. Her own footsteps thudded in her ears as she hurried along, hoping there was an innocent explanation for the loss of contact. She knew Nicky, and how she worked. She was careful, they all were. They had procedures, different options to cover all eventualities. Their training was exhaustive, and continuous. Mistakes were rare, and usually costly. If Nicky had vanished, just as Liv Hobbs had, who could be behind her disappearance? Marcus Crowley was out of action, unless he had been faking his injuries, and Caelan didn't believe he had. Why had he been attacked? He'd been hurt, but superficially compared to the agonies inflicted on Ben Rainey and Anthony Bryce. More to the point, he was still alive. Why?

She entered the station, waited for the train, working through what they knew. The picture was still hazy. Snippets of information kept coming to light, but they weren't leading in any meaningful direction. Rainey, Bryce, Crowley, Jackson Hobbs. Liv, and Adam Waits. The two men who had grabbed her to send a warning to Frankie Hamilton. Ryan Glennister, always central to the investigation but also on the periphery, impossible to catch hold of. And Aaron Jacob, murdering a man because of the threat hanging over his daughter. Caelan looked down the platform, listening for the train. She couldn't see the link, knew she was missing the truth. There were too many unknowns, more questions than answers. Lies, and half-truths. There always were, in any investigation, but there was no pattern here.

She checked her phone again, called Achebe.

'You've heard about Liv Hobbs and Ben Rainey?' she said.

'Penrith told me. Hard to believe.'

'Why?'

'I wouldn't have said it was something Liv would do.'

'Even though her husband had cheated on her?'

'Well, yeah. Goes to show, you don't really know people.'

'You've not worked with her that long.' Caelan could see the lights of the train approaching, and knew she had to be quick. 'There's still no sign of her?'

'None. And I'll be honest, I've no idea what to do next.' Achebe sounded defeated.

'There is an explanation...'

'I'm not going to like this, am I?'

'Maybe Liv doesn't want to be found.'

'Caelan—'

'I'm serious. Look, I need to get on the train, but do me a favour and think about it. Have a look at her bank accounts as well her phone records. Please, Tim.'

'You know I can't, I've no justification. Liv's clean, I'd bet my pension on it.'

'She's a missing person. You can do whatever it takes to bring her home.'

'You think she's capable of torture, of murder? Of ordering the death of her own brother?'

Caelan moved towards the train, one of the last people remaining on the platform.

'You know as well as I do that people are capable of pretty much anything if they have to be. We're talking about drugs, which means shitloads of money. Just... something doesn't feel right. Have a look, it can't hurt. I've got to go. I'll call you back.'

As the doors closed, Caelan leaned back against the side of the train and closed her eyes. She was making assumptions, flailing for answers. But several things about Liv Hobbs didn't stack up. She hadn't mentioned her fling with Ben Rainey, though that was understandable. It wouldn't have been something Caelan would have wanted to broadcast to strangers herself. Liv had shown little emotion when discussing the death of a man she had been closer to than she had admitted. Again, unsurprising, but was there a more sinister reason for her reticence?

Most likely, Caelan had to admit, Liv Hobbs had been embarrassed about her night with Rainey, and was hoping no one except herself and her husband knew about it. It seemed she and Adam were looking to their future, and turning their backs on the problems of their past. Who could blame them?

But Caelan knew she wouldn't be doing her job properly if she didn't voice her concerns. Achebe should be able to gain permission to poke around in Liv's finances and phone records without too much trouble. And when Liv came home, she could have no complaints if she discovered they had been looking. It was to be expected when someone in her position suddenly disappeared.

Opening her eyes, Caelan caught a woman seated further down the carriage staring at her. The woman looked away, blushing, and Caelan allowed herself a tiny smile. Whatever was passing through the woman's mind, she was looking at Caelan's disguise, her mask. One advantage of this job was the opportunity to press pause on her own life and step into someone else's for a time, but it could also make her head the loneliest place on earth. Until Nicky's disappearance had been officially confirmed, Caelan wouldn't allow herself to dwell on how she felt about it. She had to focus on what she could do, not on what might be happening to two of her colleagues. If she allowed herself to remember that Nicky had been the person she had imagined her future with, she would go to pieces. Better to keep pushing towards the truth.

She took a circular route towards the snooker club, reluctant to go too close to it. She had heard nothing from Penrith, but he should be there by now.

Two streets away, her phone rang.

'She's not here.' Penrith's voice was flat.

'I'm five minutes out,' Caelan told him. Her voice trembled, her mouth dry. What the hell was going on? Police officers disappearing from the streets? Torture? She felt a flicker of fear, unfamiliar and unwelcome.

'Which street are you on? I'll come to you,' said Penrith. She told him, quickening her step again. They shouldn't be seen together, not so close to Crowley's place, but this situation called for action, not following rules. She had never been part of an operation where an officer had gone missing before. She wondered if Penrith had.

She turned a corner, saw him hurrying towards her, his eyes scanning the street around them. Hesitating, she pretended to take a call, turned her back on the street, giving Penrith the opportunity to walk past her if he wanted to. She was aware of him stopping beside her.

'There's no sign of her,' he said softly. 'I've asked them to put a trace on her phone, and spoken to the Assistant Commissioner. She's... not happy.'

'I can imagine. What's the plan?'

'To find Nicky? There isn't one.'

Caelan stared at him. 'What, we're just going to forget about her?'

Penrith's lips tightened. 'There have been concerns about her state of mind. I've been told to give her some time.'

'Time? Time to reappear as a corpse, you mean?'

He laid a hand on her arm. Caelan glared at it, considering wrenching it away.

'Look at it from Beckett's point of view,' he said. 'Either Nicky fucked up and someone realised she wasn't an innocent passer-by, or she's gone AWOL.'

Caelan sneered at him. 'AWOL? You think that's likely, do you?'

'Honestly? I don't know. She's been through a difficult time, and since she's been back, she's not been herself.'

'Then why was she out here, especially alone?'

'You know why. We couldn't have you working together, not after...'

'I was told I had to work with her or be transferred out of the department. Don't lie to me, Ian.'

'I wasn't.'

'What's this new job title of yours going to be? Assistant Commissioner Beckett's puppet?'

His cheeks were red. 'We're all her bloody puppets.'

'Does she honestly believe Nicky would walk away from an assignment? From her team?'

'I don't know.' Penrith blinked, ran a hand over his forehead. 'She wants you to focus on the deal Crowley is looking to set up.'

'The... What?' Caelan struggled to believe what she was hearing. Two officers absent without leave, and Beckett was focusing on a fictional drug deal?

'It's the only lead we have. We can't find Liv Hobbs, Ryan Glennister, or the two blokes you saw earlier.'

Caelan looked up and down the street. It was half residential, half shops. They were standing outside a fried-chicken shop, closed for another couple of hours. No one anywhere near them. 'Isn't it feasible that the two of them grabbed Nicky?'

'It's possible. What I can't understand is why they would even have noticed her.'

'No idea.' Her stomach lurched as she visualised Nicky being taken against her will. She would have fought, there was no doubt, but Caelan knew that if they were the same men she herself had fended off, they would have had no problem overpowering her. 'I think it's obvious what I need to do.'

Penrith stared at her. 'You're not going in to confront Crowley.'

'How did you—'

'It's the last thing you should be doing, as you no doubt know. Let us do this our way, Caelan. Otherwise, Beckett will have you taken off the case.'

'What if Nicky's telling them everything she knows already? What if our operation's been blown wide open?'

'She wouldn't talk.'

'With a hot iron held to her back? Boiling water poured down her throat? I think she probably would. I'd sell you all out as soon as I saw them put the kettle on.'

Penrith shook his head. 'We've no reason to believe anything of the sort.'

'I've suggested to Tim Achebe he should be looking at Liv's bank account.'

'You're expecting a few hundred thousand to be stashed away in an ISA? You think she's stupid?'

'No, far from it. We should be searching her house too.'

'You mean you didn't have a poke around while you were there? I'm surprised at you.' Penrith stepped back as an elderly man hobbled towards them, dragging a fabric shopping trolley behind him. Caelan waited until he had limped past before she spoke again.

'Not easy to do with Adam Waits watching my every move. Did you find out where he was when Rainey died?'

'Working. As he was the night Bryce was killed too. Caelan, I know you're worried about Nicky.' She began to protest, and he held up a hand. 'I *know* you are. But Crowley is our only lead. If we stick with him, he'll lead us to Glennister.'

'And in the meantime, Nicky and Liv could be dead.'

Penrith exhaled. 'What do you suggest? We knock on every door in London looking for them? We have nothing.'

Caelan met his eyes. 'Then let me go and speak to Crowley again.'

'Absolutely not. If you attempt it, I'll arrest you myself.'

She laughed. 'You'd have to catch me first.'

'Listen, if whoever's behind all this has Nicky, you think they'll keep her alive if they realise we're going after them? She's useful to them.'

'If they're not wiring her up to the mains already.' An image shot through Caelan's mind – a lazy Sunday morning, Nicky cooking them breakfast, a stroll around Brick Lane market, arm in arm. One of the few weekends they had been able to spend together. She clenched her jaw. Where the hell was Nicky? 'Did you search the alley?'

Penrith looked surprised. 'I had a quick look, but I didn't want to hang around. Why?'

'I just thought… Liv's phone was left behind. They must know we can trace them, everyone does.'

'You think Nicky's might have been left too?'

'Worth checking, isn't it?'

He nodded. 'I'll go. Crowley knows you. Go and get a hot drink or something.'

She turned away. He should have looked for the phone. She dug her hands into the pockets of her jacket, scanning the street. She knew he was right, Crowley could be their way to Ryan Glennister, but the idea of waiting around for him was unacceptable. Penrith had forbidden her to approach Crowley, but what if she went above him? If Elizabeth Beckett was keen for the meeting Crowley had hinted at to go ahead, a conversation with her might be worthwhile. Caelan knew she had to act. Sitting back and waiting was not an option. If Beckett wouldn't agree to her seeing Crowley, she knew she would have a decision to make.

She took out her phone, knowing she would have to call the office to be reminded of Beckett's number. And using this phone, the one given to her as part of her Kay Summers character, was a risk. When Penrith found out, he would be furious, and Beckett probably wouldn't be too pleased either. But Nicky was a colleague, one of her team. Their personal relationship was irrelevant; Caelan knew she would have the same need to act if Richard Adamson or Penrith himself had disappeared. She stared at the ground, knowing she was denying the truth – it did make a difference. Nicky had devastated her, damaged their relationship beyond repair, but Caelan knew she would still risk everything to help her. The admission infuriated her, and she stabbed at the keys on the phone, making the call before she could change her mind.

Less than a minute later, Assistant Commissioner Beckett was on the line. Her first words weren't encouraging.

'Are you crazy?'

'Not as far as I'm aware.' Caelan waited, unable to predict how Beckett would respond. She was loyal to her officers, but also capable of dismissing the lot of them if she deemed it necessary. Their past meetings had been business-like, based on mutual respect, but Caelan knew she was already treading a fine line.

'What do you want? This is totally against protocol.'

'It's an extraordinary situation.'

'Even more reason to stick to the rules. I'm ending the call now.'

'Wait, please. The meeting Marcus Crowley wants to organise. Do I have your permission to speak to him, or see him, try to hurry it along?'

Beckett paused. Caelan wished she could see the other woman's face, though she knew from experience that Elizabeth Beckett gave little away. 'Why?'

'Because we potentially have two lives to save. Three, including Liv Hobbs's unborn child.'

'This is about Nicky Sturgess, isn't it?' Beckett made a sound of exasperation. 'I'm bringing you in, Caelan, as Commander Penrith was told to do. You're a risk to yourself, your colleagues and our operations. Stay where you are. A car will collect you.'

Caelan smiled. 'With respect, ma'am, who else are you planning on sending in? Crowley knows me, and he's beginning to trust me.'

'Because of a story fabricated by Ian Penrith. It can easily be changed.'

'Wouldn't work and you know it. Crowley is cautious. We need to act quickly.'

Another silence. 'You think the people who killed Ben Rainey and Anthony Bryce have DI Hobbs and Detective

Sturgess? Why would they take such a risk? Kidnapping police officers? It's ridiculous.'

'I agree, but what other explanation is there?'

'We've no proof.'

Caelan turned to see Ian Penrith striding towards her. He stopped, opened a huge hand to reveal an object in a clear evidence bag. Small, silver. Nicky's phone.

'I found it about five yards from the entrance to the snooker club,' he said quietly. He nodded at Caelan's own mobile. 'Who're you talking to?'

She ignored him. 'I think we might have found your proof, ma'am. We've got Nicky's mobile, abandoned like Liv Hobbs's was.'

Penrith's expression changed from concerned to thunderous. 'Is that the Assistant Commissioner? Give me the phone.' He reached for it.

Caelan shrugged him off as Beckett said, 'Then the situation has changed. What's your plan?'

'To find Crowley, tell him I've been offered a deal by someone I know from way back. Say that if the meeting doesn't happen tonight, I'm out and he loses his chance to make some commission.'

Silence. Penrith waited, hands on hips, scowling. Caelan had counted to fifteen before Beckett spoke again.

'I won't tell you it's risky, because you know it will be. I won't say it'll probably fail, because I agree we need to act. I'd prefer you to speak to Crowley on the phone, though, not face to face. What do you think?'

Caelan didn't hesitate. 'Works for me.'

'I want to talk to you. Come to my office after you've spoken to Crowley. Bring Penrith.'

'Yes, ma'am.'

Beckett ended the call, and Caelan looked at Penrith. 'Game on, then.'

He was clearly furious, struggling to contain his anger. 'Strange how you always seem to end up getting your own way.'

'Not always.' Caelan checked the time. 'She wants to see us.'

'Not in that ridiculous bunker of hers?' He groaned, some of his good humour returning. Caelan waited, knowing he would back her up however much he might disagree with the action she had taken. 'Come on then. If you're determined to throw yourself into another suicide mission, I might as well wave you off.'

30

Mulligan stared at the woman in the back seat of the car, nose wrinkled. They had fastened the seat belt around her, making it look as though she had fallen asleep.

'Who is she?' he demanded.

His men were standing by, waiting for acknowledgement, like dogs who had brought their owner a ball to throw.

'She was hanging around the snooker club,' said Andri.

'Hanging around?'

Andri nodded. 'Looked like she wanted to go inside. We didn't like it.'

Mulligan glared at them. Not too intimidating, not yet, but enough to worry them. 'It's not our club, not our business. Crowley has friends we don't want to piss off. Why did you bring her here?'

They looked at each other, frowning. Mulligan tapped his foot, wondering who had possession of the family brain today. Neither of these two, obviously. Must be their mother's turn, back in Albania. They had been useful, especially when he had been moving into what he liked to call 'live exports'. In the beginning, they had sourced girls in Albania, finding those from the poorest families, the most desperate. They had promised new lives, unlimited wages. Hope. Once the girls arrived in the UK, they soon discovered things weren't quite as rosy. Mulligan smirked. Still, it had to be better than scraping a living in the backwaters of Albania, so where was the problem? Now, though, his men were dragging him down. His vision for the future, the new direction his business was taking... The future looked rosy, but these two would have to go. The Albanians he was hoping to count as business associates soon could eat them for breakfast.

'We were being careful.' Erdi glanced at his brother, who looked away.

Clicking his tongue, Mulligan folded his arms. 'I'm still not getting it.'

Blank looks. 'Boss?'

'She's nobody. She's not the woman Crowley has been talking to. He gave you a photo of her, didn't he?'

'After Erdi punched him.' Andri nudged his brother, getting no response.

'So why didn't you check? They're not even similar. She's not the woman we want. Did she see your faces?'

Shuffling feet. Eyes flicking from side to side. He'd caught them. 'We asked her what she was doing, she didn't cooperate. We had to—'

Mulligan interrupted. 'Had to?' His voice low, dangerous. He took a step towards them, almost nose to nose with Andri, who shrank back.

'She fought us, boss,' he said quickly. 'What were we supposed to do?'

'Not bringing her here would have been a start. Ignoring her, leaving her alone would have been even better. You've fucked up, boys, you get me? She's the wrong woman. You were jumpy, and you panicked. Now we have to deal with her.'

They were red-faced, wondering how to back-pedal. Mulligan knew each would betray the other in a heartbeat, brothers or not. He could read them without even trying.

Leaning closer to the woman slumped in the car, Mulligan prodded her arm. There was no reaction. 'How much did you give her?'

Erdi gave a nervous snicker. 'Enough to keep her quiet for a while.'

'Obviously.' Lifting her wrist, Mulligan pressed two fingers to it. 'There's a pulse, but it's faint. Congratulations, boys. You've excelled yourselves.'

'You mean she's...'

'Dying?' said Mulligan conversationally. 'I'd say it's a strong possibility, you fucking halfwits. Get her out of here.'

'But boss—'

'Now.'

Mulligan turned on his heel, took out his phone. Waited.

'Where shall we...?'

He couldn't tell which one was whining at him, but they needed to stop. Fucking pathetic. He took a breath, told himself to keep a lid on it. He still needed them. 'Put her with Hobbs. If she wakes up, finish her. She's seen too much.'

'Okay. Sorry, boss.'

'And find me the right person, the one Crowley told us about. You've already spoken to her once, and she kicked the shit out of you. Kay Summers. Do you need me to write it down?'

'We'll find her.'

He looked over his shoulder, gave them a hard stare, feeling like a pantomime villain. 'Make sure you do. And remember, this woman you've brought in – if she wakes or speaks, kill her. No loose ends.'

He watched them scrambling back into the car, falling over each other to do his bidding, and smiled.

Like rats in a trap.

The office Elizabeth Beckett had summoned them to was located beneath a building on Great George Street. Various rooms were hidden away underground. What the others were used for, Caelan had no idea, but it would be high level, top secret. She had been there a few times now, but the marble floors, ornate plasterwork and crystal chandeliers were still impressive.

So were the armed officers stationed in the underground corridors.

They had been met just inside the entrance by a man, introducing himself as Simon, who asked them to follow him. As they crossed the ornate lobby, Caelan recognised a plain wooden door, tucked away beside a marble staircase. Anyone who even noticed it would assume it was a store cupboard, which was no doubt the point. Simon tapped on the door, and it was immediately opened.

'You mean there isn't a secret knock?' Caelan raised her eyebrows. 'I'm disappointed.'

There was no reaction from Simon as he stood back and waited for them to go through.

Beyond the door was a stone passageway, the air cool, a single unshaded bulb hanging above them. Penrith coughed.

'I always expect to emerge in a cell in the Tower of London.'

'Don't give Beckett ideas.'

'Beyond our budget,' said Beckett from behind them. Caelan fought the urge to spin around. Where had she sprung from? The Assistant Commissioner passed them, held open the door to her room. Inside, grey walls and carpet added to the general air of gloom. The place was empty apart from a table and six chairs. A jug of water and six glasses stood ready. Beckett picked up the jug and filled three glasses.

'Not expecting anyone else?' said Caelan. Beckett gave a terse smile as she opened the briefcase she carried and removed a laptop.

'Not in person.' She readied the machine, and after a few clicks, the faces of the two men from the National Crime Agency they were supposed to be working with appeared. Caelan had almost forgotten about them. What the hell were their names? She glanced at Penrith, who raised his eyebrows at her. No doubt he couldn't remember either.

Beckett nodded towards the screen. 'Spencer Reid and Phil Webster. You met them a few days ago, and I've been keeping them informed of our progress.'

Caelan looked at the screen. Webster sat with his arms folded, the beginnings of a beard darkening his jawline. Reid rubbed at his eyes, hid a yawn behind his hand. Caelan got the hint – they were tired, no doubt had been working hard. Good for them. They were both sitting in a warm conference room, safe and comfortable.

'We heard about your colleague.' Reid shook his head. 'Tough break.'

Webster stared at the tabletop, but Caelan caught the hint of a smirk on his face. She tensed, ready to challenge him, but Penrith's foot landed heavily on hers and she contented herself with a loud exhalation instead. Beckett turned and frowned at her, but Caelan knew she would have noted Webster's expression. Little escaped Elizabeth Beckett's notice.

'We're here to discuss the Marcus Crowley situation.' Beckett pulled out a chair and settled into it, nodding at Caelan and Penrith to do the same. 'Can you explain why Crowley wasn't on your radar when we first sent Nicky Sturgess into Edmonton?'

Reid tried a smile. 'Maybe *she* could explain why she wasn't aware of him, after spending time in the area, supposedly familiarising herself with the local dealers.'

Beckett didn't miss a beat. 'No doubt she could, if we knew where she was. If her disappearance is linked to this operation, I'll need answers.'

'As will our gaffer,' Webster said. He leaned forward. 'With respect, this isn't our cock-up.'

Beckett looked down her nose at him. 'Detective Sturgess was working with information provided by you, and your colleagues at the NCA. If she was sent in with half the intel she should have been, questions will be asked – by my superiors as well as yours.'

'Not our problem.' Webster looked unabashed.

'Had you heard of Ryan Glennister before?' Beckett's voice was taut, her anger held in check, but only just.

Webster raised his shoulders a fraction. 'Only as one of the local crackheads.'

'And Marcus Crowley?'

Reid stepped in. 'Look, if we'd briefed you on every drug user in Edmonton, we'd have been there forever.'

Caelan couldn't help herself. 'And that's why you didn't bother?' Penrith's foot gave her another nudge, but she didn't look at him.

Webster didn't bother to hide his leer this time. 'I suppose you're missing Detective Sturgess more than most?'

'Fuck off.' Caelan was succinct.

Beckett held up a hand. 'Can we get back on track?'

'Gladly,' said Reid, shooting his colleague a frown.

Webster sat back in his chair, unconcerned. 'I'm not sure what we're doing here, but yeah, go for it.'

'You requested this meeting,' said Beckett.

Webster wagged a finger. 'Not me. The whole situation is a joke. I'm all for us forgetting we were ever involved.'

'How professional of you.' There was no mistaking Beckett's contempt.

Webster inclined his head. 'I've a career to think of. And a family.'

'Nice prioritising,' said Caelan.

Webster bridled, thrusting out his chin, ready to snipe back at her, but Reid turned to him. 'Can we get on with this, Phil? I'll remind you lives could be at stake here.'

Webster forced a laugh. 'Why not? Things are fucked up enough already; we might as well finish the job.'

Beckett folded her arms. 'Good to see you so optimistic. Now, Caelan. Explain what Marcus Crowley said when you spoke to him on the phone.'

Caelan leaned back in her chair, wondering why Beckett was involving the two jokers from the NCA. Webster clearly didn't give a shit, and Reid, with his tight shirt and carefully styled hair, would do nothing to endanger himself or his reputation. They were irrelevant, and Caelan could only see them hindering their plans, not helping them.

'Ma'am, could I—' she began.

Beckett turned to look at her, her face impassive. 'This was a joint operation from the beginning, and I'm under instructions to keep it that way. Tell us what he said, please.'

Caelan had no choice. 'Well, he was happy to hear from me.' She thought back to the call, Crowley's animated tones. 'I allowed him to think I was panicking, possibly getting itchy feet about selling my phantom kilo of coke. I said I wanted the deal agreed tonight, or I'd be disappearing with the goods.'

'What did he say?' asked Reid.

Caelan smiled. 'That he'd have to make some calls. Less than five minutes later, he was back on the phone with a time for the meet.'

Reid waited. When Caelan didn't elaborate, he said, 'And?'

'I agreed to it, told him I'd see him there. Came here as instructed.'

'Now we need to decide how to play this,' said Beckett.

'I'll need a sample. To show them. They'll want to test it.' Caelan rubbed her eyes, a headache beginning behind them. Not what she needed. She would need to play her role to perfection, be on top of her game. The rush of adrenalin that usually accompanied the hours before such an operation was absent. The hum running through her body, the sense of being hyper-aware and hyper-alert. Perhaps it was too early. Maybe, as she approached the meeting place, she would feel the familiar sense of control, of power.

'Did Crowley say who would be at this meeting?' asked Reid.

'His buyer, or more likely, a representative of his buyer,' Caelan said.

'Ryan Glennister?' Reid was already looking sceptical, and Webster seemed to be hardly listening.

'I assume so.' Caelan couldn't be certain.

'But you don't know for sure?' Webster snorted. 'Wouldn't it have been better to speak to Crowley face to face, insist on hearing his side of the conversation?'

Beckett was stern. 'We decided against direct contact, for operational reasons.'

'In other words, you made a mistake.' Webster grinned. Beckett's nostrils flared, but she said nothing.

'Where is the meeting?' Reid had shifted his body, turning slightly away from Webster as though attempting to distance himself from his colleague.

'Crowley's going to text the location to me an hour before.' Caelan knew this was less than ideal for their preparations, but she had been given little option. 'The arrangements were made on the buyer's terms, take it or leave it.'

'And you accepted that?' Webster looked incredulous. Caelan told herself not to bite.

'I had no choice. This meeting could be our only chance of finding Ryan Glennister, and our two missing colleagues.'

Reid was frowning. 'Because Glennister was involved in setting up the murder of Jackson Hobbs?'

'It's the only lead we have,' said Penrith. He had been silent, watching Reid and Webster, his expression inscrutable. Now he leaned forward. 'And I'll thank you not to question my officers, or our methods.'

Caelan glanced at him. It was unheard of for him to publicly stand up for her, but also unwelcome. She could fight her own battles, and Penrith knew it. He looked back at her, and she caught the glint of mischief. Even now, with one of his team missing, he was doing his best to annoy her. Caelan ignored him, but Webster narrowed his eyes.

'Because they've done an outstanding job so far, yeah?'

Penrith sat back. 'In the circumstances, yes.'

'Really? Get a bonus for losing officers, do you?' Webster blew out his cheeks. 'Unbelievable.'

'You gave us little information and no support.' Penrith's smile was serene. 'In my opinion, my officers' progress has been more successful than anyone could have expected.'

Webster's eyes widened. 'You must have fucking low standards, mate.'

'Can we concentrate on the matter in hand?' Beckett glared at each of them in turn. 'We agreed to this meeting out of courtesy, but we don't need, or even want, your cooperation.'

Reid's lips thinned. 'Understood. What's the plan?'

'Caelan goes to the meeting, wherever it is.' Beckett glanced at Caelan, the look hard to read. Apprehension? Disappointment?

'She'll be alone?' said Reid.

Beckett spread her hands. 'She'll appear to be. It goes without saying that she'll be supported.'

'By?' Webster sat up straight, as though hoping to be asked himself. Caelan wondered why he had been so bullish. At the previous meeting he had been abrupt, but civil. Now he seemed to be out to cause offence.

'By our own officers.' Beckett's eyes were cold. 'As I said, we're here to share our plans, not to ask for help.'

'I've been involved in stings before,' said Webster. 'Why not let me go with her?'

Beckett stared at him. 'With respect, this is an undercover operation, not a drugs bust. Caelan is highly skilled, experienced. Her safety is our highest priority. Anything that might compromise it—'

'I wouldn't,' Webster interrupted. He held up a hand. 'Sorry. But we've been involved from the start. Joint operation, remember? Come on, I'll stay out of the way.'

Why was he so keen to be there? Caelan wondered. Bringing down a major dealer would be a boost to his career, but he had done his bit. Maybe the sense of danger appealed to him, or the subterfuge. From the outside, donning a mask, stepping into character for hours, days or even months seemed glamorous. Caelan had quickly learnt the truth. Watching Webster beg to be allowed to join in and knowing Beckett would never allow it felt like a waste of time. They had four hours until the meeting. Four hours that, for Liv Hobbs and Nicky Sturgess, could be the longest of their lives. Caelan hadn't allowed herself to dwell on the possibility that they were being subjected to the same punishment meted out to Ben Rainey and Anthony Bryce, but now her imagination provided a slideshow of horror.

She swallowed, attempting to shut the images down. Liv was pregnant, and Nicky... Nicky she had loved. Either of them suffering like the two men had was unthinkable. Why had they been snatched in the first place? There had been no demands for money or information. Nicky was hugely experienced, even more so than Caelan was. What had she done to draw attention to herself? Or was her disappearance unconnected to the case? Had she, as Penrith had suggested, simply walked away without looking back? Caelan couldn't believe it. She wasn't naïve enough to think Nicky wouldn't go without saying goodbye to her, because she had done it before. But the job was her life. Nicky had lost friends, family and Caelan herself because of it. Arguably her work was all she had left. Where the hell was she? And what was happening to her?

'You will not be involved.' Beckett spoke quietly but with authority. Webster looked away, pouting like a scolded child. Reid glanced at him but said nothing.

'You'll let us know where the meeting is, though?' Webster asked.

Beckett gave a tiny smile. 'After it's taken place, yes.'

'This is our operation.' Webster glared at her. 'Now you're going to grab the credit.'

'This isn't about credit; it's about finding our officers, and the people who killed two young men. If we can bring a drug dealer in at the same time, so much the better.' Beckett checked her watch. 'We're wasting time. We'll contact you again later, when—'

'When it's all over?' Webster spat. 'When the fat lady's sung? This is bullshit. I'll be speaking to—'

'Speak to whoever you want.' Beckett was calm. 'I'm telling you what's going to happen, not asking for your permission. Caelan will attend the meeting. At the right moment, the rest of our officers will move in. Everyone present will be arrested.'

'Including Caelan,' said Penrith. He smiled at her. 'Been a while since you've spent the night in the cells. Can't let Richard have all the fun, can we?'

'You're going to arrest her too? To preserve the cover story?' Reid blinked. 'Seems a lot of trouble to go to.'

'To protect her identity, and yes, to keep the story going. At no point should anyone suspect that Caelan or any of our officers are anyone other than who they've been pretending to be.' Beckett leaned forward, reached out a hand. 'Thank you, gentlemen. We'll speak again later.'

'But—' Webster began. Beckett cut the connection, the screen darkening.

'Goodbye,' she muttered. She turned to Caelan and Penrith. 'A waste of time, but we have to play nicely with them.'

'Why do you think Webster wanted to tag along?' Penrith asked.

'Fancies himself as an undercover cop. I'm surprised Reid didn't ask to be there too. He's ambitious, confident.' Beckett raised her eyebrows. 'And totally unsuited to our work. Neither of them would last an hour in the field. Anyway,' another glance at her watch, 'let's talk about what's going to happen.'

Caelan waited as Beckett and Penrith made their plans. Her job, meanwhile, was to prepare herself, to ready her mind for the task ahead. It wasn't easy. There were so many unknowns, and with them came the room for error, even for disaster. She knew that however much Beckett and Penrith discussed the meeting, in truth she was going in blind.

Blind, alone and underprepared.

Again, walking away from the job while she still could, looked extremely appealing.

31

Crying quietly, Liv Hobbs tried to peer into the darkness. The door had opened again, how long ago she couldn't have said. She thought there had been at least two men, but as they hadn't had torches, she couldn't be sure. They had carried something in, grunting and cursing under its weight, the meagre light from outside allowing Liv a second to see what it was. A large, heavy shape, wrapped in blankets.

A human-sized shape.

Allowing it to slump to the floor, they had gone without even glancing at Liv. She had tried to lean forward, willing her eyes to see through the gloom.

A body.

She was certain they had left her here with a dead body. Though the traffic noise outside made it impossible to be sure, she couldn't hear any breathing other than her own. Panic hurtled through her, and she screamed against the makeshift gag. She saw dead bodies frequently in her working life, but being locked in a room with one was a new and entirely unwelcome experience.

She forced herself to take some deep, shuddering breaths. Blinking away tears, she waited, willing whoever was there to speak, or even to breathe.

Nothing.

Liv closed her eyes. Where would this end? She knew she had only been here a matter of hours, but she was a police officer, for Christ's sake. Why weren't they looking for her? Where was Adam? And why the hell had she been abducted at all? What had he told her, the man who had fed her the sandwich? He'd said they were keeping her out of the way. But why? Liv frowned, working through the possibilities.

Anything to keep her mind off the prone figure in the corner.

Ben. It had to be.

She had discounted the possibility at first, unwilling to believe there could be a link. They had been so careful. But once he had told Anthony Bryce... In the end, he had signed both their death warrants. She had warned him, believing that once she had transferred away, he would forget about it all.

But clearly he hadn't. Ben was dead, and the knowledge would cause Liv pain for the rest of her life. Who had he been talking to? And why was she sitting here, tied up, a prisoner? She knew nothing of what had happened after she had cut ties with him. She had her life with Adam – their child, their future. Ben was part of her past.

But then... Jackson was dead. He'd had contacts, done deals. Pissed people off. Maybe one of them was taking revenge. But why take her, a police officer? She thought of her other brother, Taylor. He had no ties, was drifting through life. If Taylor was the alternative, of course they would choose her. Keeping a police officer under lock and key – what a joke. But why kill Jackson before he had a chance to see his sister captured and helpless? They hadn't asked questions, hadn't even threatened to torture her. Were they the same people who had killed Ben, or not?

Liv blinked, her head still aching. The messed-up fog of her thoughts wasn't helping.

In the corner, the blanket-covered figure still hadn't moved.

32

Mulligan checked he had his current phone and wallet, patted the inside pocket of his jacket. Grinned.

He waited for the car to appear before strolling outside and climbing into the back seat. Ryan was already sitting there, shoulders hunched, knees bouncing. Mulligan smiled.

'All right there, wee man? Feeling the bite, are we?'

Ryan licked his lips. 'Can't I have—'

Mulligan cut him short with a look. 'Not yet. You'll need your wits about you. That's assuming you have any.'

Sniggers from the front seats. Mulligan narrowed his eyes. Fucking sycophants. He was tired of the wastes of skin he was currently employing. After tonight though... Well, he was moving up in the world. Gaining respect, building a reputation. Soon he would be top dog around here. He had outmanoeuvred the competition, got rid of those who hung around. He glared at the back of Erdi's head as he changed gear. Time for a new team.

Beside him, Ryan was twitching, causing his sour, unwashed smell to fill the confined space. Mulligan turned his head away, nose wrinkling. Ryan was useful, but fuck, did he stink. He opened the window a crack, leant towards it. Soon the deal would be done and he could walk away from them without looking back. It had taken him months to initiate and then build the relationship with Marcus Crowley. Crowley was a prick: loud and brash, but well connected. Courting him had been a necessary if unappealing step in Mulligan's business plan. And now the man had made him an offer he knew he had to take. But Crowley had also made a mistake. Mulligan smiled, savouring the thought of what would happen next.

33

Penrith was fussing around her like the mother of the bride on her daughter's wedding day. Caelan slapped his hand away as he reached to check the transmitter for the hundredth time. It was attached to her bra, and though Penrith hadn't touched her, she was tired of him hovering.

'I don't want to wear this. It's a risk,' she told him.

Penrith spread his hands. 'Assistant Commissioner Beckett's orders, as you know.'

Caelan pursed her lips. 'And if it's found? Is she going to pay for my funeral?'

'Why would anyone find it? Are you planning to take your shirt off?'

'Come on, Ian. You know how these things work. They'll pat me down.'

'Okay, how about one like you wore last time out? The one attached to the…' Penrith waved a hand, 'hair thing?'

'Bobble, do you mean?' Caelan thought about it. It would be more discreet, and she knew it was reliable. 'I'd feel better.'

'Fine. I'll request it.' Penrith turned away to make the call. Caelan rolled her shoulders, feeling the tension in her neck and jaw. Here was the feeling she had once enjoyed, even craved. Adrenalin lighting her body, fizzing through her fingers and toes. Anticipation, expectation. Fear. Always fear, no matter how hard you tried to deny it. But even fear could be addictive.

'On its way,' Penrith said. Caelan's phone beeped, and he stared at her. 'Do we have an address?'

Caelan checked the message. 'Shit.'

'What?' Penrith almost knocked her over in his rush to read over her shoulder. 'The snooker club?' He rubbed his jaw. 'Is Crowley stupid?'

'I don't think so. I'm betting that once I'm there, he'll send another text with a different location, and have me chasing around.'

Penrith considered it. 'And if he doesn't?'

'We'll have to go with it, but the snooker club has only one door, one means of entry and escape. It's not ideal.'

Which was putting it mildly. Her backup wouldn't be able to sneak in through a fire door, or even approach unobserved. There were buildings around, providing some places to keep out of sight, but as soon as anyone tried to get close to the club, they would be spotted, should Crowley have lookouts. And in his position, he should. Caelan thought about it.

'I could reply saying I'm not happy, I want it to happen elsewhere,' she said.

'No. In the text, he's relaxed, confident. If you start making demands, he might panic and call the whole thing off.'

'Not with what he stands to lose if the deal doesn't happen. I think he'll go for it.'

'Even if he does, his client might not. You're not just dealing with Crowley, remember.'

There was a silence, each unwilling to give in. In the end, Caelan puffed out her cheeks, admitting Penrith had a point. If she didn't do as she was told, she could blow the whole plan. What would happen to Nicky and Liv then? 'Fine. I'll reply, say I'll be there.' She did so. 'Have you heard from Achebe?'

'They haven't found her.' Penrith didn't say who he meant, but Caelan knew. Liv Hobbs was a police officer, but Nicky was one of Penrith's babies. He was bluff, irritating and occasionally offensive, but he cared about his team. Caelan watched him pull out his handkerchief and blow his nose with gusto, wondering why she hadn't seen it before. Penrith was as nervous as she was. Nicky's disappearance had cut him to the bone. He felt he had failed her, and now he was preparing to send Caelan off into the darkness too. No wonder he was twitchy.

Putting the handkerchief away, he took out his phone. 'I'll update Elizabeth Beckett, double-check we're good to go. Or you are, I should say.' He flashed her a smile, and Caelan grinned back, each of them attempting to reassure the other. It wasn't working. Caelan's stomach was somersaulting, and Penrith's hairline was damp. This was different to any time she had been sent out into the field before. Now, people were missing, and Caelan had no way of knowing if, come midnight, her name would be added to the list.

Or if she'd be in the local pathologist's big fridge.

There was a knock on the door, and Caelan moved to open it. A young officer stood there holding out the hair bobble with the transmitter hidden inside it. Caelan thanked her, and the woman turned away. Closing the door, Caelan pulled her hair into a ponytail using the bobble. Last time she had worn one like it, she had been on her way to confront a killer. The thought wasn't comforting.

Penrith turned back to her. 'Okay. Time to go. You get out of here. I'll move everyone into position, now we know where the hell we're going.'

Caelan rubbed her hands across her face. 'I still don't like having to go to the snooker club.'

'Out of our hands. At least it's a place you've been before.'

345

'One way in, one out,' she reminded him. 'Could be a trap.' She knew it wouldn't make a difference to whether she was sent in or not, but she wanted to make the point. Penrith looked at her.

'You're jittery. I've never seen you like this. What's the problem?'

Caelan blinked. 'I'm not sure. Liv Hobbs is missing, and she's pregnant. Nicky's gone too. If I fuck up...' She tried to swallow. 'If I fuck up, they might pay.'

'And if you don't, we might finally nail those responsible, get Liv and Nicky home before they've hardly been missed.'

'If any of this relates to Rainey and Bryce's deaths.'

'You still think they're not linked?' Penrith's eyebrows danced. 'Jackson Hobbs's death proves they are.'

'What has Hobbs to do with the other two murders?'

Penrith gave her shoulder a gentle push. 'I don't know. Let's see if we can find out.'

34

Mulligan instructed Erdi to park three streets away. He sat in the back seat, legs crossed, whistling to himself. It was almost show time. He was in control and loving it. This was what it was all about. It had angered him when his men had failed to track down the woman Crowley had been boasting about meeting, but there hadn't been much time. He tipped back his head, yawning. At least this way, Crowley had done the work for him. This Kay Summers would come wandering along, ripe for the picking. He smiled to himself. She had to be stupid. If Crowley knew what her boyfriend had left behind when he'd gone to jail, plenty of other people had to be aware of it too. And now she was arranging meetings, thinking she was calling the shots. Silly bitch. This wasn't a game.

He wondered if he should take her home. He turned his head, gazing out of the window, licking his lips. It would depend what she looked like. If she'd been sampling her boyfriend's wares, she'd be spotty, scrawny and toothless. Not his type. He'd probably catch something. But if she was clean, maybe she would be worth his time. A right-hand woman, one who already knew the trade, might be what his business needed as it grew. A pretty face, someone who knew how to charm his clients, maybe his enemies too. Could be invaluable.

Could be a liability.

Mulligan stretched out his legs, leant forward to check the clock on the dashboard.

Nah. Better to stick to the original plan.

He tapped Erdi on the shoulder. 'Ready?'

Erdi glanced back at him. 'Yes, boss.'

'You know what to do? Andri?'

The brothers shared a grin. 'We do.'

Mulligan nodded, satisfied. 'Ryan? You all right, wee man?'

Hunched in his seat, arms wrapped around his stomach, Ryan managed a smile as he looked up.

'Fine.'

'You ready?'

'Listen, I—'

Mulligan thrust his face towards him. 'I said, are you ready?'

Ryan shrank back. 'Yes.'

'That's what I thought. See you back here.'

He turned his head to stare out of the window, heard the car doors open. Three slams, and they were gone. Satisfied, Mulligan closed his eyes. Nothing to do now but wait.

35

The second text, the one Caelan had expected Marcus Crowley to send changing the location of the meeting, didn't arrive. She arrived at the snooker club a couple of minutes before the hour, every instinct urging her to run. She knew she couldn't.

There were no vehicles parked outside, no one in sight. She stood on the pavement, pretending to check her phone, wishing she had an earpiece so she could speak to Penrith. The transmitter meant he would be able to hear what happened around her, but if she spoke directly to him, the game would be up. Or she'd be carted away in an ambulance.

One more scan of the street, and she pushed open the door, jogged up the now familiar steps. Her heart thumped, but she knew her face would show no signs of her anxiety. It wasn't the first time she had walked into a situation every sense was telling her to rush away from, and she knew it wouldn't be the last. The trick was to control the panic, the urge to run, and channel it into keeping herself safe, taking note of every detail of her surroundings. Being hyper-aware was an asset in many jobs, but in hers, it could save lives.

Silence. The same musty smell, sticking in her throat. Take a breath. Let it out slowly. You're fine. Repeat it. Try to believe it.

She reached the top step, and waited.

'Kay?'

Marcus Crowley appeared from behind the bar. He wore a black suit, white shirt, a plain grey tie. Dressed for business. Nice touch. Had he wanted to startle her? Put her on the back foot from the beginning? It didn't matter. Caelan raised an eyebrow.

'Marcus. There you are.'

He came towards her, smiling. 'Just checking the stock. Are you ready?'

She shrugged. 'Why not?'

His eyes flicked over her body, and he frowned. 'Where is it?'

'What?'

'Don't fuck around, you know what I mean. You were going to bring a sample.'

'Was I?'

He bared his teeth, hands clenching, all his charm disappearing. 'Don't fuck me around. You know how much money we could make here? You need to take it seriously. Where have you hidden it?'

She sneered. 'Like I'm going to tell you. Start showing me some respect, or I'll walk away now.'

He raised his hands, took a step back. Tried to force a smile. 'Hey, hey. I'm sorry, okay? It's… These aren't people you want to piss off.'

'People?' Caelan watched him blink, raise a hand to touch his hair. Nervous, or he was about to lie. Probably both.

Downstairs, the door slammed closed. They heard feet on the stairs, more than one pair. Caelan didn't move, glaring at Crowley. He turned away, pretending he hadn't seen her expression. She waited, wondering if he had set her up. She should never have agreed to come here alone, but she had been given no choice. She was vulnerable, but it had been the only way. The backup was there if she needed it, but for now, she was on her own.

Three men appeared. Two were obviously the muscle, and Caelan knew she had seen them before. Big and broad, with shaven heads. Born to be thugs. Now that she could see them clearly, she realised they must be brothers, or cousins at least. They had the same prominent nose, identical eyes and high forehead. Not pretty. The other man was shorter, thinner. Caelan assumed she was having the pleasure of meeting Ryan Glennister. He looked ill, but Caelan knew what his problem was. She'd seen withdrawal enough times. The urge to grab and handcuff him was almost overwhelming. Instead, she smirked, hands on hips.

'Good to see you again,' she called to the muscle men. 'How are your balls?'

Crowley and one of the men laughed. The other scowled, pointed at her.

'Shut your mouth. We're here on business.'

'Fine by me.' Caelan looked from him to Crowley and back again. 'How does this work?'

The man she guessed was Glennister hunched his shoulders, and the smell of stale skin and unwashed clothes wafted towards her. 'Do you have the stuff here?' he asked.

'Do you think I'm stupid?' Caelan tried not to breathe through her nose.

He moistened his lips. 'No. Naïve, but not stupid.'

She watched the other two move closer to her, one on either side. She took a step backwards, controlling her breathing, not wanting to find herself trapped.

Crowley cleared his throat. 'Where's Mulligan? I thought he was—'

A huge hand covered his mouth, the other bunching his shirt beneath his chin before he could complete the sentence. Crowley's eyes bulged.

'No names, you stupid fuck. Thought you were a professional?'

As he was released, Crowley spluttered, straightening his tie. 'I am. I thought—'

'We're not here to talk to you. Now shut the fuck up.'

Scowling, Crowley did as he was told. Ryan Glennister smiled at Caelan, his ruined teeth displayed for a second. She forced herself not to recoil.

'We'll need to go to wherever what you have for sale is hidden and do some tests.'

Caelan tossed her hair. 'Tests? What do you mean?'

'Come on, darling,' said the man who'd grabbed Crowley. 'You wouldn't buy a car without test-driving it. It's the same in our line of business. You should know that.'

'I've brought a sample with me.' Caelan patted her handbag. 'Cook it, smoke it, do whatever you want with it. It's the fucking business. My boyfriend only sold the best.'

Laughter. 'Not a chance. We take our own sample.'

Caelan turned away. 'No way. Deal's off. See you around, Marcus.'

A hand on her arm before she'd taken two paces.

'Where do you think you're going?'

A new voice, coming from behind them. Male, a Scottish accent. Everyone turned, Ryan Glennister's face showing fear. Caelan tried to twist away, to see who was speaking, but her other arm was seized and held tight. She didn't move, told herself not to panic. Other officers were seconds away.

The newcomer sauntered over, hands in his trouser pockets. He had auburn hair, cut short, and vivid green eyes. He stood almost toe to toe with Caelan, smiling at her. She stared back, unflinching, and he chuckled.

'You're not what I expected.'

She knew she had never seen him before. Mulligan. Who the hell? 'Are you Ryan Glennister?'

His eyes narrowed. 'I look like a junkie to you?'

'No, but he does.' She nodded at the thin man.

A smirk. 'There's your answer then. I'm not here to fuck around. Are you selling?' Mulligan glared over her shoulder. 'Let go of her, for fuck's sake. Let me talk to her. I don't think she's going anywhere.'

Caelan's arms were immediately released, and she rubbed them, shooting a glare at the man who'd held her. He blew her a kiss as he went to stand beside Glennister.

'Call it revenge,' he told her, nodding towards his crotch.

'Well?' Mulligan made her meet his eyes. 'I asked you a question.'

Caelan stared back. 'Isn't that why we're here? I'm selling, you want to buy.'

'I need to see the white.'

'Fine by me. But I'm not taking your boyfriends.'

His smile was tight. 'They can stay here with yours.'

Caelan threw Marcus Crowley a scornful glance. 'Boyfriend? Kidding me.'

'Like I fucking would,' Crowley snapped back. He stepped towards Mulligan, hands up as though surrendering. 'Listen, I thought we had an agreement?'

Mulligan didn't look at him. 'We did. Now I have one with her.'

'But...' Crowley opened his mouth, closed it again. Mulligan smiled, his hand on Caelan's elbow as if they were going to dance.

'What can I say? I'd rather look at her face than yours.'

Caelan knew she had to keep them talking. She couldn't leave here with this man. 'What agreement?'

'Nothing for you to worry about.' He tried to steer her towards the exit, but Caelan pulled away.

'I want to know what's going on.'

Mulligan set his jaw. 'I'll tell you. We're going for a drive. If you play your cards right, you'll be a rich woman in a few hours' time. If not...'

'If not?'

A smile. 'Then we'll have a problem.'

'Marcus said—'

He took her arm again, his grip firmer this time. She could smell him: aftershave and the scent of his skin. She had seen the look in his eyes, and it chilled her. She had misjudged Marcus Crowley – he was a coward. Ryan Glennister was weak, in thrall to his addiction. The other two had muscles for brains. This man was the real deal – cold and brutal. She knew she couldn't go with him.

'Forget Marcus.' His voice was soft, persuasive. 'Stick with me, you won't regret it.'

'I don't think—'

'You don't need to.' He smiled, but his eyes were empty. Caelan shivered, and it wasn't part of the act. She wished she had brought a gun, and fuck the consequences. No one had patted her down, or even looked in her bag. The backup wouldn't move in yet. She was alone, his hand on her arm, being dragged towards the stairs.

Crowley tried again. 'Listen, I told you I was brokering the deal.' Caelan heard him swallow from ten feet away.

Mulligan exhaled, as though Crowley was the most pointless creature on the planet. 'Brokering? Really? Shut the fuck up.'

He inclined his head at his men, and they scrambled to follow. Crowley scampered after them.

'He's on his way, I thought you could discuss it—'

Mulligan rounded on him, jerking Caelan with him, his fingers digging painfully into her flesh. 'On his way? Who? Who the fuck have you been talking to?'

Crowley was gabbling now, sensing he'd made an almighty mistake. 'It's business, you know how it is. I spoke to him after I talked to Ryan. He wanted to make me an offer, and I thought, well… we could have a drink, chat about it.' He tried to smile, but his face didn't want to join in. 'Like an auction, you know?'

Mulligan let go of Caelan's arm. She stood still, waiting to see what would happen. There had never really been a plan, but if there had, this situation wouldn't have been part of it. What was Crowley babbling about?

Mulligan poked him hard in the chest. 'You're saying you offered my white to someone else? Who?'

'I—'

Another poke. 'Tell me, you little shit. It was business? Who the fuck do you think you are, Richard fucking Branson?'

Crowley smiled desperately, looking over Mulligan's shoulder. 'Maybe you should ask him yourself. You're not the only one who wants to own Edmonton, you know.'

They all heard the door closing, the sound of more feet on the stairs. Caelan shifted position, moving so her back was against the wall, the bar on her left about fifteen feet away. Ryan Glennister watched her, but stayed quiet. Mulligan turned, hands on hips, his face set in a snarl as he waited for the newcomer to appear.

Caelan held her breath. She had no idea who to expect, but she knew it wouldn't be anyone there to help her. Penrith would be listening intently, perhaps ordering officers to creep closer to the club. But he would wait to make his final move. He had to.

Crowley's eyes were wide, a fixed smile on his lips as though he was desperate for everyone to shake hands and make friends. Mulligan's minders stood ready, waiting for a word from their boss.

In the end, it didn't matter. The man who appeared at the top of the stairs had a smile on his face and a gun in his hand.

Caelan's stomach lurched, and for a second she thought she was going to be sick.

She recognised him, had spoken to him more than once.

The man with the gun was Adam Waits.

Liv Hobbs's husband.

36

She couldn't let him see her. Caelan turned her face, her legs trembling. She had no idea how Waits was involved or what he was doing here, but if he saw her, she was dead. He knew who she was, and what she was. She had no choice but to stay still and hope he didn't notice her. Waits hadn't spoken yet, but when he did, would Penrith recognise his voice? Had he heard it? Achebe would, but was he listening? Was she too far away from Waits for his voice to even be picked up? She had no idea, had never been told what the range of this oh-so-clever listening device was. Waits was staring at Mulligan, but if he turned his head even slightly... Caelan shuffled to her left, just a pace, keeping her eyes on the ground.

Waits stepped forward, the gun aimed at Mulligan's face.

'Where's my wife?' he demanded.

Mulligan's lips twitched. 'Sorry, pal. Don't know what you're blethering about.'

'Bollocks you don't. My wife. Liv Hobbs. Sister of Jackson Hobbs. Where the fuck is she?'

Mulligan's hands went up. 'Can we slow down? I'm here to make a deal, not to have a gun waved in my face. I don't know what you're talking about, so why don't you calm down and put it away?'

Caelan took another step, aware that everyone except Mulligan was also inching away from Waits.

'Don't think I won't shoot you, you prick.' Waits sounded calm. Too calm.

Mulligan risked a smile. 'Like I said, I don't—'

The gunshot was deafening in the confined space. Caelan heard Mulligan scream, saw him fall before the sound registered in her brain. Blood on the floor, Mulligan clutching the outside of his thigh. Waits stood over him, his face pale, biting his lip.

'Where is she?' He sounded as though he was trying not to cry. Mulligan's face contorted into a parody of a smile.

'Don't know what you're—'

Waits kicked him in the stomach. Mulligan howled at his men.

'Do something, you cowardly bastards!'

No one seemed to hear him. Crowley had vanished behind a table he had upturned. Glennister seemed frozen, cowering against the wall beside Caelan, while the two heavies had thrown themselves to the ground. Caelan shoved Glennister, nodding towards the bar. He stared back, uncomprehending. Waits raised the gun again.

'Tell me where she is.'

Mulligan was panting, sweat visible on his forehead. 'Why do you care? You're always shagging around.'

Waits shook his head, his eyes wild. 'Shut up.'

'Must have been awkward for you when Jackson was sent down.' Mulligan spat on the floor. 'Your business partner gone, and no one to run the show. Had to get your hands dirty for a change.'

Caelan blinked. Adam Waits had been working with Jackson Hobbs?

Waits waved the gun, his hand visibly trembling. 'You don't know what you're talking about.'

Mulligan's body twisted, his breathing ragged. 'But I do. Your little friends told me. Couldn't wait to betray you once we started working on them.'

Caelan moved her feet again, her hand closing around Glennister's sleeve. Looked like she was going to have to drag him. She glanced at Waits, but he didn't seem to have even seen them. She hoped it stayed that way.

'My friends?' Waits stared down at Mulligan, swaying on his feet. He looked broken. Mulligan laughed.

'The two amateur detectives you had sniffing around, trying to find out who was taking over where your brother-in-law had left off. Never knew I was stealing all your business, did you? They weren't that fucking clever. No loyalty, either. When I got them in my workshop and they saw what I had waiting for them, they couldn't stop talking.'

Mulligan's hand disappeared inside his jacket. Caelan saw the movement, wondered if Waits had. The bar was still a couple of feet away. Too far. It might as well have been ten miles. Glennister was a dead weight, holding her back. But he was a civilian, and she knew she had to protect him if she could, even if it meant endangering herself. His eyes were rolling, his mouth hanging open. Was he about to have a fit? Caelan pushed him in front of her, almost falling over his feet as they dragged behind him.

'What did they tell you?' Waits was saying.

Mulligan coughed. 'Thought you wanted to know where your wife is.'

Waits ran his free hand over his eyes. 'I do. But I want to know what they said.'

Mulligan smiled. 'Rainey told me what he'd done to your wife, how she'd seduced him, begged him.' He licked his lips. 'How much she'd enjoyed it.'

Caelan moved again as Waits raised the gun, his foot on Mulligan's chest, holding him down. 'Keep talking.'

'And when you found out about it, you decided to go after Rainey yourself. Not to hurt him, but to use him.' Mulligan took a shuddering breath, blood still leaking from his thigh. 'You'd been working with your brother-in-law for years. Your wife, the fucking detective inspector, never suspected a thing, and you kept playing the Good Samaritan. Paramedic by day, drug dealer by night.' Another laboured breath. 'Depending on your shift, of course.'

Waits pressed harder on his chest. 'Very funny.'

'Not as funny as you. Thought you were being clever, didn't you, setting Rainey off on a mission? He thought he'd impress your wife, be a shoo-in for detective constable. He didn't have a clue you were using him to get rid of me. He'd get his promotion, I'd be off the streets, leaving the way clear for you.' Mulligan's throat gurgled as he laughed. 'I lied before. Rainey held out for quite a while. Didn't want to tell me anything. He thought a lot of your wife. Thought you were a piece of shit, mind, but...'

Waits was losing interest, Caelan saw. She took another step towards the safety of the wooden bar, hauling Glennister, now barely conscious, along with her.

'Where's Liv? Last chance.' Waits aimed the gun at Mulligan's face again.

'She's safe.' Mulligan was still talking, but each word was an effort, his breathing more laboured with every passing minute. His leg wound was still bleeding freely. Waits didn't seem to care.

'Why did you take her?'

'Why? Because I could. I knew you were working with Jackson Hobbs, and then he was out of the picture.'

'Because you had him killed.'

'Says who?'

Waits glared at Mulligan, his eyes venomous. 'Didn't even have the guts to do it yourself.'

'Prove it. Anyway, Jackson's death did you a favour.'

Waits shook his head. 'He was going to be inside for years anyway. You expect me to be grateful?'

'With Jackson gone, I thought you might cut your losses. Taking Liv was a safety net, in case you refused to shut up shop and piss off out of my patch.'

'Your patch?' Waits snorted. 'Who the fuck do you think you are? Jackson's been king around here for years. Now it's my turn.'

Caelan froze as Mulligan shifted position, his hand whipping through the air. Adam Waits opened his mouth to speak, but whatever he said was lost in the thunder of another gunshot. Waits staggered backwards, clutching his abdomen, blood immediately staining his fingers. Mulligan pushed himself onto his elbows.

'Should have walked away when you had the chance.'

Caelan heaved Glennister behind the bar and scrambled after him. Waits pointed a trembling finger.

'Is she the one who's got the white?'

Mulligan managed a laugh. 'Shot, and you still want to talk business? I'm impressed, big man.'

Caelan kept her head down, hoping Waits would lose interest, or even better, lose consciousness.

'I didn't know you'd be here,' Waits managed to say. 'Crowley told me the deal was done. I was just coming to collect.'

'Yeah, well, it seems he decided he'd have an auction, sell off the gear to the highest bidder, didn't you, Marcus? Fucking stupid idea, but what can you expect?'

Waits gritted his teeth. 'Not much.'

'I was going to take the white from the girl and not hand over a penny, but in the end...' Mulligan fell back, but kept talking, 'in the end, I didn't have the chance. If she's got any sense, she'll get out of here.'

Caelan stayed where she was. Where the hell was her backup? Two gunshots, not to mention the arrival of Adam Waits and the chance that he would recognise her. How much more of a hint did Penrith need?

Slumped against the wall, Waits was coughing. 'How about a deal?'

Mulligan closed his eyes, then opened them wide, his face pale, the gun still loose in his hand. 'I'm listening.'

'Tell me where my wife is, and I'll walk away, find myself somewhere else to do my business.'

'This is the woman you cheated on? Changed your mind about her, did you?'

Waits smiled, agony clear on his face. 'Just tell me.'

'What about her?' Mulligan jerked his head towards where Caelan and Glennister were hiding. 'Still a kilo of white out there. Don't think she's going to fight us for it, do you? What do you say, split it and we can both walk away?'

Waits nodded. 'Not sure I'm up to walking, but works for me.'

Mulligan turned his head. 'Erdi, get her over here. Andri, call Danzig. Mate of mine,' he told Waits. 'He trained as a medic. He'll get us patched up, no questions asked.'

Caelan sprang up, considering making a run for the stairs. With both Erdi and Andri in the way, it was a long shot, but what choice did she have? Waits might see her, but his head was bowed, blood pooling around his shoes.

Erdi was scrambling to his feet, and she knew it was now or never. She let go of Glennister and ran.

'Fucking grab her!' Mulligan bellowed, both hands clutching his wounded leg. Caelan sprinted past him, dodging Erdi, but the other man was there, blocking the way, grinning at her.

'I know you can fight, but today I've got the advantage.' He pulled out a knife. 'Better do as you're told.'

Caelan was on her toes, ready to unleash a kick, but she was grabbed from behind again, arms encircling her waist, and lifted off her feet. Erdi. He breathed heavily in her ear as Andri came forward, laughing.

'Bet you're regretting kicking me now,' he said. Caelan scowled.

'Not really.'

Mulligan chortled. 'She's a piece of work, this one. Maybe I'll give you a job, sweetheart, what do you say?'

'She's got a job,' said Adam Waits.

Caelan's stomach plummeted.

'What are you on about?' Mulligan demanded.

'Turn her around,' said Waits. Erdi did so, Andri keeping the point of the knife just beneath Caelan's chin. She stayed still. She could try to break out of Erdi's grip, but his arms were like iron, and with the knife so close…

Waits pushed himself away from the wall, staggered towards them. Caelan kept her chin down, her eyes on Erdi's boots as he dragged her forward. Do something, she ordered herself, but she knew she was out of options. Where were the others? What was Penrith doing?

Waits reached out, lifted her chin with a fingertip. Caelan stared back at him, all pretence gone. If this was the end, she wouldn't be cowed.

'Tell them your name,' Waits said softly.

Caelan met his eyes. 'Kay Summers.'

Waits laughed. 'Nice one. And your real name? Your rank?'

'What the fuck?' Mulligan was trying to get up. Andri handed the knife to Erdi, who shoved it hard against Caelan's throat. She felt the tip bite into her skin, and swallowed. She was calm, the terror of the last few seconds dissipating. Nowhere to go, and nothing to lose. Fuck you, Penrith.

Mulligan limped over, leaning heavily on Andri's arm. 'What's this about?' he demanded.

'She's a copper.' Waits was pale, his voice little more than a whisper. 'I've met her before. She was looking for Liv. Fuck knows what she's doing here.'

Crowley stuck his head up from behind the table. 'A copper? But she said—'

Mulligan turned, fired a shot in his direction. Crowley screamed, disappeared. Mulligan turned back to Caelan.

'You've been clever, haven't you?' He moved closer, smiling at her. 'Playing with Marcus and Frankie Hamilton. Blending in. That what you do?'

It took all her effort to reply calmly. 'Sometimes.'

He nodded. 'Have to say, I admire you. You've some fucking guts. Just a pity you're on the wrong side.' He took her chin in his hand, gently lifted it so she was looking at him, as Waits had. 'Now, we can't let you live. You get that, don't you? You understand? Job like yours, you'd have to. Are you here on your own?'

Caelan almost laughed. 'Very much so.'

'All right. As you know, there's been a gunfight. Unfortunately, you got caught up in it. Collateral damage. I'm sure you understand.' He turned away. 'Andri. Do it. Get rid of her, and Glennister too while you're at it.'

Andri came forward, grinning. 'What about Crowley?'

'Him too. Then torch the place. I need a doctor.'

Erdi marched Caelan to the wall, then let go, went to help his boss. Andri raised the gun, and Caelan stared into his eyes. He would do it, she had no doubt. She felt nothing – no fear, no regret.

Pounding feet. Bellowing. Another gunshot.

37

Caelan lay back, the dressing beneath her chin itching, her stomach rumbling. Strange how a near-death experience could leave you feeling so hungry. Why she had been brought to the hospital she had no idea, but it was somehow comforting to lie quietly and think about nothing for a while.

'Here you are. I'm surprised they persuaded you to stay in.' Penrith was in the doorway, digging into a packet of crisps.

Caelan laughed. 'Almost losing another member of your team hasn't put you off your food, then.'

He collapsed into the chair by her bed. 'Almost losing? Rubbish. We arrived in plenty of time.'

A flashback to Andri raising the gun, the smile on his face. Caelan blinked it away. 'Whatever you say.'

'We found Liv Hobbs. She's in a room on the next floor. They'll keep her in for observation for a few days, but she and the baby weren't harmed.'

'Thankfully.' Caelan was surprised by the ache in her throat, the tears in her eyes. She rubbed them away with a fingertip before Penrith could notice, though he was concentrating on tipping crisp crumbs into his mouth. He folded the bag and shoved it into his trouser pocket.

'Mulligan's men are singing like canaries, as they say. Blaming him, each other, everyone they can think of.'

'Crowley?'

'Dead.'

Caelan had expected it. 'Glennister?'

'Oh, he's all right. Nothing a rock or two won't fix.' Penrith smirked at his own play on words.

'How did Liv take the news about her husband?'

'They haven't told her yet. Achebe and Jen Somerville are with her. Waits is still in surgery, though they tell me he's in no danger.' He sniffed. 'Bit of a shock when he turned up.'

'You heard him, then?'

'Loud and clear. Almost fell off my chair.'

'Sorry I missed that.'

He smiled. 'Assistant Commissioner Beckett wants to see you.'

'Well I don't want to see her.'

'Thought you might not be keen. Told her no visitors today, doctor's orders.' He wagged a finger. 'You can buy me a thank-you present when they let you out.'

'What about Mulligan?'

'They're operating on him too, but he'll live. Our friends at the NCA had never heard of him.' He spread his hands. 'They're backing away from the whole affair as if it's spontaneously combusted.'

'There's a shock.'

'I'm surprised they're not trying to claim at least some of the credit, considering the stash of drugs and cash we found at one of Mulligan's hidey-holes, but...'

They had also found Nicky Sturgess, but neither of them wanted to approach the subject. Caelan pulled the thin blanket higher over her chest. She was wearing just a hospital gown, and the room felt cold. Penrith leaned forward, clumsily patting her hand.

'I've seen her.'

Caelan gulped. 'And?'

He shook his head. 'I won't lie. It's not looking good. Her parents are on their way. As you know, they've been through this before.'

'Last time, they were told she was dead.' Caelan twisted the blanket between her fingers. 'I thought I saw her die. And when I'd begun to come to terms with that, suddenly she was back.'

'I know.' His voice was soft.

Caelan looked at him, not bothering to hide the tears now. 'Forgive me if I don't know how to react.'

–

Later, after lukewarm soup and thin sandwiches, Caelan asked a nurse where Nicky was.

The room, at the end of a long, busy corridor, was silent but for the beeps and hisses of the machinery surrounding the bed. Another nurse was there, checking readings, making notes. She looked up with a quick smile as Caelan appeared. Caelan approached the bed, looked down at Nicky's face. The pale skin, the bruising around her eyes. The mask covering her mouth and nose. Nicky's hand lay on the bed, a cannula with another tube attached disappearing beneath the sheet. Tentatively, Caelan touched it with a fingertip. Cold. All at once, a surge of emotion welled in her chest, sudden and overwhelming. She wanted to throw herself into Nicky's arms and howl. They'd had such plans. The job had driven them apart, threatened their relationship, even their lives.

The fucking job.

'They're saying there could be brain damage.'

The voice came from the doorway. Caelan didn't turn. The nurse looked up, detected the tension, left the room. Assistant Commissioner Elizabeth Beckett crossed the floor to stand beside the bed.

'Have you spoken to her parents?' Caelan didn't look at Beckett, keeping her eyes on Nicky, on the machinery.

'I broke the news to them myself.'

'Big of you.'

Beckett turned her head. 'You think it's my fault she's lying here?'

'You're the boss, aren't you?'

'And the buck stops with me? No. We don't know what happened, but the ones to blame are the men who gave her... whatever it is they injected. No one else.'

'You were concerned about her, but she was still on active duty.'

'I'm also concerned about you, and here you are. If I forbade any officer I worried about from being in the field, the department would be empty.'

'Probably a good thing.'

'You think so?' Beckett pressed her lips together. 'I'll need a statement from you.'

'Tomorrow. I'll be at home, taking the leave you insisted on. The leave you cancelled. Twice.'

'And then?'

'What?'

'I'm prepared to give you two weeks, then I'll expect you back in the office.'

'I'll need longer. Goodnight, ma'am.'

'You won't be able to stay away, you know.' Beckett spoke quietly, her eyes still on Nicky's face. 'You people are all the same.'

Caelan felt a flash of fury. 'You people? What's that supposed to—'

'Once you've been undercover, nothing else comes close. It's like soldiers who've seen active service. Take them out of uniform, give them a desk job, and they don't know what to do with themselves. The adrenalin is addictive.'

'Yeah, yeah. Maybe I'll take up skydiving.'

Beckett ignored her. 'Mulligan's men have given us some interesting information. They were involved in people trafficking.' She gave Caelan a sidelong glance. 'The brothel you went to was one of the places they supplied.'

'Supplied? You've a real way with words.'

'We'll be following up on what they told us. When Mulligan's recovered, we'll be talking to him with a view to making him an offer in exchange for information. It could mean opportunities for you.'

'Mulligan knows who I am, what I do. You expect him to keep his mouth shut?'

The Assistant Commissioner's smile was cold. 'In these situations, it usually depends on what is offered in return.'

'Better make it the Crown Jewels, then.'

Beckett didn't respond, and Caelan went to the door, opened it. Stood watching as Beckett lifted Nicky's hand.

'She could still recover, you know.'

Caelan blinked, her throat aching again. 'Ma'am.'

Beckett looked up, still holding Nicky's hand. 'What is it?'

'I resign.'

Acknowledgements

Every writer is probably certain they have the best publishers in the world, but I'm sure mine beat them all. A huge thank you to the lovely people at Canelo for everything they have done to get this book out into the world. Special thanks to Michael Bhaskar for all his help, advice, support and understanding. Caelan and I couldn't have found a better home.

I'd like to thank everyone who has read the book, especially those who have taken the time to review it or to contact me about it. It means so much to know people are reading your work, and for me is a dream come true. Thank you all.

To my hugely supportive, kind and generous friends – you know who you are. Thank you.

Without the encouragement and support of my family, I would have given up writing long ago. To Tracy, who keeps me on the right path and believes in me – thank you for everything. To Mum and Grandma, who have supported and encouraged me for forty years now – thank you. A mention too for my son, the rest of my lovely family and also my furry writing companions, Evie, Poppy and Alexa. No, I can't throw your ball. I'm working.

H